We were all looking forward to a night of hard-core travel. Night travel is special. Mystical really. You're just out there in the darkness, somewhere in between places. You wouldn't even know you were moving except for the radio stations drifting in and out like voices at a party. Mark and I always preferred our long-distance, haul-ass driving to be done at night.

There is a time about twenty minutes into a trip—when the NoDoz and the night air kick in—that a highway euphoria wafts over you. And it helps if the radio transmission is still crisp and clear.

We always considered the car radio to be as important as the engine. Not only is it a companion and guide, it's the music maker and music is the road drug that keeps you going on long night drives.

PICTURES FROM A TRIP

PICTURES FROM A TRIP

Tim Rumsey

FAWCETT CREST • NEW YORK

Grateful acknowledgment is made for permission to reprint excerpts from:
"Hello I Love You" by The Doors, copyright © 1968 by Nipper Music
"Route 66" by Bobby Troup, copyright 1946, © renewed 1973 by Londontown
Music, Inc., and Edwin Morris
"Johnny B. Goode" by Chuck Berry, copyright © 1958 by Arc Music Corp.
Used by permission. All rights reserved.

Grateful acknowledgment is made for permission to reprint excerpts from:
The North Star Guide Manual, Vol. II, Jacques and George Herter, Herters'
Inc., 1961; *Vertebrate Paleontology*, Third Edition, Alfred S. Romer, University of Chicago Press, 1966; *The Minneapolis Review of Baseball*; *Osteology of the Reptiles*, Alfred S. Romer, University of Chicago Press, 1956;
Goodnight Moon, Margaret Wise Brown, copyright 1947 by Harper & Row,
renewed 1975 by Roberta Brown Rauch.

Library of Congress Catalog Card Number: 84-62074

ISBN 0-449-20954-7

This edition published by arrangement with William Morrow and
Company, Inc.

Manufactured in the United States of America

First Ballantine Books Edition: January 1987

TO ROSEMARIE AND LITTLE CHAD

ACKNOWLEDGMENTS

I would especially like to thank Jonathan Lazear, Kay Sexton, and the God-Pal of *Pictures from a Trip*, my editor, Pat Golbitz. I am also grateful to the following individuals and institutions:

Susan Barker
The Boeckmann Library
Mason Boyd
Norma Brandon
Dan Brennan
Marvin Busse
Cook County High School
    Library
Charles Dana
Merrill Davis
Terry Diebel
Kevin FitzPatrick
Roberta Flescher
John Goodell
Kathy Gray
Victoria Klose
Vicki Lansky
Dorothy Lindholm

Ronald A. Lyschik
Diana McEvoy
Billie McQuillan
Sandy Olson
Orlo Otteson
Molly Park
Bill Quinn
Barry Rosenbush
Ann Rumsey
Rosemarie Reger-Rumsey
St. Paul Public Library
    System
Tom Sinnott
Joe Soucheray
Mary Stibbe
Jennifer Williams
Beth Wollerman

AUTHOR'S NOTE

This is a work of fiction. The towns of Canaan, Beauty, and Ed are creations of the author. Dinosaur fossils have not been discovered in the area of South Dakota depicted in this book. Other historic, scientific, and geographic facts have been slightly altered. However, I am indebted to the following resources for invaluable inspiration: *Fossils and Flies*, E. N. Shor (University of Oklahoma Press); *Men and Dinosaurs*, Edwin H. Colbert (E. P. Dutton); *The Hot Blooded Dinosaurs*, Adrian J. Desmond (Dial Press); *A Species of Eternity*, Joseph Kastner (Knopf); *We Americans*, National Geographic Publications; "Experiences in the Grand Canyon," Ellsworth and Emery Kolb, *National Geographic*, August 1914; *Bury My Heart at Wounded Knee*, Dee Brown (Bantam); *The Buffalo Hunters*, Mari Sandoz (University of Nebraska Press); *The Badlands*, Time-Life Books; *A Dictionary of the Old West*, Peter Watts (Knopf); *Looking Far West*, Frank Bergon and Zeese Papanikolas (Mentor Books); *Challenge— The South Dakota Story*, Robert F. Karolevitz (Brevitz Press); *The Rolling Stone History of Rock and Roll*, Jim Miller, editor (Rolling Stone-Random House); *Cameras*, Brian Coe (Crown); *On Photography*, Susan Sontag (Farrar, Straus and Giroux); and *The War, the West, and the Wilderness*, Kevin Brownlow (Knopf).

PROLOGUE

I CAN'T REALLY EXPLAIN WHY IT'S STILL SO CLEAR TO me. It's like I saw it on film or I was there or something. Of course it happened at night. Most bad things do.

Basically we all knew the car went off a cliff. But that's where I take over. I see it leaping into the dark. Then there's got to be what, maybe four or five seconds of unbelievable quiet inside that vehicle. I'm sure he never knew what hit him, but in the air he must have known something was going to hit him. I keep wondering if he thought of me. Even just for a blink.

Then the car hits nose first.

I know he was gone the moment he went through the windshield. Then his body flies over the ground and skids and bumps into a little mountain stream. He probably had gravel ground into his cheeks and back and legs, and dirt in his mouth.

When it was all over, my version has him facing up at the stars with both hands fisting a bundle of weeds as one wheel of the car still spins and the night water of the brook jumps over a new, special boulder.

There was a newspaper photo of the accident scene. Taken the next day, I imagine. It only made the local papers, so the mortician sent us two copies. But I have never looked at that picture and I probably never will. I don't have to.

CHAPTER
1

B EN COULD DO THE NIGHT DRIVING. THAT'S WHAT my brother, Mark, said to try to get him to join us on our big trip out West. It was his way of saying that Ben's being blind wouldn't be any problem, but on the contrary, a real asset to us and our marathon driving techniques. My job was to find a dinosaur and Mark would be the trip photographer. His pictures weren't just going to be of us standing by WELCOME TO MONTANA signs or the life-size cowboy statues at Wall Drug. They would be material worthy of *National Geographic*. In fact, Mark was so convinced that *NG* would want this trip recorded, he painted their insignia on the front doors of my Ford Bronco.

More on the dinosaur in a moment.

This was all back at the end of the Glory Years of the American highway. The summer the price of gas and the cruising speed were the same as the year. Seventy-five, if you're with me. Some people say you look back with a little more affection on times that can't ever be done over. But I don't know. I think I knew that trip was special even before we left. I'm not a believer in the astrological alignment of the planets and whatnot, but with all those seventy-fives lined up in a row, you'd have to be out of it not to figure something was up.

Our old buddy Ben could care less about dinosaurs. So Mark told him to think of the trip as a two-month picnic. As an opportunity for what in those days we called experiences. An opportunity to take in the sights, both natural and un-, he said. I guess that's what got Ben to go along. It would have been enough for me too. Being around Mark, things just seemed to happen.

Let me clear up this dinosaur business right away. Mark and I weren't scientists or anything. We just wanted to dig up a dinosaur. We never lost the dinosaur fever of seven-year-old, white, middle-class males, and since at that time we were just out of college and had access to transportation and a whole shitload of time, finding a dinosaur seemed like the right thing to do. And then you can throw in things like when fossil legs and arms the size of tree trunks started a dinosaur bone rush out in the Old West in 1874 and the treasure-on-the-beach aspect of it all, which may have just been an excuse for Mark and me to get out into the Great West in the first place.

Where else but in the American 1870's West could there have been a dinosaur bone rush? Hey, I'm not kidding here! Spying, sabotage, fossil-hunting armies, sacrilegious creatures coming to light. All that kind of good stuff. Big-shot museum directors out East were at absolute war with each other trying to unearth the biggest and the most spectacular dinosaurs in the solar system. Bone diggers worked straight through twenty-below winters and fly-buzzing summers. One crew ate in shifts from plates that were nailed down to tables and swabbed out between diners. (While these guys helped the dino make its comeback, somebody else was blowing the buffalo into oblivion on the prairies nearby.)

In the right places, dinosaur bones were everywhere. A Montana sheepherder built a cabin out of dinosaur bones that sprinkled the hillside his flock grazed on.

Mark had a good story about the geologist Ferdinand Hayden. Hayden was fossiling out in the Dakota Badlands during the Gold Colic, a time when the native Sioux were not at all turned on by miners ripping open their Black Hills. A group of war-painted braves watched Hayden standing on a Badlands hill tossing fossil bones into a bag. He was dressed in a vest, suit and tie, and a top hat. Finally noticing the warriors, Dr. Hayden humped off into the distance, dragging his sack and stopping to pick up a specimen or two while he was at it. I suppose they thought he was nuts because they let him go. That's when he became the Man-Who-Picks-Up-Rocks-Running.

Friends of Mark's and mine laughed at us when we told them we were going dinosaur hunting. They joked about not exceeding the limit or getting bit in the behind. But what did they know about the Bone Cabin or the Man-Who-Picks-Up-Rocks-Running? And so what if all that was a hundred years ago and the buttes and hillsides had long since been picked clean? There was even some talk of twentieth-century Indian trouble.

"Piss on em," Mark had said of all our friendly detractors and doubters. "If there's anything left out there, we might as well be the ones to go and claim it."

WE LOADED UP MY TRUCK AT OUR FAMILY HOME. IT WAS still that time in our lives when we used the parents' place as a storage depot. My father watched in silence as the camping gear and shovels and picks went into the car carrier on top of the Bronco. He said something about Ben being the singing cowboy when he saw his guitar getting put on board, but he seemed a little upset when he noticed me carrying a wooden crate of railroad flares. The red stick kind. He thought the flares were dynamite and I told him they were just highway flares in case of a night breakdown. Then he wanted to know why we needed so many of them and Mark said that with my Bronco, there may not be enough.

Well that was cute, but wouldn't you know it, the Bronco didn't start when we finally were ready to get going. It was just a loose battery cable though and after we fixed it, Mark and I had our usual NōDōz and Coca-

Cola for the road. Ben felt his braille watch and told us it was 9:04 P.M. St. Paul time.

"Trilobites of the world unite," Mark yelled out the driver's window as we pulled out of the garage. Then he gave out a war whoop that I was surprised didn't crack the windshield.

We were westward, ho.

WE WERE GOING TO START LOOKING FOR DINOSAUR IN the South Dakota Badlands, but actually we didn't have any particular destination in mind. Just the West. As if somewhere out on I-90 where farms became ranches and time turns into Rocky Mountain, we could pull off the road in a likely looking remote spot and see piles of beautiful, broken dinosaur sculpture. Mark did have something specific in mind with regard to discovery though. He wanted a *Tyrannosaurus rex* skull the size of a Volkswagen Beetle.

"Sounds like you're after the Behemoth of the Holy Writ, sweet," I said. We had just hit the freeway outside of St. Paul.

"The Behemoth itself, my sweet," said Mark. "And I don't want to set one foot back in this town unless we've got that *T. rex* head on board."

"I have some people here I'd like to keep seeing," Ben said. (Ben talks like that, "Good to see you" and "See you later" kinds of things.)

"You seem worried," Mark said. "Like you think we won't ever be returning."

"Not *seem* worried," said Ben. "I *am* worried. Can I get out now?"

"Sure," Mark said. Then he sped up to eighty-five and leaned over and opened the passenger door.

MARK AND I HAVE ALWAYS BEEN CLOSE. WE USED TO drink out of the same pop bottle without wiping off the top and we took turns walking down the sidewalk in my dad's baseball spikes because we liked the sound. But our prepubertal closeness was mostly geographic. We lived under the same roof, played in the same yard, and went to the same school. Our brotherhood hadn't really been tempered or earned. That would come later, after several girl friends and other shared traumas of the soul, including my last two years of high school during which Mark and I barely spoke to one another.

It was probably the trips that solidified us more than anything else, that made us brothers of the soul. And the honeymoon of our reclaimed brotherhood was the dinosaur trip with Ben.

Of the two of us, Mark is really the traveler, which is kind of interesting since I'm the oldest and I guess the one who's supposed to be the trailblazer. Mark had hitchhiked to Alaska and back the two previous summers. Hitchhiked, mind you. Curling up in a sleeping bag in the woods alongside the highway at night with only a sheet of plastic over him if it rained. Wearing a bell to keep away the bears as he walked along the AlCan Highway. Bumming rides in gas stations and cafés and getting his wallet swiped in Banff. Hitchhiked! Hell, I have trouble transferring from one bus to another right here in the city.

Mark hitchhiked as easily as normal people might take a cab. He used to thumb 250 miles one way to the Minnesota–Canada border to see his girl friend, Leslie, at her summer place just for the weekend. But I'm sure that the idea of having a moving vehicle under him for the whole dinosaur trip was such a pleasure that Mark didn't want to leave the road for any longer than necessary. So he laid down some early ground rules for Ben and me, and as far as he was concerned they were set in stone. No motels ever. On the whole trip. We'd either drive all night or camp out. And we would keep the restaurant stops to an absolute minimum, maybe just for some wake-up coffee.

Now here's the funny part. Mark hated my Bronco. The Bronchitis he called it. My innocent, little, yellow Jeep on whose doors he had painted NATIONAL GEOGRAPHIC SOCIETY, INCORPORATED A.D. 1888 over a meridianed globe. It was as if the old Bronc were some kind of unpleasant, nasty person. And it wasn't the physical faults like how the radio faded under bridges or the dash lights were shorted out so that you had to open a door to activate the cab light if you wanted to check a gauge or read a map. He just deep down despised that truck.

I never mentioned this to Mark, and I'll only bring it up once here. I liked to think that the Bronco was haunted.

Sometimes in the driver's seat it would be cold as hell and two feet over it was hot and sweaty. And maybe every third time you pushed in the cigarette lighter, the windshield wipers went on. But driving alone once, and this is what really did it for me, I saw an old, wrinkly lady in the rearview with a crown on her head and wearing a long, white evening gown. She was sitting on my spare tire trying to figure out how the jack worked. I turned full around and she was gone. I'll tell you, I don't know how I kept on the road.

The Bronco is my kind of vehicle. I can relate to its shortcomings. Probably because I have often been accused of dressing shabbily. Like a grub, as Mark puts it. I will admit that my clothes are chosen more for function than style. There was a time when I wore bowling shoes because they felt so comfortable, and it's not beyond me to wear pajamas on all-night drives. But I try to keep my appearance socially acceptable.

By my senior year in college, I had the start of a flabby belly and was as tan as the fluorescent lights of a library can make a person. Of course, Mark could have been an escapee from a department-store display window. Even as an away-from-home, malnourished film student in Toronto he kept himself immaculate and dashing. He's kind of a Warren Beatty with glasses anyway. The car he had up in Toronto fit his image too. Under all other circumstances it would have been considered a limping, flatulent, student car, except that it was a rusted-out Mercedes-Benz.

WE WERE ALL LOOKING FORWARD TO A NIGHT OF HARD-core travel. Night travel is special. Mystical really. You're just out there in the darkness, somewhere in between places. You wouldn't even know you were moving except for the radio stations drifting in and out like voices at a party. Mark and I always preferred our long-distance, haul-ass driving to be done at night.

There is a time about twenty minutes into a trip when the NōDōz and the night air kick in that a highway euphoria wafts over you. And it helps if the radio transmission is still crisp and clear.

We always considered the car radio to be as important as the engine. Not only is it a companion and guide, it's the music maker and music is the road drug that keeps you going on long night drives. Sweeping across the western plains, that old radio pulls in anything that happens to be floating about. Little Rock, Arkansas, was great late-night radio. So was KOMA out of Oklahoma City. But I do hate to miss the title of a good song because the airwaves get scrambled.

Usually the radio isn't all that necessary at the start of a trip. The energy level is high enough on its own, so you go along with whatever you can pick up loud and clear. Polka or country. A local call-in show. Or you might not even have the radio on. Besides, the first hundred miles are for catching up with each other.

That's when I found out Mark was planning to move to Chicago when we got back. He had some contacts from film school there and he thought the job possibilities were more viable than in the Twin Cities. I didn't want him to go, of course. But I never told him that. Ben said he had an application floating around the state's department of education for some kind of planning position. Whatever they do there, I was sure Ben could handle it.

WE SNUCK INTO SOUTH DAKOTA ABOUT 2:00 A.M. So-Dak as Mark says. We were flying along real good and Mark said that if anybody had to take a leak it'd be out the window or hold it.

It was black out. No other vehicles. No highway lights. No cities glowing in the distance. When you're way out there on the night road, like out on I-90 between Sioux Falls and Mitchell, it can be as dark as a closet. And lonely. You could be on a space shot to the moon for all you know.

I try to respect the road no matter where it is or what the time of day. All roads have seen a lot of time. Dirt roads, four-lane superhighways, the back country roads. In former lives they may have been Indian trails or river valleys, or, who knows, maybe even dinosaur paths.

There wasn't any particular reason that I myself was to make the actual discovery of a dinosaur; Mark just wanted me to have the honor. As our trip cheerleader he felt better about each of us having special jobs. Ben's main function would be radio operator and honorary navigator. Like the sightless often do, he seemed to have some ancient, underwater sense of time and direction that would probably do more for us than any map or compass. And the boy had radio charisma. Those were pre-CB times, but with Ben at the controls we actually expected personal advice out of the speakers. I have a picture of him tucked away in my brain. He is bent over in the front seat of the Bronco, one hand on the tuner and one on the volume knob. It's late at night and as we slice across South Dakota, Ben's ear is turned toward the radio and his fingers are flying like he's cracking a safe. He tells us by the sound of the static that there's a storm about fifty miles to the southwest and then he pulls in a Beatles retrospective out of some Canadian Station.

EXCEPT FOR GASSING UP IN ALBERT LEA, WE HAD BEEN talking and driving nonstop for about five hours. We were all getting a little fuzzy. Mark was at the wheel and Ben was lying down in back in a space we had cleared out among the gear. We'd just heard our third version that night of "Raindrops Keep Fallin' on My Head" when Eric Clapton's "Layla" came to us out of nowhere. I'll tell you, even the Bronco perked up. I turned the volume full tilt and we all rocked back and forth in our seats and pounded our feet. Mark was singing into the microphone of his fist. That's a song you can't listen to at less than seventy-five miles an hour. But then it started to fade and crackle and suddenly it was gone. It was nothing but a tease. Bait dangled before tired travelers' ears and then snatched away again. Mark slowed down and started looking for a way to get to the other side of the freeway.

"Shit," he said. "It's probably just a couple of miles behind us. Let's get back there."

So we jolted across the grass center strip and headed back down the opposite side of I-90. We picked up "Layla" again just as it breaks into the piano and slide-guitar part. Listening reverently, we drove on eastward. When the song ended, Mark pulled onto the shoulder.

We were like beached fish there for a while. A good road song will drain you that way. After a breather, Mark got us turned west again.

Cassette players would eliminate problems like overdriving a special tune and Lord knows that the old nighttime car radio speaks in tongues and can barely hold one song as it is. But the commercials are as vital as the music and tapes take away the spontaneity of the search. The expectation alone of finding a road classic like "Johnny B. Goode" or "Cinnamon Girl" somewhere along the dial can keep you going for miles. It just seems too easy to pop in a cassette whenever you want to hear some favorite.

Oh, I guess a tape deck could be used in moderation.

A WEEK BEFORE WE LEFT, BEN HAD MADE MARK PROMISE that we would see the Corn Palace at Mitchell. It was about 3:00 A.M. when I saw the Mitchell signs, but since we were making such good time, neither Mark nor I said anything to Ben. Suddenly he jackknifed up like a sprung-open ironing board to remind us to take the Corn Palace exit. (Mark had recently been telling me how he thought Ben was psychic.)

The Corn Palace is a civic-center type of deal that was built in 1892. It has a bit of the Byzantine in it—minarets and spindly towers and flags and pennants. And it has quite a bit of the Midwest in it too, since every year the outside is decorated with two thousand bushels of corn and grain. Usually in some cowboy or Indian scene.

It's a famous place. William Jennings Bryan harangued there once. John Philip Sousa played the Corn Palace in

1904 and again in 1907. And Lawrence Welk is a regular. (I wonder if Mick Jagger has ever been there.) There were even several Corn Palace clones that popped up in nearby towns, but they never made it beyond a few early festivals. The Mitchell Corn Palace is still going strong.

We saw it in the 3:00 A.M. streetlight. A brown-and-gold cathedral with vegetating walls. Ben wanted to touch it, so Mark led him over to the main entrance. Then for a picture he had Ben put on some goofy, red-rimmed sunglasses and pretend he was a visiting Chicago blues man. Ben shouted out a chorus of "What I Say" and trilled his fingers over the ghostly piano walls of the Corn Palace.

FUN FACT: In 1902, two stockmen built an eighty-mile-long barbed-wire chute in western South Dakota. It was supposed to be a quick way of getting cattle back and forth and wouldn't have been half a bad idea except that a railroad came in a year later.

BREAKFAST IS USUALLY SUCH AN UNDESERVED MEAL. That is, unless you've been working the late shift or driving all night. We had been driving all night, but it wasn't a sense of worthiness that brought us to a little South Dakota café. The Bronco went bad about 5:00 A.M. and we barely made it into a Standard station next to the Kimball exit. It was there all through breakfast. Up on the rack. We were only eight hours out of St. Paul and still a long way from the old dino we were planning to chase down.

Ben was understanding. He suggested that we walk into Kimball and look around, and get something to eat while the mechanic checked out the truck.

Mark was what you call pissed. He hadn't said much, but he gave the dashboard of the Bronco the finger for a good ten seconds while we were looking for a gas station. After gathering up his rented camera gear, which he never left unattended, he took off into town five yards ahead of Ben and me.

Kimball seemed as good a place as any for a breakdown. Better, probably. The sun was warm there and the air smelled good. It was a fine, western little place. But it's the kind of place that's easily maligned and passed off as nowhere.

There are plenty of these wonderful nowheres strung out along I-90 across the whole of South Dakota. The picture is always the same. Two or three service stations are clumped around the cloverleaf ramps, and in the town itself there is one greasy, old gas station. There are several joints and cafés and a hardware and a barber shop. The post office is usually squeezed into a corner of the grocery store and a cement-block VFW hall proudly displays an antiaircraft gun out in front. You would get the sense of knowing one of these places on a single pass through, although you usually wouldn't be passing through unless you had relatives there or were broken down.

We had seen Mark turn into the Plains Café. When we joined him, he was sitting in a booth worrying over a highway map spread out before him. Probably figuring our lost time.

He didn't say a thing to either of us until we had started eating. Then he looked straight ahead at me, shaking a fork. "If we even make it to Wall in that heap, just get there is all, I'll personally hump it in the tail pipe."

This caught Ben with a mouthful. He sputtered and coughed, sending a little piece of sausage across the table.

Meanwhile, Mark poured too much syrup on his pancakes and it ran onto the map. "Mother Fox!" was all he said as he slammed down his fork and stomped out of the place.

"I guess Mark's pretty hot to get out there, isn't he?" Ben said after carefully completing a swallow.

"He'll be okay," I said. "You know how he feels about the Bronchitis. Besides, he's a little wound up with school over and not having a job."

Mark was wound up all right. So was I, actually. It was some of our catching up coming back to us. While Ben dozed off last night, we had quite a talk. Women, religion, work, parents, Vietnam. It was a great, soul-sounding brother talk. The kind of talk you had to go on a trip to have.

Mark was always going to show me what life was all

about. That was because he thought I was the straight-and-narrow, good-student type and he was a man of the world. In fact he wanted me to see the world. He kept giving me books like *The Hotel Guide to Kenya* and *Romania in All Seasons*. There was talk of Australia and Tibet and Venezuela. Mark had a beach-ball-size globe in his room with a dent in Greenland. I'm pretty sure the dent was from him stabbing his finger at the general area whenever he told me how we had to hit the Arctic Circle someday.

Before Ben met Mark, I told him all about my brother's trips and travels. Ben and I kind of lived off Mark's experiences for a while. I think Ben figured he was another Lowell Thomas or something. I just thought Mark was having a better time than I was.

Mark and Ben met about a year before the big trip. They pretty much had your basic immediate rapport. The first time I got them together I ended up just listening to this wild, Ping-Pong conversation about the state of the world and the economy and how America was still a good place to live but just barely and so much more that I can't even go into it.

Mark was very quiet when we drove home from Ben's after that first visit. Then he told me that he thought Ben had some kind of special power. Some kind of supersensitive, tuned-in-to-the-world power, and that from Ben we could both learn to see things in their real light.

Ben and I continued eating, but he must have still been thinking about Mark's reaction to the breakdown. He began to tell me his theory about cars and their owners. All about the delicate interplay between the human psyche and the car. How your car goes, you go and vice versa. If you wake up with a headache one morning, you know in advance that the old car will be sluggish and lackadaisical. Of course, it also follows that the vehicle is hot to trot on Friday nights after work. Psychomechanics Ben called it. He also said that he'd heard how some owners even look like their cars.

"That all sounds great, Ben," I said, "but it's my truck, not Mark's."

"There is also a cross involvement with the siblings of the vehicle owners," he added.

Well, the psychomechanics thing sounded pretty interesting, but all I know about cars is that I don't know a thing about them. I just turn that old key and I have no idea what's going on under the hood. It's a supreme act of faith, hope, and trust every time. Rabbits could be running on a treadmill for all I know.

BEN AND I WERE JUST FINISHING EATING WHEN MARK came back into the café like nothing had happened. He shoveled in his cold breakfast standing up, talking with a mouthful. "When you little whorelets are done, I've got something great to show you," he said. Then he gathered up his map and camera gear and paid for all of our checks. "The barbershop across the street," he said pointing out the window and jerking his head in the same direction. Then he was gone again.

THROUGH THE PICTURE WINDOW OF THE BARBERSHOP, I could see Mark behind his tripod. When Ben and I entered, he must have sensed our presence because he didn't even look up from the viewfinder; he just kept firing away and introduced us to the barber.

I saw that the window seat was crowded with several petrified turtles and other fossils and rocks. Mark got Mr. Reber, the barber, to hold a few specimens for another shot and then brought Ben over to the window. Mark had Ben run his hand over one of the fossil turtles and explained some of the other pieces to him. There was some dinosaur bone in there too. I got a little revved up myself. I also decided to get a haircut.

Mr. Reber was a distinguished-looking gentleman in his eighties. He wore suspenders and a little black bowtie and was as bald as a rock. He only used scissors during my cut, leaning on me several times to steady his hand. No electric hair clippers had ever buzzed in his shop he told me.

He was also the town's veterinarian. The fossils were

just a sideline. "I'm not really schooled in animals from that far back," he said.

The first time Mr. Reber left me alone in the chair, a rancher brought in some cattle-blood samples to be tested. The second time, he went over to the window to better answer Mark and Ben's barrage of questions. After a few minutes I joined the group myself (half haircutted and still draped). Pretty soon we were all touching turtles and passing around dinosaur vertebrae and teeth, and arrowheads. Mark and I were getting pretty worked up over all the stuff.

As Mr. Reber finished my haircut, he told us where the specimens were found and what ranchers we should talk to for permission to work their land. There were supposed to be some good dinosaur spots in the Badlands south of Wall.

The three of us were leaning toward the door by this time and after the bill was paid, we grabbed Ben and bolted out of the place. When we hit the street, Mark and I looked around like we didn't know where we were. Like we were expecting to be standing in the middle of the Badlands.

And then it hit us. The Bronco! We were one hangdog little group walking back out to the Standard station.

"That sucker better be running when we get there," I said. Affection for a truck can only get you so far across South Dakota.

THE MECHANIC SAW US COMING AND STEPPED OUT FROM under the hoisted-up Bronco; he was shaking his head like a surgeon with bad news. "You boys own this vehicle?" Mark looked at me sideways, but none of us said anything. "I'm afraid things don't look too good."

There was a puddle of oil cupped in his right hand and he held it out for us. "Metal shavings in the crankcase, boys. That's bad, real bad." Bad enough that he even suggested we try driving ahead to Chamberlain and sell the Bronco for whatever we could get for it.

"Sell it!" Mark said to me after the mechanic returned to the terminal patient. "Sell it and here we are not even halfway across South Dakota. We're broken down and this trip isn't even a day old yet."

Ben had a thought. "Let's drive it into Chamberlain— at least that's in the right direction. We'll get another opinion there and if it's just as bad, let's sell it and finish the trip by Greyhound."

"Great," Mark said. "Something I always wanted to do, take the 'dog' all over the West. Great, just goddanged great."

Actually, I couldn't imagine having to sell the Bronco. For as long as I'd had it, the inside still smelled like a new phone book. It had over ninety-nine thousand hard miles on it and it had been Mark's plan to push it the final mile before turning over a hundred thou. And it looked so helpless up on the rack. Selling it would be more like abandoning it. But at the time, Ben's idea was the only one that would get us moving.

I remember thinking that maybe we could just get it washed and waxed and then it would be okay again.

WE LIMPED ALONG I-90, GOING ABOUT FIFTEEN OR twenty miles an hour. I was driving, keeping the truck half on the shoulder and half on the road. Ben was riding shotgun and Mark was boiling in back.

About ten miles out of Kimball, the Bronco started acting even worse than it had before breakfast. In fact, it sounded exactly like a piece of silverware caught in a garbage disposal. I had Ben turn the radio up, hoping Mark wouldn't hear the awful grinding. (I remember the song that came on too, "Jumpin' Jack Flash.")

Then something happened. A stock truck blew by us on the left. Mark caught a glimpse of a curlicue pig's tail sticking out from between one of the slats and called it out to us. It turned out to be the road blessing we needed. The Bronco lurched suddenly and leaped ahead on its own. For a moment I thought the grinding was gone. I quieted the radio; it sure sounded gone. I sped up cautiously, and then slowed down. Looking in the rearview, I expected to see engine droppings strung out behind us on the asphalt. Then I stopped on the shoulder and started

up again. The noise was gone! We were sailing along at
fifty-five.

After a half hour of silent, steady running I saw a sign
that I read out loud.

"See the Badlands at Wall. A hundred seventy-five
miles." I let that linger so Mark was sure to gather it in.

"All right!" Ben said, thumping the dash. "Let's hear
it for the old Bronchitis."

"Wall Drug!" I yelled and then honked the horn. "Dinosaur city! We'll be there for lunch."

Mark must have remembered his breakfast vow about
the tailpipe business and was probably thinking ahead to
an arrival in Wall that was no longer in doubt. "Mind if I
wait until she cools down a bit?" he asked from the back.

CHAPTER
2

DAYLIGHT TRAVEL HAS ITS POINTS. LIKE YOU CAN see, and there's always plenty to see. The semis, the farm equipment, the seed ads. And that summer it seemed like cows were jumping each other wherever we looked. (Mark never failed to mention this to Ben, who would puff up and get red.)

You've got to take it all in, even the names on the campers. "Kon Tiki," "Travel Queen," "Nomad," and "True North" were all popular numbers. And then there're the bumper stickers, like Mark's all-time favorite, "Keep on Truckin'." Mark always said he'd drive into a ditch to keep from looking at one more of those bastards.

Ben is not your hard language type of guy, but somehow he tolerated Mark's and my foulness. If he was sighted, Ben would be the person who modifies lavatory-stall graffiti so it wouldn't offend future patrons.

WE CROSSED THE MISSOURI RIVER AT CHAMBERLAIN where the Bronco was supposed to have been sold. The water looked like snow in the noon brightness. The bridge wasn't marked, but I knew from a South Dakota wayside rest plaque that Mark let me read from the truck that it was named for Lewis and Clark. The boys and their forty-two-man Corps of Discovery camped nearby in September 1804. Clark bagged and skinned an antelope that went to the naturalist artist Charles Willson Peale, curator of Peale's Museum of Philadelphia. The marker says Clark thought the animal was a new type of goat and that he was very impressed with the antelope's speed. Actively made, he described it, appearing more suited for airborne flight than the motion of a quadruped.

"We have Thomas Jefferson to thank for all this," Mark said as we took off from the rest area.

"What?" I said. I was still plugged in to Lewis and Clark.

"The West," said Mark. Then he looked over at me like I should have been reading his mind. "Thomas Jefferson bought the West from the French in 1803. Then he sent Lewis and Clark to check it out."

Mark was right there. The Louisiana Purchase. Jefferson bought the land between the Mississippi and the Rockies from Napoleon, who had just won it from Spain in a card game or something, and the U. States of America had its Great West.

"Thomas Jefferson invented the dime," said Ben. "He also pioneered systematic architectural methods, and after the British burned Washington in 1814, he started a new Library of Congress with seven thousand of his own books."

Facts were flying around so fast and furious, I felt like a *College Bowl* moderator.

"Thomas Jefferson did a lot of stuff," Mark said. "He was a statesman out of duty and a gadgeteer out of curiosity, but his real love was natural history."

I expected Ben to have something to say about Jefferson because I expected him to have something to say about everything. But Mark sounded like he was an American studies expert. I happened to know for a fact that he had been reading the most recent issue of *National Geographic* before we left and they had profiled Jefferson.

Mark rambled on. He was gesturing wildly. A fine mist of spittle covered the windshield in front of him as he spoke.

"When all the hotshots gathered in Philadelphia to go over Jefferson's draft of the Declaration of Independence," Mark was saying, "he was walking through the city futzing around with America's first thermometer. And during the same stopover, he lectured to the American Philosophical Society about the fossil bones of an extinct ground sloth that were given to him by a saltpeter digger in western Virginia. And he had the bones right there with him.

"When he was President, Jefferson had mastodon bones and other Ice Age fossils stored in the East Room of the White House. The son of a bitch was a paleontologist!"

"Please don't refer to one of our greatest Presidents in that fashion," Ben said.

"As a paleontologist?" asked Mark. He actually looked hurt.

"Well, that too, I guess," said Ben.

JEFFERSON HAD BEEN THINKING ABOUT EXPLORING THE Great West for over twenty years. In 1783, he had already cooked up secret plans for an exploration of the West through a back-door approach across Siberia and the Bering Strait and down through Canada by dog sled and then on to the Louisiana Territories. Some trip. But it never pulled off.

When Jefferson took the presidency in 1801, the flame for western exploration was still singeing his brain. At the time, the area belonged to Spain, but he had another plan, this time up the Missouri River from St. Louis to as far west as it would go. Maybe all the way to the Pacific.

Mark said Jefferson would have given his left nut to go with Lewis and Clark's Corps of Discovery. The early nineteenth century was natural history's golden age and Jefferson was one of its bright lights. A handful of refined gentlemen with notebooks and cabinets of natural curiosities were quietly going about Europe and the civilized parts of the New World cataloging the land and its lifeforms. (Observations of children and natives evidently didn't count for much.) And then all of a sudden, Jefferson gets the Great American West! A whole half continent of unnamed living things and uncharted country. My God! It was a natural historian's wet dream. In 1803, woolly mammoths were still thought to roam around out there among rivers of ice and salt blocks a mile high. Nobody really knew about dino in those days, but if they did, I'm sure they would have figured that *T. rexes* and hairy elephants ran around together.

The Corps of Discovery pulled out of St. Louis on an 1804 May day for what would be a two-and-a-half-year keelboat and canoe trip up the great western highway of the Missouri River. There was a final letter from Jefferson that reminded the boys to take close notice of the country and its productions, the great mammoth in particular, and the remains of any animal which may be extinct.

"Goddamn!" Mark said as the Bronco winged us across the beautiful South Dakota prairie. "Just think if I-90 was here in 1804? Just I-90 and the Bronco and us, with everything else just like it was in Lewis and Clark time?"

"What would we do for gas?" asked Ben.

Mark sniffed and looked straight ahead without saying anything for a moment.

"Well maybe there'd have to be a self-serve Super America every two hundred miles," Mark said. "But nothing else."

FUN FACT: Edgar Allan Poe had an unfinished novel about the West that was fired up by Lewis and Clark's journals.

BEN AND MARK HAD BEEN COOKING UP A PROJECT FOR the 1976 bicentennial. A Hold Hands Across America campaign. They wanted to get a chain of people holding hands from New York to California. Mark was most excited about the ripple that would run through the two million or so people it would take to do it.

It was probably Mark's idea, but Ben was getting the details worked out. He had calculated the number of people it would take and had actually contacted several state highway patrols and local Triple A chapters. Mark was supposed to have written to the bicentennial commission for a grant but I imagine that task got pushed aside by some other grand scheme, although Mark did mention the human linkup a few more times before America's two hundredth summer.

I LOVE MAPS. I LOVE TO RUN MY FINGER OVER A MAP OF the western states and feel the magic of the Dakotas and Montana and Wyoming. I look at a map—in my room, in the car, in the middle of the Badlands— and I forget time. I forget distance. For a moment I may even think of walking somewhere that is actually hundreds of miles away.

Ancient cartographers must have gotten heady creating great open swaths of uncharted lands. And I can imagine the comfort that Columbus and Magellan must have felt in their old age as they stuck pins in globes to mark the places they'd been.

I had the usual complement of regional gas-station maps and road atlases. I also liked to page through the huge maps on file at the public library. But the premier maps, the real mind travelers, are geological section maps. These window-size projections have the elevations and contour lines and rock type all marked and colored in. You could almost step into one and walk around a bit. I have a section map of our favorite area of the Badlands, near Beauty, South Dakota.

Thirty-five miles out of Chamberlain, Mark was giving me some very poor map advice. Not that we needed much. Once you get on I-90 at Albert Lea it's just a straight shot to the Badlands, but I wanted to know what town Mountain Time started at. Mark was looking at a map in back and calling out distances that were way off or telling me that certain towns weren't even listed. I held out my hand for the thing.

"Give me that s.o.b. I'll check it out myself."

"Yes, suh!" Mark said. In the rearview mirror I could see him trying to bow.

I only needed one quick glance at the map to see what was up.

"What is this piece of shit?" I said. I couldn't believe it. It was a place mat from the café in Kimball. It had an outline of South Dakota with several highlighted landmarks. There was a big water skier near the Missouri River. The Corn Palace popped out of Mitchell and of course there was a profile of Mount Rushmore in Rapid City.

"Real fine document," I said, crumpling it and throwing it over my shoulder in Mark's general direction.

"Hey, jerko, I wanted that!" Mark said as he smoothed it out. "Lewis and Clark would have slit throats for this thing."

"Sorry, sorry."

Ben was feeling around in the glove compartment to find me a real map when Mark called politely up to the front.

"Murdo."

"Pardon me?" I said.

"Murdo. That's where Mountain Time begins. It's right here in the corner of my place mat under 'South Dakota Facts'."

"Thanks, sweet," I said.

"That's quite all right, sweet," said Mark. "I picked up a map for you too, but it may have to be the wrinkled one."

MARK IS A PROFESSIONAL PHOTOGRAPHER, CINEMATOGrapher really. But he doesn't own one piece of photographic equipment other than the light meter I gave him two years before the trip for his nineteenth birthday. He had had a nice little Pentax that he hawked during film school and then just rented whatever he needed.

Looking back over the trip slides, I see Mark got some good shots of us loading the Bronco. There's a choice one of my dad holding a red-stick flare in both hands with several more stuffed in each pocket. Like he was pretending the flares were dynamite and he was the side of a hill about to be blown away.

Ours was an audio-visual family. Like all growing-up Americans of the 1950's, we were the first generation whose every milestone could be recorded on film, photo, or tape. And my father was right there for baby words and steps, and bike riding, and graduations. He was also rather ahead of his time by photographing Mark's and my sister Anne's births. A good friend was the family obstetrician and he let my dad into the delivery room.

The home movies are great. It's like watching someone else play you. There I am on film taking a first step or sitting on a potty chair. There are Mark and me running in and out of a little rubber swimming pool or jumping in the snow. Home movies make you think you remember your childhood clear as a bell.

Mark's and my pre-high school days are one third black and white since color didn't come into widespread, practical use until 1955. That also explains why all of Anne's photos are in color, except for a couple of portraits.

When Anne was nine, she got on a local kids' TV show called *Casey Jones and Roundhouse Rodney*. Our grandmother was living with us then and took a whole roll of pictures of the TV set with her Brownie whenever Anne was visible, even though she was sitting in a big crowd. They kind of turned out, but each print had horizontal lines across it.

It's hard for me to believe that everyday photos of the present will have any meaning in a hundred years, and yet, everyday old photos are spellbinding just because they are old. In fact, the more everyday the better. Street scenes, backyards, factory interiors, mothers with babies, fathers holding pocket watches. If it's old, it has meaning. It's special.

One of the oldest surviving photographic images was made in 1835 and is now a priceless museum piece. It's of a plain and ordinary latticed window. (From a three-hour exposure by the way.) Take a snapshot of a nearby window and then will the negative to your survivors.

In grade school, Mark and I both liked to look through our grandmother's photograph drawer. She and Grandpa had home-steaded in a sod shack on the Dakota prairie until moving to St. Paul just before our father was born.

Pioneer Grandma got into those old pictures even more than we did. She especially got fired up whenever she looked at the Dakota scenes. Mark and I never knew Grandpa, since he left the planet about the time we got here.

At the time of our big trip, Pioneer Grandma was eighty-five years old. Her speech was slurred and her once-beautiful handwriting looked like sky writing in dispersion. She had already had a little stroke and a heart attack. Mark and I hoped she would make it through the summer. Before we left, Mark promised he'd find her a dinosaur bone as big as her bed. With that, she gave us both a confused look.

"What is this trip for again?" she asked. We told her once more.

She didn't say a thing for several minutes. She just picked at some blanket lint.

"That doesn't even sound right," she said, twitching her shoulders, "Dinosaur bones? You're going to drive all the way out there for dinosaur bones? Now, pretty girls I could understand."

THE GREAT PLAINS. I WANT TO GO RUNNING OVER THEM like Julie Andrews did through her mountain meadows in *The Sound of Music*. I'm talking the Great American Western Plains here. The Great Plains as opposed to the Basin and Range or the Appalachian Highlands or the Canadian Shield. The Complacent Plains, a *Psychology Today* survey called them. The region rated the lowest of all national regions in the number of negative feelings. South Dakota, North Dakota, Wyoming, Montana, Kansas, Nebraska, Iowa. Great country those Great Plains. A great palace to dilute my claustrophobia.

Major parts of the Dakotas are undeniably flat, but that doesn't preclude their attractiveness. And it also makes for safe driving. You don't have to worry about flying off a mountain pass at eighty miles an hour.

I saw Mark looking out over the prairie and then back at the road. When he knew he had my audience, he let go with a passage from George and Jacques P. Herters'

North Star Guide Manual: "'In case you have to leave the trail or road at high speed, your best bet is to head into the bush if any is available.'"

"Ah, the Herter wisdom," I said.

Only out there we wouldn't need any bush if we had to leave the trail. It'd be like driving onto one huge, shopping center parking lot.

The *North Star Guide Manual* was one of Mark's and my favorite books. It had helped take the edge off puberty by having nothing whatsoever to do with girls. From it we learned that streams that came directly from glaciers didn't have fish in them and that you should never drive over a porcupine, dead or alive, and that insects from car radiators made good panfish bait. We studied that book like our future lives out in the field would hinge on it.

By the time I was in the ninth grade, Mark and I had gone over the *Guide Manual* so many times we thought for sure we could pass the 1966 Alaska State Fish and Game Board exam right then and there. The book had an appendix listing sample questions from the test, which the Herters felt was the strictest and most complete in the country. We had our favorite questions underlined in red:

—Can polar bear liver be eaten?

—Draw a sketch of the human body showing the points where blood flow may be stopped.

—Describe how to start a fire with aluminum foil.

—If big-game meat you left out smells strongly of urine, what animal did this?

—Draw out the 18 Civil Air Patrol signals and briefly describe each one.

—Will grayling take wobbling spoons?

—In taking a photograph of a dead brown bear and your client, where would you place the client?

WALL DRUG.
DON'T MISS WALL DRUG.
FREE ICE WATER AT WALL DRUG.

Those signs must be on every other fence post across South Dakota.

"What's with this Wall Drug?" Mark asked after the millionth sign.

"That's the whole idea," said Ben.

"Wall Drug is the only true heir to Burma Shave," I said like I knew what I was talking about. "They spend a hundred grand a year on these signs."

Ben was up for Wall Drug. More up even than he was for the Corn Palace. And he had promised to get his nieces and nephews some View-Master slides at Wall Drug.

The Badlands start about forty miles before Wall at Kadoka ("The Gateway to the Badlands"). You can't see the Badlands from the highway around Kadoka, so you take it on faith. And there aren't any signs saying you had hit the Great West, but there were hints. Like how every little town beyond Chamberlain had its own gray, weathered rodeo arena.

Ben told us he heard that there were underground missile silos near Kadoka. ICBMs and Minutemen. And in the Badlands of North Dakota and Montana and Wyoming too. In fact, as Ben told it, over half of the most dangerous places to live in the U.S.A. in the event of a full-scale attack on our military-industrial targets were in the Complacent Plains.

Think about it. Dinosaur land being blown to bits. I think about it a lot.

Outside Kadoka we started seeing billboards for a Badlands museum. I was driving and reading aloud to Mark and Ben. "'See real dinosaur bones. Walk through our petrified garden....'"

All of a sudden, the museum exit popped up in front of us.

"Let's hit it!" Mark said. Then he braced himself.

I turned abruptly onto the off ramp at highway speed and we took it on two wheels. The gear shifted in back and Ben's guitar case fell on him. That jarred up the guitar enough to let an open chord ring out and then hang momentarily in the boxed-up air of the case.

I stopped with a skid in the graveled parking area and Mark shot out of the truck, leaving his door wide open.

He ran toward the edge of a cliff overlooking the Badlands that for the moment steered him away from the museum display. He hopped up on a low stone wall and was looking through a pair of binoculars that Ben had brought for us.

Meanwhile, Ben scrambled out of the back, probably thinking he had better bail out before the vehicle exploded or sank or something.

THE EXHIBIT HAD SOME CURIOUS DISPLAYS, SO I GUESS it was worth the two bucks apiece. It reminded me of a state fair exotica show. You pay at one end and walk down dark, narrow aisles with glass window displays built into the walls. But in this case it wasn't shrunken heads or lost treasures. It was hulking dinosaur bones and stumps of petrified wood. At the end of the line you came out into a little room full of boxes with signs saying DINOSAUR FOSSILS—$1.00 YOUR PICK. They were just bits of broken bone, but Mark and I gathered up handfuls and let them fall through our fingers like they were gold coins. But no way were we giving to ever buy a fossil.

"Strike me dead if I ever do anything so crass as buy some dinosaur bones," Mark said to me.

"And you me, babe," I answered. "That would be like going fishing and then just buying a few instead."

But I have this feeling that either one of us was close to buying a sackful of dino bone. Despite the pumping up the Kimball barber had given us and now this exhibit, Mark and I were still worried that we wouldn't find a single fossil during the whole trip. Shut out in dino land. And a lot of people knew we were coming out here to dig dino and had been skeptical enough as it was.

"Hell, we probably won't find so much as a dinosaur cow pie," Mark worried out loud as we pulled away from the museum.

"Hey, that would be great," I said.

"What would?"

"Dinosaur droppings—fossil scat. 'Coprolites' they're called. Man, that would be something for a museum—a real museum."

"No shit," Mark said.

"No shit."

"Well, we really will be lucky if we find some shee-it then."

"Pardon me," interrupted Ben from the back. "You gentlemen seem rather fixated on that word."

"Which one?" Mark baited.

"'Coprolite,' I believe," Ben answered.

I'M SERIOUS ABOUT THIS COPROLITE BUSINESS. PETRIFIED animal droppings really are museum specimens. And they aren't that easy to find either. Locating coprolite is more serendipity than anything else, although large accumulations have been identified. In Arizona there's a place known as Rampart cave where twenty-five thousand years of sloth dung has piled up. The arid climate preserved their droppings intact. The place was a paleontologic wonder until the dung caught fire. The Grand Canyon Park Service even suspected arson. They spent fifty thou battling the smoldering scat for over a year. The stuff burns like peat. Finally the fire went out on its own.

Coprolite tells a lot about an animal. What it ate, how it lived. Some specimens are perfect casts of an animal's intestinal tract.

Bones and teeth are what we usually think of as fossils, but soft body-part casts like coprolite are real finds. Sometimes tendons fossilize. Even fossil brain casts have been found. Then there are the deep-freeze woolly mammoths from Siberia that are so well preserved sled dogs have to be kept away from the meat.

Probably the greatest find of an intact animal was a mummified duck-billed dinosaur found by the famous fossil hunter Charles Sternberg and his sons in the Kansas chalk beds in 1914. Even the skin markings had been preserved.

Personally, I would like to find a fossil butterfly. I imagine it was an exquisite etching on a block of limestone, as if the dust of its wings had left a mark forever. A fossil butterfly I would hang on the wall.

FUN FACT: Wayne "Mr. Las Vegas" Newton has a big hunk of dinosaur coprolite on his fireplace mantel.

BETWEEN KADOKA AND WALL, A HERD OF TRAILER homes was sprouting out of the prairie. Mark hated trailer homes. To him they were a blight. A sign of man's defilement of the earth. He allowed that they probably were all that some people could afford, but a defilement nonetheless. I sent him a little pamphlet when he was in Toronto called "How to Buy a Mobile Home."

"That's enough to piss off the Pope," Mark said, shaking his head as we passed the trailer court.

"I do not understand your use of this word 'piss,'" Ben said in what sounded like broken, visiting-America English.

"Hell, neither do I," Mark answered. "It just sounds good." Then I thought he was going to try a feeble little joke with "piss" in it, but he didn't. So I sang out in fine, schizophrenic form: "We're so poor we don't have a pot to piss in."

"That I do understand," said Ben.

Mark and I had a whole litany of urological obscenities revolving around the word "piss." "Piss" is one of the better vulgarities really. It's not too crass and it actually feels good across the lips. The adjective is probably most commonly called upon, as in "a piss-poor excuse" or "pissed off." It's more rarely used as a noun and then usually with another word, like "a whole piss load." The verb form can be a nice directive— "Go piss up a rope" —and the expletive "What the piss!" is surprisingly unoffensive. Of course, "To take a piss" is self-explanatory.

EVER SINCE MARK LEFT FILM SCHOOL, WE HAD BEEN planning some way to continue the contemplative life. It's not that we had anything against hard labor or desk work or the selling of insurance and real estate. We just had a lot of other things to do. One of the first things was to win the Canadian lottery so we could retire at the respectable ages of twenty-two and twenty-three.

We even had the days measured. Mornings would be spent in the public library relishing current periodicals, contemporary fiction, and the classics. And we would take long walks about town or drives through the country in the afternoon. All the day's activities would point toward an evening retreat to one of several movie houses.

It's not only okay to mess the floor in a theater, it's expected. That's what gives those delicious places the spilt-popcorn and candy-on-old-furniture smell. There is simply no comparison between watching a movie at home and at a theater. Size of projection is one thing, but that's minor. It's the arena darkness and the collective gaze of the crowd and that wonderful smell. If I was a scientist, I would invent a scented spray of theater essence for TV watchers to blow around their living rooms or dens. It could be called Balcony or Aisle Seat.

Mark and I hit a lot of movies together. Usually on weekday afternoons when it wasn't too crowded and you could get in for a buck. We'd do our best to be early. There is a wonderful before-the-movie ebullience that you can only experience by being in your seat before the screen lights up. (Unfortunately, this is often balanced by a post-movie depression, especially if you've cut a class to be there.)

Most afternoons we were about the only people in the whole theater, but once, I think it was at *The King of the Marvin Gardens*, the place was packed. Mark and I had to sit in a sweetheart seat—one of those small couchlike things that two people can barely fit into. Mark kept his arm around the back of my side of the chair for the whole film. It was unthinkable at the time, but I really wish we had somehow gotten a picture of that.

CHAPTER
3

MARK WAS CONVINCED THERE WAS SOMETHING otherworldly about Ben. I wasn't particularly impressed that his last-second reminder to hit the Corn Palace was anything special, but I didn't get a chance to talk about it until Mark and I were alone in a truck-stop men's room outside Kadoka.

"So tell me again about Ben being psychic," I asked Mark as we stood side by side in the john.

Just then I remembered that back in college Ben had told me he could always tell if someone was sitting in the lavatory stall next to him. When he mentioned it, I wasn't sure why that was so special. You don't have to see someone to know they're one can over from you. In fact, sight would follow sound and smell as far as detecting signs of life in that setting go. But then he told me how he did it. He could *feel* a presence he said. It was warmer when someone was nearby, and the air was heavier.

Mark flushed his urinal and turned my way. He did it so quickly I jumped back thinking he was going to pee on my leg.

"Ben is psychic," Mark was saying. "No lie. My watch always stops when I'm around him."

"So what else is new," I said. "Your watch is stopped more than it runs. Hey, Ben is one special dude, but I can't go with the psychic stuff."

"He has premonitions about things before they happen. He has crazy dreams." Mark was gesturing wildly, walking around the men's room with his zipper down.

"He's been my friend for ten years and I never noticed any of this stuff," I said.

"I've just pieced it all together. You were the one who told me about how animals go to him. Birds on the shoulder. Squirrels follow him. He can hypnotize cats."

"Is that psychic?"

"It's something," Mark said. "But listen to this. He doesn't show up in photographs."

"Come on!"

"I shit you not."

"I've seen pictures of Ben," I said.

"I bet they're all of him as a kid. And in black and white."

"Yah. I guess that's right. So?"

"So, he doesn't show up in color. At the house when we were packing, I took a Polaroid of Ben and Dad. In the print, Dad's standing alone with his left arm outstretched like it should be around somebody's shoulders but isn't."

"Holy balls!" I said and must have looked scared.

"Don't worry about it," Mark yelled above the din of a hand dryer whose button he had just hit. "Ben probably doesn't know he has any special powers. Besides, I've got this feeling he'll lead us to a big, buried *T. rex* skeleton with that animal radar of his."

I'm sure there was some explanation for Ben not being in that picture. He probably just stepped out of view or something. And I'm sure Mark knew it too. I think he wanted Ben to be psychic. Ben was sharp all right. Tuned in. But I don't know about psychic.

BEN WAS WAITING FOR US IN THE TRUCK. MARK HANDED him the keys. "It's about time you did some driving in-

stead of telling the future all the time, you little whorelet,"
Mark said as if Ben knew what we had been talking
about.

"You may be a bit disappointed on either count," Ben
said.

"And which counts are those?" Mark asked.

"Driving or telling the future," answered Ben.

"Get out and walk then, man," Mark said, putting Ben
in a hammerlock. "Everybody pulls his own weight on
this trip."

I DIDN'T MEET BEN UNTIL HIGH SCHOOL, BUT I CAN PIC-
ture him as a kid from a photo his mom showed me. One
of the black and whites that did retain his image.

He must have been about four years old. He's standing
with a German shepherd, his new Seeing Eye dog. Ben
never told me about the dog; his mom did. It died when
he was eleven and he never got another one. Ben never
told me anything about his blindness. I never thought of
him being blind anyway. Ben never held back. He played
driveway basketball, rode a bicycle on an open play-
ground, water skied. He even tried serving Mass, but that
didn't work out too well. The Latin he could handle; there
were just a few too many movements and steps to ne-
gotiate.

Once last winter my bus passed him by on the street.
A fleeting glimpse was all I got. Hello, dear Ben. It was
like seeing a slide flashed up on the wall and then flicked
off again. What caught me by surprise was his white cane—
a fold-up, telescoping thing. I had never seen it before.
He told me later that he only used it in unfamiliar territory.

Mark says Ben is a reincarnated Basil Rathbone and I
have to kind of agree. Ben does have a Sherlock Holmes
sense about him. He doesn't say much, but what he does
say is always right. I think Mark would like to have seen
Ben with a curled pipe, pacing back and forth contem-
plating a weighty matter and then suddenly shouting
"Hello?" (The question mark here is important.)

Ben was our trip sage all right. But I was worried about
his health around that time. He had this continual, nag-

ging, rattly cough. The kind that makes you want to clear your own throat when you hear it. And he always looked pale. I hoped some evil like TB or leukemia wasn't lurking around inside him.

ONE OF OUR HIGHWAY STAPLES WAS PRETZELS. THE BIG long ones that look like cigars. When I was at the wheel, I kept four or five of them in my shirt pocket for ready access.

Mark had just given up smoking, so he really latched on to those pretzel sticks. I mean he'd bite off an end and spit it out the window. Then he'd run it under his nose and hold it between two fingers and rap it on the ashtray. Hell, after watching all that, I expected him to light it up.

I don't smoke, but pretzels, root-beer floats, chocolate éclairs, and a fresh stick of chewing gum take care of all my oral gratification needs. Gum chewing especially. Its got its own little rituals. Pulling the red cellophane string off the package, unwrapping the stick, smelling it, savoring that first burst of flavor. One thing about gum though: you can't make it at home.

THE BEAUTY OF WESTERN SOUTH DAKOTA NEEDS NO defense; the Badlands and Black Hills sing their own tunes. I just wish the eastern half of the state wasn't so maligned by travelers. (Maybe only Nebraska and Iowa get more of a tourist bad rap.) The highway department's entry signs don't help matters any either. From the east there is a simple, functional WELCOME TO SOUTH DAKOTA. The standard highway white reflective lettering on a green rectangle. But from the west, the traveler sees a huge billboard with a mountain backdrop and a broncobuster about to be thrown from his horse.

Let there be no doubt about it, western South Dakota is the West. The gold-mining, cattle-rustling, cowboy-and-Indian, ghost town, Frederick Remington, buckskin, Great Spirit, prairie dog, buffalo West. Mark called it the left side of South Dakota.

The great Sioux warrior Crazy Horse is supposed to

be buried in the Badlands. And the Black Hills were so special to the Indians that they considered them to be the center of the earth. They still do.

Annie Oakley, Wild Bill Hickok, Calamity Jane, and Buffalo Bill Cody all hung out on the left side of South Dakota. Wild Bill took a bullet in the back during a Deadwood card game. He's there now, becoming fossilized in Boot Hill.

The West! The God Bless America West! Every manifest destiny American likes to claim a little bit of the West for their own state, and in a way they all could. To the Pilgrims or Vikings or whichever out-of-towners waded onto the continent first, the West was anything in the general direction of the sunset. (I don't think the Indians get all worried about the West. It's the earth itself they're into.)

In 1800, the West was the Ohio River Valley, followed in a decade or so by the Mississippi. Now, I suppose technically the West is the West Coast and Alaska. But *the* Great American West covered the plains of Montana and the Dakotas and followed the buffalo to Texas. That West, the Colorful Period, was and always will be a magic and better-times place.

It was a land of excess in those glory days. Excess beauty. Excess mineral and timber wealth. Excess game and excess land. Basically it was excess excess. There was so much that the first white settlers thought they'd never run out of anything ever again. Lovely black and whites from the nineteenth-century West show pioneers in front of stark homesteads, but there are four-foot piles of antlers on the ground and carcasses hanging from cabin walls like clothes out on the line. And all around is a land that won't quit.

There couldn't have been a better setting for the digging up of the biggest and strangest beasts that ever walked planet Earth. (Pardon me, I'm taking dino again.) Mark considered himself an expert on the history of American dinosaur hunting and he had schooled me in the essentials.

Railroads opened the post-Civil War West, and some big-buck easterners were putting up museums that needed unusual pieces of natural history. The bones of furry mastodons discovered in New York and Missouri peat bogs generated plenty of excitement, but it was the reports coming out of the West of six-foot leg bones and giant sea serpents that fired up a paleontologic gang war.

That's when E. D. Cope and O. C. Marsh decided to simultaneously gather all the fossils in the West.

Both men were hotshot geniuses who jumped into paleontology with a flare and fire unknown to science in any time including the present. Cope had a personal fortune and the Philadelphia Academy of Natural Sciences to fuel him. Marsh was the director of Yale's Peabody Museum.

The show started pretty quietly. Marsh sent teams of buffalo hunters and railroad-men-turned-fossil pickers to the Kansas chalk beds to look for toothed-bird specimens. Cope and his men were nearby, daily uncovering new species of extinct fish. There was some razzing at first. One or the other of the parties would labeled items in the field such as buffalo droppings or prairie dog holes to further the other's education. Somebody even put a sign on a mound of human "bee-em" calling it "food for thought." But then there was some spying and attempted buying off each other's men. Sabotage of campsites and work sites followed.

When the word was in on discoveries farther west of bones so big they were mistaken for petrified tree logs, both Marsh and Cope sent their best men hightailing it all over Colorado and Wyoming and Montana looking for these new monsters.

Dinosaurs had actually been discovered fifty years previous in England. And the first American dinosaur, a duck-billed *Hadrosaurus*, was quarried out of New Jersey in 1858. But even those finds were nothing like the beasts coming out of the West. It wasn't just the heft of the locomotive-size brontosaurus or the three-horned *Triceratops*. It was the shitloads of perfectly preserved specimens. Their bones were everywhere. One of Mark's books on the history of paleontology shows an old black-and-white print of piles of excavated bones that look like logjams. And I already mentioned the cabin made out of dinosaur bones.

Fired up by the hype that the new finds were getting in the eastern news, Cope and Marsh had their men hellbent for dino. During good weather, hundreds of men raked Wyoming and Montana dig sites and returned from every direction loaded with dinosaur bones. Entire quarries opened and closed within weeks. Boxcar loads of bones were sent back to New York, Philadelphia, and New Haven. Complete skeletons of brontosaurus, *Diplodocus*, *Allosaurus*, and *Stegosaurus* came out of the bonanza.

Both parties telegraphed their progress back east in code. Cope even bought his own magazine to get the word of his new discoveries out as soon as possible. Sometimes from on-the-spot identification. So many new species hadn't been named in so short a time since Adam and Eve. Occasionally, Marsh and Cope were describing the same animals simultaneously, but with different names. They cooked up a scientific nomenclature mess that took years to sort out.

I was always partial to Cope because he seemed more our type. He loved to get out in the field and dig. I like the story about Cope wandering around the fossil fields of Montana all by himself right after Custer bit the dust. Cope walked straight into a camp of Sioux warriors on the run. He wasn't too worried and neither were the Indians, so he started bullshitting with them a little bit in sign language. He gave them some very nice marine fossils and then crinked a few necks when he pulled out his own teeth for a moment. Before he took off, one young man gave Cope a pair of bifocals.

Mark phoned me one night at 3:00 A.M. several months before the trip. Long distance from Toronto. He had been "reviewing the literature" and wanted to tell me about Cope's post-fossil-hunting days.

The professor retired around the turn of the century to his house in Philadelphia, which was so crowded with specimens and papers that his family had to live somewhere else. Cope wrote about and sketched specimens to the end in the studio he shared with dinosaur and rhinoceros skulls, several basketball-size meteors, and piles of manuscripts. Barely moving about the room was his gigantic Galapagos turtle.

"I hope that's how you and I go, sweet," Mark had said.

I know I was interested in the story, but I don't recall anything else Mark might have told me that night. I remember he called though, because when I woke up later that morning, the phone receiver was lying on my chest.

Mark and I developed an immediacy of thought through hundreds of late-night, sweaty-ear phone calls. He could have been in Toronto or Chicago or just across town. It didn't matter. The talk slipped between the profound and the profane, sometimes starting as if in continuation of a recent, unfinished conversation. We could speak in monotone or sentence fragments. It was soul to soul. We didn't need the external trappings of gesture or tone of voice.

I COULD SEE IN THE REARVIEW THAT MARK WAS LOOKING at some kind of a chamber of commerce pamphlet.

"What's that, brother?" I asked.

"A little promo piece on Kimball," Mark said. "But look at this great old photo postcard of the place." Then he passed the picture up to me.

"Hey, with the place mat and now this stuff, you've got a great little portfolio going on Kimball. You planning on starting a business there?"

"Sure thing. A little light industry would be right up their alley. Listen to what it says here: 'Kimball, a good place to live for good people. We have fresh air and open spaces, new streets, a willing labor force, wonderful schools, good shopping, and everything that is desirable for the good life.'"

"And a barber-dinosaur hunter," I added.

"Right you are. But there's more: 'We have the very best with none of the bad.'"

"That settles it," I said. "Let's move to Kimball when we get back. Ben, will you join us?"

"I'll write to each of you," said Ben. "And I'll pray for the return of your intellects."

"Hey!" I said, remembering the postcard and picking it up again, "this is a beaut of an old photo."

Old pictures put me in a trance. I fixate on one and start to see dust swirl in the streets and people move about. I may even get into the photo myself and walk around a bit.

Since I was still driving, I had to wait until we stopped in the Wall Drug parking lot to look at this one.

It was an aerial view of Kimball taken in 1904 from the top of a grain elevator. Black and white, of course. The whole town of about seventy folks is out on the street in four different groups with a few stragglers sprinkled here and there. Everyone's looking toward the camera. Some people are waving. It looks like a hot summer noon. Worn base paths are visible in an empty lot and a sign says to look out for the wagons. Unbelievable flatness surrounds the town itself, which rises like a little blister off the sweating prairie.

THEY ARE MIRACLES. THEY ARE TRICKS OF NATURE. THEY are magic, pure and simple. They are the daguerreotype, the tintype, the home movie, the cinema, the snapshot, and the videotape. Momentographs. Talking pictures. Mirrors that remember. Perfect shadows.

But these days we take photography for granted. No longer do we have to mess with glass-plate negatives or gunpowder flash or heads under light-shielding drapes. As early as 1900, George Eastman had been telling the world that there was nothing to it ("You push the button and we do the rest"). Mark told me the first mass-produced Kodak cameras even came loaded with a one-hundred-exposure roll of film. When you had taken the hundred shots, you mailed the camera in. They unloaded and re-loaded the camera, processed the pictures, and sent it all back. Hell, look at today. Cameras with built-in computer exposure meters. Automatic film-loading cassettes. Polaroids. Home video.

But despite never-miss color film and guaranteed picture-perfect processing, every photographer, pro or newborn, carries a deepdown dread that his just-exposed film may not "turn out." It's a mutated chromosome that entered humankind during the last half of the nineteenth century. A Mathew Brady gene.

That insecurity is perpetuated in those who know bits and pieces of photographic fact, like how moving-picture film manufactured prior to 1930 can supposedly blow up in its storage can with all the power of a hand grenade. But that is no news to me. I think almost any picture could explode and splatter emotions all around. Like home movies where you see yourself grow up, or pictures of former sweethearts that get your soul hunched up in a ball and under a table for protection. And there's always the smiling college group shots. But the most explosive photographs of all are of dead loved ones. My God, that smile, that gaze. They're looking right at you. You lean in toward the image and it leaps out of the frame at you. But then, as if on a leash, it's jerked back again. When things settle down, you can see that they miss you too.

Despite hanging around Mark and even having studied some photochemistry and optics, I am as wonder-struck with a photograph as an African native who sees the miracle for the first time. I talk to photos and halfway expect a response. I gaze in amazement at projected slides or movies and want to look behind the screen for the tricks being played. Or I'll pick up Mark's camera and hold it to my eye lens-first and expect to see a View-Master scene inside.

To me, the camera is a magic box. Actually, "camera" means a room or chamber. I looked it up. That explains it all for me. A dark little room where images are baited and trapped. The inside of a camera is like the inside of the head. Sacred, off limits. Something only for brain surgeons and professional photographers.

My sister Anne's first camera was a Mick-a-Matic, a Kodak Instamatic hidden behind the face of Mickey Mouse. Mark gave it to her in 1970 when she was in the fifth grade.

I should have had the Mick-a-Matic on the dinosaur trip. Or maybe a 1959 Japanese radiocamera. Those would have been cameras that I could have related to.

Racing through photography's history always makes

me wonder where the hell it's going. How far beyond instant home movies and perfect exposures and 3-D laser photos can you go? Personally, I'd like to see a return to fleeting images in a bottle of silver salts.

But if they really want something, they've got to work on preserving a few of the other senses. Vision and hearing have been taken care of. We need some bottled tastes and feelings and smells. Smells may offer the most interesting possibilities. There's as much nostalgia in a good whiff of a special odor as there is in a high school yearbook or Bing Crosby's "White Christmas." Cigar smoke. Warm candle wax. Turpentine. Pencil shavings. Moth balls. The smell of your mother's kitchen. Capture those essences for people to take down from their mantels or out of bureau drawers and you've got memory nailed down.

Mark's favorite photographer was a gentleman he heard about in film school. "One-Eye" Deane. Old One-Eye bought his nickname when he recorded a remarkable photograph in 1896 of two trains the instant they collided. It was a real train wreck, but staged for thousands of onlookers by a railroad official named William Crush ("I shit you not," Mark said every time he told the story). On the appointed day, fifty thousand people pressed into the temporary Texas town of Crush. The two locomotives, one green and one red, nuzzled cowcatchers and backed up their empty cars several miles apart. Then they turned loose wide open as the engineers jumped ship. The trains smacked into each other at full-steam ahead, exploding their boilers and catapulting debris out into the crowd. Three people were killed and dozens of others injured, including the photographer named Deane who got his picture and a bolt in the eye.

When I came to again, I was alone in the Bronco. Mark and Ben had slipped into the famous Wall Drug.

SOMEBODY KNEW WHAT THEY WERE DOING WITH THIS Wall Drug deal. Out front is the Old West look—hitching posts, wood-burned signs, boardwalks, and life-size cowboy statues. But inside it's all big-city department store. A whole block long. Somewhere between rock shop and bookstore and haberdashery there really is a drugstore. Mark bought some aspirin there. I also noticed him fingering a pack of cigarettes. Western souvenirs are all over the place, and in the back—so you have to walk through the whole maze of temptation—is a cafeteria that seats five hundred.

During the summer, ten thousand people a day visit Wall Drug. It's the industry in town. A third of the families in Wall work there. Ten thousand people a day! Luckily they're all on their way to Mount Rushmore and Yellowstone and not the good old Badlands.

Wall Drug is like Las Vegas for the one reason that they are both so Made Only in America. Wall Drug's not as slick as Vegas, but it's the closest a drugstore has ever come to being a state fair and a circus and a national landmark all at the same time.

I found Mark and Ben in the rock shop. There were some fine fossils on display. Ben was sitting on a five-foot-long dinosaur thigh bone and Mark was about to take a few shots of him.

"Testing out the psychic bit?" I tried to whisper.

"Except for one thing," Mark said, firing off two quick shots. "These won't be developed until we get back."

"What won't be developed?" Ben said, appearing beside us.

Ben popped up so sudden, I got goose bumps.

"It's what will develop when I give you this stolen T-shirt," Mark said. Then he put down the camera.

Draped over one arm, Mark did have a yellow T-shirt that he began pulling over Ben's head.

"Did you really steal this?" Ben asked.

"Yes and no. It was more like a trade. Some informal bartering upon which the Old West was grounded. I took the T-shirt in exchange for a golf-ball-size Minnesota agate that I put in the rock bin over there."

"Does Wall Drug know of the transaction?" I asked, looking around for any plainclothes detectives.

"Hey, they're coming out ahead on this one," Mark said. "Did you look at Ben's shirt?"

I looked. Four pink bottoms stuck out from the side of a mountain.

"It's the back of Mount Rushmore!" Mark said so loud that everyone in the rock shop turned our way.

EVIDENTLY WALL DRUG HAS GENERATED A LOT OF AF-fection. There were framed snapshots covering the cafeteria walls of signs in Shanghai (WALL DRUG, 9,066 MILES), Vietnam, the North Pole, Australia, and about every state in the Union. I've heard that London subways have spray-painted Wall Drugs signs. I wouldn't have been surprised if Neil Armstrong put a Wall Drug sign on the moon.

Mark and I got to feeling fond of the place too, because out near the freeway exit they have a life-size brontosaurus statue that stands out nicely against the horizon. Its eyes light up red at night.

Ben bought a bumper sticker for the Bronco: "I've Seen Wall Drug." We were official believers. We were also tardy paleontologists.

"Boys, let's hit those Badlands pronto," Mark said as he made his way toward the exit.

"Afraid the dinosaurs will be migrating?" Ben asked.

"You're bucking to walk again, aren't you, matey?" Mark said. "And you show yourself around town too much in that T-shirt, you're liable to get yourself arrested for indecent exposure."

I slipped Mark five bucks to buy a few fossils while I brought Ben out to the truck.

CHAPTER
4

THE CLOSEST WE HAD EVER COME TO SEEING THE Badlands was the peek of one little corner by the Kadoka museum. Otherwise, they were just kind of looming in the distance. Mark and I had read about them and seen pictures, but this time we were going to drop down into the Badlands. We were going to dip our hands into their blood. Get their dust under our fingernails.

Seven miles south of Wall, the paved road—the oil, as they say—ends at the lip of the Badlands in a national park overlook. Most people see the Badlands from there. Then they hurry back to I-90 to continue on to Rushmore or Yellowstone or wherever. I wouldn't have minded at least a little sneak preview, but Mark took a sudden right at an arrow to Beauty without even a glance at the overlook.

After leaving the asphalt, it's thirty gravelly, twisted miles to Beauty, South Dakota, along the rim of the Badlands. The road was what you call bumpy. Like if you had some gum in your mouth, you wouldn't have had to chew it. I couldn't believe the scenery. Ben wanted me to describe it to him.

The flat green prairie bursts upon an arena of pink, yellow, copper, and brown earth. In a way it looks like a drained ocean basin. The floor is sandy and white. Spindly islands of earth and grass-topped plateaus dot the view. Pyramids, spires, and clay haystacks materialize with each new vista. Solitary trees are sprinkled here and there. Even without any water in sight, it looks like one huge beach with hulking sand castles all about. I think I was starting to wish we did have a tape deck. A little Charles Ives would have been just so right.

I looked over at Mark during my narration. A bitten-lip gaze was fixed straight ahead at the road.

"Slow down, man!" I yelled to Mark. "Look at this joint! The Mauvaises Terres!"

It seemed like he didn't even hear me. He just hunched over the steering wheel a little farther and kept driving with a mission. A little too fast, I might add, noting the parachute of dust we were pulling.

Then it occurred to me that Mark was afraid to look. Afraid that we might never get to Beauty and dinosaur land because of the scenery that could delay us at every turn.

But I caught Mark take a quick glance at the holy land. Then another and another. I grabbed the steering wheel in time to keep the Bronco from leaping into dinosaur country. Mark stopped on a grassy edge of the prairie overlooking some astounding Badlands real estate.

"Holy shit!" Mark said. "Nothing like a ringside seat." Then he stepped out of the truck. He started to breathe quickly. He was staring straight ahead out over the abyss in front of us. Then he put his city-bound body in gear and ran the ten yards to the edge of the prairie and in one motion leaped into the air and was gone from sight over the rim.

"The son of a bitch just jumped off a cliff!" I yelled to Ben.

I hopped out of the passenger seat and ran over to the edge. There was Mark on a ridge four feet below. He must have known he wasn't going to kill himself, but I don't think he was jacking around. The exuberance just got to him. He was standing with his back to me, looking out over the Badlands. It was very quiet. A just-emptied stadium quiet. A sweet afternoon breeze registered and an occasional meadowlark note floated our way.

Ben had gotten out and eased his way toward me. At the edge, he crouched down and swept his hand out over the chasm.

Mark was still standing there trancelike. Then he turned around and saw us. "How about a little Badlands music?" Mark said to Ben. "Something haunting and holy."

He was serious.

"Can you do Gregorian chant on a guitar?" I asked Ben. (Actually, some classical, melancholic bagpipes also would have been nice.)

"It's church out here all right," was all Ben said.

Being out in the Badlands—or any wilderness really—has got to be a religious experience. It's just you and the quiet and that unbelievable soul-thumping beauty. I think of ancient human beings seeing rainbows or eclipses in places like that. Or maybe finding dinosaur bones as big as telephone poles. Hell, just thinking about all that makes me feel like going to church again.

ON A PURELY OBJECTIVE BASIS, A SCENIC BADLANDS overlook is probably less spectacular than one's first view of the Grand Canyon. But the Badlands are no slouch. And I've always thought the Badlands were more approachable than the Grand Canyon. You can get down into the Badlands and walk around and claim them. Of course, we also knew that somewhere out there, hundreds of dinosaur bones had our names on them.

"Badlands" is a general term for eroded grasslands with underlying rock of soft clays and sandstones and shales that undergo yearly destruction. There are badlands all over the world, but our Badlands—the dino lands—were a fifty-mile-wide trough stretching from the western Dakotas and parts of Wyoming and Nebraska to the right-hand corner of Montana.

I'm just as taken with the spirit of the Badlands as with

their appearance. To me they feel like a broken-windowed, moss-walked cathedral that's long been abandoned. The sacredness is retained, but the life that once jumped around has since moved on.

But there is new life in the Badlands. The terrain can be dotted with thick outgrowths of grass, and in the spring, prairie flowers pop up all over the place. Tough little shrubs send out mineral-seeking roots that sometimes wrap around buried fossils. And the buffalo and prairie dogs and coyote and antelope have taken the dinosaurs' place.

"If all this is from erosion," said Ben, who must have been building a mind picture of the place, "then think of what used to be here."

"Really," I said.

"How would you like to have flown over this baby seventy million years ago?" Mark asked.

Mark used to say that he would have loved to have had just twenty minutes in dinosaur time. Twenty minutes with two motor-driven Nikons strapped around his neck and a four-man film crew.

FROM THE TOP OF THE TABLELIKE PRAIRIE THAT SUR-rounds the Badlands, arms of clay drop three hundred feet below. Deep gullies with usually dried-up streams dissect the sometimes grassy, sometimes sandy plain of the floor. Here and there are clusters of parched clay haystacks. Mark said it looked like a big brain. I had another perspective.

"Looks like a whole field of breasts out there," I said in a solely descriptive vein.

"I do love a feminine landscape," Ben said.

"Let's get out there in that cleavage already," said Mark.

I'M SURE THERE ARE SOME GOOD GEOLOGICAL EXPLA-nations about how the Badlands got to be the Badlands. Volcanic accumulation, flood-plain sedimentation, uplift, differential erosion. Stuff like that. But I like the story of the cowboy 150 years ago who was riding for days across the parking-lot-flat prairie. He was nodding off in the saddle when his horse stopped at the lip of the Badlands. The cowboy shook awake and looked out over the great show in front of him. "Something happened here," was all he was supposed to have said.

I DROVE THE REST OF THE WAY TO BEAUTY, BUT WE slowed down for a prairie-dog town. Hundreds of the little buggers were scurrying around, popping in and out of the ground. Through the window, Mark put a long lens on the scene.

They say that if you shoot a prairie dog, its brothers and sisters will drag it down a hole. Social beings, those prairie dogs. Lewis and Clark called them little dogs of the prairie and barking squirrels. They say sent a live one to Thomas Jefferson via steamboat to New Orleans. The barking squirrel made it to the White House six months after having left the plains of South Dakota. Unfortunately, it expired somewhere between Louisiana and Washington. Jefferson did his own study of the critter and then sent the former little dog of the prairie to Charles Willson Peale, the artist and curator, who added it to all the other specimens from the Lewis and Clark show.

We finally started to leave the rim and drop into the Badlands. We could see the town of Beauty below. Badlands wonder surrounded us. Right then and there we needed the movie music from *The Big Country* to follow us down.

BEAUTY, SOUTH DAKOTA, IS ONE MILE OFF THE PINE Ridge Indian Reservation, smack dab in the middle of the Badlands. It seems like it's only football-field size, but we had a fine little tour up and down its several unnamed streets.

Everything looked abandoned. There were two boarded-up churches, a deserted row of numbered cabins, and an empty, stone-wall jail. Around a place called the Longhorn Saloon, a buffalo and a baby yak rolled around in the dust of a fenced-in yard. A coyote was leashed to a rusty gas pump and several hundred junked autos lay in a pasture to one side of the saloon. Behind the place was half of a train depot. The right half.

The whole town looked like a vandalized state fairgrounds. And there wasn't a human being in sight. There was one lonely looking phone booth on the main street just down from the Longhorn. Its glass was long gone. There weren't even any splinters left in the cross-bar frame.

On a later solo trip to Beauty, I called Mark back in Chicago from the Erector set phone booth. It was noon on a fine summer day. I got Mark at his office. From where I was standing, I could see the Longhorn's buffalo and yak clomping around in their pen. Winds from both oceans met over the big front lawn of the Great Plains and pushed an empty milk carton back and forth on Beauty's main street. I described it all in detail for Mark. It was the kind of day that made you want to go running and leaping toward the horizon.

"Hold your receiver out the window for a moment, buddy," Mark told me. "Put me in touch."

So I did. I held the receiver out one of the empty frames of the phone booth at arm's length. Like it stunk or something. A carload of Indians drove by and looked at me and then at each other. I smiled and waved with my free hand. I could still see them wondering through the back window of the car as they drove out of town.

BEN AND MARK AND I STOPPED IN AT THE LONGORN Saloon for an afternoon cool one.

Just let me say this about the Longorn. What we had seen outside during our little tour of Beauty was just a warm-up for this place. There was an inch of sawdust on the floor and the barstools were milk cans with mounted tractor seats. A full Baggie nailed to a post was labeled GENUINE HORSE SHIT. And there were signs everywhere. (SKI VIETNAM, SIERRA CLUB GO HOME, FUCK WALL DRUG.) I didn't get the impression that the Longorn was your basic tourist stop. A sleazy-looking Gabby Hayes type of guy was loading a case of beer into a cooler. I counted nine pens in his shirt pocket. I remember wanting to ask him if there were any ballpoint pens left in South Dakota.

"A little firewater for you men?" asked the Gabby Hayes character.

"Drugs," Mark said. "We're on drugs. We just need about three Coca-Colas to help wash them down."

Gabby looked impressed. He actually dropped the half-emptied case of beer and ran to the other end of the bar and returned with the Cokes.

"They're on me," he said.

It was dark inside the Longhorn. More surprises came into focus as my eyes adjusted. Above the back of the bar were shelves of used cowboy boots and leather belts and spurs and, I think, watches. There were even a couple of saddles on sawhorses. And all these things had a tag with somebody's name on it. This guy Gabby Hayes was running a pawn shop! Probably a pawn shop for the Indians. Lots of moral fiber there. Trading liquor to Indians for their clothes.

"Can I sell you boys anything?" Gabby asked.

"Like what?" I asked.

"Anything," he said. Then I was afraid he would offer his daughters to us or something.

"How about a dinosaur bone?" suggested Ben.

"Certainly," said Gabby. Then he whipped out this absolutely perfect, five-inch-long *T. rex* tooth.

Mark knocked over my bottle of Coke reaching for it, but Gabby snapped the tooth back against his chest.

"Two dollars to look at it," he said. "Two hundred to keep it."

"Where did you find that?" I asked. For some reason I expected him to give me the exact latitude and longitude of its discovery. Then I could go running out the door into the Badlands and find its mates.

"Badlands," was all he said.

Of course that wasn't exactly what you'd call pinpointing it. At that moment we were in the midst of five thousand square miles of Badlands.

I think that was about the time we met Clarence. We had gone back to our pops and Gabby was putting the dinosaur tooth away when somebody busted through the door.

"Who's got the magazine truck?" the man asked. He

was a sturdy, ruddy fellow even though he was probably seventy or eighty years old.

Nobody said a thing. I for one didn't know what the heck he was talking about.

"The Geographic," he said. "Whose truck is that?"

I remember thinking in a moment of panic that he was a National Geographic Society board member who had been trailing us across South Dakota. Now we were done for. I was wondering how many years in prison you could get for false representation. Mark had never really checked in with *NG*. He just kind of assumed an official role as one of their photographers. He got mad at me when I asked him if he had gotten a go-ahead to use their insignia. "Why should I?" he had asked. "We're not just subscribers to their magazine; we are members of the National Geographic Society. We represent them in our daily lives, in everything we do." Fine, fine, I remember thinking. But members just don't send in their family photos. I figured there was something you'd do before saying you were doing a piece for *NG*. Mark was the professional photographer. He should have written them or called or whatever you do before starting an assignment.

So there we were. Caught with our pants down in a little So-Dak bar.

"It's my brother's truck," Mark said. "But I'm the official photographer."

The dumb shit! There he was giving us away.

"Then you're probably looking for me," the older gentleman who was Clarence said. "I was wondering when you'd come."

He sat down by Mark and started unleashing his life in the Badlands. I had this feeling that Clarence was ready to tell his story to anyone. I'm glad we were the ones. Mark was taking notes on a napkin.

Clarence was seventy-seven years old. I am always a little in awe of people who have had a foot in two centuries. He and his wife, Goldie Junior, had lived all their days in Beauty.

"You name it, boys, I've done it," Clarence said. "Farmed, ranched, dug wells, built bridges. I was a U.S. Weather Service recorder for twenty-five years and the

janitor and truant officer for our school until it shut down
in 1962. All I've had myself is six months of education."

I think it was Mark who asked Clarence if he had ever
come across any dinosaurs.

"Dinosaurs!" Clarence said. "Dinosaurs. Ackerman,
have I ever come across any dinosaurs?"

Gabby Hayes just nodded. It looked to me like maybe
Clarence was stealing his thunder.

"I've walked and rode over every foot of these Badlands," Clarence told us. "And guided for all the big-shot
field parties that have been through here from 1920 until
the last one came out five years ago."

We were all leaning into Clarence with wide-open eyes
and ears.

"I found the *Triceratops* that today stands in the museum at Harvard College. Just a nubbin of one of the leg
bones was sticking out of the clay. I told the crew to dig
right there and they'd have themselves a whole dinosaur."

"Did they?" Mark asked.

"You know they did, friend. It's in the Harvard museum like I just said. And my name is on a little plaque
there too. My name is in a lot of museums."

"Are there any good fossil-hunting spots left?" I asked.
My palms were so sweaty I had to keep drying them on
my pants legs.

"There are some good ones left," Clarence said. "Mostly
on Indian land though. And there's a real beauty two miles
south of here where this guy from Rapid City used to
dynamite for fossils. I wouldn't go in there myself though.
It's a mine field. There's at least eighty pounds of blasting
caps still buried around there."

Just then we were distracted by Gabby Hayes yelling
into a telephone to one side of the bar. We only heard
half of the transaction of course.

"When? Goddamn, I knew those bastards would stir
up with all these Feds around. You know I'll be ready."
Then he slammed the phone back on the cradle, reached
under the bar, and pulled out a carbine that he slipped a
clip into.

"Excuse me, sir," I said. I stood up and looked around.
"What's going on?"

"Indians on the Pine Ridge are pissed off at some FBI agents," Gabby said. "That means they'll be coming around to knock the hell out of white folks' property." Then he disappeared in the back of the saloon carrying the rifle with him.

I was ready to jump into the Bronco and floor it all the way back to St. Paul.

"He's full of crap," Clarence startled us by saying. "Just showing off his weaponry. He'd do that if he heard there was a band of Boy Scouts on the way. Sure, there's some Indian trouble. But just stay off their land and they won't bother you. They're decent. They don't go into the Badlands too much anyway."

Clarence didn't seem worried about the call. He just went on talking. Then he invited us to his house.

"It's just down the street," he said. "I have some items to show you men."

ON AN OUTSIDE WALL OF HIS HOUSE, CLARENCE SPIED something that must not have looked right. He opened up a pocketknife and pried whatever it was out of the plaster.

"Twenty-two caliber slug," he said. "Goddang it. Indians shot at the house again."

"I thought there was nothing to worry about," I said.

"It happens all the time," Clarence told us. "They don't mean anything. Sometimes they're just not too careful."

Great place, Beauty. Bartenders pulling out carbines. Bullet holes in houses.

Goldie Junior wasn't home. She was in Rapid City with the grandchildren for the day. Clarence told us we were missing a chance for her to show us the finest state capital plate collection around. And newspaper clippings. For fifty years his wife had been cutting out things from papers and magazines that had anything to do with South Dakota, Beauty, or dinosaurs.

"Well, we might as well see my junk then," Clarence said.

Junk, mind you. Junk like a garage full of dinosaur limbs and huge veterbrae and a four-foot horn core of

Triceratops. The barber in Kimball had some okay stuff, but this was museum material. Junk!

"I didn't even have to dig up that horn," Clarence said. "It was just sitting on top of a ridge. Almost tripped over it. Of course that was fifty years ago."

Clarence told us he had always collected fossils and that after a while they just kind of took over the garage. Goldie Junior got some old bakery-display cases and they were on their way with a little museum.

"A lot of big-shot gynecologists have looked at my things and drooled," said Clarence. "And not just the fossils. In 1911, I found a meteorite the size of a doghouse that I later sold to a French outfit. The wife and I bought this house with that money. I heard the ship carrying it back got sunk in World War One."

(Gynecology I thought? Why not? Mother Earth, right?)

Clarence also had coprolite and petrified wood and arrowheads and Badlands agates.

"Everything stays right here when I die," said Clarence. "It's in my will. Make a little historical place out of all this."

A tooth fell out of Clarence's upper plate as he was talking. He picked it up and walked over to a workbench off to one side and squirted something on the tooth.

"Elmer's glue," Clarence said. "Fixes dinosaur teeth and my teeth." I wonder if Clarence had ever thought of putting a big *T. rex* fang in his mouth.

We asked Clarence if he wouldn't mind showing us a few Badlands hot spots, but he told us that he didn't dig dino anymore. The legs didn't go like they used to and he suffered from dizzy spells. And Goldie Junior didn't want him falling off a Badlands cliff and joining the dinosaurs. So we got a little pep talk instead.

"First off, you want to stay on private land," he told us. "Get down in among those haystacks that you can see from above and look at the strata. The dinosaur layer is between two coal seams twenty feet apart from each other. Go above or below that and all you'll find is rattlesnake droppings. Oh, I could teach you boys a book if I had the time."

He gave us directions to a rancher five miles south of

town who would let us work his land if we wouldn't start any fires or leave a mess. Paul Jordan of the Bar J.

"How will we know if we're on reservation land?" Mark asked.

"Planes will start buzzing you," Clarence said. "The Indians watch from the air."

"What if that happens?" asked Ben.

"Then get the hell out of there," said Clarence.

When we pulled out of town, I turned around and saw Clarence watching us from the middle of the street. He just stood there with his arms by his side. I think he would have liked to have been on board.

"Do you believe it?" Mark asked as we headed for the ranch Clarence had pointed us to. "We just walked into a gold mine. Clarence, dinosaurs, the Longhorn. Hell, if this isn't *National Geo* material, nothing is."

"I didn't notice you doing any pictures," I said.

"We'll be back," Mark said. "After the fossil hunting. I can see Clarence on the cover of *NG* in a year or two."

I LOVE THE *NATIONAL GEOGRAPHIC* MAGAZINE. MY PARents have fifteen years of those yellow treasures weighting down several bookcases. And then my mother bought fifty leather-bound volumes from about 1900 to 1930. But there's a "but" coming. Everything in a *National Geographic* is almost too beautiful, too perfect. As if a rainbow over the Grand Canyon weren't enough, there's as likely as not a soaring eagle included in the frame. Animal close-ups are so good you can smell them. The children are perfect and smiling. The old people are perfect and smiling. The towns, the cities, the countrysides—they're all quaint and lush and sunshiny. Perfect and smiling places that seem to have no drudgery or day-to-day plodding. I've heard people say that places look better in *NG* than they do in real life.

In 1979, *National Geographic* did a piece on Minneapolis and St. Paul. It was as beautiful as *NG* could do it. But speaking as a proud and realistic Twin Citian, we have drudgery here. We have gray days.

But that's as far as I go in knocking *NG*. Some people—political activist types—think that the magazine or the society itself doesn't have any bite. That it's too slick. That there's no responsible social critique. No guts. But you know, maybe the beauty is statement enough. And *NG* has put money into the explorations of Perry and Byrd and Amundsen, and of Cousteau and the Leakeys. They helped save Sequoia National Park and the Lost City of the Incas. And hell, who knows, *National Geo* may have even funded half of the moon shots.

No one will fault the *National Geographic* for lack of information though. It's put geography back on the map (taken it off the map?). It's been used in grade schools since 1906. FDR followed the course of World War II on *NG* maps mounted on rollers beside his desk.

You ever see someone throw away a *National Geo*? *NG* puts out for its readers. It always has. We're talking about a world leader in popular geography and natural history and photojournalism. Just look at some of their early breakthroughs:

—First major color feature ever printed in a magazine (individually hand-tinted, by the way): 1910

—Longest attached foldout (eight feet of Canadian Rockies): 1911

—First underwater color photos: 1926

—First aerial color photo of U.S. Capitol: 1930

The *National Geographic* is all right in my book. I was still worried about them trailing us through the West though.

CHAPTER
5

WE DROVE THROUGH THE BAR J'S GATE AND WERE met by a yapping, scrubby dog who peed on all four tires of the Bronco as soon as we had stopped.

"Let's get the spare out so he can wet that down too," Mark said opening his door and stepping down from the truck. But the little mutt bit him on a booted ankle. Mark shook the beast off and slammed the door. Mr. Dog stood guard, keeping us hostage.

Neither of us had noticed Ben slip out the back of the Bronco and feel his way around to the front. All of a sudden, there he was in a catcher's squat with a hand extended in the dog's general direction. It looked like they were long-separated master and pet judging by the slavering that took place. Mark turned my way with an I-told-you look. I just hunched my shoulders.

A peacock in full bloom was strutting around the backyard. Maybe it was an escapee from the Longhorn.

* * *

WE WERE CLEARED TO PARK THE TRUCK ON MR. JOR-
dan's tableland overlooking the Badlands and camp down
below for a couple of weeks. Now, this was no fenced-in
back forty we were going to be walking around in. The
Jordans had twenty-five thousand acres of Badlands. And
that opened up onto the government range. The free grass.
Eroded prairie that rolls all the way to Nebraska.

First, we had to drive a mile and a half over the grassed
table to the edge of the Badlands. There were no roads
or fences out there. There were no people and there was
no water. (The Jordans told us they had lost a hundred
head of cattle in the previous summer's drought.) This
would be hard-core fossiling. We get lost out there in
ninety-plus heat and run out of water and that's all she
wrote.

You don't mess with nature in the raw. You've got to
respect the terrain, the weather, the time of day, the animals in the area. You don't take a single thing for granted
out there. Sometimes the most beautiful places are the
toughest.

At the end of the table is Badlands as far as you can
see. Except for the sounds that the earth makes when
humans aren't around, it was powerfully quiet again. It's
hard to believe that the Badlands came about in silence.
It seemed like we had just arrived on the scene as the
dust was settling from an earth-splitting explosion.

Ben cupped his right hand to the side of his mouth and
yelled out a "hey" so loud that it lifted him up on his
tiptoes. It's kind of mandatory to yell at solitary, scenic
overlooks. Just your name or a long, drawn-out "hel-
loooo" is usually enough.

I asked Mark about the mechanics of making a film
using the Badlands as a setting. A Hollywood feature,
35mm, big-time film. It could be done he said and should
be. They could build tracks for the cameras, haul lights
and generators out. Bring in portable dressing rooms and
movie-crew caterers. No sweat, they could do it. Spring
would be the best time, when the prairie flowers are out
and the grass is still lush. But they could make fall look
like spring too by greening the grass and bringing in some
trees and foliage and even touching up negatives if nec-

essary. Then they would always have spring within the frame and the viewers would never know it.

Buffalo Bill Cody himself did some Badlands filming in the area where we were headed. Between bankruptcies and Wild West shows, he founded two film-production companies.

His fanciest moving picture project was *Buffalo Bill's Indian Wars*, which included a Badlands sequence for the famous Ghost Dance. In October 1913, the Colonel W. F. Cody Historical Pictures Company took off from the Pine Ridge Indian Reservation for the Badlands. The hike took a week and a half while a blizzard looked over their shoulders the whole time. For three days the colonel choreographed several hundred Sioux extras reenacting the Ghost Dance on top of Cuny Table.

Men and equipment were lowered down steep crevices by rope. Hours of climbing were necessary to get the right camera angles, and the darkroom tents blew away in a sleet storm. But the film got made.

A *Denver Post* reporter wrote that the Badlands filming was the greatest achievement in the history of motion pictures. Of course, the history of motion pictures wasn't all that old in 1913.

Buffalo Bill met the great O. C. Marsh during that stint in the Badlands. Evidently they had quite a visit. Bill didn't put it past the Old West that something like dinosaurs used to run around out there. He even got kind of excited about having a dinosaur in one of his traveling shows, but never could get something mobile enough to follow him around.

MARK AND I LOOKED OUT OVER THE BEAUTIFUL SOUTH Dakota earth two hundred feet below us.

"You're wonderful!" Mark yelled.

I had this feeling that I should grab Mark by the arm to keep him from jumping off the ridge we were standing on.

I think even Ben was itching to get out into dinosaur land, but it was dusk. We would be camping on top for the night. The next day we'd climb down and make our way to a new site.

We set up the tent and ate dinner. Ben said something about a recreational activity for the evening and Mark sounded like he had it all worked out.

"Trilobites. Tonight, we're going midnight fossil hunting."

"Hey, come on," I said to Mark taking him aside. "It would be tough enough for you and me to climb down in the dark, let alone with Ben. Any one of us could fall into a ravine and be lucky if we just got a broken leg."

"Wait'll the moon comes up," Mark said. He was oblivious of my hush-hushness. "It'll be light enough."

I looked up at the moon. An early June, fingernail clipping of a moon. I couldn't see it illuminating our way down the side of a cliff.

IT WAS LIGHTER AROUND 10:30, BUT I DON'T KNOW ABOUT light enough. We formed a little mule train with Ben in the middle and Mark and me tied to him. Mark led us down.

"Just what are you guys looking for?" Ben asked once we got going.

"Scraps of fossil bone, I guess," said Mark.

"I'm looking to not bust my butt falling off a cliff," I said.

Mark had a lantern, but didn't light it on the way down. The moon was surprisingly bright.

We reached the sandy floor intact, but still decided to stay hooked together. We were in a steep-walled canyon that was only shoulder-breadth wide. Moonbeams didn't reach the canyon recesses, so Mark lit the lantern and we snaked in and out along a dry stream bed hoping it would open up onto the plain we had seen from above.

We were all very quiet. The canyon branched, and we drifted right. It was still narrow and deep. It was pretty much fast-pulse time down there. I had read that during heavy rains, entire walls of Badlands clay can collapse. Then all of a sudden Mark tripped. The light went out and Ben and I dominoed on top of him.

"Get up, get up!" Mark screamed. "I think I landed on a skull. We've got our first fossil!"

I helped Mark light the lantern again.

It was a skull all right, but no fossil. More like an old, bleached horse skull with its cranium recently crushed. Like as recent as a minute previous.

"Hey, you've got the right idea," I said. "The next one will be a brontosaurus leg bone."

"Maybe I should lead the way," Ben said, "so we don't fall over them."

That was the end of the night's fossil hunting. And a good thing. It took us two hours to climb back up to our temporary camp.

THE NEXT DAY, MARK AND I LOOKED AT THE ROUTE OF our night descent. Mark let out a low, drawn-out whistle. About halfway down, we had walked along a ridge with a sheer drop of 150 feet to one side.

"Sweet, if we had gone down that way when it was light out, we would have fallen off for sure," Mark said.

"It was a good thing we did have Ben with us," I said. "He probably kept us going the right way."

"Say, where is the Wonder Boy?" Mark asked.

We looked around and saw him a hundred yards off in the grass socializing with about fifty head of cattle.

"Look at that guy!" Mark said. "A regular Francis of Assisi."

The cattle had formed a circle around Ben. He was scratching backs and patting muscular necks.

"He's probably going to drown in cattle spit," I said as we got closer and saw the animals nosing and licking Ben.

When the herd noticed Mark and me drawing near, they broke up their little meeting and started peeling off the circle in threes and fours. By the time we got there, only one little, wobbly-legged calf was left.

"I think this one is lonely," Ben said, sensing we had arrived. "Otherwise he would have bolted with the others."

Ben turned the little guy around in the direction of the

herd's exit, and then gave it a get-into-the-world nudge on the backside.

Our plan was to establish a base camp somewhere out in the Badlands. But first we had to haul the gear down below the table in several shifts and then try to carry it in one trek to wherever our new campsite would be. The water was tricky to climb down with. We used five-gallon army surplus cans and as the fluid sloshed around, it lurched us with it.

It was easier going on the flatland below, so we loaded ourselves up. Ben had a pack in front and back, and carried his guitar and a camera tripod. Mark and I had big-frame packs and stumbled along with the two five-gallon water cans that we carried between us with a pick handle threaded through the hand grips.

It was hot. By noon we reached the clay haystacks— the breasts where the dinosaur strata are. A half mile away there was another table that rose several hundred feet above us.

Mark and I were sufficiently pleased to be in the middle of this wonderful place. We both thought that the farther away from civilization we were, the better the fossil hunting would be. We dismissed the fact that Clarence had found the Harvard *Triceratops* ten yards off the road between Wall and Beauty.

I am a stickler for campsites. Be it the Canadian boundary waters, the Badlands, or a highway wayside rest, everything must be just right. For starters, the tent has to be on a site with good drainage. If it rains in the Badlands, it rains hard and the water rushes over that cementlike, thirsty ground in a flash flood. I don't care how waterproofed it may be, no tent keeps you dry if you're being undermined by a river.

The gear must be organized. Pots and pans and utensils are set aside. Food is kept out of the sun. Fossil-hunting tools herded together. At night, it's all got to be covered. We had a couple of old shower curtains that never failed us as tarps no matter where we were. A pick and shovel and frying pan were all we needed to hold them down.

And nobody littered. We hauled any refuse out with

us, except for what you would call your self-generated organic waste, which we buried on the spot.

FROM STORIES I HAD READ IN THE *NORTH STAR GUIDE Manual* about grizzly bears tearing wings off float planes and opening the entire flank of a moose in one swipe, I developed a healthy respect for all bears. There used to be grizzly bears on the Great Plains too, but that was 150 years ago.

Lewis and Clark had some grizzly bear tales. (They actually claimed the grizzly bear for science, since they were the first white men to write down its name in a little notebook.) Their men put eight musket balls into a charging grizzly that still chased the group a quarter of a mile before limping back across the plains.

The great Long Hair Custer was photographed with a monster bear he shot in the Black Hills in 1875, one year before the Little Big Horn fiasco.

I think Mark had present-day Alaska and early nineteenth-century South Dakota on his mind when I noticed him starting to urinate in a big circle around our tent. (It was the Herters' manual again and their guaranteed method to keep bears out of camp: "Simply go to the latrine in a fifty-yard circle around the camp using a different spot each time you go until you have a circle completed around the entire camp.")

"Hey, buddy," I called to Mark, "I appreciate your thinking of our safety, but there aren't any bears out here these days."

"Nuts," Mark said, ignoring me and not looking up from what he was doing, which at that exact moment was trying to shake out every last drop that he could. "I couldn't make it all around. Could you or Ben scare out some bilge water?"

I explained the situation to Ben who immediately retreated into what looked like a well of deep thought.

"There aren't any bears, I know that," Mark said all of a sudden, looking very teed off. "But there are coyotes. I figure the same would hold true for them too. How would you like it if our food was gone when we came in from fossiling one day? Or the tent ripped to shreds? Or one boot missing or something?"

"Hey, I can dig it," I said, throwing up my arms and walking over toward him. "Where did you leave off?"

AFTER THE CAMPSITE WAS FINALIZED, WE WERE READY for some real fossiling. So I thought. But Mark wanted us all to climb the nearby table first.

"Don't bring anything and don't say anything," Mark said. "Just follow me."

We followed. Ben held on to my arm. It was a short walk to the table and then a twenty-minute climb. Mark did bring one thing, his new rock hammer. And I snuck a canteen and the binoculars along.

Up top, we witnessed another beautiful Badlands panorama. I focused the binoculars on our tidy little camp way down below. The blue tent. The water carriers. I could even make out a can of Campbell's soup on an overturned pot.

"Hey!" I suddenly yelled in faked anxiety. "There's a grizzly bear down by the tent!"

"What?" said Ben.

Mark tried to grab the binoculars away from my face, but I fended him off with an elbow and pretended to still be looking at the campsite.

"Now he's . . . he's taking a dump right in front of the tent!"

After I calmed down, Mark grouped us together for a little ceremony that he said would ensure plentiful hunting.

"Boys, we are on sacred ground here. We must make ourselves worthy of our prey."

I remember thinking at the time that Mark was going to ask each of us to cut off an extremity and throw it into the Badlands below.

"Everyone hold on to my hammer," he said.

Three fists wrapped around the handle. It was a nice hammer. A brand-new Estwing rock hammer with a wood handle and molybdenum shaft.

"This instrument will lead us to a history-shaking find," Mark said. "Now please stand back."

Mark flexed his shoulders a few times and windmilled his right arm in increasing circles and then let the hammer fly out into the Badlands. He looked like a pointing springer spaniel as he watched the arc of the Estwing. Then he fixed a bead on it when it hit the earth. It looked to me like it was 150 miles away.

"Okay, let's go get it," Mark said. "Under that hammer lies the sweetest dinosaur skeleton any museum has ever seen."

I started to believe it too and I wanted to be the first one to the hammer. I mountain-goated ahead of Mark and Ben down the 45-degree slope in front of us. I fully expected to find the hammer amidst an entire hillside of splendid dinosaur bones lying about as if just having been strewn from a dynamited Florentine statuary.

UP AND DOWN THE RIDGES AND RAVINES WE WENT. Twenty minutes and no hammer. It was noon and we were all cooking in the sun. After forty-five minutes I started getting a little worried.

"You didn't happen to tie some fishing line around that puppy, did you?" I asked Mark.

By 1:30 Ben and I had separated from Mark. Ben just stuck close by me but I was actually expecting him to find the hammer. When I asked him where it was, he laughed, but I was serious.

We must have been only one ridge over from where Mark was because every now and then a litany of obscenities would float our way when the wind was right. One of them was surprisingly loud and clear.

"Jesus H. Christ!"

"Think he found it?" Ben asked me.

"Nope," I answered. "That's the wrong tone, the wrong inflection. It'd be more like this—" and then I let go with the same exclamation, but more in the discovery mode.

Mark himself came running over the hill.

"Did you find it?" he asked. He was sweaty and out of breath.

"Sorry," I said. "I was just warming up in case I did."

Mark took a pull from my canteen. I tried to get him to forget the hammer, but he threw the canteen back at me and stomped off down a ravine. Ben and I went back to camp.

I WOULDN'T SAY OUR EXPEDITION WAS OFF TO A BAD start, maybe just a little shaky one. Of course, I was a bit impatient myself. I was ready for one of us to locate the paleontologic find of the century on that first day.

There are still headliner finds being made. In northwestern Texas, a paleontologist found a huge wing bone from a pterosaur, the flying dinosaur. That was in 1971. From just that bone alone it was estimated that this creature had a wingspan of forty-two feet. About the same as a McDonnell Douglas F-15 fighter jet. (The extinct reptile was nicknamed 747.) Mark and I were hoping for a similar act of serendipity. A single bone from some new, extinct beast was all we asked for. *People* magazine profile material. The stuff of *NG* covers.

BACK AT THE CAMPSITE BEN AND I HAD SOMETHING TO eat and then took a nap on the warm sand. At about 4:30, I saw Mark walking toward us. He was maybe three hundred yards away. I could see him swinging his arms and stepping smartly. As he got closer, I heard him whistling, *The Bridge on the River Kwai* theme. I put the binocs on him.

"Oh, oh," I said to Ben. "No hammer."

"He sounds happy," Ben said.

I wasn't going to be snide. I wasn't going to be smartassed. I would be supportive and understanding. I would forget that Mark ever put his hammer into orbit.

"Hey, sweet," I called out when Mark walked into camp still whistling. "We kept some RyKrisp and cheese out for you. How about it?"

I interpreted a short little whistle as a yes. I gave him the food.

A whistle with an inflection like "Thank you" followed.

I tried to think of something encouraging to say. "We're going to have a great day tomorrow," I tried.

Mark started to whistle another answer but all that came out was a fine mist of crackers. Then he coughed. "Yes, I imagine it will be a good day," he said. "but I hope we don't find something that needs too much chiseling out."

THE FOLLOWING MORNING A TREMENDOUS EXPLOSION about blew Ben and me out of the tent. I say only Ben and me, because the first thing I noticed was no Mark.

"Mark, Mark, you okay!" I yelled.

My immediate fear was that a meteor had hit the earth and Mark was lying beneath it.

"I'm okay, kid," he answered from somewhere outside. Then another explosion boomed around our corner of the Badlands.

I jumped out of the tent bare-assed naked and stepped on a little prickly-pear cactus that sent me hopping around on one foot.

"Where you high steppin' to, bud?" Mark asked.

"What the hell's up?" I asked, limping over to him. Then I saw the hammer stuck in his belt. "When did you get the hammer?"

"Got going at sunrise and rustled it up," Mark said. "I started all over again. Hiked back to the table, climbed up, did my routine, and went to where I thought it would be and there it was."

"How about the T. rex head?" Ben asked from the tent.

"You still in there pulling your crank?" Mark said to Ben. "I was just glad to get the hammer. I picked it up and pretty near ran all the way back to camp. Now I'm commemorating the event with a few cherry bombs."

"That's a great little wake-up service," I said. "Could you rouse us like that every morning?"

I GOT OVER MY CACTUS LIMP IN A DAY OR SO, BUT THOSE little thorns stayed in my foot for months. Callus built up and walled them off. They didn't hurt, I just noticed them

on occasion, like when I bathed or clipped my toenails.
I know it was months because I still had my cactus needles
when Mark took a film-editing job in Chicago with a small
production company. He lived in the studio until he found
an apartment. Slept on a chaise longue in the projection
room for two weeks.

Noticing my cactus always reminded me that I had
part of the Badlands in me, but it also brought back the
cherry bombs and Mark in his new Chicago apartment.
That's when I bought Mark a wake-up service. I called
long distance to set it up with this Chicago outfit I had
read about. They will wake you whenever, wherever, and
however you want, provided it can be done over the phone.
They suggested several packaged versions. A simple "Time
to get up." Any number of sexy calls (male or female).
An explosion. Or that old standby, a rooster crowing. I
arranged for a more sophisticated custom selection.

Like any of the other calls, Mark's phone would be
rung at the designated time. But the first thing he would
hear when he answered would be the sound of two trains
approaching each other. I had Mark's old buddy One-Eye
Deane in mind here. Then steam whistles would blow
distant warnings. The rumbling keeps getting louder and
louder and then *wham*! The two engines hit and the twisted,
crumpled iron heaves and groans. After a moment of silence, a nondescript voice says, "Up and at em, sweet."

BEN GOT OUT OF THE TENT AND DID ABOUT FIFTEEN
creaky jumping jacks. Then I saw him turn toward the
sun. Mark elbowed me and pointed at Ben. We both
watched him like we were invisible men. He kind of lifted
his chin and closed his eyes. He was feeling the sun on
his face. Then he shivered a little bit, like he had just
come out of a trance. Mark and I knew that Ben played
this little game about guessing the time by feeling the sun
on his face and then checking his braille watch. But before
he put his hand to his wrist, Mark called out, "Don't
check! What time is it?"

"Eight-forty," said Ben. "Plus or minus five."

"That's good enough for me," Mark said. Then he turned

around and walked out of camp. Probably to take his morning toilet.

AFTER BREAKFAST, MARK WAS GETTING ANTSY.

"Do we need reminding, friends, that we have a decided purpose for standing on this hallowed ground?" he said, hitting the palm of his hand with his recovered hammer.

"You needn't remind us," said Ben.

"They're out there, men," Mark said. "Dinosaurs. Great leaping lizards of long ago, whose bones now lie scattered about like the blown-apart fuselage of a nose-dived airplane."

"Hey, that sounds nice," I said.

"It is nice," Mark said. "Actually, it's great. That's why we drove twelve hours straight across two states and hauled all our crap out here on this pilgrimage in the first place."

Mark and I can get a little sentimental about the past. As long as it's millions of years ago. We both agreed that the recent past of high school and college and former girl friends was too painful to dig into. But give us the seventy-millions-of-years-ago past. The great sweep of time back to *Tyrannosaurus* and *Triceratops* and some of those other wonderful house-size animals and we were rubbing our hands together with glee. Geological nostalgia Mark called it.

Mark Twain would have known what we were talking about. He knew there was solace in the contemplation of antiquity.

WE WOULD BE IN THE FIELD FOR MOST OF THE DAY, SO we supplied ourselves accordingly. Everyone had his own canteen and a day pack with food, knife, rope, and old rags to wrap any fragile finds in. I also had the binoculars and a first-aid kit and a compass.

I really don't know how to use a compass, but it's so reassuring to have one on hand. And I have this little rule for the trail. I always insist on a three-day supply of food, shelter, and clothing in case we get lost.

We left the heavy-duty fossil tools in camp—the pick and shovel and the plaster to protect large or broken fossils. This would be more of a get-acquainted-with-the-Badlands hike.

Ben was tied to Mark by a four-foot rope. He looked like Mark's slave. I scouted ahead. A dry, cleansing heat actually made it kind of cozy. A grasshopper buzzed by. My pack rested on my back like a reassuring hand.

There was no method to our initial exploration. It was easy enough just going up and down one haystack after another, expecting a huge dinosaur bone to be looming over the next ridge. When we were eating lunch, Ben remembered some earlier advice.

"Didn't Clarence say that we had to find those two coal seams?"

"Holy shit!" Mark said, shattering a rectangle of Ry-Krisp that he was spreading peanut butter on. "Well, we've been having fun thinking we knew what we were doing."

THE COAL SEAMS WERE EASY TO FIND, SO AFTER LUNCH we just stayed within a twenty-foot horizontal swath looking for fossil sign.

"Look for bone chips," Mark said. "Clarence told me that's how you know you're getting warm."

I went off by myself into a little ravine and found a beautiful flint arrowhead half buried in the clay. It was white and perfectly symmetric. I looked around the great country we were in and imagined an Indian firing off a shot at a bounding antelope or deer. This was a miss I figured. A two-hundred-year-old miss.

The arrowhead was within the two coal seams, but that doesn't mean it was ever pointed at a dinosaur. Erosion can bring artifact and fossil together. Human beings and dinos never looked at each other. The great beasts went extinct seventy million years before the first cowboy or Indian ever set foot on the old earth ball.

Mark was very impressed with the stone missile. "Wow! Holy balls! Is this great!"

"You can have it," I said and handed it to him.

"Hey, come on now. I wasn't..."

"No, really. I mean it. It'll give you something to remind you of your older brother."

"Man, thanks," Mark said.

I heard Ben laugh through his nose. "What are you guys going to be like if one of you ever finds a dinosaur?"

"For your continued lack of respect," Mark said to Ben, "no water for you for the next three days."

LOOKING IN THE RIGHT STRATA STILL DIDN'T BRING US any fossils, but Mark found something very intriguing.

"This ain't no deer rifle shell," Mark said, holding out a large, blackened cartridge casing for me to see.

"No lie, that's a military shell," I said.

"Can I see it?" asked Ben.

Mark gave him the five-inch cartridge to check out.

Ben turned the thing around in his hands. "You could just throw this at someone and hurt them bad," he said.

"Here's another one!" Mark yelled. "And another."

Clarence told us later that they were 50-caliber machine-gun shells. During World War II, fighter planes from Ellsworth Air Force Base in Rapid City practiced strafing runs over the Badlands for about two months. One plane every five minutes unloaded its machine guns into the clay hills. ("Hell, it was like the war was being fought right here," Clarence said.) No doubt the machine-gun bursts also shattered a few dinosaur bones.

I HAVE PRETTY MUCH BEEN GLOSSING OVER THIS FOSSIL-hunting business. There actually is quite a bit to it. When you're going big time, like for dinosaur, you aren't just out for a stroll.

First you look for marker fossils—chips of fossil bone that let you know you're in the right place. In dinosaur country those markers might be dino themselves, but usually they're bits of fossil turtle shells. Clarence said there used to be so many hunks of busted-up turtle fossil that they were used for fence braces.

Turtles have a very strong ancestral line. Back to the dinosaurs and beyond. I picked that up from somebody a lot smarter than me, Alfred S. Romer, in *Vertebrate Paleontology*:

> From the Triassic, turtles have come down to present time relatively little changed; they have survived all the vicissitudes which have swamped most of the reptilian groups and are in as flourishing a condition today as at any time in the past.

The Plains Indians knew this. (Maybe Romer learned from them.) The turtle is their symbol for longevity. The Mandan Sioux even had a Keeper of the Sacred Turtles and a special tepee where they kept the little reptiles for religious ceremonies.

Mark and I used to have a little turtle. The dime-store pet shop version that lived in a plastic dish with a palm-tree island.

After some markers have been identified, what you really want to find next is part of a dinosaur bone sticking out of the clay. Every spring rain and snowmelt uncovers brand-new suites of specimens. It's best if they are only partially exposed. Even though those bones have been in the ground for seventy million years, once they're uncovered by erosion they may last only a year or two before crumbling to bits.

This is all if the fossils are close to the surface. Sometimes the bone layer may be in the middle of a cliff and extend back into the hill like a drawer. But that doesn't stop the major league diggers. If they figure there's a productive seam of dinosaur relics, they might get out the dynamite or call in a Caterpillar and take off the overburden right down to just above the paydirt.

The bones are petrified of course, but they're still very fragile. No way could you just pull one out of the ground or pry it up. When you've got your specimen located, you start a careful dissection around it with dental tools, brushes, and small chisels. If you've really hit the big time, the single bone is a flag for a whole beast buried within.

There's notes to take too. The strata from which the specimens are collected, the positions in which they lie, pollen samples, rock samples, and other bones or plant fossils they are found with. For a major dig, like for a complete dinosaur, whole areas are roped off in meter-square grids and specimens are tagged and numbered according to where they were found within that scheme.

As the bones are dissected out, they're treated with a hardening mixture of shellac and alcohol. Then, wet paper is placed over them, followed by burlap strips soaked in plaster to form a protective cast around the bone. Only when the plaster hardens do you start in with the heavier tools like the picks and sledgehammers and crowbars. Digging for dino was a long way from the times Mark and I pried shells and coral out of the Mississippi River limestone near our home.

It may sound like I know what I'm talking about. It sounds like it to me too. Mark and I both took a few geology courses and I had a field anthropology lab. And Clarence had given us that little chalk talk back in Beauty.

We were geared up all right. Doing like the big boys do Mark said. All we needed was a dinosaur bone sticking out of the side of a cliff.

CHAPTER
6

OUR FIRST DAY ACTUALLY SPENT IN THE FIELD PRO-
duced more weaponry than fossils. The arrowhead
and machine-gun cartridges were interesting, but they
weren't dino. Mark said at least we didn't find any beer
cans or gum wrappers.

At dusk, Ben took his boots and socks off and tiptoed
out on the silt plain beyond the table and haystacks. He
made a big loop and came back to where Mark and I sat
watching.

"Is it pretty clear out there?" Ben asked. "Any boul-
ders or branches?"

"Clear as a virgin beach, kid," said Mark. "The flats
go for a mile to the south and a half day east and west
with nothing in the way."

"Here I go then," said Ben, taking a deep breath and
curling his toes into the sand. He swayed a little bit, like
he was stoking up enough courage to jump off a high dive.
Then he sprang away, running and jumping in the air, arms
flailing like a set of spastic windshield wipers.

"Looks like Ben's got the disease now," Mark said. "The first signs of Badlands fever."

Mark and I weren't the slightest bit worried about Ben running off into the desert. We just assumed he'd find his way back.

I went into a little nostalgia trance about then. I was somehow onto baseball. Softball actually. My sister, Anne, was a fast-pitch softball star. a pitcher. Just before the trip, Mark and I went to one of her games. We got there in the second inning. Anne was on the mound.

She was hummingbird fast. I didn't realize a softball could be thrown so quickly. And underhanded at that. In the poetry of baseball it would have been said that she could "bring it."

"Think we could hit Anne?" Mark asked. We were sitting in the stands along the first-base line and Anne had just struck out the inning.

"Man is she fast," was all I said.

I remember Mark and me teaching Anne to play catch in our backyard when she was about four or five. Of course, it was baseball all the way then. Mark was trying to make her ambidextrous. She went from baseball to softball and got good real quick. But nothing like we saw at that game.

"I can't believe that's really her," I said as Anne was winging the ball over the plate again. "She either got real good or we got real old."

"I wonder if we could hit her?" Mark asked again. He said it like maybe we couldn't. And since we were the ones who taught her how to hold the ball in the first place, the possibility of not getting a hit would verge on the sacrilegious.

Anne's team won 3–0 on her two hitter and ten strike-outs. Mark went out on the field after the last inning and was talking to Anne with his arm around her. I waved and sent a little rah-rah, way-to-go hand pump out toward the mound. Mark pointed back to me and both of them started to laugh. I looked around to see if I was missing something. Then Mark waved me over and pointed at home plate.

"You hit, I'll catch," he said.

Most of the crowd and players had gone. In the lovely orange dusk a couple of little kids were running the base paths. I waved a bouquet of bats around in the air like I was King Kong.

"Move those kids out," I said to Anne. "I don't want them getting hit with any line drives or anything."

Anne's first pitch was a fast ball that seizured. It sailed over my head and stuck in the backstop. And I mean stuck. I suggested we end batting practice right there, but Mark pounded the ball out of the wire with a bat.

"You got a batting helmet?" I asked Anne. I laughed a fake laugh. Actually I would have preferred a full suit of armor.

So then Anne whips about ten perfect strikes by me. I didn't even touch the ball. Hell, I could barely see it. I think if the ball would have just brushed by the bat, it would have singed the lumber.

"Next batter," I said to Mark. I handed him the bat and pretended to knee him in the groin. "Hope you have a nut cup on, boy."

Mark shifted from foot to foot in the batter's box. He reached out with the bat and touched the corner of the plate and then finalized his nervous Little Leaguer act with a quick Sign of the Cross.

Anne threw a change-up on the first pitch. Anticipating another one-hundred-mile-an-hour fast ball, Mark had taken a big stride forward just as she released the ball. But it came toward us in slow motion. Mark could have swung at it about three times. As it was, he did get a limp-wristed piece of the ball and sent an impotent pop-up toward the pitcher's mound. That was enough for Mark to run all the bases and then slide head-first into home plate. He looked up at me while he was still on the ground. "She is something else," he half mouthed and half said.

So there it was, another of life's lessons clearer than all get out: baby sister will eventually handcuff you at the plate. But actually, I was kind of proud that we had guided Anne through the formative years.

Softball is one thing but it's baseball that I'm out and out in love with. Small-town, out-in-the-country baseball. Triple A, State Amateur Men's League, Southern Minny.

That's the kind of ball that gets me all sentimental and goosefleshed. I don't have the *Encyclopedia of Baseball* committed to memory or anything. I just like to sit in beautiful old ball parks in the middle of plowed fields. Hell, I could sit there for an hour by myself with nobody but the sparrows and the prairie and the flagpole halyard clanking in the wind. Baseball for me is just one more part of that magic business of the past.

Pioneer Grandma loved baseball. Our grandfather was a town ball hero. Like I said before, Mark and I never knew him in person, but we saw plenty of old pictures. Team shots. Blurry, running-the-bases shots. Bats-over-the-shoulders shots. And Grandpa standing in a backyard, proud and uniformed with a glove that looked like a limp starfish hanging from his belt. He had a stroke and died while listening to a 1948 Red Sox–Senators game.

So, Mark and I and Pioneer Grandma and our own father hit the road on Sunday afternoons and saw a lot of good, small-town ball in magic, little towns like Hanska and Sleepy Eye and Stark. Especially Stark. Ten of the fifteen players from Stark were all brothers or cousins and the park was a real beauty that sat at the intersection of two country roads. The only building in sight was the grandstand. If you arrived late for a night game, you could see the field lit up from five miles away, a UFO hovering in the black Minnesota farmland night.

"Hey, boy!" Mark said to me. He was shaking my shoulder like he was trying to wake me up. "Where you been?"

"You could have a great ball game out here in the Badlands, couldn't you?" I said. I felt drugged. I looked around and saw that Ben was still gone.

"What?" said Mark.

"Baseball," I said. "There could be some great baseball played out here on the flats."

"Yah, I guess there could be," Mark said. Then he must have thought about it. "Sure. Just draw in the base paths. There could be some great slides into home plate."

"The World Series should be played out here." I was really sick now.

"I'm with you," Mark said. "Helicopter the teams in with a TV crew so the fans wouldn't have to rough it."

"There'd be no night games of course," I added. "But think of the bonanza of advertisers like Coppertone, Foster Grant, and Miller Lite."

Just then Ben came huffing and puffing back into camp. "Look at this," he said handing Mark something. "I stepped on it and went flying."

"Bejesus!" Mark said, dropping it like he had just been handed a glowing charcoal briquette. It was a naturally occuring oddity known as a mud ball. They're perfectly round, sandstone spheres formed in the cliffs. Erosion weathers them out and they roll down to the Badlands floor. This one was the exact same size and shape as a baseball.

HOW CAN I BEGIN TO TELL YOU HOW BEAUTIFUL BADlands sunsets are? Maybe you could start by thinking of the finest ocean sunset you've ever seen and then drain the water. A Maxfield Parrish blue-and-pink sky dances around silhouettes of castles and buttes, which are planted on a beach that goes forever. Finally, a surrealistic light breaks through some ghostly clouds. Better yet, get yourself out to Beauty, South Dakota, and walk straight into the Badlands, alone, and wait for the sun to go down. Spring or fall are the best times.

MARK WOULD LIKE TO HAVE WIRED BEN FOR SOUND SO he could give us some rock 'n' roll out in the old Badlands. Ben was in a local rock band for three or four years. He was the lead guitarist. They did good early Beatles and Rolling Stones and The Byrds, but Chuck Berry was their forte. "Roll Over Beethoven," "School Daze," "Johnny B. Goode," "Too Much Monkey Business." Ben even learned the Chuck Berry duck walk and could play the guitar between his legs and behind his back. I'd seen him cutting loose like that at high school dances or parties. That was a whole other side to our Sherlock Holmes. He even knew the real words to "Louie, Louie."

But since Ben wasn't electrified, Mark did what he could on his own. "One, two, three, four!" Mark yelled. Then he jumped off the tailgate of the Bronco where he had just introduced himself as the great Chuck Berry and starting singing:

Down in Louisiana down in New Orleans,
Back up in the woods among the evergreens.
There stood a little cabin made of earth and wood,
Where there lived a country boy name Johnny Be
    Goode.
He never learned to read or even write so well,
But he could play the guitar just like a ringing bell.
Go, go. Go Johnny go . . .

It's hard to say what's *the* greatest rock 'n' roll song ever written, but it just might be "Johnny B. Goode." Watch a dance crowd go snake shit when "Johnny B. Goode" gets cranked out. It was even made into a movie, *Go Johnny Go*, starring Chuck Berry himself. That was back in 1958. Jack Kerouac time. I bet old Jack dug Chuck Berry.

Parents used to think rock 'n' roll was something evil and primitive. Jungle music. I think they were right. It is powerful. It is basic. I've seen one-and-a-half-year-old babies bob their heads to rock 'n' roll. I've seen animals prick up their ears. I've seen high school gymnasiums full of convulsing dancers as a rock band lets fly with the old back beat. It's not always pretty what rock 'n' roll does. And rock 'n' roll, real rock 'n' roll—none of this punk or glitter shit—is not something you whistle. It's moving music, down and dirty. Dancing, snapping fingers, get in the car and go music. Rock 'n' roll is voodoo.

WE HAD THE MAKINGS OF A COZY LITTLE CAMPFIRE SCENE. Mark was throwing the mud ball from one hand to the other. I was lying down and Ben was strumming his guitar. The Coleman lantern stood in for a blazing fire.

"How about some music, Ben, my boy?" Mark asked, suddenly looking up and putting the mud ball in his pocket.

"Yes, sir," Ben answered. Then he hit a few chords with a little more volume.

"But none of that hootenanny shit," Mark said.

Ben broke into a very loud Kingston Trio medley (the "MTA," "It Takes a Worried Man," and "The Sloop John B").

"At least the little whorelet didn't do 'Michael Row Your Boat Ashore,'" Mark whispered to me when Ben started the guitar lead to "Michelle."

Ben can play good rock 'n' roll on his acoustic too, which is not the easiest thing to do. He couldn't honor Mark's request for "Layla," but he cooled down with a few more great, early Beatles numbers.

Ben taught Mark the guitar part to "Memphis," Lonnie Mack style. All Mark came away with was the intro. Dunt-dunt, dunt-dunt, dunt-dunt diyadda-dunt. All through the trip Mark played it. Over and over and over. Later, whenever he saw a guitar in a music store or at a party or something, he'd have to play "Memphis" (that is, the first three bars of "Memphis"). "Hand me that sumbitch," he'd say. Then he'd take the guitar and if it was one of his on-the-weeds time again, he'd take a big puff and put the smoldering cigarette under the strings by the tuning keys and let it hang there until he was done. He did it all so well, like he was an old Chicago bluesman ready to let some sorrow fly, that even I thought he'd play something recordable. But no, it was always "Memphis."

Mark bought an old beater guitar, but it didn't expand his song list any.

Later that same year, I was the night cashier in a twenty-four-hour grocery. Mark was in Chicago by then. I was checking stock one night late when the phone rang.

"Piss on it," I thought, "let it ring." I was surrounded by cereal boxes and laundry detergent and a push cart full of frozen pizzas.

But the phone rang and rang. Hell, it was 2:00 A.M. Maybe it was some emergency! I jumped up and tried to hurdle the cart of pizzas. Over we both went.

Then I mashed a box of Post Grape Nuts Flakes and broke a broom handle getting to the phone, but I got it in the middle of a ring.

"Ladies and gentlemen," was all I heard from the other end of the line, "Mr. Lonnie Mack!"

Then I could hear the guitar intro to "Memphis." Over and over.

"Not bad, eh?" Mark said when he finished.

"Not bad for an asshole," I said. But I loved it, of course.

MARK TURNED OUT THE COLEMAN AND HE AND I LAY on our backs looking at the sky. Ben lounged Cleopatra style, sifting sand through his fingers.

"Lordy, look at that sky," Mark said. "And that moon!"

"Goodnight Moon," I said.

"Goodnight cow jumping over the moon," Mark said, continuing the story line to one of our favorite kids' books. "Goodnight stars and goodnight air. Goodnight noises everywhere."

It was quiet until Ben coughed.

The stars blinked and tweaked like I'd never seen before. It was the kind of view that made you think you were in church.

"Think of how far away those bastards are," Mark said about the stars. "Light-years. Light travels a hundred eighty-six thousand miles a second. That's miles per second! And the distance to a star is measured in the distance light travels in years!" Mark was almost comatose with his own revelation.

Actually, astronomy makes paleontology look easy. At least you can hold on to those old bones. Dig them up and put your hands on them. I'm still trying to comprehend man on the moon. (Our Pioneer Grandma thought the moon shot was a TV hoax.) Hell, now rockets have landed on Venus and Mars and passed through the rings of Saturn and headed out of the solar system.

"Try this out," I said. "Some of those stars have already burned out. It's just taken this long for their light to reach us."

"Now, that is something," said Ben, throwing down a handful of sand. "Fossil light."

"Hey, that's good," I said.

Mark told us that the first daguerreotyped celestial body was a star named Vega. Its image was recorded in 1850 at Cambridge, England. Astronomers of the time calculated that the star's light had taken twenty years to traverse the distance between it and the earth. Since Daguerre made his discovery in 1837, that particular light ray left Vega seven years before the daguerreotype process was even invented.

Mark and I looked up at the night. Ben rolled over onto his stomach.

"The infinite numbers do me in," Mark said. "The distance to the farthest star, the age of the earth, the speed of computers. We throw these seven-, eight-, and nine-digit numbers around like they were the ages of our brothers and sisters."

"I know what you mean," I said. "The earth is four billion years old. Billion! Shit, the last four years of my life have gone so slowly, I'd believe it if somebody told me the earth was only forty years old."

"Four billion years," Ben said. "All the time in the world."

Ben stood up and his knees cracked. "Fifteen minutes is a long time to be in pain," he went on. "Three weeks is a long time to be away from someone tender. But four billion years?"

I knew what Ben was getting at. I can actually handle about a hundred years. Back to cowboy and Indian and dinosaur bone rush time. And if I don't think about it too closely, I can kind of take in the four thousand years between now and the heyday of Egypt. But the time behind that, forget it. To me, ten zeroes after a number are the same as three.

Mark and I didn't say a thing for the next five minutes. I think we were both waiting for a little more wisdom from Ben.

"This is why people go to church," was all Ben finally said. But he said it so magnificently, with breaks between every few words, that the tone itself would have conveyed the thought.

Ben's sentence temporarily cleaned the slate for any deeper discussions, so Mark eased into the next topic.

"The Badlands are beautiful enough," he said. "But it sure would be nice to see a few women. Nothing raucous. Just see them. Maybe talk a little bit. Tell them of our fossil-hunting exploits."

Mark was no lech. He just deeply appreciated the female countenance. He looked at women reverently, with open-mouthed, wide-eyed, amazed-little-kid looks. Never a slit-eyed leer. He looked at them as one might gaze upon a castle on the Rhine.

Mark could actually tell when a woman was having her period. I don't mean the she's-on-the-rag crap or because someone may be a little extra emotional. He knew from the subtler effects. Puffy eyes and cheeks. Rings tight on the fingers. A minute change in voice. He was tuned in to women.

"Aren't tan women something?" I said.

"They knock me out," Mark said. Then he took a deep breath. "And think of all their white areas."

"Like under their wristwatches?" Ben said. Mark rolled over and lobbed the mud ball onto Ben's lap.

"What's Leslie doing?" I asked Mark about his old sweetheart.

"She's in Aspen." I think there was a little ache in his voice.

"Doing what?" I wasn't really sure how far to pursue the topic.

"Waitressing. Ski instructing in winter," Mark said, but then he switched gears. "Say, what would you guys want your last dying gesture to be?"

"What?" Ben said.

"What?" I added a half second later.

"The last thing you would want to do or say before you left the world."

Mark is, of course, crazy, which is to say nuts. But this has certain inherent advantages to me, because I've always maintained that to make it in this world, you either have to be nuts or stick close to somebody who is. I had planned on sticking close to Mark.

"I guess I'd want to die out here," I said after some minor reflection. "Reaching for a huge, exposed dinosaur limb with an outstretched hand and clutching a coprolite to my bosom with the other."

"I would want to go in the early morning with my head facedown in new-mown wet grass," said Ben.

"Well, I've been thinking about it for a while," Mark said. "I don't care where it takes place. It's the sound I leave with that matters. First, I want to gently clear my throat and then follow that with a quiet cough. My finale would be a high-pitched, discrete sneeze. The kind that feels good down to the belly button."

Ben gently cleared his throat.

I pretended to cough.

Mark missed his chance to complete our setup by letting out a very loud, and I must say crude, burp.

CHAPTER
7

MOTHER NATURE HAS A WAY OF PROTECTING MEN-who live together without bathing. I'm talking about trappers, miners, maybe lumberjacks, and definitely amateur paleontologists in the field. After the third or fourth day without changing clothes or washing, you quit noticing your own smell. After several more days you can't pick up your partners' scents. Either the odors harden into the fabric or the olfactory receptors burn out for those smells.

I think Ben retained his sense of smell though. Unlike Mark or me, he changed clothes every day and tried to wash himself each morning with a face cloth. He never said anything to us, but I could see his nose twitching like a rabbit's when we passed by.

After our first nine days of fossiling, we ran out of water. Not from Ben's bathing. From bad planning.

Mark hiked back to the Bronco with the canteens and one five-gallon water can. Thankfully, we did have ten more gallons back at the truck.

Mark was gone for three hours. It was a dry, water-

appreciating three hours. Even though it was still before
noon, my saliva was getting pasty.

"Mark was reading to me from the *North Star Guide
Manual* a few nights ago," Ben said. "He read where
Halazone tablets can be used to drink your own urine."

"That is complete horse shit," I said. I think I was
actually disappointed with the *Manual*. "All Halazone
does is kill germs. Urine's got a lot of poison in it that
Halazone won't touch."

"I thought you swore by that book," Ben said.

"I just did," I said. "No, it's a good book. Just a little
inaccurate in places. I suppose Mark was ready to try it?
The Halazone in the pee bit?"

"He was. He asked me if I'd do it if he did."

"What happened?" I asked.

"Neither of us had to go."

I LIKE TO THINK OF WATER AS A ROCK. A MINERAL. WHY
not? Ice could be a rock. It just has a lower melting point
than granite or copper or quartz. Look at mercury. Water
happens to be a rock that we can drink.

Water. Life is water. Water is life. Just add water. Don't
go near the water. Water on the knee. Water on the brain.
From water we came and unto water we shall return. H
– 2 – fucking –0.

The Indians simplified the elements of life right down
to the earth, which is to say rock and water. Human beings
and buffalo and the prairie grasses were all animated bits
of rock and water. Carbon, nitrogen, calcium, iron, sulfur,
hydrogen, oxygen. And water. You don't have to be a
chemist to figure it out. Rock and water are where it's at.

I WAS DAYDREAMING OF JUMPING INTO SWIMMING POOLS
full of root beer and Ben said he'd give anything, especially a dinosaur bone, for a cherry Popsicle. We didn't
even notice Mark had returned.

"Time to cut the dust, my little whorelets," Mark said.
"Water's warm, but a cold Budweiser wouldn't taste any
better."

Ben and I handled our full canteens like they contained nitroglycerin. We savored it molecule by molecule. Mark looked at us as if he had just delivered a sack of toys to an orphanage.

"Say, how is the Bronco?" I asked, tightening my canteen so tight that later that day I had to use a pliers to open it.

"Never looked better," Mark said. "All the tires are flat and the windows are punched out."

"Come on."

"Nah. I'm shittin' ya. It looks great. I even gave it a little pat on the hood."

IT WAS HIGH NOON BY THE TIME BEN AND I HAD RE-covered from near dehydration. Mark was walking around taking light-meter readings and swearing.

"The light is terrible at noon," he said. "Horse-shit light."

"Looks fine to me," I said.

Mark held a hand out in front of his face and squinted through it at the sun.

"For the photographer, it's bad news. Too harsh. It washes out detail and contrast. Ansel Adams says noon is the most uninteresting time of day."

"Really?" I said.

I always kind of liked that warm, reassuring noon sun. It reminded me of twelve-year-old summers when Mark and I sat on the concrete steps in front of our house and ate peanut butter and jelly sandwiches and carrot sticks.

"Maybe it wasn't Ansel Adams," Mark said. "Maybe it was Leonardo da Vinci. Or Rembrandt. Sure, it was Rembrandt. He knew light. Can you imagine Rembrandt with a camera in his hands? The guy invented available light before there was such a thing."

"What, the sun didn't shine before Rembrandt?" Ben asked.

Mark looked at Ben for a second and then at me.

"You ever see those side-lit portraits he did?" Mark asked. "I'm telling you, Rembrandt knew light."

Mark's cheeks were flushed. He was walking around

waving his hands and shouting. I picked up his rented Nikon and followed him through the viewfinder. I snapped a picture of him and he stopped dead in his tracks.

"I know, I know, the light is horse shit," I said, holding up a hand to calm him down. "but the moment was right."

FUN FACT: The optics of photography were all worked out in Leonardo da Vinci's time. Image inversion, ground-glass lenses, focal planes. They had it all. They just needed a few more centuries for a light-sensitive plate to be discovered.

PEOPLE CAN GET ANTHROPOLOGY, PALEONTOLOGY, AND archaeology kind of mixed up. Paleontology is basically old animal bones. Ancient veterinary medicine, if you will. The other two have to do with artifacts and culture and civilizations. But no matter. They're all part of the study and collection of the past that covers looking at old high school yearbooks and coin collecting and wanting to touch ancient knickknacks on display in big museums.

Mark and I got the collecting bug early, from my mother, I guess. In a way, she was sort of an anthropologist herself. She kept our baby teeth in a jewelry box, along with strands of first curls and other little artifacts of childhood. Mark and I would sneak in to look at the box from time to time. Eventually we reserved a top drawer for our own treasures of the past. We had fossil shells and petrified wood and several very nice Indian arrowheads. But the little replicas of dinosaurs were the most special. We knew all their names by heart and not just the biggies like brontosaurus or *Tyrannosaurus rex*. We could rattle off *Diplodocus* and pterodactyl and ankylosaur as if they were the names of major league ball players. (Aunts and uncles were more impressed with our Latin than our paleontology.)

Pioneer Grandma cut something out of the paper for Mark and me when we were still in grade school. Something about pygmies in equatorial Africa having sighted a huge animal deep in their rain forests. Kind of a landlocked Nessie the article said. A scientific search team was sent out from the University of Chicago. I remember

Mark and me wishing we could have gone with. The scientists tentatively verified the animal's existence as dinosaurian through tracks and animal signs. But that was all I ever heard about it. I'd watched for any more news for several years afterward. The only actual sightings had been by the pygmies themselves. Of course, things do look bigger to pygmies.

Aside from reports about monster sightings, there are a goodly number of burning paleontology questions yet today. Dinosaur extinction has always been right up there, but added to where the dinos went is whether or not they were warm-blooded cousins of birds. And evolution is still hot. Supernovas and amino-acid sequencing take a little heat off the monkey myth between announcements of early man discoveries by people like Donald Johanson or the Leakeys.

But these are only the questions of the last ninety years. The longest running paleontology question, the one that confounded all the great minds for the longest time, had nothing to do with evolution or dinosaurs. And it was very clean and simple: how did seashells get on the tops of mountains?

Herodotus thought fossil shells were sports of nature. Results of lightning bolts striking the ground high above the earth. That theory was gospel for about five million years. Joan of Arc eventually had a go at that one. She bought a notion that former oceans had dried up and receded. But wouldn't you know it, Leonardo da Vinci had it right. Uplift of earth's crust. That boy wasn't the Renaissance Man for nothing.

ANOTHER WEEK AND A HALF WENT BY WITHOUT ANY fossil sign. Mark and I quit talking dinosaur. Even Ben didn't jive us anymore.

"How could we get Clarence out here?" asked Ben one morning.

"Why don't you send him one of your telepathic messages," said Mark.

We needed Clarence all right. The fossils just weren't popping out at us.

TWO LUNCHTIMES LATER, I NOTICED A CLOUD OF DUST moving our way from the northeast. "Somebody's coming!" I yelled.

Mark and Ben stood up. Ben was facing the opposite way of the vehicle's approach.

"Hope it's not Indians," Mark said.

"We aren't on the reservation, are we?" asked Ben.

"You got me," Mark said. "We've been wandering around out here for three weeks and I've never really known exactly where we are."

It was an old Jeep pickup generating the cloud, but we couldn't tell who was driving until it stopped right in front of us.

"Glad to see that you boys are still kicking." It was Clarence. Our guru. "I was getting the feeling that you might be needing me," he said. "And the pictures for the *Geographic* would look a lot better out here anyway."

CLARENCE LIKED MY ARROWHEAD. AND HE WAS SURprised to see that there were still some machine-gun shells around. Mark wondered how he drove all the way out to where we were, and he said it was from knowing the passes and the right stream beds but that it wasn't something for just anybody.

Clarence said Goldie was okay with him spending a day with us to help find a big one. Then he started walking around our campsite, eyeballing cans of food and tools and Mark's camera gear.

"God-Lord, I feel good out here," Clarence said. He closed his eyes and took a deep breath. "I'm at the height of my glory down here."

"You want something to eat?" I asked. Clarence was holding a can of Campbell's Bean with Bacon soup.

"Hell no," he said. "Heck no. Just checking out your groceries. You boys been living off airtights?"

"Pardon me?" I said.

"Cans," said Clarence. "Canned goods. Dog food, I call it."

"What else is there?" I asked. "The Longhorn doesn't cater, do they?" It was kind of a disrespectful answer, but

I laughed anyway. So did Clarence. Mark just looked at the ground and Ben picked at something in his teeth.

"Say, boys," Clarence said all of a sudden, "I'm going to find a fossil in the next two minutes. Time me."

Ben snapped open his braille watch. I expected Clarence to run out into the Badlands with a shovel, but he started sifting through an anthill at his feet.

"Got one!" Clarence said. "That was quicker than I thought."

He held out a half-inch piece of what looked like a jaw on the palm of his hand.

"Ancient rodent there, boys. Wrap this in Kleenex and put it somewhere safe."

Here's what Clarence told us about anthill fossils. Red ants excavate these pretty big mounds, more like gopher hills really, and kick up little fossils. Birds, rodents, seeds. In one anthill, there might be thirty or forty little treasures like that.

After Clarence's find, we were all on our hands and knees tearing apart that anthill. Ben got bit up pretty bad, but Mark found some fossil hackberry seeds and I found a small thigh bone. Small, like the size of a watch's hour hand. The anthill fossils were pretty impressive. We filled five empty film canisters with them. But they were hardly the kind of trophy you could hold up for the folks back home after having been dinosaur hunting for half the summer.

Mark was getting some shots of Clarence by the anthill.

"It's okay to get a few pictures now," Clarence said. "But save a few for when we get the big stuff."

Big stuff. We were so ready for big stuff. But Clarence said to hold on a bit. Where he wanted to take us was too far away for that day. "Tomorrow the big stuff," he told us. "Today we just get warmed up."

WHAT A DIFFERENCE CLARENCE MADE ON A BADLANDS hike. We'd been walking around like idiots for three weeks expecting to find complete dinosaur bones all but packaged and labeled for us. And there was more than dinosaur to see. Clarence showed us probably fifty different layers of volcanic ash and a vein of quartz that ran through the Badlands clay for miles. He showed us chips of turtle-shell fossil that we'd walked over every day and old wagon-train ruts.

"Twenty years ago you boys couldn't of kept up with me," said Clarence. "But I could still break your necks if I wanted to." He had crouched down for a moment to take off his hat and wipe his forehead. I was having trouble keeping up with him right then and there.

Near a semicircle of clay haystacks Clarence stopped and told us to climb one of the hills. We did. He waited down below and shouted out some directions.

"Train your spy glasses to the west," he said. "Those are the Black Hills fifty miles out. You should be able to make out a patch of white in their middle. Mount Rushmore."

We climbed back down and sat around Clarence. He told us that he used to be able to see Rushmore from that same spot without glasses or binoculars. He had seen Mount Rushmore before it was carved out too. Back in the early twenties when South Dakota planted four flags on top hoping that a national shrine to democracy would be blasted from the mountain's granite face.

Clarence and some friends got a little sparked up one night and climbed up top to take a leak over the side (about where Lincoln is now, Clarence said).

Then I had a little story to tell. Since I'd never been to Rushmore, I had to defer to *National Geographic* to flesh out some of the facts. Originally, a western theme was planned for the mountain. A trapper or cowboy or such. But as the project grew in scope and notoriety, something a little more weighty was suggested. Sculptor Gutzon Borglum finally came up with the four presidents whom he considered represented everything the U.S. of A. was about. I basically break them down this way:

Washington, founding father

Lincoln, champion of freedom

Jefferson, fossil hound

Theodore Roosevelt, North Dakota Badlands rancher (a little more about this much later)

The Mount Rushmore basics are all there in about four different *NG*s if you want to check it out. Up until his death, Borglum worked continually on Rushmore from 1927 to 1941. He supervised everything from the dynamiting to the fine chiseling to the location of portable toilets for his crew. When he wasn't on the mountain, he was looking at it from an observation post down below. If the morning light or afternoon shadows didn't fall just so across the faces, he zipped back up top to fix it. He would have been a helluva dinosaur bone digger.

Borglum's son finished the great project six months after his father's death.

FUN FACT: Jefferson was originally hacked out to Washington's right, but three serious cracks in the rock opened up, so Borglum decided to erase the great paleontologist and put him on the other side of General Washington.

WE WERE SITTING ABOVE CLARENCE IN A NATURAL AMphitheater. Like in those old lecture halls with students on benches that rise 45 degrees away from some distinguished professor. Only this was a Badlands classroom.

"The Badlands will cure whatever's ailing you," Clarence was telling us. "Just walking around in them will do it. But throw in a little digging and you have heaven."

Clarence was getting into it good. I bet it'd been awhile since he'd been out there.

"Let me tell you about the digging," he said. "It's a privilege, you've got to understand. Something special. You're digging up mysteries, if you follow me."

Good God, the man was a poet!

"Putting the shovel to the earth, the pick to the Badlands clay. It's something special. A privilege. And then, goddangit yes, then the clink of hammer and chisel undoes the treasure! A leg bone. Five vertebrae strung together. O, God bless us, a whole head!"

I think Mark and I were misty-eyed and holding hands.

(If we weren't, we should have been.) I looked over at Ben. He might have been into it too.

"Whatever happened to the dinosaur?" asked Ben. It was the first serious paleontology question I had heard Ben ask.

Mark hopped on that one himself. He began a harangue so eloquent and formal it sounded like he was reading from some highly respected paleontology text. All about the parallel evolution of mammals and the effects of plate tectonics on weather. Even the latest stuff about an asteroid colliding with the earth and killing the large lifeforms but sparing small animals and aquatic life.

"That all sounds pretty good," said Clarence, "but let me put it to you this way: what did the passenger pigeon in? And the Irish elk?"

"I know what you're getting at," said Mark. "But..."

"And how about the buffalo," Clarence said. "Who almost did them in?"

"Men and dinosaur never lived together," Mark said. He looked like he was getting mad.

"Just telling you my thoughts, is all," said Clarence. "It wasn't no asteroid that chased the grizzly off the plains."

"I got one," I said. I stood up and walked down to where Clarence was sitting and faced Mark and Ben like I was a guest speaker. "The dinosaurs were done in by constipation."

Everybody laughed but I wasn't kidding.

"Really. It's something I read. In the late Cretaceous, dinosaurs changed their diet from conifers [Grape Nuts, if you will] to the soft, sweet-flowering plants [Hostess Twinkies by my analogy]. They gave up fiber for junk food and got terminally bound up. Hey, I read it somewhere. *Smithsonian* I think."

School was out after that note and we all headed back to camp. Clarence was getting a little tired by then, but he didn't have to be carried in or anything.

Clarence saw something a couple hundred feet off to our left just before we hit camp. He had Mark run over and check it out. It was an old muffler. The only piece of trash we'd seen in the Badlands in three weeks.

"It was mine," Clarence said when Mark rejoined us. "Fell off an old Ford pickup I used to have." He looked kind of proud of the muffler and its still being around.

CLARENCE WOULDN'T EAT ANY OF OUR FOOD. HE PULLED out a canvas bucket that had a sandwich wrapped in wax paper. After the sandwich, he cut and peeled an apple that he ate in small pieces.

We all watched some shooting stars and then we had another kerosene lantern campfire.

Clarence asked Mark what it was like to work for *National Geographic* and how much did the cameras cost and where was he going to shoot pictures after the Badlands. I was glad Mark didn't carry it out too far. He fielded the questions so ordinarylike, though, I was beginning to think that maybe Mark did square things away with *NG*. A day or so before, I had found a pamphlet in Mark's camera bag, "Photographic Requirements for *National Geographic*." It had info about subject matter, rates of payment, captions, and how to submit material. Maybe Mark was holding out on me.

I wanted to know what was ahead for the next day and Clarence said we were going big-time digging. That was all I needed to hear to not get a night of sleep.

CLARENCE SLEPT IN HIS JEEP. SITTING UP STRAIGHT IN the front seat. I'd heard once that some older people had to sleep upright. Something to do about breathing and the heart. It must have worked out okay because he was the first one up and at em the next day.

"Let's get going, men," Clarence said. He was walking around our tent pounding a fork on a plastic dish. I'm sure that if he had found our frying pan he would have been beating on it with a hammer.

CLARENCE AND I PACKED THE BACK OF HIS JEEP PICKUP. Shovels, picks, plaster. We were going for it all right.

Ben and Mark got in back and I sat up front with

Clarence. We took off over the hard bumpy ground and headed south. Clarence said we were headed south. I wouldn't have known.

It was a long ride. Two hours anyway. Up and down gullies. Snaking a path around the little prickly-pear cactus. Finding a pass through the haystacks. This was Clarence's country.

I looked through the back window at Mark and Ben. A bump sent them up in the air like they were on a trampoline.

"I wasn't going to mention this," Clarence said to me, "but I might as well tell you. We're headed to the pot at the end of the rainbow."

"You mean we're going onto Indian land?" I said.

"Cuny Table," Clarence said. "I call it Ghost Dance Butte."

I didn't know where or what Ghost Dance Butte was, but if Cuny Table was the same Cuny Table that I knew about, it was the place where Buffalo Bill made his movie. But then it all fit, because that's where he filmed the Ghost Dance.

I knew about the Ghost Dance. So did Mark. We had both had our whiteman guilt cranked up real good by *Bury My Heart at Wounded Knee*. We read it one after another, Mark using my underlined copy.

By the 1880's the Native American was on the way out. Eastern tribes had long been just names of sporting teams and tobacco products and fancy hotels. In the southwest and northwest, Indians were cramped into reservations. And the mighty, free-roaming Plains Indians were also getting claustrophobic. The buffalo were out, railroads in. Fences, roads, and city blocks were sneaking across the prairie. And the U.S. Army had to protect all that real estate.

The Plains Indian came to represent the whiteman's stereotype of the red man. They were the painted buffalo hunters. The Sioux and Cheyenne and Blackfeet. The noble savage that Buffalo Bill romanced the hell out of in his Wild West shows. The Plains Indian gone vaudeville. (Today there would have been T-shirts and souvenir programs and millions in merchandising. Buffalo Bill's traveling shows were probably the closest thing of that time to rock 'n' roll tours.)

Buffalo Bill took his Indians and cowboys to the east and then on to Europe. They played for Queen Victoria and rode gondolas in Venice. The holy man of the Sioux himself, Sitting Bull, went on the tour. (That's like Solzhenitsyn winding down his career by doing Harlequin romances.)

Times were bad on the home front, is what I'm getting at. 1890. So out of the southwest comes a Paiute prophet named Wovoka who tells the Indians that if they dance the Ghost Dance the buffalo and antelope would return, the fences would go down, the railroads fall into a hole, and the white folk go back to Europe or someplace far away. It was an attractive idea at the right time and when it caught up with the Sioux, the Ghost Dance had become a religion. Hundreds of Sioux on the Pine Ridge Reservation took it up. Dancers went into frenzies. Didn't eat for days. Let their Christianity go to hell. So the Indian agents and the U.S. Army did the best thing they knew how to do to put an end to it. They outlawed the Ghost Dance.

Sitting Bull (back home, but farther north) told his people to keep at it. Buffalo Bill was called in (he was a good man actually; he cared about the Indians) but he couldn't calm anybody down.

Things were getting what you call hot. Six hundred Ghost Dancers snuck into the Badlands and camped out on an arm of Cuny Table called the Stronghold. They spent a cold November and December there with the Ghost Dance.

History is a mess after that, but the main heartbreaks were Sitting Bull's murder and our nineteenth-century My Lai, the Wounded Knee massacre.

So. Clarence was taking us to Cuny Table. Ghost Dance Butte. Maybe we'd see the ghosts of the Sioux and the buffalo and dino. Mostly the latter, I hoped.

Clarence headed down a steep, rocky slope. I'm sure we left the ground several times. I thought his Jeep was going to double somersault when he finally bolted to a stop. He got out and walked around to Ben and Mark.

"How's that for a ride?" Clarence asked them. He was smiling big. I think he was personally proud of how tough the Badlands were.

"I think I confused my sitter," said Ben.

"You're lucky that trail didn't bounce your nuts off," Clarence told him. Then I noticed Mark look down at his own lap.

Clarence told us that we weren't in the Promised Land yet. That this was just a little break. A little leg stretcher. Mark went up and over the ridge we had just come down, and Ben and I stuck with Clarence.

Clarence found some bits of fossil turtle and just nodded his head. He told Ben and me how he'd thrown out his right shoulder carrying a three-hundred-pound turtle out of the Badlands. That was in 1952 he said. The same year he almost lost Goldie Junior. He didn't get to say what happened to her because just then Mark came running up to us and said he had found a dinosaur egg. He gave something to Clarence that he was holding in his cupped hands.

"Mud ball," Clarence said after he checked it out. "Does look like an egg, but it's a mud ball."

Back in the Jeep. Down another dry stream bed. Clarence and I were in the cab again. I hadn't noticed before, but the right front window-turner-upper was a rusty crescent wrench.

We entered the beginning of a steep canyon.

"There's no signs of fireworks," Clarence turned to me and said. "But we're on Indian land now."

Suddenly I wanted to crouch down and tell Mark and Ben to shut up in back. I figured that even though we were all very in tune with the Indian way, if you will, in this setting we were just four measly trespassers.

Clarence stopped the Jeep and had us all get out.

"Let's pack it in from here, boys," he said. "Dinosaurs."

WE WALKED DOWN A LONG, NARROW RAVINE THAT WAS supposed to lead us to the base of Cuny Table. The mother lode would be anywhere from that point on Clarence said.

I know I personally saw myself sweeping in armloads of fossils.

A helicopter buzzed by, but Clarence told us not to sweat it. We were just walking and breathing he said. No laws against that.

As a kid, Clarence said, he came out here a lot because that's where the best fossils were. Just sitting there waiting to be had he said. He sold most of them to a builder in Rapid City who mortared one or two nice ones into every stone fireplace he put up.

Mark was plowing ahead of us and Clarence hollered up to him to branch left at the next fork. Then Mark was out of sight.

It was probably five minutes later that we caught up with him. I should say we got to a place where we could see him. Clarence and I stopped dead in our tracks. Ben banged into my back. At the end of the canyon ahead of us was a landed helicopter. Its blades were still turning slowly and Mark was being led by the arm by an Indian with a rifle strapped on his back. Several companions sat around the chopper.

"Let me do the talking," Clarence said to Ben and me. He was looking straight ahead at the formerly seated Indians who were trotting toward us.

I was breathing fast and shallow—hyperventilating I guess. I have claustrophobia bad and was not exactly treasuring the thought of even one night in jail.

We didn't know it then, but the business back at the Longhorn with Gabby Hayes pulling out a rifle had to do with the reheating of some old AIM and FBI problems at Wounded Knee.

INDIANS ARE BADLANDS PEOPLE. THESE INDIANS ANYway, the Oglala Sioux of Pine Ridge. The Lakota. Mark and I knew that from our reading. Like good liberal arts students of the early seventies, we had studied *Black Elk Speaks*, *Lame Deer: Seeker of Visions*, and *Seven Arrows* in order to raise our Native American consciousness.

We loved the Indian world view. How they were part of the earth and everything on it. They apologized to the buffalo before killing them and then prayed for their brothers in the buffalo nation. And they knew the power of the rocks and the old bones. (I bet they found dinosaur.)

I like Indian names. They have some kind of innocence and freshness. My favorite was one signed in Sioux to an 1875 treaty: the Buffalo-Who-Urinates-and-Smells-It.

Mark was particularly taken with the Indian and their measure of days. (The Moon When the Snow Drifts into Tepees, the Deer Rutting Moon.) He himself went without a watch for several months. I'm on Indian time he would say when he showed up about an hour late somewhere. Indian time is fine in the Badlands, but in the big city it's not at all conducive to meeting bus schedules or catching planes. Mark went back to wearing a watch before the start of the trip. The watch that supposedly stopped around Ben.

It was these people, these people of the earth with the beautiful pastoral history whom Mark and I held in nothing short of awe. And they got screwed real bad back there in the 18-whatevers. But what do we do now? Give them back the West? (Was it ever theirs? Is it ours now?) Paying them millions in the 1960's didn't help. Maybe they're a people too close in time and place to the original screw. And now bingo is going to save them for godsake.

I let out big sorrowful breaths whenever I see members of the all-too-visible stereotype of that new tribe, the Urban Indian, in the bad parts of Minneapolis or St. Paul. Mark does too.

Mark and I didn't know any Indians personally, but we were driving around downtown St. Paul once and picked up an Indian boy of about sixteen who was hitch-hiking. Like I thought he would, Mark went right to the bone with the young man.

"What's your tribe? What do you think of white people? Do you long for the old days?"

The poor kid would have had to tape record all those questions in order to have answered them.

"Really now," Mark said, "what do you think of white people?"

"What can I say?" the Indian said, looking from one of us to the other. "Here I am getting a ride in your car."

"Ah, don't sweat that," Mark said. "Are whites ass-holes or what?"

It became silent and sweaty for a moment.

"No," our rider said. "People in general are assholes. White folks haven't cornered that market yet."

Mark nudged me and nodded with excitement like we had picked up another Sitting Bull or Crazy Horse or something. Maybe we had.

So there we were, amateur dinosaur hunters. More whitemen violating Indian land in some new way. Tres-passing on their last little bit of earth. Digging up dead animals even.

It was bad enough that the Indians were booted off the prairie and allowed to keep the Black Hills. But that was only until gold was discovered. Then they got the Bad-lands. Even two hundred thousand acres of that was taken away in 1942 for a bombing range and never returned. And then, exploration for coal and uranium was getting under way. Hell, they had every right to salt us away in their jail. My claustrophobia was getting real bad and I loosened my shirt to breathe better.

Clarence didn't have to do any talking. Mark was con-versing with the Indian who had escorted him down the canyon. We were even offered some water. My respira-tory rate slowed from sheer fright to simple anxiety.

I'm sure they thought we were Feds at first. The men were having a hard time believing we were just looking for rocks, as Mark vaguely put it.

"What kind of rocks? Gold, coal, uranium?" asked one of the men. Then he laughed and looked at his friends.

"No, no, none of that," Mark said quickly. "Bones. Dinosaur fossils."

Then all the Indians laughed again and looked at us as if we were wacko, which wouldn't have been too far off. Then I suppose they figured that a seventy-seven-year-old guy and a blind kid and two brothers with geological hammers couldn't be too much of a threat.

They must have believed us because they shrugged their shoulders and offered to fly us back to the Jeep. My claustrophobia popped up again with the thought of a crammed helicopter ride that to me would be like flying in a phone booth filled with college students. I gratefully declined for our party. Mark kicked me, under the table so to speak.

We about-faced and set off for Clarence's Jeep.

I DIDN'T RELAX UNTIL WE WERE IN CLARENCE'S TRUCK bouncing back to our camp. Then I started taking in the scenery.

Those Badlands still looked all the same to me. Wonderful and beautiful, but the same. Clarence tested me when we came to a valley that split off in two directions.

"Which way, badlander?" Clarence asked.

"Left," I said. I actually believed it.

"Sorry," said Clarence, turning the Jeep to the right. "There's five days of Badlands your way."

When I asked Clarence how he remembered all his landmarks, he said he didn't put any faith in landmarks. He just knew the land.

BACK AT CAMP I WAS RUMMAGING AROUND FOR SOMEthing to eat when I heard Mark ask Clarence if we could sneak back onto the reservation that night. I let a perfectly delicious dried apricot fall from my mouth at the suggestion.

CLARENCE LEFT THAT NIGHT APOLOGETIC AS HELL. "I could have showed you boys the real thing," he said. "The best."

We knew it and told him so. Maybe next time we'd get permission from whoever you'd get permission from to do something like that.

I wanted to bawl as I watched his Jeep pull away across the Badlands. In just the two days that we spent with him, he had become like our grandfather or something. At least we'd get to see him once more back in town before we left.

CHAPTER
8

AFTER CLARENCE LEFT US, WE PRETTY MUCH FELT like the ball game was over. We were fizzled out. Mark was even talking about heading to Montana to try to find the Bone Cabin. But we still had a long night to wait out before we could break camp and hike back to the Bronco.

Mark played "Memphis" on Ben's guitar for probably an hour straight. I've never ever seen Ben get mad, but I think he was close that night. He was fidgety and blowing his nose and getting up and down. Finally, he quietly asked Mark if he could play something himself. As soon as he got the guitar, he snapped it up in the case and brought it into the tent with him. The party was over for Ben. We wouldn't see him until morning. I rapped Mark good on the shoulder when he started whistling "Memphis."

I COULDN'T IMAGINE HAVING TO WANDER AROUND IN THE desert for thirty years or whatever the Jews had to do when Moses led them out of Egypt. Just carrying our crap five miles through the Badlands and then climbing up onto the table where the Bronco waited was quite enough for me, thank you.

Mark decided we'd go on to Montana after seeing Clarence one more time.

We hit Beauty at about 9:00 A.M. and headed straight for the Longhorn. I don't know why, except that maybe we were thinking it was too early to drop in on Clarence. The Longhorn was wide open. It probably never closed.

Gabby Hayes looked glad to see us. He said he had something to show Mark and asked him to come into the back.

It was quiet for a while, then I heard some laughing from behind the door where they were. Then more laughing and suddenly the door busted open and Gabby and Mark came out slapping each other on the back.

Time out. Here's what Mark told me later. Gabby showed Mark four blue capsules that he said were LSD. From California (where else?). But Mark had been a nursing-home aide once and he could see that the things were just a commonly used stool softener. So he tells Gabby that we're off drugs on account of our having had a religious experience out in the Badlands. Then Mark sells him fifteen Halazone tablets that he said were d-amphetamine from Minneapolis for a buck apiece. Mark said he never saw three fives get pulled out of someone's pocket so fast.

Time in. Mark wanted to take some photos in the Longhorn and Gabby said to go ahead but that he would be kind of busy because Social Security disability checks came in that day. I figured Mark would take about fifteen minutes, ten minutes even, but no, we were there until past noon. Mark set up reflectors and remote flash units. I had to take light-meter readings off Ben's face several times. Tripods were placed on tables and chairs. I was kind of impressed. Mark looked like he knew what was up.

Between doing whatever he was doing, Gabby Hayes asked us if Clarence had gopher-holed half of the Badlands looking for bone. I got the feeling he didn't like Clarence.

We left the Longhorn when it started to get busy. Then

Mark began immortalizing the town of Beauty on Kodachrome 25. By that time Ben had gear strapped across him like he was a photo-equipment hat tree. I was my usual first-assistant self. The session continued until we wound up at Clarence's.

GOLDIE'S MOTHER'S NAME WAS GOLDIE, SO SHE WAS Goldie Junior. Hard to find fault with that. Or the state capital plate collection that we finally got to see. ("Every one but Hawaii," Clarence said. "And one of the grandkids is going to take care of that pretty soon.")

It looked like Clarence was the collector and Goldie Junior the collectee. What I mean is that Goldie was kind of curator for the stuff Clarence dragged home. She had all the fossils recorded in a ledger and tried to keep the actual specimens tidied up. She had also made an agate-faced clock and some ballpoint pen holders that were anchored to a base of a shellacked wood with a piece of petrified wood glued onto it. (A nice touch there, the fossilized wood on wood. Kind of like parent and child, if you follow me.)

Clarence took Mark aside and I heard him ask if he could please try to get his wife into the *National Geographic*. Maybe with her newspaper clipping albums or state capital dishes.

There was a big book on a coffee table and Mark started looking through it. It was Alfred Romer's *Osteology of the Reptiles*. Signed by the author himself, who was out to Beauty in 1962.

Mark and I have it too. It's a paleontologic bible full of taxonomy and physiology and comparative anatomy, which is all to say that it's not your basic everyday reading material. Here's what I mean:

The dinosaurs are divided into two orders, the Saurischia and the Ornithischia, both included in the subclass Archosauria. . . . The Saurischia have the triradiate pelvic structure developed in so many thecodants, and the early Ornithischia had a two-pronged pubis, resulting in a tetrartadiate type of pelvis....

"You have the classic right here," Mark said.

"You're telling me," said Clarence. "There's a lot of chemistry and adjectives in that book."

WE ENDED UP SPENDING THE NIGHT AT CLARENCE'S. WE showed him some of our books and Mark took more pictures. Ben kept us all going with his own stories of how his mother and aunt taught him the different types of trees and wild flowers and rocks around their lake cabin.

"That man's a wonder," Clarence said to Mark and me when Ben left the room for the can.

"That's not the half of it," Mark said, but I sent a nasty look his way that meant no more of that psychic shit. Clarence didn't catch it because he was nodding off in his chair and Mark let it go. I saw that it was 3:00 A.M. Ben never returned and we figured Goldie had put him up in a guest bed, so Mark and I snuck out to sleep in the truck.

THE DEPARTURE WASN'T AS DISMAL AS I THOUGHT IT would be. I guess everyone figured we'd be seeing each other again. Mark gave Clarence and Goldie his card, which was really just an unused check deposit slip. Clarence told us that this place in Montana where we were headed might be good, but that no place could be like his Badlands in the old days. The last thing he told us was that we would never ever forget him.

Good-bye Clarence and Goldie Junior. Good-bye Longhorn. Good-bye wonderful, nutsy Beauty, South Dakota.

I DON'T THINK I TOOK ONE SINGLE PHOTOGRAPH WHILE we were out in the Badlands. I let Mark handle the photography in places like that. I learned early on that whenever I did attempt to take up a camera, pictures of the grandest places didn't always turn out. There you are on a cliff, gathering in a Lake Superior sunset in fall. You take a whiff of the pine air. A wedge of flying geese passes overhead. From someplace far away, a dog barks. I'll look through the viewfinder and get ready to snap the scene, but then shake my head and put the machine away feeling like a fool.

There was a time when I even tried some black-and-white landscapes a la Ansel Adams. My God the pictures were sorry. But my standards had been set at the apex. Ansel Adams *is* black-and-white landscape photography. His views are so beautiful and yet seem so simple that you want to run out and do one yourself. Then you learn he waited three months for the right light and best shadows.

Mark can get good landscape shots. As he tells me, you can't take in the whole panorama at once. In the Badlands, for instance, he would get Clarence to lean on a pick next to the side of a clay haystack. In the background is just enough great-looking terrain so that the viewer realizes our guru is not a construction worker standing by the excavation of an apartment-complex basement.

As we drove to Rapid City, Mark was getting a tad sentimental about him and me becoming a tight little film crew. He even had us on lecture tours, traveling under the banner of Twin City Triceratops. (When that happens, the Bronco will probably get a second insignia.) We'd be like Ellsworth and Emery Kolb, he said, two brothers who made early silent films and lantern slides of Grand Canyon river trips between 1911 and 1923.

Mark said we'd always be on the road, either making films with a paleontologic bent or touring with them. He envisioned us booking big old exhibition halls, and advertising in the local papers for adventure films. We would revive the turn-of-the-century lyceum circuit. The films would be silent to reinforce the extreme difficulty and danger under which they were made. Mark would narrate live. For an orchestra, we'd hire a rock 'n' roll band.

Adventure films were always auditorium busters at the

turn of the century. Early film audiences were motion-picture neophytes who were so fooled by cameras placed on the front of trolleys and trains that they yelled at jay-walkers on the screen. When full-frame facial close-ups were introduced, Mark said that people ran out of the theater.

Mark wasn't discouraged by my reminder that people today are better traveled and more video minded (not to mention TV pampered). Or that they could give a crap if a photographer had to hang upside down over Niagara Falls to get a shot. He didn't care. We'll slay them with our pressence was all he said.

I wanted to hear more about the Kolb brothers and the Grand Canyon, but Mark said to hold on to my shorts, that the topic was too special for anything less than a two-hour discussion.

CHAPTER
9

IN A WAY IT WAS GOOD TO BE ON THE ROAD AGAIN. IT'S the balm of motion I suppose. I remember my mom telling me that Mark was a colicky baby and that my dad had to bring him for middle-of-the-night rides in our '51 Ford to quiet him down. I guess it worked every time.

An automobile trip across America is a moving foxhole with its own universe and its own time. There is an intensity out there that can't quite be regained in circles of the everyday world. Mark and I have always been closest on our trips.

Long-haul car trips are funny. You have the two ends, of course, and then the big, big in-between. Maybe that's even the best part, the driving itself. The living, eating, sleeping, and breathing together in a little room on wheels. Mark and I think America would be a lot better off if families started taking long drives together again. Disneyland, Yellowstone, Washington, D.C. The destination makes absolutely no difference. It's all in the going. That's how kids should be raised. Take them on a three-week drive once a year.

Even when I'm with Mark I can get lonely when I'm gone from home, so after a few days out I make a list of family and friends whom I miss. I write jam-packed post-cards and a few long-winded, emotional letters. But by then I'm usually well into the trip mode and feeling like I never want to return. I don't seem to get my messages in the mail until I'm on the way back and then I beat them home.

Change of place on a long trip brings its own sadness. You're always leaving somebody or someplace behind. But thankfully in our part of the world we have something called road continuity to ease the transition coming and going. Every big town has a McDonald's and a Pizza Hut and a Kentucky Fried. This can be reassuring in a harsh, changing world. No matter where you are, all these places have the same basic layout with maybe a little regional decor thrown in. They even seem to face the same way. Mark always sits in the southwest corner of every Pizza Hut that he goes into. I think he gets offended if someone else is sitting at what he considers to be his table.

Then there are the white highway lines themselves. Those lines are really what hold a trip together. Every-where you go, there they are. You get to thinking that they were put there just for you to follow right to your destination.

There are classic road songs too. Songs written for the road. "This Land Is Your Land" is classic road material. More recently we have Eddie Rabbit ("Driving My Life Away") and Willie Nelson ("On the Road Again"). Bruce Springsteen knows the road. He's got "Drive All Night" and even one called "Badlands," although he doesn't men-tion dinosaurs. There are plenty of others, but the classic of road classics is "Route 66." It was a swing tune orig-inally, but any rock 'n' roller who is anybody has done it. It's the national road anthem. ("If you ever plan to motor west, travel my way, take the highway; that's the best. Get your kicks on Route 66.")

Route 66 was John Steinbeck's concrete road to the Promised Land. And it was Jack Kerouac's hipster road. Actually I've never heard "Route 66" while I've been driving. When I do, the radio will be full blast and I will be violating the speed limit.

Route 66 is kaput now. The highway that is. Interstate 40 has taken over, but it doesn't have its own song yet.

MOUNT RUSHMORE WAS NOT IN THE CARDS FOR THIS TRIP. We were trying very hard to avoid blatant tourist traps, even though Wall Drug and the Kadoka museum had led us astray. (The Corn Palace didn't count, since we saw it at 3:00 A.M.)

I know that Rushmore is supposed to be some kind of special monument, but the tourist holes around Rapid City were unbelievable. Reptile gardens, dinosaur parks (I'm talking fake, bloated objects of buffoonery here, not real dino). Restored gold mines or frontier towns wherever you looked. There was even a Life of Christ Wax Museum.

Mark wanted to check out a mammoth dig south of Rapid City that he'd recently read about. It was in Hot Springs. Even though it wasn't dinosaur, I could be open-minded. And it wasn't a tourist trap then.

Actually, the furry elephants, which is to say mammoths and mastodons, have quite a story of their own. The Reverend Cotton Mather made first mention of an American mammoth in 1714. Three fist-size teeth and a four-foot-long thigh bone were dug up in an Albany, New York, peat bog and brought to him for study. Only the Reverend Mr. Mather didn't know the remains were woolly mammoth. He thought they were the holy relics of a scriptural race of giants.

In 1770, Thomas Jefferson shipped some fossil bones to Ben Franklin, who was in England at the time playing around with politics, electricity, and European women. Dr. Franklin eventually received the bones and brought them to Paris and the great Georges Cuvier, the founder of paleontology.

Jefferson had sent the specimens with equal parts New York pride and scientific wonder. Some European hotshots like the Comte de Buffon had described the New World as a continent overloaded with noxious vapors and whose animals were so chickenshit that they bore no ardor toward the female. Jefferson knew that the saber-toothed tiger bones and elephant limbs he had sent to Franklin should clear that up.

Cuvier was impressed. He recognized the sloth fossils that were also part of the packages as a new species that he named *Megatherium jeffersoni*.

Well, I could go on and on about how farmers and road diggers and construction workers still come upon ivory tusks in upper Michigan and mammoth teeth in Minnesota gravel pits or even freeze-dried specimens of woolly mammoth meat and hair on the Alaskan tundra. (P. T. Barnum toured a mastodon skeleton.) But in Russia, where Siberians have been exporting tons of ivory for three hundred years and where entirely preserved mammoths have been thawed out of the permafrost and nibbled on by dogs and wolves, they actually have a government-run Committee for the Study of Mammoths. They had to have somebody explain where the hairy elephants and all that ivory came from. Between 1660 and 1915, fifty thousand mammoth tusks were found in Siberia. Some of the specimens were ten feet long. Most of them were sent to China and Europe. Cultured Europeans thought they were unicorn tusks. Before the Committee for the Study of Mammoths, most Russians figured the tusks belonged to giant moles.

Siberia is still the woolly mammoth gold mine of the world. I saw a 1906 black and white of a Siberian train depot. I shit you not, gondola cars as far as you can see are loaded to the gills with mammoth tusks and bones. The earth alongside some Siberian rivers even today is so densely packed with mammoth fossils that the bones actually deter erosion of the banks.

FUN FACT: Charles Willson Peale exhibited America's first mastodon in 1802 in Independence Hall, along with the Liberty Bell and the Declaration of Independence.

THE FIRST THING I WANTED TO DO IN RAPID CITY WAS head straight for a pizza joint. But Mark was driving and he said he had to show Ben and me a few things about personal hygiene on the road before we did anything civilized like eat in a public restaurant. I remember hoping that he wasn't going to make us bathe in a river or something like he probably did during his Alaska days. Then, before I knew it, we had driven into the student parking lot of the South Dakota School of Mines and Mark was out of the Bronco talking to a group of college boys. Ben and I just kind of stood around while Mark went on and on about football and frats and how we were visiting geology students from Washington, D.C., it being the home base of *National Geo* and all. (Of course, the Bronco had Minnesota license plates.) Pretty soon we were walking to a dorm and going up to this very nice person's room and using his shaving gear and towels. Then we took a shower down the hall. After we were all cleaned up, Mark had some other guy take a picture of the three of us fossilers with our lavatory captain.

I don't know how Mark can do stuff like shave and bathe in some complete stranger's room, but I guess that's how you hitchhike back and forth to Alaska twice.

THE ONLY OTHER THING WE STOPPED FOR IN RAPID CITY was that pizza. At the Rapid Pizzeria yet. We ordered two large mushroom and Canadian bacon units. Since we didn't call ahead, we had to watch the other patrons burning their tongues and groping at mozzarella cheese strands hanging out of their mouths. It's not a pretty sight to watch someone else eat a pizza, especially someone hungry. It's kind of like watching a lion on the Serengeti tearing into a zebra.

Our pizzas arrived with a little something extra that Mark noticed right away.

"There's a hair in the s.o.b.," Mark whined. "I can't stand hair in food."

Mark's observation caught Ben with a mouthful. He stopped in mid-chew, as if waiting for further verification.

I looked closer. "That's not a hair, that's an eyelash. Just a harmless little comma."

"I can't stand punctuation marks in food," Mark said. Then he reached for a slice.

Like the reactivation of a freeze frame, Ben's mouth took up where it left off.

THE NEW ITINERARY WOULD BE SIMPLE ENOUGH. DROP down to the Hot Springs mammoth site for a several-hour inspection, then backtrack to Rapid City, and head up to North Dakota with a left at I-94 to Big Sky country. It was only four hundred miles from Rapid to where we wanted to go in Montana, but mostly over secondary highway. We figured on six or seven hours of straight driving once we left Hot Springs.

There would be some great-sounding cities above Rapid City. Sturgis, Deadwood, Spearfish, Belle Fourche. And north of the Black Hills we had Castle Rock, Buffalo, and Center-of-the-Nation to look forward to.

Mark and I were getting accustomed to civilization again. Civilization as represented by the Rapid City pizza joint anyway. Our own pizzas were on their way to becoming bone and muscle when we ordered another pitcher of beer to assist that miracle. Mark invited the waitress to sit with us but she said she was too busy.

"I can see that," Mark said looking around at the typical pizza-parlor vacancy of a weekday afternoon. She giggled but her smile was gone by the time she had turned 90 degrees.

"If we don't get on the road pretty soon, we'll be sucking hind tit," said Ben all of a sudden. Mark choked so hard on a sip of beer that I had to slap him on the back.

"Okay, let's go," I said, standing up and brushing off pizza-crust droppings. "Let's get ourselves a woolly mammoth."

"I don't know," Mark said, looking at our waitress who was then returning to clear off the table. "Ben's idea doesn't sound all that bad."

ALL WE KNEW ABOUT THE HOT SPRINGS DIG WAS WHAT Mark had read in a newspaper clipping my mom had given him. In 1972, some construction workers uncovered the teeth, skull, and one six-foot-long tusk of a woolly mammoth as a housing development project. The landowner had the amazing grace to delay the project for several years while a team of students and paleontologists from a nearby college studied the area. By the third year of the dig, fifteen mammoths had been uncovered.

It wasn't any problem finding the site. A Texaco station attendant gave us directions. The elephant hole he called it.

EVEN THOUGH IT WAS GETTING DARK OUT WHEN WE GOT there, we could see that the place didn't look like much. The skeletons of four or five houses surrounded an empty lot with a fenced-in pit in the middle. A small Caterpillar sat off to one side and a lit-up shack probably housed a few students on that night's watch.

We parked the Bronco on the edge of the lot and walked to the shack. Mark was ahead of us, and for some reason he looked in a window before finding a door to knock on. Suddenly he ducked down and slowly raised his head to the bottom of the window. Then he motioned for us to keep low and quiet.

"I think there's a guy and a girl in there going at it," Mark breathed to Ben and me. "But I left my goddamned glasses in the truck. What do you see?"

I carefully spied through the window and narrated for my two sightless partners. It certainly looked like the couple was going at it. "Well, for starters," I said, "she has her shirt off." Mark grabbed my arm.

Activity in the shack evolved according to the natural order of things and I was getting a little worked up myself. "Oh . . . boy," was all I could manage.

"What's happening?" Mark asked, digging his fingernails deeper into my arm.

Then there was a little moan inside and the couple rolled over. Silverware and plastic cups hit the floor.

"What's going on?" Ben whispered.

"I'm going to get my glasses," Mark said. Then he took off in a crouched run across the empty lot.

I thought we had been pretty quiet, but I saw the guy suddenly look around. I don't know if he saw me. I don't think so, because through a knothole, I could see that he didn't come over to the window. He and his friend were covering up though. Then he stood up and walked to the door.

There was no way to get word to Mark, who was at the moment crawling toward the front door. I don't know why. Maybe he expected a better angle through the keyhole. The door swung open and bonked Mark on the head.

"You wouldn't happen to have a bathroom we could use?" Mark said pointing to Ben and me who were then coming around the corner.

WE FOUND OUT THAT ALL THE REST OF THE CREW STAYED in a motel while two people took the night shift.

"Must get lonely out here," Mark said to the students. He was lucky he didn't get kneed in the gonads right then and there.

Formalities were quickly dispensed with and we got down to business. (Most people wouldn't understand, but paleontology can rate right up with sex.) A Coleman lantern spotlighted an amazing collection of partially excavated limbs, hip bones, and vertebrae. Some specimens were already wrapped in plaster. They used toilet paper to wrap the bones in before applying the plaster. Pink toilet paper whose only significance was that they got five cases of it cheap.

The woman told us that the red clay in which the mammoth bones were found was once a hole. Once, like ten thousand years ago. It probably had a spring in the bottom too, because they had also found freshwater clam and snail fossils. Somehow, a group of mammoths fell into the hole. Paleontologists figured that they fell because a lot of the bones were fractured. Trapped mammoths that weren't killed on the spot eventually died of starvation. Since the end of the Ice Age, the hole became impacted with hard clay. Hard enough so that when the surrounding earth eroded away, a red clay mound that used to be a hole was left behind. Topographic inversion I think she called it.

I couldn't help but sneak glances at the young woman.

She had a big red mark on her neck. I was picturing her without a shirt on when the premier find was lit up by a swinging lantern. An accumulation of five or six huge tusks that lay in a half-buried pile.

"Those are some nice tits, er, tusks," I said and cleared my throat.

Ben crouched down and ran his hand over one of the six-foot pieces of fossil ivory. We all joined him. Suddenly, the whole scene struck me as rather peculiar. In my mind, I pulled back and looked around. Through the windows of the nearby homes I could see TV screens beaming their goods into living rooms. A car honked. Crowd noises and marching band sounds floated our way. I even thought I smelled barbecued hamburgers. And all the while, we earth brothers and sister fondled an old elephant bone.

WHAT HAPPENED NEXT I CAN ONLY PARTLY PIECE BACK together. We left Hot Springs late. Maybe around midnight. Mark was rather insistent upon driving. With the beer we had utilized and the longer stay at the dig than expected, I figured we should find a motel and at least be fresh in the morning.

"No way, mother!" Mark said. He looked teed off. "If we were staying, we could camp out. None of this motel shit. But we aren't staying, so forget it."

Yes sir, maestro, I thought. Well, I was beat. So was Ben. We both squeezed into the back of the Bronco and stretched out as best as we could. Mark was up front alone with his NōDōz. The last thing I can remember for sure was all three of us singing "You've Lost That Lovin' Feeling."

I dreamed that Mark was working in a pizza place back in St. Paul. He worked the counter and there was a big contest going on. A customer got one stamp with a pizza. The stamps were put on a game card and if the right spaces were filled, you could win stuff like a color TV or a ten speed or even five hundred dollars. People were always asking Mark to slip them a few extra stamps.

"Can't," Mark said in the dream. "One stamp per pizza."

"Come on," somebody would say, "nobody'll know."

"God will know," said Mark.

"I don't believe in God," the somebody said.

"Yah, but I do," Mark said. Then he laughed, but he still didn't give out any more stamps.

Mark is not your religious type, but he has his own private theology. Judeo–Christian–Rock 'n' Roll–Paleontology he calls it. He would like to hear choirs do things like "Blue Suede Shoes" or Aretha Franklin's "Respect." (He didn't know how the fossils fit in though.)

There must have been more to the dream than that, but nothing else comes back.

WE WERE STILL MOVING WHEN I WOKE UP. THE SUN WAS squinty-eyed bright. I had a tinny taste in my mouth and an acidy gut. My Jockey shorts were riding high. All the signs of a night on the road. I creaked up on one elbow to look outside. The terrain was very familiar. Mark was driving with only one hand on the steering wheel. He was sitting almost sideways, his right leg propped up on the empty passenger seat, the left on the gas. He was the most comfortably placed driver I had ever seen.

"Morning, kid," Mark said to me when he noticed I was awake.

I didn't answer right away. I had to let things register first. Particularly the strange landscape.

"You must be using that place mat again," I said about Mark's famous map. Then I laughed, but not too long. It didn't look like we were on the great western plains anymore. More like the foothills of the Rockies.

"Where the hell are we, bud?" I asked nervously.

"Three hours from Independence Pass and five hours from Aspen."

"Jesus H., man!" I said. "What about Montana and dinosaur city?"

"We'll get there. You told me you've never seen the Rocky Mountains."

"Well, shit, I've..." I started to say but stopped right there. I was going to say I'd never seen Mexico either, but I didn't want to plant any more ideas.

"We're going to see Leslie," Ben suddenly said out

loud. He had just woken up but, as usual, he was sharper than a tack.

"We're going to see Leslie," Mark repeated. "We all talked to her last night.

Then I vaguely remembered talking to someone from a truckstop phone booth. I thought that was another dream.

Mark must have seen my bitten lip. "Hey, it's not that far off the track."

Not that far to Mark is a few inches on a map or someplace you can get to by driving twenty-four hours straight.

"Going to see Leslie is fine," I lied. "The unscheduledness just threw me." I took a deep breath and sat up. The scenery outside was giving the Badlands a run for its money.

MARK AND LESLIE WERE COLLEGE SWEETHEARTS. THEY were hot and heavy for several years but went their separate ways about the time Mark headed to Toronto for film school. I saw Leslie from time to time in the post-Mark period.

I always had what you would call a crush on Leslie. Neither she nor Mark ever knew it. Hell, I never told anyone. Coveting your brother's girl friend seemed to be kind of an ancient no-no. Leslie is one fine woman though. Blond, beautiful, and brilliant. She had all the bases covered, if you follow me. When I think of Leslie, I think of a line that must be from the Old Testament: "She was dressed in garments of her gladness and was a wonder to behold."

Leslie was an English major dabbling in journalism, drama, and music. I heard that her parents had her geared to be a concert pianist. She played the piano every day from age six on. But then she gave it all up in a huff by freshman year in college. I didn't know if she had anything to do with music after that. She got into the peace movement in 1970 and became kind of a clean-cut hippie. She wrote a great Ellen Goodman-type column for the school paper, but when Mark went to Toronto and they split up, she moved to Aspen right after graduation.

I couldn't tell if Mark and Leslie were getting back together again. Kind of hard to believe they would be from just one phone call. But like I said, they used to be very close.

WE COULD SEE THE ROCKIES AHEAD OF US. IN LEWIS and Clark's time they were known as the Stony Mountains. I suppose they were a good sixty or seventy miles off.

"Emery and Ellsworth Kolb," I said to Mark. "Now I want to hear about the brothers who filmed the Grand Canyon."

"Does it have anything to do with dinosaurs?" asked Ben.

"Maybe and maybe not," Mark said.

"Well, if you don't mind," said Ben, "could you lower your voice during parts of the story that have anything to do with paleontology."

"Ben, my boy," Mark said after a little sniffle of the nose, "some night I'm going to get you so drunk you'll be able to see..."

"Hey, cool it!" I said, cutting Mark off.

Suddenly it was very quiet. Ben squirmed a little bit and Mark stared straight ahead.

"as I was saying *to Ben*," Mark said looking my way like he'd just disowned me, "sometime I'll get him to see what the dinosaur fire is all about."

"Sorry everybody," I said. I guess I'd spoken a little too soon. Mark went ahead with the story.

Actually, I knew a little bit about the Kolbs myself. From the great, leather-bound *National Geographics* my parents had. Mark had found the Kolbs' story in the August 1914 *NG*: "Experiences in the Grand Canyon" by Ellsworth and Emery Kolb. Seventy black-and-white photographs and their accompanying text took up the whole issue. I had breezed through that gold mine a few times myself, but Mark was still the authority. He even did his own biographical research and found out that the brothers built a cabin and photographic studio at the head of Bright Angel Trail in 1903. In those days there were still mountain lions in the area. And camels. Jefferson Davis (of Confederacy fame) had an idea back in 1857 that Arabian camels would be good pack animals. A thousand or so were shipped overseas and eventually made it to the southwestern United States. But the camels were too independent for the prospectors or vice versa and the beasts ran wild through the canyon lands of Arizona and Nevada until they eventually died out. Emery Kolb photographed a camel, but broke the glass-plate negative to smithereens before he got a print.

The Kolbs' most famous work was their still and motion photography of the Grand Canyon.

"These guys were no pussies," Mark said. "They'd leave their family back at Bright Angel Trail while they took off for one-or two-month hikes. Hikes, I love that. Carrying a hundred pounds of photographic supplies and enough water and food for the whole trip. Hikes! I love it."

The brothers were gearing up for a big boat trip that retraced Major J. W. Powell's famous trip in 1869 from Green River City, Wyoming, through the canyons of the Green River and the Grand Canyon itself and finally to the Gulf of Mexico. Powell was a one-armed Civil War veteran who was the first man to boat the entire length of the Grand Canyon.

The hikes the Kolbs took were scouting trips down side canyons to find ways off the river in case they lost their boat. The Kolbs weren't wimps, but they weren't maniacs either. There are stretches of the Grand Canyon where the walls are two- to four-thousand-feet high. And it wasn't the age of motorized rubber rafts or park services or portable-radio contact. Of the five trips that preceded the Kolbs, lives had been lost on each one, including the entire Stanley and Berg party in 1903. Stanley and Berg had set out to survey the Grand Canyon by boat. Survey it and then study the feasibility of draining the entire canyon and running a railroad through it.

"Those boys thought they'd fuck with nature a little bit," Mark said. "But they ended up fucking the dog."

"Did it say that in *National Geographic*?" Ben asked.

After two years of scouting around and even a short

two-week trial run, the Kolbs brought all their gear by roundabout railroad to Green River City, Wyoming, where they stocked up provisions and hired a local boy named Fergus as their assistant. Local people warned the brothers of bad guys living in caves along the river.

They left Green River in two sixteen-foot wooden boats on September 8, 1911. On board in airtight chambers were one motion picture and five still cameras, one hundred glass photographic plates and three thousand feet of film.

Fergus was an able enough hand, even though the Kolbs had to remind him to crank the movie camera and keep the still camera still. But he got terminally homesick three weeks into the trip and the brothers let him off before the Green River entered Glen Canyon. They were actually very understanding. They gave him overland directions to Jensen, Utah, and twenty exposed glass-plate negatives that he was to send to Emery's wife. Each brother then took a boat.

"So after they let their assistant pack it in," Mark was saying, "they entered the unbelievably beautiful Split Mountain Canyon, not known as Dinosaur National Monument."

For half a second, Mark looked over at Ben. I could tell Ben was getting into it. He was sitting up straight, waiting for Mark to continue.

"The Dinosaur National Park thing," Mark went on, "is a whole other story, but let me just say this. At the end of Split Mountain Canyon, there's an upturned stretch of sedimentary rock about a quarter of a mile off the river that bears the richest accumulation of dinosaur bones ever found in one place. Clarence would have been in fossil heaven down there."

Mark stopped at that point and looked over at Ben again. Ben leaned closer during the moment of silence, so Mark continued.

The paleontologist Earl Douglass was sent by the Carnegie Museum in Pittsburgh to check out the site in 1909. It looked promising enough so that he moved his whole family down and built a cabin on the banks of the Green River. At the time the nearest town was thirty miles away.

When the Kolbs passed by the Douglass cabin in 1911,

ten complete dinosaurs had been uncovered, including two new species, *Apatosaurus louisae*, after Andrew Carnegie's wife, Louise, and one for the old man himself, *Diplodocus carnegiei*. In its day, *Diplodocus* was the biggest dinosaur ever and it tickled Mr. Carnegie so that he had fifteen casts made of the entire eighty-foot-long skeleton and presented them as gifts to the major museums of the world. (That cost him a measly four hundred grand.) The *Diplodocus* skeletons became leading attractions throughout Europe and the cities of South America, and *Diplodocus carnegiei* became the best known dinosaur in the world.

Then J. P. Morgan got into the scene, but too late to get his own disonaur. He gave Earl Douglass free railroad cartage for 350 more tons of dinosaur bones that eventually made their way back to Pittsburgh.

"I couldn't find a thing about whether the Kolbs ever stopped at the Douglass homestead," Mark said. "I don't see how they could have missed it, but neither Emery nor Ellsworth mentions it in anything that I read. Actually, they never mentioned a thing about dinosaurs on their whole trip. Indian pictographs and artifacts, but no dino."

Major Powell had found dinosaur remains during his 1869 river run, probably in the same area.

Anyway, Earl Douglass and his family worked the rock and lived there for fourteen years. President Wilson dedicated the site as Dinosaur National Monument in 1915 and in 1958 a museum was built over a side of a cliff with hundreds of exposed dino bones.

The Kolbs had been left stranded for the last fifteen minutes at the end of Split Mountain Canyon and we ourselves didn't seem to be any closer to the Stony Mountains than we were when Mark started his story.

Ben was actually on the edge of his seat, his brain tape recording every word.

"Earl Douglass sent out twenty-three new species of dino," Mark said.

"Which is a genus and which is a species again?" Ben asked Mark.

It seemed to me like Ben was weakening on the dinosaur issue.

"You know that high school biology business about kingdom, phylum, genus, and species, and whatever?" said Mark. "All I really remember is that if you're of the same species you can screw—I mean mate—but if you're only in the same genus or higher you can't."

"Too bad," I said.

"That's right," Mark said to me. "I forgot. You were the one who liked sheep."

"I believe we were talking about the Kolbs," was all I said. I pretended that I was insulted. I think I have mentioned that my brother was a pervert.

The Kolbs had been gone about three and a half weeks when they passed Earl Douglass's homestead. The one-hundred-mile stretch of their trip to that point had been desolate and beautiful. But navigable enough that the brothers wrote in the *Geographic* that they had no doubt that boating down the Green River would eventually become a popular pastime. But the Big Ditch itself—the Grand Canyon—was a different matter. It still lay ahead.

When they reached the Colorado River (the actual beginning of the Grand Canyon) they had already done 850 miles. One day into the canyon they found a clothed skeleton on the bank. On Christmas Day, one of their boats broke up in a rapids and Emery almost drowned. Loss of both of the boats at once in that section of the canyon would have been the end of the road since the walls were a sheer 3,000 feet. Two cameras and a case of glass-plate negatives bit the dust, but a great sequence of film of the smack-up made it through.

Emery started having fitful dreams that were stoked up whenever they camped by a rapids. Rushing water on rock spooked him all night long with the sounds of women screaming and babies crying.

Their darkroom was set up inside a sleeping tent. Clean solution for developing came from centrifuging muddy water in a twirling bucket that also had a secret ingredient in it—a slice of prickly-pear cactus.

Their patience and presence on the river gave them pictures of the Grand Canyon and its cousins in snow, fog, rain, sun, heat, and sandstorm. They were fascinated by incredible lightning storms and worked by pure ex-

perimentation to find that one-and-a-half-minute exposures cemented the spectacular views of their photographic
plates.

Mark was particularly fond of a photo of Ellsworth
Kolb hanging by a rope from a log laid over a Grand
Canyon crevice with a one-thousand-foot drop below him.
Emery Kolb is balancing on the log above and lowering
a camera to his brother by another rope. "There's you
and me, kid," Mark would always say about the shot.

The brothers reached the Gulf of California in March.
In five months they had covered 1,012 miles.

"I don't know how the sons a bitches ever got home,"
Mark said. "You ever see where the Gulf of California is?
In the literal middle of nowhere is where."

The Kolbs always called it their Big Trip. Emery was
still lecturing on the Grand Canyon and showing bits of
their Big Trip film and lantern slides into the 1960's. He
always told people that he and his brother looked on their
journeys, hard as they usually were, in the light of a va-
cation.

"Right on!" Ben said at the end of the Kolb story.

Mark stretched back away from the steering wheel and
took a deep breath and smiled the smile of one who has
just brought an unbeliever into the fold.

CHAPTER
10

"INDEPENDENCE PASS AHEAD, LADIES AND GENTLE-men," Mark said to Ben and me in a pilot voice. "We will be climbing to twelve thousand feet. Please hold on to your genitalia."

I figured that this last bit of crudeness was a setup for one of Mark's favorite epithets. Something he picked up in an intro psych course. A term meaning one whose testicles have not descended.

"All cryptorchids to the rear of the cabin, please," Mark said.

"What about you, numb nuts?" I asked.

"Very clever, brother," he said. "A bit base, but very clever."

"Don't listen to any of this," I said to Ben.

I'm not sure what Ben's response was, but I think he gave Mark and me the double finger. The double whammy as they say. Ben! But like I said, I wasn't sure.

* * *

WHEN I TOOK THE WHEEL, I TRIED TO GET SOME CLASsical music out of the smorgasbord of our radio. I figured it would be good mountain music.

On the road, there's a time and place for every type of music. You can't live by rock 'n' roll alone. Lawrence Welk, Peggy Lee, Ella, Ray, some vintage Bing. Even Fred Waring and the Pennsylvanians have their place. But classical music in the proper spot can be so perfect. I think of it as music to announce the coming and going of the sun. At dawn once we caught an orchestra warming up. Those hypnotic strings sawing on one collective sustained note. The bird-chirping woodwinds, the far-off, thunderstorm tympani. I think classic orchestration is the only music for an unraveling sunrise. Except for maybe a single French horn.

Classical music is a commitment though. We're talking thirty to forty minutes here, not the quick-hitting minute, twenty seconds of the pop format. It'll fool you too. You turn it up, up, up during a lull, and then a fortissimo blows you out of the front seat.

I'm pretty sure Mark likes classical music, even though he calls it tippy-toe shit.

Beautiful-listening stations can help too. They'll fill out gray, rainy days on the highway for you. I hear a Mantovani version of "Summer Place" or "Moon River" and I want to close my eyes and take a deep breath and let myself float back to high school dances with lost loves, which is all okay unless you're at the wheel.

Music is a time warper that way. Everybody's got his own places that an old song brings him. Our grandparents fondle their courting days by listening to Victor Herbert or Gershwin. Our parents put on Sinatra. And in another thirty years, John, Paul, George, and Ringo and Aretha Franklin will be our Glen Millers and Artie Shaws and Kate Smiths.

I'll tell you though, the punk rockers of today have a lot to learn. For one thing, they blast their music all the time. Hell, you've got to play with that volume knob, turn it up at just the right moment and for only the most appropriate tune. That's what Ben does. Of course, he is a radio maestro. But the ultimate desecration is that some of these young punkers actually think that Joni Mitchell and Chuck Berry are old farts.

And disco. I really can't say much about disco. It's in there somewhere at the end of the seventies.

You hear a lot of music on the highway. Mark calls the five-hundred-mile stretch of I-90 from southern Minnesota to Wall the rock 'n' roll road because once you hit Albert Lea and point west there's a good ten hours of radio ahead. You get to be a pop music expert. You can pick out songs by their first note. You know who wrote what when. And you can tell live pieces from session and not just by the crowd noise.

Part of the magic of road music is the radio itself. It materializes song out of thin air. And you don't know what's coming or how long you can hold on to it. I always wondered if the highway patrol could listen to the radio. Real radio. Music, news, local call-in shows. It'd be a shame if they couldn't. That old car radio keeps you sharp.

Mark has a pet theory about the evolution of music. He thinks it all started a few billions years ago with waves on the beach. There was no one around to hear it, of course, but the pounding of water on the earth's shores for aeons put a beat into the earliest life-forms. He figures the first notes were actually a few tentative, underwater squeaks emitted by ancestral fish. Maybe dinosaurs sang or maybe they didn't, but Mark says they gave us music itself by giving rise to birds. Mark's theory then gets a little shaky when he takes a quantum leap to the 1950's and Little Richard and T-Bone Walker and B. B. King.

Mark unraveled this hypothesis to me late one night through another miracle known as a long-distance phone call from Chicago. I could just see him gesturing wildly on the other end. He actually dropped the receiver once. Then his voice faded for maybe a full minute, which it turned out was because he had set the receiver down but had kept talking while he got undressed. When he picked up the phone again, he was shouting so loud I had to hold the earpiece out a foot or so from my head. After a moment of silence that I was sure signaled the end of the harangue, I told him that I didn't know what the hell he was talking about, but I sure liked his tone of voice.

The radio—or rock 'n' roll itself for that matter—doesn't always keep us flying. During a few hours of highway burnout, Mark and I have been known to snap off the radio and sing Shirley Temple songs.

Songs I'd like to see made into movies:

"Taxi" (Harry Chapin)

"Chuck E's in Love" (Rickie Lee Jones)

"Tapestry" (Carole King)

"Heat Wave" (Martha and the Vandellas)

"Dance of the Fossils" (Saint-Saëns)

"Norwegian Wood" (Beatles)

"Dock of the Bay" (Otis Redding)

"Battle of New Orleans" (Johnny Horton)

"Rhapsody in Blue" (George Gershwin)

"Lola" (Kinks)

"MTA"; "Tom Dooley" (Kingston Trio)

"Abraham, Martin and John" (Dion)

"One Last Kiss" (J. Frank Wilson)

"Fun, Fun, Fun" (Beach Boys)

Mark was vigorously describing snowcapped peaks and soft mountain meadows to Ben. If I hadn't been at the wheel myself, I could have closed my eyes and watched a narrated slide show of summer in the Rocky Mountains.

Independence Pass was the last up and down before Aspen. I was proud of the way the old Bronco was powering back and forth up the mountain switchbacks.

Mark suddenly turned off the radio. "Who's for driving off a cliff and dying happy?" Then he yelled an ungodly loud war whoop and stepped on the gas. On top of my surprised right foot, the lawful keeper of the gas pedal.

THERE WAS STILL SOME DIRTY SNOW AT THE SUMMIT. WE stopped for a mandatory romp in the stuff and I dropped a grapefruit of a snowball into Mark's pants. It took a disappearing sun to bring back a little reverence to the scene. Thousands of feet below, the lights of Aspen tweaked at us. I looked over at Mark. I'm sure the smile on his face was for Leslie.

"HOW'S THE GAS SITUATION?" BEN ASKED MARK WHO was back at the controls for the descent.

"I hope it's a lot better down there than it is up here, which is empty."

This was no immediate cause for alarm. Mark and I were experts at driving on the big E. The only problem was how long had we been on it. There were still twenty or thirty miles left to Aspen. Luckily, most of it downhill.

"We'll coast as long as we can," Mark said, shutting off the engine. "We'll make it."

Ten minutes later, Mark erupted with a loud expulsion of intestinal gas. He ripped one off, to use the vernacular.

"Splatt!" Mark said and laughed.

"Too bad we can't harness you up to the engine," I said.

"What's splatt?" Ben asked, but then he must have figured it out because he rolled down the window and put his face to the wind.

THERE ARE A LOT OF FACTS BOUNCING AROUND IN BEN'S head, and he let a few of them out from time to time to enrich Mark and me.

"There was a survey taken by one of the reputable polls," Ben said to us right after the splatt business. "Maybe the Harris or Gallup. Anyway, it was about what people do when they're alone in their cars."

"Pass gas?" Mark asked, turning his head full around to look at Ben.

"That was one," said Ben, "but passing gas was actually third on the list. It was beat out by picking noses and singing."

"Hey," I said to Mark, "I wish you'd get in line with the rest of the country."

The splatt thing goes back to grade school, but it was revived around the time of Mark's first Alaska hitchhike. I helped him pack the night before he left. When he wasn't looking, I slipped little "splatt!" notes into his socks and shirt pockets and his boots and any other place that would hide a folded piece of paper.

Mark told me later that the best splatt he pulled out was on a rainy, spooky night in the Yukon. He had just gotten his first ride all day. In the dark of the car he reached into his billfold to give the driver a few bucks for gas and almost gave him a splatt note instead.

WHEN WE REACHED THE VALLEY FLOOR, MARK KEPT THE Bronco at a steady thirty miles per hour. We hit Aspen running on vapors I'm sure, because we kind of seizured and stopped a block from a Phillip's 66 station. Then we could only go about ten feet at a time with each turn of the ignition.

Mark was anxious to see Leslie. Since those were pre-self-serve days, he wasn't going to wait around for any attendant. He jumped out and activated a pump and gassed up the Bronco himself. Ben and I limped off to the men's room. Ben was all rumply haired and had on a holey, white T-shirt. He was also walking stocking-footed across the oil-stained driveway. The final debasement keeping him from Mark's and my plane was foul language in public places.

IT WAS ABOUT 10:00 P.M. WHEN WE GOT TO THE RESTAU-rant where Leslie worked. A little Swiss café. We sat in her section of the outside patio after the appropriate affections were exchanged all around. Then she had to get to some other tables.

I watched her walk away. She was looking her usual wonderful self, even in her waitress outfit. More like a writer-musician in exile, I thought, than a hippie. She slipped in and out among the tables, turning heads wherever she went. Waitress uniforms were still kind of tight and short-skirted then, and when she bent down to pick up some fallen silverware, I saw London and France. I think I was in love again.

Mark began a long-winded discussion about seeing your image right side up on one side of a spoon and upside down on the other. He was drawing diagrams on the tablecloth and turning silverware this way and that trying to figure it out when Ben explained the nature of convex and concave mirrors. All about how they reverse or reflect the angle of incident light and so forth.

Leslie wouldn't be off until closing, so she gave us the keys to her apartment. Mark handed her what I presumed to be a little love note he had written on a matchbox cover.

"I see your stationery hasn't changed," I said to Mark when we hit the street.

LESLIE'S PLACE HAD A BALCONY OVERLOOKING A SKI run at Aspen. I sat on the porch for maybe an hour just staring at the evening mountainside. After we had all taken lingering, luxurious showers, Mark made us one of the oldest and most reliable of all dinosaur-hunter's staples. The root beer float. Then he went to get Leslie.

There were dinosaurs in Colorado. I don't know about Aspen, but Colorado, yes. Cope and Marsh's gang war was warmed up by the early dinosaur finds at Morrison and Canon City during the seasons of 1876 and 1877. A hundred years later, near Crested Butte, Dr. Jim ("Dinosaur Jim") Jensen and his workers uncovered the largest animal to ever walk the earth: the sixty-foot-tall and eighty-foot-long *Ultrasaurus*. (The *CB Pilot* said that *Ultrasaurus* was as long as the Crested Butte post office and twice as tall.) Its shoulder blade alone was nine feet long. The giant had two small brains: one in the cranium, of course, the other in the tail, like the steering wheel in back of a hook and ladder.

BEN WAS LISTENING TO THE TV AND SINCE MARK AND Leslie weren't back, I started looking around her apartment. In a little sewing room, I saw an alto recorder next to a music stand. I knew that's what it was because of the music book nearby: *Classical Transposition for the Alto Recorder*. It also looked like she had a lot of college textbooks on some low shelves made of bricks and planks. Beautiful art history books, fifty or sixty paperback novels, history books, sociology books, theology books. It was a nice little selection, but rather deficient in science.

Leslie's bedroom was a sunny little place with a double bed, a rocking chair, and a chest of drawers. A picture of her family hung between two framed photos of fruit. On the floor, a big straw hat with a blue ribbon partially covered a dainty-looking pair of hiking boots.

From the top shelf of the bedroom closet I took down a bundle of envelopes that were rubber-bindered together. I was in sacred territory here but kept going anyway. It looked like they were letters Mark and Leslie had written to each other. I suppose Mark gave his batch back when they broke up the last time. I took out one of Leslie's letters to Mark and read it. It looked like her last letter before she went to Colorado.

Mark, you dear wonderful crazy man,

I'm not moving from you to get farther away, I'm moving to get closer to you. If you can't see that I am your one love when you're with me, maybe you will when I'm gone. If not, I know that I will recover, even though it scares me to think that someday you won't be important to me.

> I love you, love you, love you
> and can't understand how
> you can let me go,
>
> L.

My eyes were misted up at the end of the letter and I kept thinking what a jerkoff Mark was to leave such a wonderful woman. But I forgot that at that very moment Mark was probably walking through downtown Aspen holding her hand.

THAT NIGHT BEN AND I BED-ROLLED IT ON THE FLOOR of the sewing room. We were probably both asleep when Mark and Leslie got home, but before I conked out I remember I had the feeling that they were no longer ex-sweethearts.

THE FOUR OF US TOURED ASPEN THE NEXT DAY. WE SAW a lot of people with turquoise growths all over their bodies. Blue seemed to predominate the Aspen summer and not just in the jewelry. The Levi jackets and jeans. The wonderful sky and the mountain streams. But green made it all happen. The green frog skins of developers, real estate agents, and the blessed people who nested in this old silver-mining town part of each year.

I insulted a gift shop jeweler by asking if his turquoise was real.

"Is your money real?" was all he said. Then he went over to some other customer.

What the hell did I know? You hear a lot about fake turquoise these days. This particular place, Nickel Pete's Wonder Store, wasn't exactly oozing with consumer-centered ambience as it was. On the way out I noticed a big hand-printed sign: YOU TOUCH IT, YOU BOUGHT IT.

At a little corner pharmacy, I got Mark a box of Zoom laxative.

I had this feeling Leslie would be joining us for the remainder of the trip. Mark was getting her all excited about digging for dinosaur and getting into *National Geographic.*

"The way Mark talks about the *Geographic,*" Ben said to me when Mark and Leslie walked ahead of us, "you'd think he was the publisher."

"And founder and chief of photography," I said.

MARK AND I DROPPED BEN AND LESLIE OFF AT HER apartment and went on to a little bar down the street.

There's quite a bit of beauty in Aspen. Maybe too much. I didn't see anyone but tanned, smiling, beautiful people. People who skied and sailed and rode horses and played rugby and climbed mountains. It was all like a beer commercial or cigarette ad that came to life. No, forget it. I'm just being a superior asshole. Aspen is okay. What can you really tell about a place from just one night and part of a day anyway?

When we got back to the apartment, it looked deserted. Mark yelled out but nobody answered. He went into the bedroom. The sewing-room door was closed, so I knocked and then opened it. As the door swung open, I saw Leslie playing the recorder and Ben sitting cross-legged on the floor in front of her. I quick shut the door again but Mark was just coming out of the bedroom.

"What the hell's up?" he said as he stiff-armed the door. "Everybody in there have their clothes on?"

Leslie and Ben did look a little caught-in-the-act, but then they both started laughing so hard that Mark and I caught it and pretty soon we were all about terminal with the hee-haws.

WE LEFT ASPEN THAT NIGHT. WE WERE ALWAYS LEAVing at night, the prime driving hour. Leslie quit her job to come with us for two weeks. Quit her job and broke her lease. It was definitely on again between her and Mark.

Ben and I got the back of the Bronco, but that was just fine because we were both planning on conking out real soon. I didn't dare ask where we were going, although I presumed it was Montana. Just in case, I prepared for the possibility of waking up in Louisiana or New Mexico.

CHAPTER
11

ACTUALLY, I DIDN'T SLEEP MUCH. IT WASN'T THAT I had to make sure we were traveling in the right direction or anything. I just couldn't sleep.

I listened to Mark and Leslie until I lost them in the whine of the tires. Then I watched the stars fly by in the side window. But mostly I did some thinking. Thinking about how I feel more comfortable in the seventy-million-years-ago past than in the past five years of my own life.

How is it that our own past can be so unsettling? Maybe it's just me. Take college. Or high school. Those were generally good times, but I'm worthless at alumni gatherings. There's too much emotional luggage back there for me. It's all too close, too nostalgic. And besides, there's no way to recapture those days.

Grade school is even a little hard to handle. The good old days of puberty and long division, and learning to ride a bike. I visited my old grade school a couple of years ago. Right away I was hit with an overload of long-buried animal sensations. The look of the low drinking fountains. The smell of the collective peanut butter breath of the student body. The feel of the worn linoleum. I was back somewhere where I'd been before. It was an ancient, puzzling feeling. Like a salmon must feel returning to the stream where it was spawned.

Photography is rooted in the past. (Ever see a picture of the future?) Even a ten-second-old Polaroid records a moment that has already been used up.

I see an old photo, like a color-tinted postcard from 1900 or a brown, soft 1890's street scene, and I'm there, smelling the road dust, hearing feet on boardwalks, and watching wagons roll by.

The pain of my personal past is most intense whenever I dwell on old sweethearts and friends and family who are not in my daily circles anymore. Now we're talking about what life is all about. Call it love if you will, especially in its more powerful varieties. But it's a love moved on. Spent and unrecoverable to the shifting geography of the years. All those comfortable paths set down and then—bingo—you're shot into a different world. I guess it's the processes we know as graduation, breaking up, leaving home, and growing old.

Part of the pain of nostalgia has to be because modern human beings have it tougher than any previous peoples. We live longer. We simply build up more memories. Hell, the average life-span in Roman times was twenty-two years. And not only do we live longer, we can't get away from the past. Old songs on the radio, home movies, tape recordings of baby sounds, family albums, TV specials on the fabulous fifties, or sixties, or seventies. I can barely open a closet without finding some high school or college artifact.

The biggest shockers for me though are pictures of former loves that suddenly burst out from under something in a drawer or from a shoebox in the attic. I have to shield myself at first, like from a blinding light. Then slowly I take a glance. Maybe if a wallet photo and I'm feeling up to it, I'll read the back. Those "Love always" and "To my best friend" startle me when they come from someone I haven't seen in ten years. The notes are so warm and trusting, I have to restrain myself from calling the old girl friends who wrote them, some of whom may not even remember my name.

"I love you's," written down can fool a person. They're tracks set in stone. Petrified feelings if you will.

So give me the dinosaur past anytime. Give me the Golden Age of Rome. Give me post-Civil War America. Those are times that I can get into. There's no sentimentality back there to fool with. My own past leaves me weak-kneed and limp-wristed. My mind is a lavatory wall with nostalgia scribbled over every square inch.

But don't get me wrong. There are cherishable days that I can call upon just to bring a private smile to my face. Mark's and my trips for instance. I love to watch mind slide shows of any of our fossil pilgrimages. Mark gives me a lot of grief about things like that. The way he says it is that I like things better after they've happened. "You can't wait to get home and start savoring all this," he might say to me in the middle of one of our expeditions.

There is some truth there. But Mark should talk. He, a professional photographer and documentary filmmaker. The guy makes his living selling the past. Just who does he think he is anyway?

"Just who do you think you are anyway, you little dipshit!" I suddenly yelled, as if Mark had been following my thoughts for the last ten minutes. My outburst even startled me. Ben jumped in his sleep. Mark and Leslie turned around from the front to see what the hell was up. I closed my eyes and pretended I was out cold. I hoped they would just let it pass for a bad dream they thought I was having.

ON THE NIGHT ROAD BETWEEN ASPEN AND MONTANA, we pulled in an Iowa station rebroadcasting the 1959 Rose Bowl. Iowa and the University of California.

There's nothing quite like a good athletic event on the radio to dissolve about two and a half hours of windshield time. After the game really gets going, you can even read the cheers. Maybe the static blurs the play by play, but by then you can tell a home run or long jump shot or TD by the roar of the crowd. Actually, the unintelligible transmission heightens the suspense. Sometimes you jerk your head toward the radio and look at it for a moment as if that would help.

Iowa won that Rose Bowl. Even though I've only been to Iowa about four times, I have a real romance with the place. I think Iowa is every bit as beautiful as golden California, but the old Hawkeye state needs a little more commitment than the average passing-through motorist is willing to give.

The whole place is two-way highway and beautiful countryside, and fierce, little towns. (Denver, Iowa: BIG-GEST LITTLE TOWN IN AMERICA. Vinton: THE POPCORN CAPITAL OF THE WORLD. Osage: A PLACE TO GROW.)

Speed limits in some of the towns that the highways whiz through are posted at ten miles per hour. You ever try to go ten miles an hour?

Iowans are God-proud of their high school and college athletic programs. There are no major league sports in Iowa, so the folks rally behind their football and basket-ball teams like they were liberating armies. And wrestling. High school wrestling is very big. Framed 11 × 14 black-and-white photos of Iowa State wrestling champions hang in gas stations and grocery stores in every corner of the state.

I like Iowa a lot. So does Mark. If Iowa had dinosaurs, it'd be our second most favorite spot on earth.

MARK TOOK INTERSTATE-25 NORTH FROM DENVER JUST to make some time, but from Laramie on up we'd stick to the two-way highways. The backroads. They give you a little better feel of the land and the people.

We were in cowboy and Indian country again. After I woke up from a real nap, I scanned my *Rand McNally Road Atlas* with a flashlight. The lists of Wyoming and Montana towns read like an honor roll of the Old West. Cody, Lame Deer, Black Eagle, Warren, Terry, Miles City, Spotted Horse, Sundance, Ten Sleep, Cheyenne, Roundup, Sheridan (in both states), Plentywood, Shawnee, Bridger. I wandered a little bit off our route and found a Fossil, Wyoming, and a Dinosaur, Colorado.

Somewhere out in the middle of nowhere, Mark slowed down and jockeyed halfway onto the shoulder. We bumped to a stop. He left the motor running and got out of the truck. Suddenly the back gate swung open. It was still black out.

"Get up, men," Mark said in a loud whisper. He sounded like my dad did when he used to wake us up early in the morning to go fishing. "The Bronchitis is about to turn a hundred thousand."

There were some real good miles on the old Bronco. Mark and I had put in a great trip around Lake Superior in 1972. I drove up to see Mark in Toronto once, and since he was moving to Chicago, there were quite a few Windy City trips left in her yet.

It had been understood from the start of the trip that Ben would take the wheel when we hit that golden moment in an automobile's life.

Mark led Ben by the hand and plunked him down in the driver's seat. The poor guy seemed dazed. Leslie was just getting out of the passenger's side.

"We'll get this thing back on the road," Mark yelled to Ben above the engine, "and then all you do is keep the steering wheel steady."

Ben put his hands on the wheel, but his face looked pretty tentative. Leslie and I were standing on the highway next to the shoulder. Leslie reached in through the window on our side and gave Ben a little squeeze on the arm. A big semi suddenly roared by like a speedballing freight train. The Bronco actually rocked from side to side in its wake.

"Good Lordy!" said Ben as he climbed out of the truck.

"Get back in there, matey," Mark said, pushing him down on the seat again. "This highway is as flat as the Dead Sea. We can pick up something coming or going from ten miles away."

"Maybe you can," said Ben, "but I'm the driver."

"Honorary driver," Mark said. "We'll keep the engine running in neutral. The three of us are going to push this puppy for the last tenth of a mile."

Once inertia was overcome, we got rolling along real good. We were actually running full tilt. Leslie and I were laughing so hard we had all we could do to keep from falling flat on the highway. Mark ran up and pushed alongside the driver's door. I saw him talking to Ben and trying to look at the mileage.

"This is it, whorelets!" Mark yelled. He reached in through the window and started honking the horn. I noticed he had a flare in his back pocket.

Leslie and I quit pushing and trotted alongside the slowing-down Bronco whooping and whistling. Ben suddenly found the brake and hit it so hard that the truck screeched to a whiplash stop. The three of us ran about ten yards beyond it. I pictured a comic little scene of Ben putting it in gear, doing a U-turn, and then burning rubber down the opposite lane.

Mark lit the flare and threw it high in the air. It cartwheeled through the dark like a flaming baton and when it hit the highway it busted up into drops of red fire.

"How'd I do?" asked Ben when he got back to the truck.

"Not bad," Mark said. "How are you on mountain roads?"

IT WAS TIME FOR A SMALL CELEBRATION. A CRACK OF light was appearing along the eastern edge of the earth. An all-night café in Wyoming, Wyoming, seemed like the right place.

Looking out the picture window of the café, Mark noticed the Bronco's headlights were still on.

"Bronco's lights are on," he said.

I didn't even look up from my menu.

"They cut out on their own," I said. "You know, like those Cadillacs do."

"Yah," Mark said. "Except in the Bronchitis, they don't cut out until the battery goes dead."

Mark went out to turn off the lights. I had Ben order for me and went to clean up in the fountain of youth that is any men's room along the road early in the morning. The faucet of the waist-high sink went spastic and got me real good right where a big water spot would do the most damage socially. On the way back to the table, I grabbed a menu from an empty booth and strategically placed it over the spot which seemed to be getting bigger and bigger. But Mark noticed it anyway.

"Get a little excited in there?" he asked.

"Nope," I said. "Just thinking of you."

"Hey," Mark said suddenly, "Leslie and I saw a dead badger on the road south of Laramie."

"We should've stopped," I said.

Mark was referring to something we had read about in one of our Indian books. I think it was *Lame Deer: Seeker of Visions*. As he reexplained it to Ben and Leslie, a person could supposedly tell how long they were going to live from the body of a dead badger. You had to slit open its abdomen and let the blood pool. Then, looking into it as if it were a red mirror, you would see yourself at the age of your death.

I had a dream two nights later. The four of us went back and found the badger and prepared it for the vision. Leslie and I saw ourselves with white hair and wrinkled faces. Mark brought Ben over to the badger and they both leaned over it. I saw that Mark looked like he did just then and Ben's face didn't reflect at all. "You're going to live forever," Mark yelled to Ben. "And I'm already a goner." Then he put Ben in a hammerlock and wrestled him to the ground.

"Looks like neither of them is going to live another five minutes," Leslie said to me in the dream.

AFTER BREAKFAST, WE HEADED NORTH THROUGH WYoming following one of the four main migration routes of the buffalo. That is, the buffalo of 150 years ago. They used to head up and down a big natural chute. North in summer. South in winter. Rivers crossed their path like the rungs of a ladder. The Platte, the Laramie, the Medicine Bow, the Powder, the Cheyenne, the little Missouri.

The whole area used to be a regular Garden of Eden for the Plains Indians. Hundreds of thousands of buffalo played on the prairie. The buffalo were the heartbeat of these people. Their tents, their utensils, their clothes, their fuel, their bowstrings. Buffalo cells became Indian cells. The buffalo were big medicine. Massive wintering herds would appear out of clouds of their own assembled breath, as if they were dropped from the sky. And on stormy nights a phosphorescent light was sometimes seen on their horn tips and ears.

The buffalo almost joined the dino. Their numbers petered out from twenty million in 1830 to only several hundred in 1890. And that wasn't from divine intervention. There was a new set of mammals on the plains. Railroaders, the U.S. Cavalry, and the hide hunters. But we all know that story.

Mark always reminded me that our fossiling had all the elements of what they used to call the trophy hunt. Elaborate preparation. The cross-country trek. The advice of a local guide. And, of course, the traipsing through the field looking for that big dino bone or *T. rex* skull.

An even more uncomfortable thought suddenly hit me in the gut. Were Mark and I any different from those nineteenth-century disturbers of the ecology? Sure, we were only a harmless, little fossiling party, but the first hide hunters probably didn't do much damage either. What if we set off another Dinosaur Bone Rush? 1975 style. Hell, there'd be campers and four-wheel-drive vehicles all over the Badlands. Hillsides would be dynamited away and Caterpillars would level that corner of the earth. Busloads of schoolchildren would be raking the countryside. Fossils would go on sale at outrageous prices. Museums would be broken into and specimens snapped up for the black market. I had to bury that thought real quick and real deep.

Mark and I continued a tag-team narration of the natural history of the buffalo for Ben and Leslie. Surprisingly they were still listening. They weren't asleep anyway. I looked out at the sunshined hills and river valleys that were flying by and saw heaps of bones and waves of stampeding buffalo.

When the military was making the plains safe for the invading pioneers, it was quickly figured out that the Indians would be in real bad shape without the buffalo. So grazing land was torched and more buffalo were slaughtered and the Indians fizzled out along with their buffalo brothers and sisters.

In 1883, hundreds of hide hunters and outfitters waited in northern Montana for the annual buffalo tide that had once been reported as so huge that you couldn't see beyond a countryside of brown fur. But that year, no buffalo came. It was said later that by that time there were more people in buffalo robes than buffalo.

The wiping out of the buffalo left a skeleton-littered prairie looking like it was covered with white driftwood.

Several summers of bone harvesting followed. They were shipped east to be ground into fertilizer and minerals. (Then the buffalo became part of the whiteman's front lawns and daily tonics.) But after only two or three seasons, all the bones were gone too. Now, it's easier to find a dinosaur bone than a buffalo bone, although Mark and I couldn't have backed that up at the time.

HISTORY OOZES OUT OF THE GROUND IN THE WEST. Arrowheads, buffalo skulls, rusty beer cans, wagon wheels, dinosaur teeth. History. Not kings and queens and charters and dates, but something you can grab on to. Something you can put up on the shelf.

To us midwestern Americans, fifty years is a long time. And a leap back to cowboy and Indian days is ancient history. Not like Europe where your hours might be three hundred years old and your church a grand or so. And nothing against the pyramids or coliseum, but history takes on meat in your own backyard.

WE TOOK A GASOLINE STOP IN NORTHERN WYOMING. I had a pop machine root beer. An Uncle Jake's. I love to sample regional soda pop. There's always your Pepsi and your Dr Pepper and Coca-Cola. But the fruit drinks and root beers take on a local flavor. I would like to write a book someday—*A Guide to the Local Soft Drinks of the West.*

CHAPTER
12

WYOMING IS GLORIOUS COUNTRY. PLAINS, PRAIRIE, mountains. New World Symphony country. The whole place gives me a cleansing feeling. Like I've just sucked in two lungs full of cold, mountain air. Wyoming's range country is desolate though. There are hundreds of miles of nothing but flat, brown fields and barbed-wire fences. No signs, no trees, no people, no buildings. Not even any cattle that you could see. Because of its sameness, Mark thought this was some of the loneliest country in America. At least pine forests have trees, and the Badlands have ups and downs.

The only hints of life are the occasional clusters of mailboxes where a dirt road meets the asphalt. I'm talking about twenty or thirty mailboxes in one place with signs on them like DOUBLE CROSS RANCH—45 MILES, JAMES R. JOHNSON—70 MILES, or BLAINE'S REGISTERED HERE-FORDS—32 MILES.

Distances in those see-forever spots are actually gauged more by time than mileage. Casper might be two and a half hours away. A ranch forty-five minutes off the high-

way. Or it might take a day to cover somebody's spread
on horse.

SO MUCH OF THE LANGUAGE OF THE WEST IS A LAN-
guage of the land. *Arroyo, butte, canyon, coulee, dry
wash*. A little Mexican and mountainman and a whole lot
of Indian and cowboy. *Gulch, gully, draw, hogback, mesa,
table, plain, prairie, paha*.

It's a geological circus out there in the West. Earth so
beautiful that when you show up, you wonder if its ever
been seen before.

There's been some nice things said about the West.
Like its being a country of the mind and something forever
fleeting before our grasps and whatnot. Good stuff. But
there's a real West all right. There's a real Grand Canyon
and a real set of Rocky Mountains. And then there's that
sleeper paradise out in our Badlands where the earth lies
sliced open like a club sandwich. The West. It makes me
want to go running naked through Marlboro Country yelling, and waving a geological hammer over my head.

Goddang I get fired up about the West. Right now I'd
like to be slingshotted out there and end up standing on
the side of a two-way Wyoming highway looking at a
historical marker. It might be cold and rainy and getting
dark. A semi blows by while I read about how two miles
from here there was once a great buffalo crossing. And
before that, I add, maybe dinosaurs and woolly mammoths. It would be a special moment, standing there with
goosebumps and respectful profanity for the history of it
all.

LESLIE WAS DRIVING EVEN THOUGH SHE DIDN'T KNOW
how to work a clutch. After a pit stop on the side of the
highway for a "Dr. Leaky," as my brother calls it, Mark
had shifted up through the gears and traded places with
Leslie while cruising in fourth at about fifty miles an hour.
She would drive as long as she could or until we had to
get gas or whatever. Actually, it would be a whatever
because Leslie had heard of a very interesting spot in Ed,

Wyoming. An antigravity hill. You park your car in neutral at the bottom of this hill and end up on top after about ten minutes. An old miner in Aspen told her about it. (I knew there were old people somewhere in Aspen.) Well, that was all we needed to know about the place. We were going to find it. The town was basically on the way to Montana anyway.

I looked at Leslie in the driver's seat. She had Mark's red sunglasses propped up on her head and was wearing a goose-down vest of mine. She was tapping her left foot and humming Beethoven's "Song of Joy." My Bronco had never been so blessed.

Mark had been doing all of the driving since we left Denver and was getting comfortable in the passenger seat.

"Hey, let's break out the Coors," Mark said. Leslie had given us two six-packs. To us midwesterners, Coors beer is a symbol of the Great West. I was supposed to have put the cans in our beverage cooler under the front seat, but I had absentmindedly put it in the roof-top carrier. No doubt it was boiling in the noon sun.

"Ah, it's, that's not really a driving beverage, you know," I said, trying to get Mark to go for a Coke instead.

"I'm not driving," he said.

"Well, it's in the car carrier."

"Oh, I see. Simmering on top, is it? I believe I'll have a sniveling of caviar instead." He took it rather well I thought.

"Say, pass me the fossils," Mark said forgetting the Coors.

"Fossils?" said Ben. "I didn't know we had any."

"Courtesy of Wall Drug," Mark said without any shame.

"Another piece of Old West bartering?" asked Ben.

"I paid for them myself," I cut in. "In fact, Mark still owes me for his share."

Mark was going through the pieces. He found two rib fragments that fit together and lifted them up.

"Man, it would be something to do a little Kirlian photography on these puppies," he said.

Kirlian photography records the electric life-force that supposedly surrounds living or once-living objects. Two Russians did the original work on the phenomenon. Using electrosensitive film, they photographed one section of a leaf that was torn in half. The whole leaf showed up on the print.

"Just think," Mark said. "All you'd need is one or two bone fragments of a dinosaur. Then you could do the Kirlian photos to see what else is supposed to be there."

It sounded great, but I couldn't help but think that dinosaurs were about seventy million years too inert to give off any life-force.

SMALL WESTERN TOWNS ARE MOST OFTEN RAMSHACKLE and dusty. There's trash in the streets, windows are long broken, old tires and pieces of car engines are strewn about. And the weather-beaten buildings are a part of the eroded land itself. Yet, these places seem clean. Maybe it's the openness and brightness and beauty of the surrounding land. Or the good-smelling air. Otherwise, you'd think you were deep in a city slum.

There's usually a classic structure around somewhere too. Like an old jail or an entrance to a mine shaft. The kind of setting that rock groups of the late sixties liked to pose in front of for album covers.

In the bars there is talk of shooting prairie dogs at 150 yards without a scope and how the government has ruined the West. Radios advertise predator call records and greet people in the hospital by name.

Beauty, South Dakota, is like that. So are Kimball and Kadoka and even Wall. So were all the Wyoming towns we zipped through. But not Ed, Wyoming.

Mark was convinced that the whole town of Ed was constructed as a movie set and then left to be lived in. It's a New England hamlet dropped in between some wooded Wyoming hills. Ed is a regular sweetheart of a place.

It has a town square and a city hall with a bell-tower clock. Think of some classic New Hampshire or Vermont town and I don't have to go any further.

Mark took it upon himself to personally find the antigravity hill since there weren't any tourist-trap signs to guide us. First, he parked at the base of a likely looking spot outside of town, but we just sat there like a boulder. He tried three more places, and if anything, we moved downhill. But Mark only got more set on finding the spot. I was losing faith.

"Do you think the Indians knew about this place?" asked Leslie. It looked like she was worried that she had led us astray.

"They didn't have cars to check it out," I said, but then added that they probably did know about it and that it must have been a sacred place.

Mark finally drove back into town for information. We stopped at a gas station-general store. I think there was a card game going in the back room. Through the store window I could make out a table of four men anyway. This Ed place was almost too Norman Rockwell to be true.

Mark would do the talking. He always did in the crucial situations on the road. He was good at it. He knew you couldn't just barge in someplace and ask for directions, particularly to an obviously special place.

An attendant gassed us up and Mark went inside. The rest of us waited in the Bronco.

Mark bought some candy bars and four cans of pop. I saw him and the manager talking, but I sensed right off that it wasn't going well. The guy made too many sideways looks at the truck. And he wasn't smiling. Mark suddenly busted out of the store without even bringing the goods. He looked real pissed.

"Hey, why didn't you bring the treats?" I asked as Mark climbed into the truck.

"Hey, why don't you get bent," Mark said. Then he slammed the door. He started up the engine and patched out of the graveled driveway.

Well, I sure wasn't going to ask what he had found out. Ben cleared his throat and Leslie looked out the window.

Mark stopped in front of a phone booth and jumped out leaving the motor running. He didn't set the parking brake and we started moving backward, but as gravity would have it, downhill.

"Hey, sweet, you found it," I yelled to Mark. He didn't

look up from his phone book rummaging. I hit the brakes myself.

While Mark made several calls, the rest of us listened to the "Mystery Voice" contest playing on Ed's KBIL. Listeners phoned in trying to guess what fellow townsperson's voice was being sent out over the airwaves. I looked back at Mark in the phone booth and wondered if he was playing "Mystery Voice."

After finishing several calls, Mark was back at the wheel in a more civil frame of mind.

"Okay, we got it now," he said. "One of the old guys in back told me to call a Zimmerman who might know."

Obviously, Mark and the store manager hadn't hit it off well. The guy told him he barely sells gas to tourists let alone give out valuable information.

Mr. Zimmerman was a different story.

"Hell, yes, I know where the hill is," he told us when we found his place. "It's on my land. I haven't had anybody ask directions to that spot in eight years." He seemed glad that we had.

I was starting to wonder about what was going on. Maybe there really was an antigravity hill. Keep cool, I had to tell myself. Be objective. Call upon the scientific method.

Mr. Zimmerman packed himself into the front seat with Mark and Leslie. He told Mark to drive across the front lawn and go around the house. I was getting the impression that Mr. Z meant business.

We drove a couple of miles over a field and then stopped at the base of a 35-degree slope.

"This is it," Mr. Z told us. "Turn your buggy around and put it in neutral. And you might as well shut off the engine while you're at it."

It was a humble enough place. A hill in a cow pasture. No signs, no hotdog stands. Not even an engraved marker.

I remembered to throw out a marker on my own. A crumpled Mountain Dew can. I didn't want to be taken in by any optical illusion.

The old Bronc just sat there. I heard a grasshopper buzz by.

"Something's happening," Ben whispered to me.

"Not yet," I said. Then I realized that Ben wasn't asking me, he was telling me. But I still didn't notice anything going on.

There are spots in the Black Hills that supposedly did weird things to people's senses. The countryside whirls around you and rocks roll uphill. Something to do with the depolarization of magnetic fields and whatnot. The Indians knew about those places. As far as they were concerned, it was all in keeping with the Black Hills being the center of the earth. We weren't in the Black Hills, but maybe this was the same type of deal.

Then, almost imperceptibly, we started uphill. Backward. I grabbed on to the window ledge.

It was a strange feeling. Like looking out the window and seeing the world spin around. We moved slowly and steadily. I got that floating, tickly feeling in the low abdomen that you get driving quickly over a bump or on the downswing of a Ferris wheel. But we were going backward. Uphill. Without power.

It was over in about ten minutes. We were all silent. Dazed I suppose. All but Mr. Z.

"Some ride, huh," he said. "You tell the folks back home about your antigravity trip, but don't tell them where it is. I try to keep it special."

I got out and looked for my Mountain Dew can. It wasn't there.

BACK AT THE ZIMMERMAN HOME, MARK GAVE MR. Z both sacks of our purchased fossils. That was okay with me. They were beginning to feel like tainted goods whenever I remembered that we had actually bought them.

Mr. Zimmerman appreciated them though. And before we left, he gave Leslie a beautiful fossil leaf. Fossil leaves are so elegant—works of art, really. Delicate etchings in shale. Remnants of a dinosaur autumn.

Mark and I used to make pseudo-fossil leaves as kids whenever a sidewalk was being poured. We also usually left some fossil thumbprints or names for the reading of future sidewalk users.

Mark drove back into town. Without saying anything,

he stopped in front of the only movie theater and jumped out of the truck. I suppose the matinee was just ending, but I couldn't figure out what he was up to. I don't remember what was showing either. Then he came running out with a barrel of buttered popcorn (a "monster bucket") and several boxes of Dots and one extra-large Lotta Lemon with straws. He drove us to a little city park and we all got out.

"Party time, kids," Mark said. Then he passed around the units of delight. Leslie and Ben split the lemon drink. Their heads clunked once when they both leaned into it at the same time.

I could tell that Leslie was becoming fascinated with Ben. Not in some geeky, gawky way, but like Mark and me, Ben's silence pulls you toward him. Mark probably told her about the psychic business too.

WE WERE SITTING QUIET AND PEACEFUL IN THE WON-derful Wyoming dusk when Leslie moved close to Ben. He knew she was nearby because he stiffened up and leaned away. Leslie was looking right at Ben's face and picked up his right hand and brought it to her cheek.

Mark and I looked at each other and couldn't believe it.

Ben moved back, but Leslie held on to his hand. Ben loosened and then brushed her forehead with one finger. It was a privileged moment for anyone to be watching all this and Mark and I knew it. Ben touched her hair with an open palm. Then her nose and lips and neck and shoulder. It was all so beautiful and sensual, I thought they were two innocent little eight-year-olds checking each other out for the first time.

WE PULLED OUT OF THE MAGIC TOWN OF ED AT SUNSET.

"There is only one explanation for all this," Mark said to the rest of us about the antigravity hill. "I always thought that the West was a semihallucinatory drug. And we just took a real good hit of it."

We still had 250 miles to navigate before we got to

Montana dinosaur country. Mark hadn't slept since Aspen but insisted on driving again. Ben and I rode up front with him. Leslie was out cold in the back. Fifteen miles out of town I caught Mark nod and then jerk his head back up.

"How you doing?" I asked.

"Great. Just great. You got any chewing gum?"

I gave him a piece of Juicy Fruit. He threw the gum out the window and put the wrapper in his mouth. He knew it was time to hand over the reins.

"If I don't get horizontal in about five seconds," he said, "the Bronco's going to end up in a ditch."

He stopped on the side of the highway and crawled in back with Leslie. Ben and I and the Bronco faced Montana.

"Work your magic on the juke box, will you?" I asked Ben.

Within a minute he had pulled in that classic of classic Everly Brothers tunes—"Cathy's Clown."

GODDAMIT WE HEARD SOME GOOD MUSIC THAT NIGHT. Vintage stuff. Gerry and the Pacemakers, Del Shannon, The Supremes, Sam and Dave. We even got the Ventures' "Walk Don't Run." I don't know what station or what state it was coming from. Maybe it was Ben. Or maybe it wasn't even coming from any station. Maybe it was just music that had been flying back and forth between the coasts for fifteen years and had finally found a home in the night air of the Great West. I wanted to put my hand out the window and feel the notes buzz by.

Some beautiful music floated up to us from the back of the Bronco. It was Leslie humming again. If Mark left her once more, I would shoot him.

Ben turned the radio down and asked me if Mark and I had always been close. I gave him a yes and no on that one. As kids of course we were, but around my junior year in high school he and I hated each other's guts. I was the studious one. Mark was the young rebel.

"What got you back together?" asked Ben.

I told him I didn't really know. It wasn't like it was

any one thing. After his sophomore year at Minnesota, Mark went to film school in Toronto for a couple of years. Sometime in there we started to miss each other.

"How'd you keep in touch? Did you write?" Ben was beginning to sound like Mark's and my biographer. I had to look over his way to see if he was recording our conversation.

"We almost never write," I said. "But we sure have a great phone relationship. When something hits us, we usually can't wait three or four days for a letter. Mark calls a lot after one A.M. Usually collect."

"I guess I'd like a brother like that," Ben said.

"Hey, it's not that great. He passes some foul intestinal gas. Makes your eyes hurt."

"Well, that must be a family trait then," said Ben. Then I remembered him furiously rolling down the passenger window of the Bronco every time Mark or I not-so-discreetly erupted.

"This is no lie, Ben," I said, "the Romans outlawed farting in public in forty A.D."

"Sounds like something this country should look into," Ben said and laughed.

"I can see it now," I said. "The highway patrol pulls us over. 'Roll down the windows, boys,' the cop would say. 'Pretty ripe in here. Who did it?'"

"No one, sir. It's just some old food."

"Food, my foot. I saw the steamy windows. Step out of the car. I'm taking you in for an analyzer test."

"What's the fine for driving while flatulating?" Ben asked.

"Say, Ben," I cut in, "what do you think of Mark?" It was my turn to get philosophical.

"What?"

"What do you think of him? What kind of guy is he?"

Ben cleared his throat and pulled at his right ear.

"Well, he's something like I've never seen before. He's got so much zip. The guy's always go go go."

"He's a good kid though, isn't he?" I asked.

"You know it," said Ben.

"I know this will probably sound strange," I said, "but Mark is the most important person in my life. I mean, more important than any woman ever was or ever will be."

"Yup," said Ben. "That is different."

"I can't explain it. I'm proud of him. He's the first person I think of when anything important comes up, and I miss him when he's not around. But sometimes I could wring the little bastard's neck. He's always got some task he's never finished up after blitzing through town. I'll have to deliver this or pick up that at the bus depot or call So-and-so about such and such. But then in the end I don't really mind doing it anyway."

"You two are something else," Ben said. "It's almost abnormal, really."

"Yah, I know," I said. "Does Mark, ah, ever talk about me?"

"If I could play you a tape of what he says, you'd swear it was all that you've just gone over. All except for the picking up after him part."

Just then a muffled explosion burst from the back of the Bronco. It could only have been escaping intestinal gas. Ben yelled, "Splatt!" and we both rolled down our windows in a seizure.

"When the air clears," I told Ben, "you better take a body count back there."

I DIDN'T GO INTO THIS WITH BEN, BUT MARK BORROWS money all the time. He always needs it. He'll even borrow money to give it away.

In high school I'd slip him five or ten bucks here and there. But by the time he was in film school, the loans took a more than inflationary leap when I became an investor in his student film to the tune of $875.

I gave him the money when I went to see him in Toronto. The very night of the transaction, Mark and I and a group of his friends ate dinner at a highfalutin restaurant. Two bottles of champagne. Oysters Rockefeller. Fancy steaks. Mark snatched the bill when it came, and I knew for a fact that it was over ninety dollars. In front of the waiter, Mark pulled out a single, unattached check from his shirt pocket. It was a move that I could see did not instill great confidence in the gentleman. Mark scribbled out the proper amount and handed it to him.

"May I see some identification, sir?" he asked Mark.

"Right on," Mark said, whipping out a picture he always carried around with him. It was a black and white of Mark and me on a teeter-totter. We were both skin-headed grade schoolers.

"That's me there," Mark said, pointing to himself on the teeter-totter. "And that's my brother up in the air."

I REMEMBER DRIVING AROUND TORONTO IN THE BRONCO with Mark on a Sunday during the film investment visit. There seemed to be women everywhere. Pretty and not pretty. Young, old, infirm, healthy. Mark was driving but still taking in the scenery.

"I love women," Mark said as we passed a woman at a bus stop. "All of them. But they'll screw you up good if you let them, won't they?"

"I think I know what you mean," I said.

"I'm not getting into anything real heavy here," Mark said. "More like how they get you all flushed and fired up." He honked and waved to a group of older women on a park bench.

"I can follow that," I said. "The blood leaves the brain for the middle of the body."

"You got it now. You can't think straight. You make promises. Say outrageous things." Mark was gesturing with both hands off the wheel.

"They know," I said.

"They know what?" Mark asked, suddenly looking confused.

"Women. They know all about us and that we don't mean what we think we do in the heat of passion."

"What are you talking about?"

"Women are smarter than men," I said. "Not only that, they are physiologic superiors."

"Come on."

"Maybe not muscle-wise," I said, "but for overall durability. They outlive us by eight to ten years. And babies. I'd like to see men have kids."

Mark chewed on that for a while. Then he had a fact of his own.

"I've heard that three fourths of the wealth in the United States is in the hands of women," Mark said. We were waiting at a stoplight. Suddenly he turned to look out the side window down into the driver's seat of the car next to us. I leaned over him to have a glimpse too.

"Oh my," I said. "I think I'm in love." All I could see was an extremely comely pair of nyloned legs whose viewing was facilitated by the driver's skirt having slipped way up on the seat.

Mark sang the start of the old Doors hit:

"Hello

"I love you

"Won't you tell me your name..."

"I feel so good, I don't feel good," I said. I think there was a lump in my pants and it wasn't cancer.

"I'd give her half a chance naked," Mark said.

Then the light changed, and our angel drove off. The Bronco killed and some cars behind us started honking.

"See what I mean?" asked Mark with a pained look as he got us going again.

"Life offers more consistent pleasures than sexual excitation," I said. "Like three squares a day and a cozy bed with clean sheets."

"And a reliable evacuation of the bowels every twenty-four hours," Mark added.

"I don't go to the bathroom," I said with fake snobbery.

"Oh, I'm sorry," Mark said playing along. "Where do you go? In your pantaloons?"

CHAPTER
13

Somewhere in the dark we crossed into Montana. The magic Montana of Yellowstone and Glacier and Little Big Horn. Just saying "Mon-tan-a" slowly and deliberately can be as pleasing to the palate as warm custard.

For such a pristine place, I thought Montana had a surprisingly materialistic state slogan: Oro y Plata (Gold and Silver). But what the hell do I know about it? There are good uses for money. If somebody laid a couple hundred thou on me, I could put it to good use.

I guess the backroads of Montana are pretty much the same as Wyoming. But I can only guess. It was pitch-black out and we wouldn't be seeing any light until we got to Canaan, the last town before dinosaur country. And there were no highway signs. I actually pulled out my compass once to make sure we were at least heading north. (I knew that much about compasses.)

Mark got up after a two-hour nap when I stopped at a truck stop in Billings. Ben was still next to me in the passenger seat, but had a bit of a glazed look to him.

Mark noticed as soon as he got up to the front.

"Get in back and take a snooze," Mark told him.

"Don't mind if I do," said Ben. "Is Leslie still back there?"

"Yah, but she's dead to the world," Mark said. "You won't bother her."

Ben faced a minor dilemma here that Mark and I weren't going to help him out of. He could feel his way to the back okay, around the outside of the truck. But we knew he was worried about slipping into the crowded rear compartment. I had taken out the backseat before the trip but I could see that Leslie was spread-eagled over every square inch of available space.

"Do what you've gotta do," Mark said slapping Ben on the back. Then he and I went to look for the men's room. I turned around and saw Ben still standing by the passenger door.

WE FORGOT ABOUT BEN AND LESLIE AFTER OUR OWN revitalization, and took off into the highway blackness.

"Say, I need a pop," I told Mark, who was sitting in Ben's navigational spot.

"What d'you want?" Mark asked. He pulled out our little cooler from under the seat.

"Coke. Orange Crush. Dad's. Anything."

"You got it," Mark said taking off the lid and reaching into the cooler.

Out of the corner of my right eye I saw Mark pull something out of the cooler that was long and stringy. He was holding it delicately between his index finger and thumb, like he was holding a dead rat by the tail. I turned toward him. His eyes were as big as hubcaps. He was holding Leslie's halter top.

We both craned a look toward the back. All I could see was Leslie with her arm around Ben's waist.

"Your watch stop again?" I asked Mark.

I COULDN'T STOP LAUGHING EVERY TIME I THOUGHT about Leslie and Ben back there in the Bronco's love nest, but Mark actually looked worried or pissed or jealous. I did look back again. It was a beautiful, innocent sight. Like a brother and sister at a grade school slumber party.

"Hey, babe," I said to Mark. "You aren't really worried, are you?"

"About what?" He did look worried.

"About Ben and Leslie."

"Should I be?"

"Don't look at me," I said to Mark. "And don't look at them either." Then I laughed again but saw it wasn't the right time.

"Let me out," Mark said.

"What?" He was starting to open the door and I was still doing sixty-five miles an hour.

"Stop the Bronco," Mark said. "I want to drive."

MARK HAD ONE HAND ON THE WHEEL AND DRUMMED A cigar-size pretzel against the dash to a 1969 remake of "Baby, It's You" by Smyth. It's kind of a sexy, earthy song. Not the words, but the pulsating bass and moaning organ and the piercing female lead. I remember the song quite clearly because it came out when I was very much in love with the teacher's assistant in an organic chemistry class. She was about twenty-six and beautiful and brilliant and 1969 was mini-skirt city. Tight sweaters were also big then. Especially hers. Need I say any more? Yes! I know that her seated presence in our lecture halls directed most of the blood away from the collective male brains gathered there. And being the TA she sat in front, next to the podium. Sideways. I bit a lot of pencils in that class. Mark almost took chemistry just to be able to see her every day.

I got as far as eating one table over from her in the cafeteria. She was engaged to somebody in dental school and the guy sometimes met her for lunch. I could see her rubbing his thigh under the table and it fairly drove me insane.

Anyway, that was my sophomore year and "Baby, It's

You" was out. I was sure it had been specially commissioned for me and Miss Huxley (those were pre-Ms. times).

This delightful little recall was suddenly interrupted when the Bronco swerved off the highway. I turned to see Mark jerking back up after groping around the floor for his pretzel, which must have shattered on a down beat. He stopped the truck on the shoulder and brushed some crumbs off his lap. The song was over when we got going again.

Sounds, not just songs, can be worthy bearers of nostalgia. Kids playing voices on the wind; the slamming of flimsy, wooden screen doors; and faraway cheers from a full stadium all strike melancholic chords in me. But the classic, the one sound that raises the gooseflesh on my very soul, is the eerie, lonely cry of a loon bouncing across a north woods lake.

AT LEWISTOWN I TOOK THE WHEEL AND WE TURNED east. Lewis and Clark left their names all over Montana. Maybe they didn't actually leave their names, but somebody did. There's a Lewis and Clark National Forest, a Clarksville, a Lewis and Clark County, and a Meriwether Lewis Memorial Park. Montana's state flower is *Lewisia rediviva*, the bitterroot. Hell, everywhere they went, living things and rivers and future towns would be named after the boys.

They identified over two hundred new species of animals and plants including the antelope, the coyote, the prairie dog, and the western sagebrush. Some of the discoveries weren't even recognized as theirs until a hundred years laters. A partial listing of Lewis and Clark's zoobotanical finds looks like a Jack Kerouac travel itinerary:

> California hazelnut
>
> Pacific blackberry
>
> Missouri milk vetch
>
> Roosevelt's mountain elk
>
> Oregon white-tipped ash

Saskatoon serviceberry

California newt

Montana horned owl

Lewis's northern woodpecker

Hutchin's Canada goose

Plains gray wolf

Missouri beaver

Columbia River chub

Western hog-nose snake

Desert rose

Most of Lewis and Clark's natural history collection was sent to Charles Willson Peale in Philadelphia at Jefferson's suggestion. Peale's museum was making a lot of news with its fully assembled mastodon skeleton, the Great American Incognitum, but Lewis and Clark's treasures were fitting roommates. Peale eventually did their portraits.

BEN AND LESLIE WERE STILL OUT COLD IN BACK, BUT I didn't dare look at them again.

"If Peale were still around," Mark said to me in a low voice, "I'd commission him to do our portrait. Maybe standing by the Bronco on an empty stretch of Montana highway at four A.M."

"It's a nice thought," I said. "Maybe when we do become famous, Annie Leibovitz will do us for a *Rolling Stone* cover."

"Famous for what?" Mark asked.

"For the scientifically renowned theory that dinosaurs went extinct because they didn't have rock 'n' roll."

Just then "Yummy, Yummy, Yummy I Got Love in My Tummy" came on the radio.

"Shit, what a horse-shit song!" I said as I flicked it off.

"Stuff like that may make the human race go under," Mark said.

MARK AND I GOT TALKING A LITTLE BIT ABOUT HOW YOU have to get away sometimes to appreciate the folks back home. Then I mentioned something about Pioneer Grandma's health. I think I said it was lousy to be gone knowing that she could die any second. Mark told me to stop the Bronco right then and there. We happened to be in front of a small-town Montana gas station. He jumped out and went to a phone booth and called home for Grandma. It was midnight back there.

Pioneer Grandma and my brother were real close. In 1972 she got some kind of female-organ cancer and had to have a radium implant. She had to lie perfectly still for about three days in this hospital room with leaded walls. Mark and I went to see her. We both gave her a big squeeze when we walked into the room. "You can't kiss me," Pioneer Grandma said. "I'm radioactive." So then Mark kisses her right on the lips. When she got back home she was still pretty down and out and said that she just wanted to crawl under the bed and die. Mark told her he hoped that wouldn't happen because it would make it awfully hard to vacuum her room.

WE PULLED INTO CANAAN AT ABOUT 5:00 A.M. EVERY-body was still asleep when I stopped in front of a closed Standard station. I sat in the driver's seat for a while listening to the metal of the engine contracting. A semi rumbled through main street. Some birds chirped.

The windows of the old Bronco were steamed up and the closed-in air was pretty gamey. I quietly stepped down from the truck but my driving legs immediately buckled under me. I dropped to both knees. Alongside the curb I saw an empty Copenhagen chewing-tobacco tin that I picked up and put in my back pocket. I always liked the look of cowboys with that hockey-puck bulge on their backside. I got up and went to check out the town myself.

Canaan is probably no different from any other out-of-the-way western town, but it looked a little more run down than the rest. I base this on nothing more scientific than the fact that there were a few too many broken-windowed shops and empty billboard frames. From our standpoint, though, one thing looked very hopeful. There was petrified wood lying all over the place. (Paralyzed wood, Mark and I affectionately call it.) It lined gas-station entrances. Big stumps sat in front yards and shop windows. There was even a Petrified Park that was built during the Depression. It had petrified picnic tables and campfires. There were two petrified log cabins and several petrified bird houses. It looked like it'd be tough to find some real wood around that place.

Mark and I always check out the fossil sign in the towns we pass through. What the rock shops are selling, the number of decorative petrified tree logs in gardens—just something to let us know that we were in the right ball park.

On the edge of town I saw a plaque remembering the passing of Crow, Assiniboin, and Sioux Indians through the region on their yearly buffalo hunts. Even the great Sitting Bull himself had been here. But that was long before there was a Petrified Park or a Canaan.

There was too much good stuff to take in alone, so I trotted back to the truck to get the others.

BEN WAS SITTING ON THE TAILGATE OF THE BRONCO WITH his guitar singing "Good Time Charlie's Got the Blues." Mark had his arm around Leslie and was whispering something into her ear. Just then a passing wreck of a car jolted over a bump and its hood flew all the way open and then snapped back shut. I took it as a good omen, a little welcome-to-Canaan salute.

"Let's hit town," I said to the group. "There's some good shit here."

"Coprolites?" asked Ben.

"Where are the puss in this dump," Mark said in a beat-on-the-chest, fake macho voice.

More good signs followed. Some Canaanite was using a piece of dinosaur extremity for a garage doorstop and

the local bank had a shale front wall with dinosaur footprints in it. And the café where we ended up was selling
petrified toothpicks for seventy-five cents apiece.

"OUR FIRST ITEM OF BUSINESS, TRILOBITES," MARK WAS
saying as he looked over a menu, "is to find out where
this Bone Cabin is."

"That place sounds like our ticket, all right," I said.

Ben and Leslie were sitting on the same side of the
booth we were in. I remember checking them out for a
hidden glow, but then I saw her and Mark playing footsie
under the table.

"Hey, look at this," Leslie said, pointing to a poster
on the wall near our booth. "They're having a Dinosaur
Daze here."

"Now that's something we've got to miss," I said.

"That's something we can't miss," said Mark.

"Come off it."

"When is it?" Mark asked.

"August fourteenth and fifteenth," Leslie said. "That's
this weekend."

"We'll be back for it," Mark said. Then he turned to
me. "*National Geographic*, my boy. We've got to remember our mission."

"Too bad *NG* doesn't remember us," I said.

AT THIS PLACE YOU HAD TO ORDER THROUGH A LITTLE
microphone box on your table. It wasn't any modern in-
novation by the way. More like fallout from the 1950's.
Ben collected all our orders and Mark activated the
speaker. A buzz like a sick doorbell sounded.

"Your order, please?"

Ben ticked off all our requests without a hitch. "Two
stacks of buttermilk cakes and one order of honey-stung
chicken. One hash brown, one order toast with no butter,
two fried eggs sunny side up and two scrambled and a
plate of bacon for the table. We'd also like two orange
juice, a glass of milk, and one small grapefruit juice."

"Ever think of being an air traffic controller?" Mark said after Ben had finished.

While the order went down, I left the table to call home. I noticed that Leslie must have been using the spare tire as a pillow. She had a red, backward "32 psi" embossed on her left cheek.

Our food hadn't yet arrived when I got back. Mark was studying a travel folder on New Zealand. He had a Lewis and Clark look in his eyes. I didn't dare say a thing. I tried to put it out of my mind.

Another one of Mark's great plans for the two of us was to drive to South America. Drive, as in automotive vehicle. Down to Mexico and through Central America and on into Venezuela. He had cooked this up when he was still in Toronto. He said the trip had possibilities for an *NG* article, a book, *and* a TV special. I had offered the Bronco.

"No offense," he had said, "but we need an ass-kicker for this one."

"What? The Bronco's not good enough?"

"We need a vehicle that plows through jungle and desert and snowbound mountain roads. We need one of those British Land-Rovers."

"The Bronco can do that stuff," I said.

"Take my word for it, boy. Land-Rover. You can ford streams with one of those things. You put this periscope dealy on the exhaust pipe and you can head into five feet of water."

So there we were in a little Montana café in the middle of a perfectly delightful fossil hunt and Mark is looking at a travel folder about New Zealand. The only way I could reassure myself about the New Zealand thing was that since we couldn't drive there, we wouldn't be making it this trip. Unless the Bronco suddenly turned into a seaworthy Land-Rover.

"How are the 'rents," Mark said putting down his pamphlet. "Did you get them on the line?"

"Good. They're good," I said. "They were still in bed, but glad to hear from this part of the country."

"Did you tell them Leslie was on board?"

"I did. They were glad to hear it. 'Hello to Leslie.' 'Hello to Ben.'"

"They been getting my cards?" Mark asked.

"Yah, about ten or twelve at least. What the heck you doing, writing from every truck stop?"

"Sure, why not."

"I never knew you to be such a letter writer," I said. "They wanted to make sure we were going to church too."

"We've been in church ever since we hit the South Dakota Badlands," Mark said looking up.

"Yah, I basically told them that."

"I smell honey-stung chicken," cut in Ben. Our food arrived about five seconds later.

CHAPTER
14

WE GASSED UP AT AN OLD TEXACO STATION ON THE south edge of Canaan. Mark and Leslie filled our water containers while Ben and I went into the little cashier area to attend to the whereabouts of the Bone Cabin.

The guy we talked to had heard of it, but didn't know if it still existed. The town it used to be near didn't. Rock River. It folded up when the railroad went out in 1958. Other than that, I didn't find out much. I think the guy was sizing me up. Maybe I hadn't sounded trustworthy enough and he wasn't telling me everything. I was thinking that Mark should have done the checking when the other attendant came in and opened the cash register.

"Hey, Loren," the guy I was talking to said, "you know anything about that dinosaur house?"

Loren was writing up our sales slip and didn't answer. He picked up a pair of binoculars by the cash register and looked out the window toward the gas pump. "Eight-oh-five," he said to nobody. "Eleven gallons."

"He doesn't know," my guy said.

"Know what?" said Loren.

"About the Bone Cabin," Ben said. "Could you please tell us where it is?"

"Why?" said Loren. He was checking Ben out real close, like he thought something wasn't right.

"Because the gentlemen I'm traveling with are looking for a dinosaur," said Ben.

Loren looked at Ben and then at me. He pointed to his own eyes and then to Ben. I hunched my shoulders and nodded yes.

Loren then spoke directly to Ben, mouthing every word like Ben was hard of hearing or not with it or something: "I . . . imagine . . . it's still there. . . . It used . . . to . . . be . . ."

Then Loren looked back over at me like he wasn't getting through. Mark and Leslie were inside now. The place was getting crowded. Mark took over the discussion.

"Any dinosaur bones out there?" he asked. Then he lit a cigarette and handed it to Loren. (I don't know where he got the cigarette. I thought he was off them.)

Loren held the cigarette in mid-shaft and looked at the lip end and then up at Mark before taking a drag.

"Just find that cabin first," Loren said. "If it's still there, it'd be on the Baker ranch, fifty miles north on the dirt road. Follow it all the way out."

Then my guy got back into it. "I heard the dinosaur bones left with the buff at the turn," he said. "A few buffalo came back, but I can't say the same for the other guys."

So we were back in the Badlands. The Goodlands Mark sometimes called them. Montana, South Dakota, it didn't make any difference. The Badlands, or the West itself for that matter, are places that melt away state lines and city limits.

Mark and I always felt like the Badlands were our very own personal Valhalla. There are more awesome places. Certainly there are more beautiful places. But the power of the Badlands is where it's at for us. The dinosaur, Indian, cowboy power. The power of the West. I told

Mark that if I was dying of cancer to put me on a Badlands hillside and let me be.

AN INTEREST IN THE LAND AS FIERCE AS MARK'S AND mine is not at all conducive to safe driving. It didn't have to be the Rocky Mountains or the Grand Canyon. Road cuts, newly plowed fields, and pine forests were all subjects of our wonder. But the Badlands were particularly treacherous since out there neither Mark nor I could keep our eyes on the road.

This portion of the Goodlands was carved out by tributaries of the Missouri River over the last ten thousand years. It was known as the Hell Creek region after one of the bigger streams in the area.

Bad guys in the Butch Cassidy and Sundance Kid days holed up in the Hell Creek Badlands, but not to fossil hunt. Lewis and Clark passed through the area in the summer of 1804, one year into their trip. Sacajawea was with them by then.

(It seemed to me like we were chasing Lewis and Clark. No matter that we were a 170 years too late. I fully expected to meet them at some river crossing. Maybe even give them a lift, or rap for a little while.)

Clark found a dinosaur rib fragment in a Badlands cliff. No one knew about dinosaurs then and the captain only described it in his notes since he left the fossil behind. It wasn't hard for future readers to suppose that he had found dino though, because the fragment was four inches wide and three feet long.

I keep thinking it's a shame that Thomas Jefferson never knew dino. It wasn't until thirty years after his death that the first American dinosaur was uncovered in New Jersey and seventy years later for the great dinosaur bone rush. If Jefferson had been around in the 1870's he would have been out there at the Bone Cabin and all those other dinosaur bonanzas. Hell, yes! To use a crude expression, he would be shitting in his pants to be out there.

There should be a dinosaur named after Jefferson. The Mount Rushmore thing is nice, but I bet he would have really appreciated a dinosaur. At least the extinct ground sloth he first described is named after him. In fact, the first shipment of dinosaur bones Marsh received from the Bone Cabin area was thought to be from *Megatherium jeffersoni*. Only they really were six-foot-long brontasaurus femurs.

"WE'LL HAVE TO GET CLARENCE OUT HERE," MARK SAID looking at a passing BUFFALO AT LARGE sign that must have reminded him of our guru. "He had a sterling idea for an improved nickel. He said it should have an Indian on one side and a buffalo and a dinosaur on the other."

Leslie was fiddling with the radio. A fundamentalist preacher was fire and brimstoning about evolution.

"May God Almighty open your minds to the light of the truth," the preacher said flexing his vocal chords. "And close your ears to the heresy dispensed by the evolutionists."

"Hey, turn that up," I said.

"This should be interesting," said Ben. We all leaned into the radio. "We probably picked up Nashville."

"Get down!" Mark yelled.

Mark loves bad radio. He heckles it. He yells out profane answers to deathly serious talk-show questions and he edits commercials. I don't know if he made this up or not, but he swears he heard a radio ad late one night somewhere in British Columbia on his first Alaska hitchhike that said anyone who could smile could have a future in motel management.

The preacher was getting hot.

"There may still be some souls out there who adhere to the blasphemy of the monkey myth," he yelled. "We are no more related to the monkeys than we are to the rocks."

"The monkeys probably don't want to admit they're related to us either," Mark said.

"Or the rocks," said Ben.

"We were created, not evolved. If you want to see your origins, if you want to know who you are, there is only one place to seek the unchanging truth, dear friends.

And that's in the holy word of God. There is your missing link. Stand fast against the brainwashing of the Darwinists, and let us pray that the theory of evolution is never proved."

"Or if it is, that no one ever finds out about it," said Ben.

"If evolution can explain the unfolding of this world and its living things, then we have no need for a divine creator at all...."

This guy was into it.

"And there are even those unfortunates who would have us believe that mankind arose from the amphibians. Now, I ask you, friends, to ponder this short verse from Genesis: And God created *man* in *His* image and likeness. Now I ask you again, would God consider himself a frog? Would God consider himself a monkey?"

"Would God consider himself a dino?" Mark shouted.

"Would God consider himself a herself?" Leslie said and we all cheered.

"God has a place for blasphemers."

"The Badlands!" Mark and I both yelled.

"God has given us his word..."

"Her word," corrected Leslie.

"And we are not to tamper with it. Let me give you this simple fact..."

"Let me give you this simple coprolite," Ben said.

"The earth is no more than four thousand years old and Adam and Eve..."

"Turn that crap off," Mark said but then he reached over and did it himself.

We bumped along in silence for a while resting our voice muscles and probably pondering our own interpretations of creation.

"There are actually some fundamentalist types trying to prove that dinosaurs lived between the time of Adam and the great flood," I said. "They say they found dinosaur and human footprints together in the same rock strata."

"I look at it this way," said Mark. "God—whoever he, she, or it is—probably started the whole ball of wax rolling and then let it unfold according to this amazing plan.

So why beat off over the blasphemy of evolution and whatever? Let's save our brains for some real problems."

End of lecture. Mark snapped the radio back on forgetting that the preacher would now be hitting full stride. Three people reached for the tuner at once. Loud polka music replaced the creationist harangue.

"Those kind of people," Mark said of the fundamentalists, "ought to get out here themselves and put their hands on a few dinosaur bones. That would make real believers out of them."

"Yah," said Ben. "And then they could show us where they are."

AROUND A HAIRPIN CURVE, WE CAME UPON A CLUSTER of low hills. Hills with about a 35-degree slope. Mark looked up from his driving and I knew exactly what was going through his head.

"Nope," I said. "They probably aren't antigravity."

"You're right," Mark said. "But they sure looked likely."

Just then we flew over a big bump in the road and I landed hard on my Copenhagen tin. That temporarily shorted out my sciatic nerve and a jolt of pain shot down my leg. I pulled the flattened container out of my pocket. It was as thin as a can lid.

"Chalk up one good fossil container," I said turning it over in my hand.

"Whoa," Mark said recognizing the former function of my piece of crumpled metal. "Did you go cowboy on us?"

"Nope. Just thought it looked good in my pocket. And I was going to use it for a specimen carrier."

We were easily an hour out of Canaan by then and except for the splendor of the Badlands, things were what you would have to call desolate.

"We are in the literal middle of nowhere," said Mark.

"Nowhere and everywhere," I said.

There is a certain magic to being somewhere where you think no one else has ever set foot. I knew there used to be a town out here someplace, and we hoped we'd be coming to the Bone Cabin sooner or later, but it didn't exactly look like picnic grounds.

The radio was drifting terribly and we had to get Ben up front to fix it. He was able to hold on to a local station long enough to hear an ad for Screwworm Ear Tick Bomb, but then all he could get was static.

"Man, we are out here, aren't we," said Mark.

"Are we lost?" asked Leslie.

"Hardly," Mark said. I think he took that personally. "All we have to do is turn around and follow the road back to Canaan."

I love the glory of a good dirt road. The gentle bumps, the curves, and ups and downs. The weeds and grass centerline. And especially that rug of soft, cool dust.

"THERE'S A CROSSROADS AHEAD," I SAID. "WE BETTER check it out."

We all got out for a little stretch and a walk around. A warm wind lapped up against us. Lonely crossroads are special places, especially in the middle of a dinosaur graveyard.

"We're breathing the same air that the dinos did," Mark said in a more poetic than scientific vein. Hearing that, Ben went into a coughing spasm that set off a chain reaction. I started hacking and Leslie couldn't stop clearing her throat. It sounded like the whole Russian Army was being checked for a hernia at the same time.

"A pubic hair go down the wrong way?" Mark asked us.

"Reptilian air went down the right way,' said Ben. Then he took out a plastic box of Dynamints and shook one or two out and popped them into his mouth.

"Ben's into the amphetamines again," Mark said.

Ben ignored Mark and started doing some deep knee bends in the middle of the road. Leslie got out Mark's rented camera and took pictures.

"I have a dinosaur type question," Ben said. "But I'd hate for you to get the wrong idea, like I was actually interested in the subject or something."

"Shoot," Mark said. "Quit dicking around and shoot."

"All I want to know is, what's the difference between reptiles and mammals?"

"Tits," Mark said right off like he had been waiting for the question.

"Sir?" asked Ben.

"Mammary glands. Mammals, mammary glands, milk. Dig?"

"I think so," said Ben. "Sorry to have had to ask."

Mark joined Ben for some calisthenics. "We can talk openly here. Besides, it's one of my favorite subjects, the difference between reptiles and mammals."

THE CROSSROADS OFFERED NO CLUES TO THE BONE CABIN, so we hopped back into the Bronco and continued on down the road. Ben shook out another Dynamint.

"Could I have one of those L.A. Turnarounds?" Mark asked.

Ben gave him three of the mints.

"Good little sumbitches," Mark said.

"Thank you," said Ben.

On a long trip, it's easy to lose track of the days and weeks. I guess it had been almost two months since we left St. Paul. Leslie was only going to be with us for about eight more days before Mark had to bring her to Miles City to catch a plane to Minneapolis. It also left us with only two and a half weeks to find some keeper dinosaur bones.

"We better find that Bone Cabin," I said, "or we're going to have to pillage some rock shop before we ever show our faces back in San Paulo again."

"What's a fossil worth, anyway?" asked Leslie.

"Turtles go for a hundred bucks in the rock shops," I said. "A nice *T. rex* tooth could be seventy-five bucks easy. A whole head, maybe several thousand to some museum. But generally speaking, fossils really don't have any commercial value."

"Thank God," said Mark.

"But we aren't out here to buy and sell fossils," I said. "That's kind of like selling tickets to watch a sunset."

Ben rattled his Dynamints case and passed around several more of the little bullets to all of us. Mark played junkie again.

We really did have our own drugs out there. Like Mark says, the West itself is a mood-altering chemical, but there's also the night air with the smell of rain in it, and Badlands dust taken under the fingernails, and music.

Music is especially powerful. For me, driving with a good song on the radio is like driving under the influence. I go through stoplights, make wrong turns, and drive beyond my destinations. Mark had a fender-bender once with our family car driving and singing along with "Diamond Girl."

LESLIE AND I WERE LOOKING AT A GAS-STATION MAP OF Montana for any clues to the Bone Cabin. Since the town of Rock River was eased off the face of the earth, we weren't surprised to not see it listed, but sometimes historic spots are at least asterisked. We were so busy squinting over the map, we hadn't noticed that we had stopped and that Mark and Ben were out of the truck.

I looked up. A God Bless America blue sky was the perfect backdrop for the shining white structure we saw through the windshield. The road seemed to end right there. The Bone Cabin had found us.

We got out of the Bronco and joined Mark and Ben. Mark reverently walked ahead of us up to the shrine and touched it. Even I could see from where I was standing that hundreds of dinosaur bone fragments and even several complete extremities were mortared into the walls. A sign above the door read THE ORIGINAL BONE CABIN. PLEASE HONK.

"Son of a bitch," Mark said in a low monotone and then repeated it a little louder. "Son of a bitch!"

He looked back at us in a trance. He put his arms up in the air and turned slowly around looking at the sky and at the cabin and then at us again.

"This is it!" he yelled jumping up and down. "The goddamn Bone Cabin itself!"

The Bone Cabin stood to the side of a larger structure that had its own sign on the door: PRIVATE HOME. Two four-foot dinosaur femurs flanked the entryway. The rest of the house was a dirty stucco. I saw someone peep from behind a curtained window.

"Hey, cool it," I said to Mark, who was now trying to get into the fragile-looking Bone Cabin by rattling its shaky wooden door. I could just see him knocking over the whole structure and being left standing there with only the doorknob in his hand.

"It's been awhile since anybody but a busload of school kids from Canaan ever made it out here," said a voice from the doorstep of the main home. "Looks like you've heard of the old Bone House."

It was the owner, Mr. Baker. He walked us around the cabin. I wasn't as vocal as Mark, but I was about to drop my drawers for the beautiful pieces cemented into the wall. Under a window I noticed a portion of a *T. rex* jaw with three chipped teeth in it.

The place was being used as a storeroom. There were tools and bales of fencing and seed bags and whatever else goes along with trying to eke out a Badlands ranch living. Mark asked if Mr. Baker could direct us to the fossil fields.

He told us that the people in town didn't want him showing any outsiders where the bones were found, but that he really didn't know anyway.

"Hell, when I was cowboyin' out in the Badlands twenty years ago," he said, "I'd see something like a fossil and pick it up and say, 'Well, I'll be goddamned,' and then toss it away. My wife's the one who knows more about it."

Mrs. Baker grew up there and her father had done quite a bit of dinosaur digging. Once inside the real house, she started in on the background of the place. We were sitting around the kitchen table while Mr. Baker fixed lunch. Evidently they liked us. Or maybe they just hadn't seen anybody in a few years.

The Bone Cabin and the ranch had been in her family for eighty years. She wasn't sure who actually built the cabin but it was a sheepman like the history books said. Back in the 1850's. She got out a ragged, Bible-size *Ripley's Believe It or Not* and showed us a full-page entry labeled "The Dinosaur House."

"They kind of duded it up a bit," she said looking at the page. I could see a frothing-at-the-mouth carnivorous dinosaur looming in a cloud behind the Bone Cabin.

She also showed us a beautiful *T. rex* claw that she kept in a china soup terrine and a yellowing black and white of her father and the great paleontologist Barnum Brown standing beside an excavation.

"Father helped Dr. Brown and his men dig out two *Tyrannosaurus* heads in the summers of 1902 and '03. The first two ever discovered."

She said her father got so taken with the digging that he didn't get all his hay and feeder corn in for two seasons. Sometimes he even dug bones all through the night. He built a winch to lift out the first skull, which, with the plastered-up block of earth that it was contained in, weighed two and a half tons. When it was being hoisted onto a wagon, a strap broke and the block of dinosaur skull swung free and knocked her father out cold. Everybody and everything turned out okay and Dr. Brown said that her father was the first human being ever injured by a dinosaur.

A bird chirped within our circle of huddled bodies. A canary had landed on Ben's shoulder. Behind him I saw a slowly swinging bird cage. It looked like it was made of dinosaur bone. Leslie stood up and reached for the little bird and it flew off into another room.

Mark started in on how birds were thought to be descendants of dinosaurs.

T. H. Huxley suggested it a hundred years ago because of the amazing similarity between bird and dinosaur anatomy. The two-legged dinosaurs are even called bird-hipped (Ornithischia). And they made birdlike footprints. Huxley was particularly fascinated by Archaeopterix, the fossil bird that is still thought of as a glorified feathered reptile.

The bird-dinosaur thing has been fired up again and added to the in-thinking these days that dinosaurs were warm-blooded. Fancy stuff like predator-to-prey ratios and vascularity of bone marrow and discovery of dinosaur fossils within the Arctic Circle are all supposed to help solidify this warm-bloodedness business and the similarity to the birds. And true reptiles are motionless 90 percent of their lives. Just to get a creature the size of *T. rex* to stand up would evidently have been a major event based on a purely reptilian model.

"There are paleontologists today," Mark was telling us, "who are proposing a total realignment of the animal kingdom. In their minds, there are only amphibians, reptiles, fish, and mammals, and a new order that includes birds—the dinosaurs."

There was some commotion by the stove and then Mr. Baker appeared at the table.

"Clear the decks for some dinosaur meat," he said. Then he set a plate of baked chicken on top of the *Ripley's*.

THE BAKERS WANTED US TO STAY WITH THEM. THEY SAID we could use their place as base camp. Mark said we appreciated that, but in our profession we had to get out and live with our quarry. He did say we might come in from time to time to get some water.

I was glad Mark didn't start BS'ing about *National Geographic* or that the Bakers didn't say anything about the insignia on the Bronco. (But I must say, here was another place ripe as hell for the *Geographic*.)

Mark did start on some photos. He took a whole thirty-six-exposure roll of color slides just on the Bone Cabin and then he tried a roll of black and white. For the artsy look he told me in an aside.

I think black-and-white photographs are sad. They're beautiful you understand, but sad. And lonely. Margaret Bourke-White's Africans. The Civil War of Mathew Brady. Dorothea Lange's Depression families. The panoramas of Ansel Adams. My yearbooks. My grandmother's engagement picture. Artsy shots of weather-beaten barns and old men's faces. Lonely. Beautiful. Sad.

Mark told me once that the black-and-white negative was the score and the print was the performance. I told him how great that was and how it should be put in a book somewhere. It already was he told me, in Ansel Adam's *The Eloquent Light*.

But look what's happened to black and white. Color used to be what you had to wait for. Take a roll of black

and white to your photo processor today and they tell
you two weeks. In the same place where you could get
your color prints back later that afternoon, it takes two
weeks for black and white. Loneliness and beauty and
sadness are not as easy to record these days. Not in less
than two weeks anyway.

FUN FACT: In 1941 the only two *T. rex* skulls in the world
were from the Bone Cabin. They were kept at the American
Museum of Natural History, but the curator sold one to the
Carnegie Museum because he was afraid that if the Germans
bombed New York, the universe would be minus two dinosaur
treasures.

CHAPTER
15

WE DROVE ABOUT FIVE MILES STRAIGHT WEST OF THE Bakers'. Right through the Badlands, since the road ended at their house. We picked our way around short, stubby cactus plants and down and over several dried stream beds. We stopped near a grouping of clay haystacks and saw the two coal seams that marked the dinosaur layer. Mark jumped out of the Bronco and scaled a hill to the level of the first seam. Ben and I and Leslie sat in the truck and visited. We were all sitting close with knees touching. Ben and Leslie got going about Vietnam and the draft and how Nixon had brought America to new lows. I just took it all in and felt honored to be there.

It was probably no more than fifteen minutes later that Mark was whooping and hollering.

"We got one!" he yelled.

I ran up the hill to take a look. Ten inches of a perfectly preserved *Triceratops* horn core stuck out of the earth.

"You little piece of shit!" I said. We hugged and danced around.

"If that's attached to a skull somewhere underneath," Mark said, "I'll kiss you on the lips."

I ran back down to the truck and told Ben and Leslie to get ready for a party. After rummaging around in the back of the Bronco, I zipped back up to Mark with a couple of dental picks, a trowel, and a whisk broom.

There's a good story about a *Triceratops*'s horn. In 1893, O. C. Marsh named a new species of extinct buffalo from just a single three-and-a-half-foot fossil horn that had been sent to him from Wyoming. (Describing an entire unknown animal from just one bone was an exercise nineteenth-century anatomists loved to follow through on. Acts of creation.) Two months later when the rest of the skull arrived, Marsh backtracked and reidentified the owner of the horn as a new dinosaur he called *Triceratops*. He also correctly assumed that the *Triceratops* had been herbivorous, stagecoach-size beasts which probably were once as plentiful as the buffalo.

We carefully dissected the clay around the horn for a couple of hours before either of us noticed that it was pitch-black out. Mark went to get the Coleman, but after another twenty minutes we decided we'd better wait until daylight to go any farther. We hadn't botched the excavation and the bone still looked like it went deeper into the hill.

Mark took off his undershirt and laid it over the exposed horn. Then we covered it up with an inch of dirt.

GODDANGED WE HAD TROUBLE GETTING TO SLEEP THAT night. Mark was convinced there was a whole beast attached to that horn. He was hoping that we could get the Bakers to help us with the really big digging. Maybe they could even borrow us a little bulldozer. Mark figured that we had a new species of *Triceratops* and that we should name it after Ben or Leslie or Clarence or maybe all three of them. He went back up the hill in the dark with Leslie and Ben to show them the site with a flashlight.

While they were gone, I was playing out a little delusion of my own. Remembering something else that happened to O. C. Marsh once when he was uncovering a dinosaur in Connecticut and had to delay his digging, I started thinking we would never get our horn out. Marsh had partially exposed a dinosaur thigh in a bank of the Connecticut River. It was in shale and had to be carefully quarried out. He left it in place over the winter and when he returned in the spring, a bridge abutment had been cemented over the exact site where his bone napped. I was worried that overnight a row of condos would go up over our horn or the hill would be blasted to bits by some uranium miners. (John Ostrom of Yale knew about Marsh's dinosaur, and when the bridge was torn down in 1972, he actually got the thing dug up. But I didn't want to wait any hundred years to find out what we had.)

THE NEXT DAY, BEN AND LESLIE HAD FIFTY-YARD-LINE seats to a dinosaur dig. The baked clay actually came away from the bone pretty easily as we dug a grotto around it. The horn looked so solid and perfect Mark and I decided it wouldn't have to be hardened with shellac or even need a plaster casing.

We had three feet of horn exposed by noon and went back down to our campsite for lunch. Then the four of us climbed back up to the dig site.

Several roots with no visible attachments bogged down any further digging, so Mark and I grabbed one near the specimen. Enough of it came up so that we had Ben and Leslie latch on to it with us. All four of us pulled like a group of tug-of-warrers. The root suddenly ripped out of the ground and kicked up a line of dust in the direction of the bone like a lit fuse. It happened in a thousandth of a second, but I watched it all unfold in slow motion. We were all on our butts of course. Unfortunately the root was wrapped around the still-buried portion of the bone and the whole horn shattered into a hundred thousand pieces. Like a vigorously and badly cracked nut, one moment it was there, and the next it had disintegrated.

Mark and Leslie and Ben went silently back to camp. We hadn't even taken a picture of what it had looked like.

I started digging through the rubble to see if there was anything left. After extending the hole another three feet and coming up with zip, I called it quits. It was getting hard to look at the zillions of minute bone fragments any longer. It must have been just a solitary horn. A nice, solitary horn. Clarence would not have approved of our technique.

WHEN I GOT BACK TO CAMP, THE OTHERS WERE SITTING around the tailgate of the Bronco. I guess Leslie thought the gathering was a little too solemn, so she got out the six-pack of Coors. I downed one in about three swallows.

"Jesu H. Christus," I said. I crumpled my empty can and threw it into the back of the Bronco.

"If you'll pardon the expression," Mark said, "we have just fucked the proverbial dog."

"And sold the puppies," said Ben.

Leslie stood up and hopped from one foot to the other.

"I'm sorry to have to ask such a mundane question at a time like this," she said, "but where do you go to the bathroom around here?"

"Anywhere," said Mark. "Just take a shovel with you." I was surprised he didn't tell her to go in a circle around the campsite.

"That's right," Ben said. "You can go anywhere. The whole world's a bathroom to these guys."

In a roundabout way, Ben was right. Whenever I get back home from a long campsite trip, I have to be extremely careful for the first few days not to take a leak out in the backyard or behind some handy bushes.

ACTUALLY, MARK'S INSTANT FIND WAS A GOOD SIGN. A capital sign. We were both still shaking from what all had happened. Even though that one got away, our dinosaur fuses had been lit again.

When Mark and I talk dinosaur, it's usually more poetic than anything else. We get worked up by the feel and look of a beautiful bone. We wonder if dinosaurs squeaked or roared. We suppose how they mated. Dinos to us are hardly slithering reptiles or objects of buffoonery. They are works of art. Precious pieces of sculpture. Fragments of beings that lived and breathed seventy million little years ago. Just holding a dinosaur bone could bring mist to our eyes.

Kids have a tough time relating to actual dinosaur bones. They can't abstract a connection to the images in their picture books or their little plastic models or even fully assembled museum skeletons. Myself, I only think in dinosaur parts. A vertebra, a tooth, a piece of a femur. I can just hold a single bone fragment and imagine the connections. But I know I couldn't feel any affection for a live dinosaur. They look like they might have been too slimy or cold. I'm not the type of guy who would keep pet snakes.

OUR FOSSIL EXPEDITION WAS LIKE ANY HUNTING TRIP. First, there's the preparation and then the long drive out to the hunting grounds. There's the looking for sign, the stalking, and the sighting. There's expectation, disappointment, and loud talk around evening campfires.

Out in the Montana Badlands, we were based around the Bronco. Ben and I slept in the truck; Mark and Leslie occupied the honeymoon suite of my pup tent.

"I won't tell Mom," I called out to Mark before hopping into my sleeping bag on our second night.

I heard zippers go up in the tent (or maybe down). Mark or Leslie turned on a flashlight and I saw a very interesting silhouette and it wasn't my brother's.

It was your basic beautiful Montana summer night and it was nice that somebody was in love and able to do something about it. Ben wanted the tailgate of the Bronco left open for some air but we got more than a little breeze. You didn't have to be Masters and Johnson to figure out what was going on ten feet away. Soft yips and moans. Fast breathing. Some absolutely delightful giggling. Once or twice I know I heard cloth being torn.

I looked over at Ben. He was lying on his back absolutely still, but I know we were both tuned in to the same station.

I remember wondering then if Ben was going to get jealous. Or me. (For me it could have been of either Mark or Leslie.) It was all getting a little too much like a made-for-TV movie.

Twenty minutes later another round started up. Ben and I were sitting on the tailgate by then. When things were quiet again, I think Ben and I were as exhausted and love-satisfied as our teammates. I suggested to Ben that the least we could do was light up a cigarette.

WHENEVER WE CAME IN FROM THE FIELD, MARK OR I went right to the cooler, which we kept in the shade of the truck. (This was not unlike a visit to my parents' house where we always looked in the refrigerator before saying hello.) Sometimes we just took a reassuring peek inside. But most often it was to down a quick soda. In Montana we had a particular hankering for Tahitian Treat. The two units of Coors that were left were reserved for the hopeful uncovering of a keeper dinosaur.

Ben brushed his teeth every day of the trip. Whether we were on the road or out in the middle of the South Dakota or Hell Creek Badlands made no difference. Ben was at those teeth. Flossed them too. Mark told him he sure had the dental hygiene thing dicked. He really did have the brushing down pat. He took a short swig of canteen water and then kept it in his mouth while he brushed. Then he didn't have to keep rinsing all the time. He didn't waste the water either. He swallowed it, but he purposely only used a little bit of toothpaste.

Mark was a toothpaste swallower as a kid. I taught him how to brush his teeth, but all he usually did was suck the toothpaste off the brush and then swallow it. I pana it was. I don't think I pana is around anymore, although Mark probably downed enough of it so that there's still some floating through his body.

I LOVE IT, BUT I REALLY DON'T KNOW WHAT THE HELL the big deal is about camping. Maybe it's a back-to-the-basics gene that we all possess. A thread extending to our ancestors in the caves and deserts and forests. Or maybe it's an unidentifiable urge to play at soldier or cowboy or Indian. All I know for sure is that it's great to be out in the middle of the boonies with only the bare essentials and get so dirty and sweaty and out of it that warm water tastes like champagne. (Actually, I can't stand champagne.)

I always thought that we had more water in one of our canteens than there was in the whole of the Badlands. Clarence told us that sometimes homesteaders had to wash their hands in milk. I laugh remembering back to the Longhorn. Gabby Hayes was selling instant water. He had these plastic bottles with a hash mark on the neck. The instructions said to "Just add water. Fill to line."

BEN AND LESLIE WENT FOR A BADLANDS STROLL LATE one afternoon while Mark and I sat around on our butts. Our camp was in a grassy little meadow with clay haystacks surrounding us on three sides.

I asked Mark as a joke if he thought that Ben and Leslie were going to get throttled again.

"What do you mean again?" he said and I could see that he was as serious as I've ever seen him. I didn't say anything, so Mark did. "Leslie is her own woman," he said. "She can make up her own mind."

Christ, I thought to myself, I'm joking for Christ sake. I let it drop and for sure I wasn't going to bring it up again. Not to Mark. Maybe I'd check it out with Ben or Leslie.

BEN AND LESLIE AMBLED BACK TOWARD CAMP AT DUSK. Fifty yards off I could see them back-lit by a disappearing sun. Leslie had her arm looped through Ben's. Ben looked like he was carrying something really heavy. He dropped it and they each picked up an end.

Leslie was pretty worked up by the time they got to us. "Ben found something," she said. "It's a big dinosaur bone."

"I bumped into it, really," Ben said. He held up his end of a three-foot-long specimen that must have weighed at least fifty pounds.

Mark ran over to check it out.

"It's a dinosaur dick!" he yelled.

The two of them dropped the thing like it was a live grenade and it landed on Mark's right foot.

It was actually a very nice petrified tree trunk that would give Ben much solace in the future as it lay in his den or someplace where he could reach out and touch it and let it take him back to dinosaur land.

With Ben's find and Mark's horn core, we had been rather spoiled in our first several days of Montana fossiling. The next two days we came across plenty of small fragments, but no more keepers.

WE SEEM TO RELISH OUR FOOD MORE ON THE TRAIL. Canned stew and chili, cheese, sausage, RyKrisp, peanut butter, tuna, dried fruit, nuts. Even the dehydrated foods taste like chef's delights out there. I wish somebody would hurry up and invent campfood pizza though.

Mark had recently been sprinkling something on his food from a plastic bag. Something I didn't recall having seen in our food pack before.

"What's that stuff?" I asked when I saw him use it again.

"Plankton."

"Plankton? Let me see that pecker!" I grabbed the bag to check it out.

Mark snatched it back. "Hey, don't knock it. It's the most concentrated form of protein known to human beings."

"And whales," I said. "Plankton is goddamned whale food!"

"So? They seem to do all right on it."

"Where'd you get it?"

"A health-food store in Aspen."

"Say no more," I said. "That explains everything. You better watch out. Your fingernails may be turning into turquoise inlay pretty soon."

* * *

THE PLANKTON TURNED OUT TO BE ONLY THE BEGINNING of one of Mark's new leafs. He went vegetarian on us about the fourth day in the Hell Creek Badlands.

"No more bacon. No more fast-food burgers. No more pork chops," Mark told us at breakfast. "I'm done eating muscle."

"What about the salamis you brought for trail food? And the chili and the stew? We still have a ton of all that stuff left," I said.

"No way for this kid. You can eat it up if you want, but I wouldn't recommend it."

Then we got a lecture about the fat content of meat and how meat contains blood products and injected hormones. He even threw in a bit of evolution.

"The teeth of human beings are not meat-eater's teeth," he said opening his mouth and pointing to a molar. "They are the crushing and grinding teeth of herbivores. Look at a dog's tooth or a cat's or *T. rex*'s for that matter—those are the teeth of carnivores."

I figured it would take about a week for Mark to break down and join the rest of us meat eaters and junk-food addicts, but the very next day I awoke to an unmistakable smell. I looked through a side window of the Bronco and saw Mark poking a fork into a frying pan of sizzling bacon. So much for vegetarianism. I was going to spy on him until he put the first morsel to his mouth. Then I would jump out from the truck yelling some appropriate taunt.

As he drained off the grease, I got poised to jump into the scene, but I still can't believe what happened next. He took the pan and a shovel to the edge of our campsite, dug a basketball-size hole, threw in the bacon, and covered it back up.

What the hell, I thought, putting on my pants and getting out of the Bronco, trying not to wake Ben.

"Hey, sweet," Mark called out to me. He didn't look the least bit caught in the act.

"What's with the bacon burial?" I asked.

"I love the smell of bacon," he said as if that explained it all.

"So what'd you throw it away for? I thought you had

gone soft on your new way of life, but at least you could have saved it for us."

"Bacon is one of the unhealthiest types of meat there is," Mark said gesturing with a cooking fork. "It's rude. Full of nitrates. And it's mostly cholesterol. No way could I make bacon in good conscience for anyone else anymore."

"I appreciate the concern, but maybe we want to die of cancer or hardening of the arteries and enjoy it."

Ben and Leslie were up by then and had gathered around us.

"I smell bacon," said Leslie.

"It's a new deodorant I'm wearing," I said.

"Mind if I gnaw on your arm?" Ben asked.

"See what meat will do to a species that can't handle it," Mark said jumping around and waving the cooking fork. "Cannibalism. Right here, folks, in the United States of A."

Actually, I can see Mark's point. I love the smell of coffee in the morning, but never could stand to drink the stuff. On occasion I'll have a pot brewing while I read the paper.

CHAPTER
16

THE INDIANS HAD IT RIGHT. THERE IS NO TIME IN THE Badlands. (I don't know if the Indians really thought that or not. It seems like something they would have come up with.) Sure, the sun goes up and down and the seasons fly by, but dinosaur bones surface near rusting washing machines. Cattle eat the grass of buffalo which rolled in the dust of millions-of-years-ago volcanoes. And three men and one woman drink Orange Crush in the night and silently look up at the stars.

"You folks are pretty quiet," said Ben. "What's up?"

"The goddamn solar system, I believe," said Mark. "It's lighting up the world like a Chrysler showroom. I think I need my shades."

It was quiet again for a moment. Then Ben coughed and rubbed his nose. "You know, I used to think that your profanity was an indication of an unretrievable loss of self-control. But lately I've been thinking that with its exuberance and appropriate usage, it borders on prayer."

"God bless you, dog nab it," said Mark.

A scream suddenly sliced through the night. Leslie

jumped. My heart skipped ten beats. A sweat broke out on Mark's forehead, and Ben's jaw clenched so tight I heard his teeth grind.

The scream sounded again. Like a high-pitched baby cry.

Mark stood up slowly, looking and listening into the dark. "I suppose it's a bobcat," he said. "But it's enough to scare the kee-rap right out of you."

Pioneer Grandma told Mark and me once that in her Dakota sod-hut days, bobcats and coyotes would come right up to the shack at night and whenever they howled like a baby, somebody young was going to die.

Ben took out his guitar and did a little mindless playing. Leslie got her recorder and started loosening up.

"Can you folks do 'Dueling Banjos'?" Mark asked. Then he laughed and looked over at me. I didn't think it was so funny.

Perfect-pitch Ben chorded along with whatever Leslie did. Some old medieval rounds and madrigals. A little improvising. I don't know what it all was but it was very nice. I think Mark even kind of liked it. But then Leslie started in on something so beautiful and haunting that I thought I was going to keel over. Mark sat up straight.

"Hey, that's not classical," Mark said. "That's movie music."

"Try Mozart," I said.

"Try both," said Ben, keeping up the rhythm section. "The theme from *Elvira Madigan*. Mozart's Piano Concerto Number Twenty-one in C Major."

"Right on!" I said.

"No shit," said Mark. Then I thought he was going to say something dumb like "Where's the piano" but his head was bobbing slowly and his eyes were closed.

What else can I say? I'm sure the lovely music swirled up and away from us and out over the Badlands like smoke from the campfire we didn't have.

Ben and Leslie could have played for fifteen minutes or fifteen days for all I knew. It was so, so beautiful. And sad. Rainy day, lost love music. But their playing had me in love. In love with Ben and Leslie, with Mark, with the Badlands, and with Wolfgang A. Mozart.

WE TOOK TO THE FIELD EVERY DAY LIKE WE THOUGHT we were pros. Mark and I were always functionally attired. Wearing our dinosaur-hunting suits Mark said. Ben burns easily so Leslie always made sure he had a little zinc oxide on his nose and that he was wearing a wide-brimmed hat.

"They're out there," Mark said to us each morning to instill the proper sense of our mission. "Let's go get em."

Mark usually led our little party and Ben was tied to his belt. Leslie and I kind of stuck together and dawdled behind Ben and Mark. It was funny to watch them from a distance. You couldn't hear anything, but Mark might stop suddenly and pick something up and start jumping up and down. Or he'd spurt ahead and the rope to Ben would go taut and Ben would have to grab on to it and start running. Then Ben might trip and fall and Mark would be reined back in like a dog straining at the leash.

We had glorious weather. It was hot, but dry. Most nights got down into the forties and every A.M. was a see-your-breath morning.

The whole thing was like a big treasure hunt and we were walking one continuous beach looking for washed-up presents from the sea.

Lunches were eaten in the field. Standing up, squinting into the sun with crumbs on the chin. After a swallow of canteen water, you close your eyes and take a deep breath. You are higher than a kite.

Mark and I tried our best to do a Clarence. We scanned the ridges for fossil sign, licked rocks to bring out their highlight. Sometimes Mark even walked like Clarence, and back in a Wyoming gas station I reached into my pocket for some change and laid three quarters and a prairie agate on the counter.

THE BAKERS CAME OUT ON HORSEBACK ONE AFTERNOON. Ben told them we weren't ready for the winches yet, but luckily while they were there we found a *Triceratops* vertebra lying bigger than all get out on the surface of a haystack ridge. We were hot stuff, all right. The genuine article.

ONE DAY IT WAS UNBELIEVABLY HOT. I MEAN IT WAS over a hundred easy. A regular fever Mark said. (Boner weather he called it. Weather that in the cities makes so many women wear so few clothes.) He tried to fry an egg on the hood of the Bronco, but it just kind of hardened into a coagulated mess. The least he could have done was crack it in the middle of the hood so I'd have gotten an ornament out of the deal.

I decided to stay in camp. I was flushed and sweaty and gritty as it was, but had that feeling that something great was going on. So I just wanted to sit back and savor it all. Leslie wanted to stick around too. I think she was getting a little down about having to leave in a few days.

We watched Mark and Ben return to the fossil fields. "So long, dogies," I called out to them as I opened a cold can of 7-Up from the cooler. I love the feel of a cool aluminum can as it gives way a little bit when you're downing a soda real quick. I like that burn in the throat and buzz in the nose too.

Ben and Mark were hitched together as usual. Ben walked with one ear turned to the ground, like a robin in search of worm.

"It looks like Mark should be following Ben," Leslie said to me.

"You ain't just a-kiddin'."

Leslie was looking what you might call ravishing in her halter top and tight shorts. Horizons of white around her magic places were nicely set off by a deep, dark tan. I don't know where the hell they came from, but I had to squelch some animal desires that suddenly snuck into my physiology. I couldn't believe it. The blood was rushing to my waist. I got up to look for some wood to chop and then remembered that we hadn't seen a tree in about ten days. A cold shower would have helped, but I settled for the desert-camping-trip equivalent. I brushed my teeth. Vigorously.

Leslie's voice slowed down a little mind film I was watching of me and her whooping it up in the pup tent. "I didn't know Mark had sold all his camera equipment," she said. Her voice sounded like an echoey airport page.

I garbled part of an answer and started choking on a

mouthful of water and toothpaste. Leslie had to slap me on the back and was about to do the Heimlich on me when I caught my breath again.

"Whoa, I'm all right," I said spinning out of her reach. "That toothpaste is strong stuff."

I cleared my throat a few more times and sat down. "In Toronto," I said continuing my answer, "Mark was in some financial straits. The camera went to some guy he owed money to. He sold me his stereo, a nice throw rug, and a reading lamp. He bought the stereo back a few months later. I'm his pawnbroker, you know."

"Yah, tell me about it," Leslie said. "You're a lot more than that. I don't know two brothers—or two friends for that matter—as close as you two birds."

"I'm not only his pawnbroker, I'm his slave. Remember that big, honking sculpture of his on display on the twenty-first floor of the First National Bank Building? He had left for Canada by the time the exhibit ended. Naturally, I had to go get it. I had to go up and down two different banks of elevators. Me, the claustrophobe who hates elevators."

Then Leslie told me that Mark was actually proud of me. That he bragged about me when I wasn't around. But she said sometimes I overpowered him with all my favors and that I didn't give him a chance to return them.

"And I bet you call Mark the most," she said.

"Yah. I guess I do."

"When you get back home and if he goes to Chicago, wait for him to give you a call."

"I'll probably have to wait a year," I said. "Well, maybe not. Maybe he'll have something at the airport for me to run after."

Leslie told me to get off the negative stuff. She said Mark had told her that he and I would be living in a shack in Dinosaur, Colorado, when we were eighty. That I did believe. Mark and I just talked about it the week before. We figured we'd both probably be a couple of flatulent old coots who would be swearing all the time and combing public parks with metal detectors on sunny afternoons. Then nights we'd play vintage Beatles and Rolling Stones and Diana Ross. Loud too, since we probably wouldn't be hearing too well.

"You two will have a lot of good times to look back over," Leslie said.

I laughed and told her that reminded me of a talk Mark and Pioneer Grandma had had before we left. Mark told her she must have seen quite a bit in her time since she'd watched trains and automobiles and rocket ships all take shape. But Grandma said that she'd seen too much.

"I haven't seen your grandma in maybe five years," Leslie said and then I remembered how she had been part of our family during her and Mark's high school dating days.

The blood had returned to my brain, and I was thinking deep platonic thoughts about my brother's sweetheart.

I wanted to ask Leslie about Ben but then I figured why bother. I was sure that she and Mark were tight again. Maybe there was a little magic between her and Ben, but so what. Trips are like that. Magic and special times where somewhere else something wouldn't have been right.

"You come with us to Dinosaur, Colorado!" I said standing up with all the urgency as if we were about to turn eighty in another minute. Leslie was on her feet too and we hugged long and hard. It was a familial embrace that I knew wouldn't generate any more ignoble desires, but just the same I couldn't help but think how only three items of clothing separated us. Leslie's shorts and I assume her underthings, and my jeans. I had been out of underpants for two weeks.

CHAPTER
17

I WASN'T GOING TO REMIND ANYBODY ABOUT DINOSAUR Daze, but I should have known that Mark wouldn't forget about it. And Ben, Mr. Elephant Brain himself, had wanted to go to church that same Sunday.

"I think I'm sick," I said the morning of the return to town. "I have a tummyache."

"Fine," Mark said. "Stay here and pick the lint out of your belly button. Maybe you'll feel better then."

I don't know if it was Mark or the thought of a chocolate malt that got me motivated to join the church- and partygoers, but there I was, on board with the rest of the crew.

During the hour-long ride in to Canaan, Mark and I were both formulating reasons why we couldn't go to Mass. Leslie had already said she was going with Ben. We just couldn't seem to give a simple answer for not joining them.

"We've got to stock up on our food supply, don't we, babe?" I said to Mark.

"You got that right. And we better hit those stores early before all the hoopla starts."

"It's Sunday," Leslie said. "The only places that will be open are the gas stations and bars and probably that little restaurant we went to."

"Right," Mark answered. "But we should still get to one of the joints early so we can save a place for you and Ben."

"Maybe we should just stay with the truck and discourage any vandalism," I offered.

Ben straightened up and cleared his throat. "Why don't you guys just quit pissing and moaning and get your asses in church."

"Hey," Mark said, "I have nothing against church. There are just some realities that have to be faced here."

Mark is a proponent of facilitative speech. The bending of the truth ever so little so as not to disturb other people's lives. Not really lies. More like lubricated words or greased sentences. Like how he always told my mother he was going to church on Sundays for noon Mass. He'd pass through the church parking lot and buy a Sunday paper. That was his going to church. Then he read the paper in a nearby drugstore for the next forty-five minutes. This wasn't for his personal gain, mind you. This was to ease my mother's conscience. As far as she knew, a son of hers would not burn in hell because he missed weekly Mass.

I DON'T EXACTLY RECALL WHAT HAPPENED AS WE DROVE around Canaan looking for the Catholic church, but saving seats for breakfast or warding off vandals didn't seem like viable options.

The town hall was the church. Lutheran services at 8:00 A.M. Baptist at 9:30. And Catholic at 10:45. Mark led our gathering into church and sat us all down in the very last row of chairs.

Since we didn't know what times the Masses were until we got there, we just kind of showed up. Mark and I exchanged painful looks when we realized that we were about twenty minutes early. Leslie and Ben knelt down side by side.

The Baptists had cleared out and a young priest was leading early arrival Catholics in the Rosary. In a perfect exchange at the end of the fourth decade, an older priest took his place without breaking cadence. Mark noticed this too and sent me a little not-bad look.

I know it had been awhile since I'd hit church, but the familiar movements and smells all came back, even though this place was just a part-time church. Still, I was really more of a passive observer than a participant that day. A liturgical voyeur so to speak. But it was kind of peaceful.

There was a quaint touch to the collection. One of the baskets that was sent around was an empty ice-cube tray. It made its way down our row and Mark whipped out a bill and dropped it in with the ones and fives and loose coins. He noticed the denomination of the bill as soon as the money left his hand. It was a twenty. Mark had to ask the usher for change.

We actually stayed right up to the very end of Mass. Mark and I were more used to bolting by the time Communion came around.

"Not too bad," Mark said outside the church. "We ought to do that more often."

"Yah, like every Sunday," said Leslie.

"It's something I wouldn't want to jump into right away," Mark said putting the key in the Bronco's front door.

He opened up the vehicle and then looked at the window. He slowly put his hand through the open frame. "Hey. The window was wide open all the time!"

I know he was alluding to the fact that a thousand dollars' worth of photographic gear was sitting on the front seat.

"Were you planning on giving this stuff away?" he said to me since I was the last one out of the truck before Mass.

"It's the illusion of security," I said. "Lock the door and it doesn't matter if the window's down."

"Sure. You put the key in the lock yourself," Leslie said.

"Yah, well," Mark said. "It's a good thing this is the West. Somebody probably would have come by eventually and rolled up the window and then locked the door for us."

A BIG NOON SUN AND A MONTANA BLUE SKY BLESSED Canaan. A marching band was warming up somewhere. Concession booths were being opened. Dinosaur Daze was getting cranked up.

There was a fossil hunt, float judging, foot races and games for young Canaanites, and general hell raising for anyone felt left out.

We returned to the café where we first learned of the celebration. So as not to crowd our stomachs for the coming delights of corn dogs and popcorn and carameled apples and malted milks, we all just had coffee and tea. There was a copy of *Hoard's Dairyman* left out on our table and Mark was leafing through it. He stopped in the "Job Openings" section.

"Here's something for Ben. 'Elderly couple with twenty-one-year-old daughter and ideal beef spread desire a herdsman who might be responsible, experienced, reasonable, and of Christian persuasion.'"

"No need to illustrate anything further," Leslie said knowing Mark's mind was chalking up items to embarrass Ben with.

"What's the time factor?" Mark said suddenly getting business-like.

"It feels about noon," I answered.

"Eleven fifty-six," said Ben.

"Let's ambulate, trilobites," Mark said. "Parade starts at twelve."

PEOPLE WERE LINING THE STREETS. LITTLE KIDS WERE running around with balloons. Older ones were blowing off firecrackers.

"Ah, the carnival atmosphere," Mark said sniffing the air, which I'm sure at that moment smelled like we were standing under the exhaust fan of a greasy spoon, which was in fact exactly what we were doing.

I saw three hard-guy, cowboy bikers giving Leslie the lecherous eye from across the street. I walked in front of her as if to protect her from their laser gazes.

The parade was led by a chicken-wire and papier-mâché *Triceratops* float that a local guy told us was left over from the 1966 high school homecoming and was so good that they've used it ever since. Pickup trucks with streamers and two marching bands and a platoon of decorated horses followed. I saw the three tough guys again, riding their big Harley choppers at the tail end of the parade, but I don't think they were really part of it. One of the cowboy-hatted bikers stared right at me when he passed. His belt was a bike chain. I nodded and sent back a nervous, ridiculous smile.

Mark was all over the place with his rented Nikon. Climbing up on platforms. Running in front of floats. I even had to hold him on my shoulders for a few minutes. All for the right shot. The best light. The *NG* photo.

The remainder of the afternoon was spent pigging out, as gluttony is commonly known in some circles. I think the most nutritious thing that I had in my mouth all day was a piece of Juicy Fruit gum.

Somebody had a hunk of dinosaur meat on display in a glass case. Mark thought it was really just a slab of marbled gneiss. As might be expected, there were dinosaur burgers for sale. They weren't supposed to be petrified.

Mark called Clarence long distance and asked him if he could get out to Montana somehow. I guess Clarence asked him why we just couldn't come back to Beauty. Then they had a little paleontology consult over the phone and before Clarence hung up he wanted to talk to Ben.

THAT NIGHT LESLIE SUGGESTED WE SEE A MOVIE. MIGHT as well make a full day of our little R & R she said. It was Kubrick's *2001*. I don't know if it was billed as a retrospective or if it was on a first-time run in dino land.

Ben goes to a lot of movies. He can pretty much follow

the dialogue on his own and then whoever is with him fills in the gaps. But *2001* is not what you call loaded with dialogue. "The Blue Danube Waltz" and "Thus Spake Zarathustra" are dynamite, of course, but it's a visual event. The colors, the space craft, the time warping. Halfway through I suggested that Ben and I hit the Hell Creek Bar and wait for Leslie and Mark.

THE FIRST THING BEN HAD TO DO WHEN WE GOT TO THE Hell Creek was go to the can. We slipped through the packed saloon and pushed into the men's. One of the tough-guy bikers was in there taking a leak. I assume he was taking a leak, because I didn't think he was the lavatory attendant.

There was only one urinal in the windowless, closet-size place, so Ben and I had to kind of line up behind him. Suddenly, I had to go to the bathroom bad. Both ways.

Mr. Hell's Angel-Cowboy Joe turned around and bumped into Ben and me. "Back off, pricks!" he said shoving each of us against the wall and kneeing me in, shall we say, a vulnerable spot.

"Hey, we didn't mean anything," I said. My lower pelvic region was starting to turn inside out.

"Neither did I, syph. Next time maybe you and your gimpy friend can check into a hospital after we meet." Then he busted out of the can without washing his hands, which figured.

"Nice guy, huh," Ben said.

"Super," I said. "I think he was one of the altar boys today." I was still taking slow, deep breaths.

THERE WAS NO PLACE TO SIT IN THE PEOPLE-PACKED joint, so Ben and I just wandered around. The Hell Creek Bar looked like Canaan's finest.

There were some fossils on display in a glassed-in shelf on one of the walls. Gar scales and dinosaur teeth. A yellowed, curling index card lay next to the specimens. Ancient fish and dinosaur pieces the card said in legible script. The thought was nice. Refreshing, actually. Paleontology for the people. But I must say, what was exhibited was not all that impressive. (Clarence told us he had sold a section of a *T. rex* jaw to the owner of the Ace Pool Hall in Sioux Falls. The jaw sat in the window until someone borrowed it for good.)

I wasn't really enjoying myself too much since I was walking bent over at the waist and still trying to keep an eye out for our new pal. Then I saw him at the bar with his two buddies from the parade. He saw us too and elbowed the other choir boys. They all slid off their stools and headed our way.

Shit. These guys had contact in their eyes and I don't mean handshakes. We couldn't go outside. We'd be sitting ducks for sure. Just stay with the crowd and hope Mark would be over real quick-like, I figured.

Ben and I kept easing in and out of people and tables. Every time I'd look around, the three dudes were just a few bodies away. Of course, Ben sensed what was up, but all I could do was keep an arm looped through one of his and steer him out of their reach.

Every town has what you call your undesirables. And every country and every time in history since mammals learned to walk erect and double up their fists. They're usually males just passing through town or working for a season. Our motorcycle captains didn't look like they worked. Greasy long hair and beards. Bags under their eyes. Pasty white skin and yellow teeth. They were either movie extras or the real thing.

I remembered that Mark had met up with an undesirable in an out-in-the-middle-of-nowhere Yukon bar. Some big, intoxicated linebacker type who was too loud and rude for even that environment. After throwing up on a pool table, the guy went outside to cool off, and the bartender locked him out. Pretty soon, the outsider was bashing against the door. Mark said every eye in the place was on the vibrating door. Maybe the collective gaze made it impenetrable. Not being able to knock the building over, the guy gave up and everybody went back to his saloon business. Mark remembered hearing a chain saw start up and thinking nothing of it. Then the noise got closer and closer. run-Run-RUN. And then there was the sound of chain link to wood and a four-foot logger's blade slides right through the center of the locked door.

Undesirables. They're everywhere and they always have been.

I'd never been in a fight in my life. Never hit another human being even once, but I figured I was about to at least have that opportunity. I've had a little body contact in my time. I used to play hockey and football. Come to think of it, I was wishing just then that Ben and I had both been dressed in full football gear.

"You two pussies going steady?" one of the bikers asked. He moved in close and I could smell dirty underwear. "You been walking around here all night holding on to each other."

What would Lewis and Clark have done in our spots? They were brave men. They were practical. I bet they would have coolly surveyed the scene and then summed it up in a split moment: outmanned and outmuscled in unfriendly territory. Then they would have flagged their kites out of there and hit the trail. Unfortunately, Ben and I no longer had the opportunity for quick exit.

"I'm having a sex change next week," Ben said in a high voice. My eyes probably went to hamburger-patty size.

"Isn't that cute?" the biker said. "Could we dance?"

"In a couple of weeks," Ben started to say, but the guy put a knee to Ben's solar plexus and doubled him up.

"That's it, fuck nuts!" I yelled. I launched my fist into the jerk's face. Man, my hand hurt. But not half as much as the crack to my head that somebody gave. That was bye-bye for this kid. The lights went out in Montana and I didn't come to until I was laid out in the back of the Bronco and we were heading back into the Badlands.

WHAT I PIECED TOGETHER LATER FROM LESLIE WAS THAT she and Mark had been looking for us in the crowd and saw the preamble to my loss of consciousness from across the room. When I went down, Leslie said Mark pole-vaulted onto the back of one of the gorillas and was flailing about like a ceiling fan. I understand there was some general head knocking and gnashing of teeth and garment rending while Ben and Leslie pulled me out to the Bronco. Mark came running after us a few minutes later and we patched out of the parking lot.

I'm sure it wasn't much of a fight by movie standards. No down-and-out saloon brawl with people crashing through balcony railings or getting cracked over the head with chairs or bottles. No standoff between gang leaders as the rest of the place cheers and places bets. In fact, it was probably a real dud as far as any kind of fight goes.

WHEN I WOKE UP, IT WAS STARTING TO RAIN. MY HEAD hurt and I put a hand to it, but the hand didn't feel any better. Maybe I did get hit with a chair.

"Welcome back, kid," Mark said from the driver's seat. "That was a nice little ruckus you started with those beat-offs."

"Ben started it," I said. "His drug-polluted mind just kept churning out these wise-ass remarks."

"Thanks for the new words," Ben said to me.

"What?" I said.

"Thanks for the new words," Ben said again. "What you called that gentleman before you hit him. I couldn't repeat them just now, but in the right place and at the right time, I couldn't think of anything better to say."

I burped silently and was reminded of the day's nutritional sins.

IT WASN'T DRIZZLING ANYMORE. IT WAS DELUGING. Looking out the back window of the Bronco was like opening your eyes under a shower head at full throttle.

This was one of those rains that they must call a fence lifter. A prairie dog drowner. The kind of rain that uncovers boxcarloads of new fossils.

"I can't see a thing," Mark said. Then he slowed down and stopped. He got out to check the road.

As soon as one foot touched the ground, Mark was on his butt. Just like everybody'd been telling us, Badlands

roads in the rain are bad news. It's the clay-based soil.
When it gets wet, it's slippery and gummy. Gumbo.

Mark got back in and started off at about ten miles an
hour.

The road was hump-backed and the Bronco kept slipping toward the three-foot gullies on either side. Putting
it into four-wheel-drive seemed to make it even worse.
We started going sideways on the greased road. Finally
we just had to sit there in the Bronco until the downpour
fizzled out. Leslie had her recorder, so she played us some
more Mozart.

It took three hours to get from Canaan back to camp.
Fifty miles in three hours. It continued to sprinkle through
the night, although one more torrent was unloaded before
the morning. Badlands weather is a definitive statement.
The place is sincere.

IT WAS STILL MISTING THE NEXT MORNING. I COULD SEE
that no one else was up, so I quietly got out my rain gear
and left the Bronco without waking Ben. I figured Leslie
and Mark were still incubating in the tent.

Rain will make or break a camping trip. You get somebody whining and complaining and it spreads to everybody else like a yawn. But weather it and the trip is
solidified. Of course, it depends on what you're doing
too. Clarence says as long as he's finding fossils, he doesn't
mind if it's snowing or if a volcano is erupting.

I remember Clarence telling us something else about
the rain other than what it does to the roads. Never to
go near a herd of cattle on the prairie during a lightning
storm. The animals' collective body heat draws electricity
to them like a lightning rod. Maybe that's how the dinosaurs got it. They were electrocuted.

I did a little scouting around despite the rain and found
some duck-billed dinosaur teeth just fifty yards beyond
our campsite. By noon the drizzle stopped and a wind
came up and the sky cleared. My boots were caked with
a mud that turned into cement. Within an hour, the thirsty
ground sucked up all the water and you would have sworn
that the previous night's cloudburst was a dream.

CHAPTER
18

On the day of Leslie's flight out we all over-slept. Leslie rumpled her things together and Mark swept pots and pans and dishes off the hood of the Bronco where we always put them to air out. I moved gear out from under the truck and slid it over to Ben.

"What the hell time is it now?" yelled Mark. He was flinging silverware around the campsite.

"Eight forty-five," said Ben with a finger on his braille wristwatch like he was taking his pulse.

"Jesus H.!" Mark said. "Can we make it?" He was in the driver's seat by then.

"It's two hundred twenty to Miles City, the flight's at noon," I said. I was trying to figure it out in my head. "You're looking at eighty miles an hour. Luckily the tank's still on three quarters."

Mark gunned the engine as Ben and I hugged Leslie. Actually, Ben got a very large kiss on the lips. Then he leaned his head on her shoulder. Mark put the Bronco in first gear before Leslie even had her door shut. The Bronco hopped three times and then killed. He started it again, and they spun out, leaving two divots on the Great Plains. The left turn signal blinked all the way out until I lost them in a poof of dust.

I like to watch the Bronco drive off. I stand tall like a proud dad as it pulls away. And it looked so good in distant profile against the Badlands panorama.

I asked Ben if he was going to miss Leslie and he got a look like I had just socked him in the gut. Then he walked away and didn't say a thing.

I HAD A LEISURELY DAY PLANNED. AFTER BREAKFAST I set out two folding lawn chairs we had brought along and Ben and I rubbed each other down with Coppertone. Ben was taking braille notes. I was finishing *On the Road*.

Mark had been after me to read Kerouac's classic for some time. Read this book and you'll see what life on the go is all about he kept telling me. He brought his copy along on the trip to finally settle the matter. It was a swollen and bloated paperback with the front cover torn off. He must have read it in a sauna. It was full of Mark's underlinings along with notes and exclamation points in the margins. I will say this, I enjoyed it very much. It is a vibrant, vital little book. But it contains no direction in life and absolutely no practical advice on travel. Not like our *North Star Guide Manual* anyway.

Hell, I love a book. Any book. A tidy little paperback or a big, glossy-paged scientific text. I love their smell and feel and heft. I could eat books.

With a particularly good book I'll cultivate a relationship. It becomes a trusted friend. Toward the end of a special novel like *To Kill a Mockingbird* or *Catcher in the Rye* I'll actually slow down a bit to savor it. When it's over and if it's a library book, I sometimes want to phone a few of those names listed on the back flap to see if they were sad to see it end too. And you can't read just any old book after that. It's like losing a pet.

FUN QUESTION: Why don't today's books say "The End" at the end? They used to in the good old days.

I FIGURED MARK WOULD BE GONE FOR ABOUT EIGHT hours. While he was in Miles City, he was also going to restock our food supply since we were down to only a few crackers and a jar of olives that we have taken with us on about five different trips but have never opened. It was an unspoken thing, but either Mark or I just kind of hung on to the olives. I know for sure that they made it around Lake Superior and back and forth to Toronto. Between trips I had them in my refrigerator, although I think Mark had them once too. Anyway, Ben and I were getting mighty hungry and after finishing off the crackers, the sacred olives were about to be inhaled.

Something else was making it on all our trips too, but not something to eat. It was one of those little, wing can openers. And this one really worked. It was an olive-drab, army-issue item. A P-49. Mark got it from his Alaska friend, old Norman Gray. Mark lived in Norman's shack outside of Anchorage when the two of them painted a shut-down army base in the summer of 1972. Norman found a crateful of P-49's and more or less borrowed the whole lot. He gave Mark ten of them and told him to strap one on his belt and to never be without it whenever he was in the field. I know why. You ever try to open a can of tuna with a geological hammer? Mark had the P-49 on him now, of course, but we didn't need it for the olives. They had a screw-top lid.

Actually, I was in the mood for two Swanson's Fried Chicken TV dinners. Maybe Mark would bring some back, although about the best we could do with them out there was to thaw them out. I figured if we made the olives last until Mark returned, we could at least think of them as appetizers.

They were the big, green juicy kind with pits. We savored them one by one and sucked the pits dry before spitting them around the campsite. The Bronco rumbled into our cocktail party about the time Ben and I were wondering if we should drink the juice.

Mark did a whiplash stop right in front of us and jumped out of the truck. He started walking quickly in the opposite direction. I ran after him.

"Don't follow me," he yelled over his shoulder. "I've got a rude dump coming."

Well, I didn't need a picture drawn for me. I went back and joined Ben, who still had a final olive pit pouched in his cheek like a chipmunk.

Mark was yelling to us from the latrine of the moment. Words wafted our way on a stiff breeze between noises like the birthing of a calf.

"Get ready to pull out for some sightseeing."

Then Mark stood in front of us again.

"Did Leslie make her flight?" Ben asked.

"Yah. No sweat. We got anything bad to eat around here?" Mark was ransacking the gear assembled around our tent.

"Man, you better have brought something good or bad back," I said. "We are plain out of groceries."

Ben expelled his pit and it ricocheted off a hubcap of the Bronco with a ping. "If you gentlemen can wait about twenty years, we ought to have a nice little olive grove right on this very spot."

"Well, listen," Mark said, not seeming to mind that we had consumed the relics, "I've got food all right, but we've got to get back down the road real quick. Don't we have any Twinkies or salami left?"

I wondered what had happened to the plankton and vegetarianism. One trip back to civilization and Mark's stomach was re-Americanized.

We all hopped in the Bronco and Mark drove off. I noticed several candy-bar wrappers and a crushed Coca-Cola can on the floor.

"Here's some nuts," Mark said holding out a blue Planters can. "Cashews."

"What's up, captain?" Ben asked. He cut his finger on the edge of the can but didn't know it. A trickle of red ran down his index finger.

"I saw a sign on the road on the way back from Canaan. I swear it wasn't there when we all came out or when I took Leslie in."

I put a Band-Aid on Ben's finger.

"I don't remember any signs when we went in for Dino Daze either," I said. "What did it say?"

"Dinosaur Footprints," Mark said. "With an arrow pointing into the Badlands. I think somebody put it out there because they know we're here. Really."

"Not the Bakers?" I asked.

"Nope. Leslie and I stopped at the house to say good-bye and a note on the door said they would be visiting their daughter in Glendive for a week."

WE PASSED THE BONE CABIN AND GOT ON THE DIRT ROAD to Canaan. Mark was driving about sixty miles an hour and the only place we could see was straight ahead. Ten miles down the road from the Bakers', Mark slowed down and I saw a splintered plywood sign pointing straight into the Badlands. Mark stopped and he and I got out.

"Not even any tire tracks," I said looking out over the terrain.

"Well, let's just drive slow and easy," Mark said, "and see what turns up."

We joined Ben in the Bronco and Mark activated the left turn signal. On probably the most desolate road in North America he signals a turn. He noticed me noticing.

"For the dino and buffalo," he said to me with a nod and then he turned into the prairie.

We hit an unexpected gully and almost tipped the truck over. The top carrier didn't weather that blow too well and we had to repair it on the spot with some rope and fence wire.

After the carrier was made somewhat travelworthy, two little kids a hundred yards off waved us toward them and we set out in their direction on foot. Ben had the honor of carrying the camera gear.

"Except for the Bakers," I said, "I didn't know anybody else was out here."

"Maybe they're Indian children," Ben said.

They were. Two boys. One about six and the other maybe four. The little one was riding a stick between his legs like a broom horse. Neither of them said a thing. They just hopped away and we followed. Then the guy on the play horse reared back and started jumping up and down pointing to the ground.

On a big slab of shale we could see ten or twelve almost perfect footprints.

"Balzac!" I said.

"Holly balls" said Mark dropping to his knees for a closer look.

They looked like giant, three-toed bird tracks and were a little bigger than an outstretched adult hand.

"Small- to medium-size carnivores I'd say," Mark said. "Do we have any plaster in the truck for impressions?"

"It's all back at camp," I said. "Should I go get it?"

"Let's wait and get some pictures now. We'll come back later for the casts."

FOOTPRINTS ARE VERY SPECIAL FOSSILS, A RECORD OF the living, of something happening. And like coprolites, they're rare too, although bonanzas have been happened upon. In Massachusetts and Connecticut of all places. People don't think of these states as dinosaur country, but a hundred million years ago they were.

In 1802, a New England kid named Pliny Moody started taking note of some large fossil tracks he knew about in the Connecticut River Valley. He found them in limestone outcropping and quarries and even the village flagstones. The boy's finds turned on the president of Amherst College, the Reverend E. B. Hitchcock, so much that Hitchcock spent the next thirty years cataloging and collecting what he thought to be Before the Flood bird tracks. He identified forty-nine different species, the most common set of prints coming from a bird he called Noah's Raven.

Those were the days when paleontology and geology were collectively known as Natural Philosophy. And there was always a little religion thrown in too. The giant bird tracks became minor scientific and theologic wonders. Hitchcock's collection was outshone momentarily in 1822 when a Missouri preacher claimed to have found the footprints of the Savior himself along the banks of the Mississippi north of St. Louis. They turned out to be real footprints, but made in cement by a local twelve-year-old.

Hitchcock carefully drew and casted thousands of the

Connecticut Valley footprints. He started a collection at the Amherst library with the help of Emily Dickinson's grandfather. They called it the Stoney Library. Huge quarried slabs of shale and limestone eventually took over the first floor of the building.

The Reverend Mr. Hitchcock never knew it, but his tracks weren't made by birds. They were dinosaur tracks. The thought wasn't a bad one though. He was right up there with Huxley and the other hotshots who officially mated the dino and birds.

There have been plenty of dinosaur tracks uncovered in the eastern United States, but very few bones. America's first dinosaur was discovered in New Jersey in 1833 and the headmistress of Mount Holyoke College found a complete, little dinosaur skeleton that was destroyed in a 1916 fire. But that's about it. If it's dinosaur bones you want, go West.

Despite the lack of actual bones in New England, the Connecticut River Valley is still a dinosaur footprint wonderland. In 1950, two thousand more dinosaur tracks were discovered at a construction site in Rocky Hill, Connecticut.

MARK PHOTOGRAPHED FOOTPRINTS AND I ASKED THE Indian boys if they knew what dinosaurs were. They shook their heads and shrugged their shoulders. The youngest got back on his stick horse and ran around in tight little circles. For some reason I turned around and what I saw about knocked my socks off. Close to thirty adult Indians were congregating along what would be our return approach to the Bronco. They had baskets and piles of blankets laid out over some boxes and even several tables. It looked like a double row of carnival booths had suddenly materialized.

We walked between the hawkers feeling like fools and not knowing what to do. Should we buy something or just give them some money? I really just wanted to stop in front of one of the folks and tell them that we knew their souls, that we dug their past and their land and the power of their spirit. But what the hell can you do? Mark bought a pottery dish for Leslie and we took off, not able to look back on the sorrowful little scene.

HUNGER SOON DISPLACED WHATEVER WE WERE FEELING, and Mark was already planning the evening meal as we bumped along in the Bronco back to camp.

"Tonight I want something green with a red side dish," he was saying. "I think that would go nicely with my sweat shirt."

"You going to eat your sweat shirt?" I asked.

"No, but that's not a bad thought. I could use the roughage and it is such a pretty thing."

"May I request something brown?" Ben asked.

"What the hell is this?" I said. "Eating by color?"

"You know those mood rings?" Mark said. "Well this is mood food. Right, Ben?"

"Yah. Sure. I guess so. How do those colors go again? Blue means you're happy . . ."

"Red goes with anger, white means you're depressed, and brown is indeterminate," Mark filled in.

"How about mood underwear," I said looking at Mark. "If you had a set, they'd always read indeterminate."

"Isn't there a yellow too?" asked Ben. "What color is coprolite?"

"Let's see," I said reaching over and unbuckling Mark's belt and trying to pull the jeans off our driver.

"Hey, dippo, you want to get us all killed?" He was fighting me off with one hand.

"Is your underwear white?" I asked. "Because any hospital emergency room would know how you felt at the time of your passing."

"This man is sick," Mark said.

"This man is a brilliant, unrecognized high priest and defender of the gastrointestinal tract," I said.

"You're nuts."

"How about yours?"

"Say, I just thought of another benefit of mood underwear," Ben cut in. "When they change color, it's time to take them off."

"Yes, of course," I said. "Mood underwear. One of America's great renewable resources."

THREE CANS OF HORMEL CHILI WITH BEANS WERE OUR main course that evening. A brownish-orange meal. I like canned chili a lot, even though it looks like dog food before you heat it up. For dessert, we finished off a bunch of bananas that Mark had bought in Miles City.

One of the great things about bananas is that you don't have to wash them; they come all ready to go in their own little wrappers that you just zip open. But bananas have three strikes against them as far as being good trail food: (1) they damage easily; (2) they spoil after just a few days; and (3) they aren't all that amenable to being crammed into a knapsack.

AFTER ALL THE BANANAS IN THE HELL CREEK BADlands were on their way to becoming parts of our own bodies, we had another campfire talk. A campfire talk, without a campfire, just the Coleman lantern. But the kind of gathering nevertheless where you felt you needed a nicely weighted pipe to cradle in your hand.

"The footprints were okay, weren't they, my little whorelets?" Mark said. He was lying on the Badlands grass, his right elbow two inches away from a cow pie.

"Indeed-o," I said. "Petrified motion. Frozen footsteps. That's righteous stuff."

"I have to believe," Ben said, "that Emily Dickinson saw those footprints...."

I think Ben was considering the topic more in the light of history than paleontology.

"...I mean, she lived in Amherst all her life and you said this Hitchcock and her grandfather were tight. And nature was her thing. The garden, the animals, the wind."

"And there are birds in her poems," I said.

"Lots of birds," said Ben.

"She must have seen the fossil tracks," Mark said. "I bet she touched them and ran her fingers over the rock.

And I bet she wondered hard about what the hell they were all about."

"I bet she's got an unpublished dinosaur poem in her notebooks somewhere," I said. "Done in her clever little way."

Ben stood up and faced away from us. He looked like he was in a trance.

"Speak to me of dinosaurs and falling stars . . . ," Ben said as if he were starting a poem. His voice was low and sleepy. I was beginning to think he had just contacted the spirit of Emily Dickinson.

". . . of hummingbirds and who we are

"of why we live and why we die

"and how to taste a piece of sky."

On the last line, the Coleman lantern went out.

"Holy shit," Mark said. In the dark I saw my brother swallow hard. I picked up the Coleman.

"Out of fuel," I said.

Ben was standing there like an Old Testament prophet, face to the wind, eyes squinted, fists clenched. Mark and I tiptoed around him in the dark. Finally, I just walked over to Ben and carefully touched him on the shoulder.

"Ben, Ben," I said like I was trying to wake him up. "You okay?"

"Yes," said Ben. Then he took a deep breath. "Just thinking about something sad."

I sat him down on the ground.

"Have a Mountain Dew," I said, "or a Strawberry Crush. Settle down, buddy."

"Thanks anyway," he said. "Just point me to bed. I'm out of it."

At least the guy really was human. He needed sleep just like the rest of us *Homo sapiens*.

CHAPTER
19

UNDERWEAR HAS HAUNTED ME AT DIFFERENT TIMES in my life. I remember one of my Chicago visits after the dinosaur trip. I flew into O'Hare. Mark was going to pick me up. It was a Friday afternoon and the airport was rock concert crowded. I had a piece of a duck-billed dinosaur jaw that broke in two in my carry-on bag. But now I'm off track again. When Mark and I went to the baggage claim, we saw a pair of white undershorts circling around and around on the baggage merry-go-round. I laughed. Mark laughed. Everybody near us laughed.

"Nobody's going to claim them now," I said to Mark and I laughed again. Then I realized that they were mine.

Since I was never overendowed with undies, I had to get them somehow. I kind of walked around to the backside of the carrousel and stuffed them into my pants pocket and then walked away smiling.

To this day, I wince whenever I see my luggage come barreling down those baggage chutes. I imagine my suitcase exploding and sending personal items flying about the airport that I then have to retrieve one by one.

THERE ARE PEOPLE WHO THINK MARK AND I ARE CRASS. I will admit that we do have a tendency to use frank language, but only in the right places and with the right people. Like we don't swear in front of the elderly or little kids. And it's those real little kids, like two or two and a half years old, that you really have to watch your language around. The phonetics of cussing make perfect baby words. Sometimes, though, I have an almost uncontrollable urge to stand up and yell a dirty word in some totally inappropriate place—like church.

We're probably more earthy than obscene. Our profanity is grounded in exuberance.

Mark swears real naturally, almost inoffensively. Some people just don't sound right using obscenities. What they say might be a little too hard or a little too forced. Like attempts at foul language in a bad made-for-TV movie. Mark can give the finger as if it were a gesture of friendship. And this is no lie, he can actually give the finger with his middle toe.

I read somewhere that one out of every nine words used in the home is obscene. In the workplace it's one out of twelve. I'll tell you, our foul to clean language meter must have registered 50–50 that whole summer. Although it was probably no different from the old mountain men who swore so much that the Indians called them goddamns.

Despite what I think is appropriate use of foul language, Mark and I will probably both wind up in a halfway house for cursers. We have all the signs. We swear alone, we miss work because we swear. We swear while driving and sometimes we can't even start the day without swearing.

ONE NIGHT, LATE, WHEN EVERYONE ELSE WAS ASLEEP, I got in the front seat of the Bronco and switched on the radio. Much to my surprise, I didn't even have to fiddle with it; some Montana station was coming in loud and clear. Even though the radio transmission had been unintelligible when we drove out from Canaan, this was a different story. Simon and Garfunkel sounded so close that I thought they were standing on the hood singing "The Dangling Conversation." Darkness does it I guess.

Shit. The folk-singing sixties. Simon and Garfunkel. Judy Collins. Peter, Paul and Mary. Joan Baez. Bob Dylan. A crew-cut and loafer and wool-sweater time. The Pill, Vietnam, campus unrest, race riots, men on the moon. The Kennedys, Martin Luther King. And Simon and Garfunkel. I hear now that they may be getting back together again. Peter, Paul and Mary too, after ten years of layoff. I guess enough time has passed that we need the folk singers back again.

When I'm in my apartment trying to nurture along a little melancholy, I'll put on something like *Send in the Clowns* or *Dionne Warwick's Greatest Hits*. Then I let the nostalgia waft over me. It helps if I get out old yearbooks and page through them at the same time. This is all done best on late Sunday afternoons.

"ANYBODY GOT A MATCH?" MARK ASKED ONE MORNING as he walked around the campsite in just his shorts.

No answer. I heard him like he was underwater and far away. Ben didn't say anything either.

"Okay," Mark said. There was an unlit cigarette bouncing between his lips. "I'll use one of my own."

"There's farmer matches in the first-aid kit," I said, suddenly feeling a need to get out an answer I had inside me all along. "I didn't know you started smoking again?"

Mark ignited one of the big matches off the hood of the Bronco. He took the still-unlit cigarette out of his mouth and held it between two fingers. Then he put the match to it like he was lighting a firecracker. I fully expected him to drop it and run. I even put my hands over my ears to muffle the explosion, but the only thing I heard was Mark saying "Piss on it!" as he threw down the smoke and stamped it out with a bare foot. "Son of a buck!" he yelled, hopping around the campsite. I could tell he was already missing Leslie.

* * *

IT WAS A GIVEN THAT WE WOULD EVENTUALLY DRIVE
back and take casts of the dinosaur footprints. I halfway
expected the sign to be gone, which it was, but I'll be
dog-nabbed if we couldn't find a trace of the site four days
later. I mean not even a single solitary tire track turning
off the road. There were no more little boys on stick
horses or carnival booths either. And there wasn't much
time left before we had to bolt back to St. Paul.

CHAPTER
20

SUNRISES ARE SPECTACULAR ANYWHERE. ALASKA. Montana. Even your own backyard. Mark's slides showed me that. Sunsets can be equally glorious, but we see them all the time. You have to put out a little to get at a good sunrise. And there's something special about being up when everyone else is in the rack. I don't know why I'm sounding like such a sunrise expert though. I have trouble getting out of bed before 9:00 A.M.

Mark was going to capture a Montana sunrise. Nail it down and pull it in. He had the site picked, knew the exact hour for that time of year, and even had exposures worked out. He was ready. But knowing Mark, he probably figured it would be too beautiful to view alone.

"You've got to see it with me, buddy," he said. "The spot's not far away and we'll camp right there. I'll get you up at the prettiest moment."

"Thank you, no."

"Come on! The desert is unbelievable at that time. It'll knock you out."

"It's against my religion to get up that early," I said. "So, I'll just wait to see them in *National Geographic*."

"You," Mark said, "are a hopeless, terminal dork."

Ben got excited though and wanted to go along. This uplifted Mark, some of his faith in humanity evidently restored.

"Not wanting to see a sunrise," he said to Ben.

I helped them get their gear together. Ben carried the tripod and camera gear along with a small day pack of his own. Mark had the tent, the water and food, and the sleeping bags. He tied a five-foot section of rope from his frame pack to the front of Ben's belt.

It's kind of funny, but even though Ben was really my friend, he and Mark had this little extra spark between them. I don't know what it was. I know Mark and I were solid, but there was something different between them. I swear they could face each other and send smoke signals back and forth. I'm not really saying it well, but how do you explain something like that? Ben probably understood it better than me or Mark.

"Send me a postcard," I yelled to their little mule train as they set off.

"Sleep well," Mark called back, not looking around. Then he held his right arm high and let an extended middle finger linger in the air.

I SLEPT GREAT. AFTER LESLIE LEFT I STILL BEDDED DOWN in the back of the Bronco while Mark and Ben slept in the pup tent. Of course, that previous night they were on location, so to speak, about five miles to the southwest. I awoke around nine and after breakfast decided to find their campsite.

I hiked for maybe an hour and a half before I saw the tent twenty yards ahead of me. I decided to stop there and watch. Somebody was moving around inside the tent like he was trapped inside a bag. Finally, the tent was unzipped and out popped Ben. He was stretching as if he had recently crawled out of his sleeping bag; he probably hopped in the sack again after the sunrise to catch a nap.

Mark was not around. Somewhere being Ansel Adams no doubt.

Ben sniffed the air and did some deep knee bends and arm whirls. I continued to watch from a distance without saying anything. Then he started ambling around the campsite. He tested each step with a leading, groping foot. He was getting farther away from the tent and I started getting worried. How would he get back? All I could think of was the farmer who got lost for good in a blizzard going between his house and the barn. But then, Ben suddenly did an about-face and walked, strode really, right on a bee line for the tent. He stumbled once on a birthday-cake-size rock he hadn't counted on, but stayed on his feet. He felt around for the opening of the tent and went back inside.

Psychic or not, Ben was something else. He probably could have found his way out of the Badlands alone if he had had to. Smelling his way or remembering how we got there in the first place and then doing another one of those about-faces.

I could see Ben rummaging around in the gear. He picked up an open bag of oranges from the wrong end and spilled several. One rolled out of the tent in my direction and sent me off on a tangent, back to my undergrad days at Minnesota.

I had an anthropology teacher, John G. Woodell, who was a real spellbinder. He was very respected in his field and people said Leakey had consulted him regularly. Even the local medical examiner's office used his expertise from time to time. Some hair, a tooth, a maybe a patch of clothing would be presented to him from a difficult homicide. He could come up with such an intricate description of the victim that you wondered if he himself had witnessed the event. And all from such scanty evidence. ("I wish I had that much to go on for my Paleo-Americans," he would say to the press.) Woodell was flown to Attica in '71 to search through the rubble of the collapsed prison gymnasium for victims' teeth or identifiable artifacts. A newspaper photo showed him and a crew of grad students tagging specimens they had sifted through coarse screens. The whole area was roped off in meter-square grids just as if some ancient civilization were being unearthed. But back to the oranges.

For our opening lecture on field techniques, Woodell silently peeled and cut an orange. He put the naked fruit aside and gathered up the peels, shaking them like dice between his cupped hands. Half of the peels he put in the wastebasket and the remaining ones he threw into the air. They fell on the floor and on book shelves and on some of our desks. One little piece landed right in front of me.

"Your assignment today," he told us, "is to systematically collect those orange peels. Work as a group. You are anthropologists on the verge of a significant find. Record where each fragment was found, sketching them as they lay. Then attempt to piece them together again."

Without further word he left the room, taking the wastebasket and peeled orange with him.

Half the class thought he was nuts; the rest of us, a genius. (Oh, I imagine there were one or two who thought he was just a litterbug.) Nevertheless, it was an impressive lesson, and to this day I still think of orange peels as priceless pottery shards. I even saved the piece that landed on my desk. I still have it in a little bottle.

Ben coughed and I saw that he had gathered up what oranges he could locate and returned all but one to the bag. Back outside again he sat cross-legged in front of the tent and began peeling the orange he had kept aside. (Opening an orange Mark calls it.) He bit into the rind to get it started and made a nice little pile of peels on his lap. He ate the orange section by section. All very deliberate, very neat. When he finished he looked like he was going to stand up. The peels! I jumped up myself and started running toward him.

"Don't throw those things away!" I yelled as Ben was about to sweep the pile off his lap.

At first, he must have been more startled by the anxiety-stricken command coming out of nowhere than by the request itself. Then, as my voice registered and words settled in, the poor guy probably wondered what kind of violation he almost committed.

Ben hadn't taken Woodell's class nor heard of its famous opening day, so I told him the story. I repeated it to Mark when he returned to camp from what turned out to be just a little scouting around. ("The sunrise was something else," he said to me. "You should have been there, whorelet.")

Mark wanted to put Ben's orange together again. We used tape and Elmer's glue and some straight pins and got kind of a cracked, halfway dish out of the process. "A real fruit bowl," Ben said.

CHAPTER
21

IN LATE AUGUST WE HIT WHAT YOU CALL THE END OF the road. It was time to go back home.

Getting into *National Geographic* would have to be the saving grace for that trip. What we had to show for a whole summer of fossiling wouldn't have filled a shoe box. An arrowhead and a few machine-gun cartridges. A handful of broken turtle shell fragments. Some loose duck-billed dinosaur teeth, a vertebra, and a little insectivore jaw. But no biggies. No *T. rex* jaws or *Triceratops* horns. No five-foot femurs. No pieces for the trophy room, so to speak. Ben's petrified stump was a nice find, but nothing unusual. We didn't even get any coprolite.

"It wasn't meant to be," I said as we tightened up our gear for the return trip. "But we'll be back. We'll get one of those big buckos next time around."

"Maybe next year we should go somewhere else," Mark said. "I hear the Red Deer River basin of Alberta is choice dinosaur country."

Whatever you're looking for, someplace else always seems better.

"I thought this Bone Cabin was supposed to be the pot at the end of the rainbow," said Ben.

"How about Australia?" Mark said. "They're uncovering some amazing new dinosaurs down there."

"Hold it," I said. "I suggest that in the future we go back and hook up with Clarence. We should never have left him in the first place."

SINCE WE WERE RETURNING ON A STRAIGHT SHOT through Montana and North Dakota, we were closing kind of a circle trip, although it looked more like a distorted boomerang when I actually traced it out on a map. St. Paul to Rapid City, then the swing down to Aspen and up through Wyoming and Montana followed by the North Dakota return.

I think even Ben was getting a little nostalgic about the end of the trip. He said it didn't seem right to just pack up and leave. With that, I could see the fireworks go off in Mark's cranium. I knew he was planning an exit ceremony.

"You going to throw your hammer again?" I asked.

But Mark did come up with quite an idea. He wanted to bury some exposed film of Ben and Leslie and him and me. One of the rolls of black and white, since that would probably last longer. (All those undeveloped images just waiting to hatch and then buried in the same dirt as our dinosaur brethren. A nice touch, I thought.)

The durability of the first roll of film was discovered when several cartridges of black-and-white negative that recorded the fatal 1897 Salomon Andrée balloon expedition to the North Pole were discovered and processed after they had lain in the polar snow for thirty-three years. There were smiling faces all around and some pretty amazing aerial photos of Greenland and Baffin Island. A group shot of the explorers standing in front of the downed balloon was especially poignant. They were smiling big and had their arms around each others' shoulders despite knowing that the bucket was about to be kicked.

But we were planning on getting back to St. Paul in

one piece, so Mark's film burial was just a nice, poetic gesture.

I also suggested that we each swallow a hackberry seed, one of the BB-size fossils that Clarence had found for us in the South Dakota anthills. So after the film was sunk into the earth, Mark passed out one little pellet to each of us.

We all stood by the loaded Bronco with the tiny petrified seeds resting on upturned palms. A warm Badlands breeze lapped up against us. There was one can of Coors left and Mark passed it to me. I was the first to take my offering.

"For Clarence, for the buffalo, and for the dinosaurs," I said in a little toast before swallowing mine. Then I gave the Coors to Mark.

"For Crazy Horse and Sitting Bull," Mark said.

"For Sacajawea, Billie Holiday, and our wondergirl, Leslie," said Ben.

I remember thinking again that maybe Ben and Leslie did have something going.

WE TOOK OUR USUAL PLACES IN THE TRUCK. BEN WAS shotgun and I was the reserve pilot waiting in back for my call. Before Mark climbed into the driver's seat he yelled out into the Badlands: "We'll be back, you little whorelets."

A return trip is usually purely functional. It's hardly the upper that the way out is, and as a matter of fact, it's probably approached with more dread than anything else. I would have preferred to just have been time-warped home.

We were trying to get psyched up for the twenty hours of road time ahead. We certainly had all the essentials. Mark did a good job of resupplying us when he took Leslie in. NōDōz, red licorice, malted milk balls, graham crackers, big stick pretzels, lemon drops, a six-pack of Coke, chewing gum, and the right attitude.

"If you two don't mind," Mark said as we drove off, "we're heading straight through to St. Paul. I'd like to see Leslie tomorrow night."

Actually it probably wasn't so bad that we were driving home. Cars help ease you back from a trip. The old jet airplane gets you there a little too suddenly. It's not natural being catapulted across time zones. Your bowels get confused.

WE WERE LEAVING AT DUSK, OF COURSE, FULLY EXpecting the night magic of the road to kick in at any time. But it didn't.

The Bakers were still in Glendive and after putting a note in their mailbox and then hitting the dirt road, I could tell that something wasn't right. There wasn't the usual electricity in the air like our other night departures. We probably should have slept over one more night at the campsite and then left fresh in the morning. We definitely were not up. Even Mark. We just weren't sharp.

We made it to Canaan in an hour and a half. Somehow Mark kept going until Wibaux, the next Montana town a hundred miles down the road. I was going to beg him to let Ben and me spend the night in a motel. If it would have made him feel any better, I was all set to help our hard-core, Alaska hitchhiker pitch a tent in the parking lot. But I didn't have to do any more than just point to a blinking motel sign. RONDE-VU...RONDE-VU. Mark actually sped up to enter its parking lot. The Ronde-Vu had a pink neon glow to it. I looked at Mark when we stopped. He was in a daze.

I signed in for all of us. On the registry I recorded that I was representing Twin City Triceratops. We got the cheapest room they had, which is to say the smallest.

When I say the room was small, I mean an ashtray would have taken up too much space. The whole room was filled by one double bed. A tight aisle led to the bathroom and a TV was mounted high in one corner.

Mark hit the bed fully dressed and was out cold before he was horizontal. I untied his boots and slipped them off. Ben took a shower and I watched some TV. (The channel numbers always seem so strange in another state.)

Mark was so out of it I considered seeing if he still had a pulse. But then I got a hankering for some cocoa, so I went out to the Bronco and brought back the Coleman stove. When Ben was done with his shower, I fired up the stove and put it in the bathtub. Ben and I took in the late news with a cup of hot chocolate. That's an old trick of Mark's, cooking in motel rooms. He would rather camp out, but whenever he did check in at some place of lodging, he maximized his stay there.

During grade school winters, Mark and I used to split a whole loaf of toasted Wonder bread that we dunked into cups of cocoa.

I ended up in a sleeping bag on the floor and Ben snuck in beside Mark.

WE ALL SLEPT UNTIL A KNOCK SCARED THE CRAP OUT of us. A young woman opened the door and peeked in and then shut it again. Probably the maid. It was 1:00 P.M. Checkout time. We were up and dressed and out into the afternoon in almost one motion. All we needed right then was a little food and we'd be ready to drive around the world.

There was only one other vehicle in the parking lot, an empty, unattached trailer that leaned 45 degrees on its hitching arm. In big, black letters on the wooden sides was printed WYOMING DEER HEARSE.

"Cute little outfit," Mark said after telling Ben what it said. "Probably belongs to a local chapter of the Sierra Club."

I could see a group of great white hunters in a liquored-up caravan making an annual migration somewhere west and then returning with the carcass-laden trailer. I remember reading in the 1974 *World Almanac* that a hundred thousand deer a year are shot in Wyoming alone. Then they're carried out in pickup-truck beds and over car trunks. Like casualties being evacuated from the front.

"Not exactly *National Geographic* material, is it?" I said to Mark as we passed it on the way into the Ronde-Vu's coffee shop.

"No shit," Mark said. He was looking at the trailer over his shoulder. Then he tripped on the curb.

IT WASN'T THE BREAKFAST HOUR, BUT IN OUR HEARTS and stomachs it was. I went with my old standby of hash browns, whole-wheat toast, and two eggs over easy. I ordered a large glass of grapefruit juice.

One of the greatest deceptions along the road is the supposed large glass of grapefruit juice. You'd expect it to come in a huge soda glass, but every time it's in a container hardly bigger than a vigil light. Every now and then I think a place will truly have a large grapefruit juice. When that happens, it will probably come in a bucket.

Two guys in their forties were sitting one booth away from us and talking about our second favorite topic. All we got between mumbles and laughs were a few ear-opening phrases like jiggling tits and wet pussy. Mark was leaning and straining their way so obviously that I suggested he join them. So he did. The talk got even more unintelligible after Mark started them up again. Ben had been following the conversation with interest and probably heard every word up until then. He set down a fork and turned to the group.

"Would you whorelets mind speaking up?" he asked.

CHAPTER
22

WE WERE ALL THREE SQUEEZED INTO THE FRONT OF the Bronco when we pulled away from the Ronde-Vu. "Nice vehicle you got here," Ben said to me, "for a dinosaur hearse."

I noticed Mark was driving barefoot. That is, no shoes, no socks. I always thought that was something you could get a ticket for, but I wasn't sure so I let it go and just continued to watch Montana fade away in one of the side mirrors.

IT WAS A BRIGHT, WONDERFUL AFTERNOON FOR A DRIVE. Mark tapped his foot on the gas pedal to "Suite: Judy Blue Eyes" as we sailed into North Dakota. Ben had his arm out the window and was letting it go spastic in the wind.

Mark turned the radio down for a moment and looked over at Ben. "Why couldn't you have been a woman with big knockers?"

"Why couldn't you have been an A and W Burger-basket and large root beer?" Ben said.

"Ah, hah!" Mark said. "Tit for tat."

"More like tit for A and W," said Ben. Then he himself turned the radio full blast. We got a carful of the Monkees doing "I'm a Believer."

At this stage of the trip, we had developed kind of a pilgrimage mode. Whenever Ben snapped open the cover of his braille watch, Mark or I would yell our own guess at the time. And if Ben rattled out a Dynamint for himself, he automatically got some for us because he knew Mark would be asking for some truck drivers, or speed balls. We had our own trip lingo that would sound funny somewhere else like at home or work.

Ben liked to guess our speed too. He'd ask us how far it was between towns. Then he'd put a hand out the window or listen to the engine. He was right on every time.

I think just when I was starting to miss the possibility of Ben being psychic, I heard him whistling an old tune. Something like "Teen Angel." The radio had been off for hours. Well, I'll be humped if Ben didn't activate the old unit and there's "Teen Angel" on the airwaves.

JONI MITCHELL MUSIC IS NORTH DAKOTA TO ME. THE summer of the big trip, my favorite songs were "Help Me" and "Free Man in Paris." I heard them over and over as we went from radio station to radio station across North Dakota. No-Dak. The land of speeding-by clouds and waving prairie. Willa Cather says that the whole country seems to be running.

North Dakota has its own set of Badlands. Teddy Roosevelt had a ranch there. The Elk Horn. He spent a lot of his young-man summers at the Elk Horn. He became a fellow badlander of a French count, the Marquis de Mores, who built a twenty-seven-room château overlooking some fine North Dakota fossil country. The marquis's place is still standing in Medora. It's got canopy beds and Oriental rugs and a wine cellar. It's not exactly a sod hut if you know what I mean.

T.R. learned horsemanship in the Badlands, so I had

always figured he must have happened across fossil bone out there. I knew he did for sure when I read a 1916 *NG* article he had written about extinct animals like the Irish elk and saber-toothed cat and other creatures that lived during what he called the hoary antiquity of man.

Oil was rediscovered out in the No-Dak Badlands and made a lot of instant millionaires and sprouted a few trailer-home cities. Little oil wells with bobbing horizontal arms dotted the prairie. They looked like grazing dinosaurs. The wells were surprisingly inoffensive and clean.

But Mark must have been formulating a scene of pollution and destruction in his head based on what we had just passed by, because he came out with a pseudobiblical quote that he thought appropriate. "And God saw all this happening, and He saw that it was questionable."

That was clever, but I thought uncalled-for. Mark was a user of petrol from those very wells.

"Before you get too high and mighty," I said to him, "maybe you want to recall that this truck doesn't run on soda pop or Dynamints."

"Maybe you want to get screwed," Mark said. I could tell he was pissed because his knuckles went white around the steering wheel. And he just kept looking straight ahead.

"Maybe we should all know some North Dakota facts," Ben said trying to clear the air. "Did you know that the North Dakota legislature meets only once every two years and that half of the agenda is spent on mineral rights?"

"My brother knows all that kind of stuff," Mark said to Ben. "The little whorelet is probably a major shareholder in some wildcat oil company that's ripping open that prairie."

"You are too if I am, sweetheart," I said. "I sign everything in both our names for Twin City Triceratops."

WE HAD TO TAKE A FIFTY-MILE DETOUR OFF I-94 ONTO an old two-way highway. We met a semi barreling toward us on a narrow bridge and our mirrors clicked. Looking across Mark, I could see that our mirror was cracked so badly it looked like an expert-level jigsaw puzzle.

"Almost lost the old Bronco there," Mark said.

"Would you care?" I asked.

"Hey, I have to take back a lot of what I've said in the past. The Bronco's done real well by us this trip. The clock runs, the emergency brake works. Ben can keep the radio honest."

Then Mark stopped for a moment. "But there is one thing I'm still sorry about."

"What's that?" I asked.

"I'm sorry that it's still a piece of shit." And then he threw back his head and laughed and gunned the engine. I poured a little canteen water on his lap.

"Where's your Mercedes-Benz now, asshole?" I said.

WHIPPING ALONG THE HIGHWAY, UNPLEASANTRIES LIKE a dead animal or a wrecked car can be passed by subliminally, like they never happened or like you were switching channels on TV. But coming over a hill on the detour we saw something ahead that we couldn't ignore. A cluster of cars were gathered along the edge of the asphalt and five people were standing over a prone body. We slowed down and bumped along the shoulder. I didn't know which human compulsion we were going to answer, the urge to gawk or to help out.

"Doesn't look like an accident," I said as I set the emergency brake.

"Heart attack or something," Mark said and I ran through my mind what to do if that was the case.

"Stay with the truck," I said to Ben. Mark and I ran over to the scene.

A middle-aged man, Mexican American I think, lay faceup on the pavement. It looked like his family was gathered around him. There were tears falling and hands being wrung. Mark was leaning over the victim. Some motorist was holding two battery cables up in the air.

"Should we shock his heart?" the motorist asked. "I'll hook up to my car battery."

No one answered him. I joined Mark and we gave the man CPR, Mark doing the mouth-to-mouth and me doing the chest pumping. An ambulance arrived on the scene just as the guy's heart started up again on its own. He was whipped away along with a couple of family members who insisted on riding in the back of the ambulance.

People shook Mark's and my hands and slapped us on the back. They must have thought we were doctors or something because some of them started asking us about rashes and coughs and skin bumps. I mean stuff that had nothing to do with the accident. We could have started a roadside clinic right there.

It's times like those, first-aid scenes and people asking body questions that I can't answer, that I think it's worth going to medical school just to relieve the anxiety of facing those inevitable situations.

BEN STRETCHED OUT IN BACK WHEN WE GOT GOING AGAIN and I nodded off in the passenger seat. I must have dreamed that I was driving, because I woke up in a fright, grabbing for the wheel. My little seizure even startled Mark.

"Whoa," he said with a shiver. "You brought me back from a road trance yourself there, sweet."

I sat in silence, not knowing the time of day, the country we were in or why. A nap usually screws up one's internal gyroscope but good.

IT WAS STILL LIGHT OUT WHEN WE COMPLETED THE DE-tour and intersected the freeway again. I think I had counted at least four or five dead skunks along the old highway. We saw another one on I-94. (Clarence called skunks "wood pussies.")

"Smell must travel as slow as sound," Mark said, "because like a high airplane that you hear after it's passed, you don't smell highway skunks until you've whizzed by."

"Skunks have gotta be dumb," I said, thinking about the most recent furry black-and-white mess on the highway.

"Do you think dinosaurs were that dumb?" asked Ben from the back.

"I don't know," said Mark, "but they probably didn't stink."

"That'd be a helluva deal if dinos crossed the roads

today like skunks do," I said. Then I played out that little scene in my head. I could just see those hulking creatures ambling across American freeways. Collisions wouldn't hurt them any. It'd be the crumpled auto bodies that lined the shoulders like dead animals.

SKUNK SMELLS REMIND ME AGAIN WHAT A SENSUAL EXperience road travel is. The gasoline aroma of truck stops and the sound of idling stock haulers with all their scared meat inside. The rumble of the highway, the whine of the tires, the feel of the steering wheel in your hands for ten hours. And there's nothing quite like the revitalizations of a 4:00 A.M. leak off the side of a freeway followed by a few profanities and creaking calisthenics. Do you think you could get all that in a passenger train? Do you think you could smell manure from a 747? The world is yours for the sampling from a car.

GAS—FOOD—LODGING. IT'S ALWAYS SO REASSURING TO see those particular highway signs when you're far away from home. What else is there except for maybe love and affection? But you can't really advertise for those things.

I COULD TELL IT WAS GETTING NEAR THE END OF THE trip. The passenger seat was not so desirable a place to be anymore. Whoever sat there had to reach out the window and hold on to the wounded car carrier whenever we hit a bump.

My right boot sole separated from the main body of the shoe. It flapped in front and made me walk with a limp, so I bound it up with white adhesive tape. Provisions were also getting mighty thin. Mark was developing quite a cold and we didn't have any tissue left. The poor guy had been blowing his nose on aluminum foil for the last two hundred miles.

We stopped for a late-afternoon breather in Bismarck. At a bus depot. After a can of pop, Mark led me by the hand to a photo booth.

"We need some derelict photos for posterity," Mark said to me as we both slipped behind the curtain and sat down. Mark got three different sets of those dull, black-and-white instant photos. He had his tongue out in several and was draped around my neck, kissing my cheek in a few others.

"Wholesome," I said looking at the strips of pictures. "We could get arrested for this kind of stuff."

"Maybe we could sell them," Mark said with a lecherous laugh. Then he tried to get Ben in a booth with him.

"I'll give you a burger basket," Mark said pulling on Ben's arm.

"I'll give you a picture of Leslie naked," Ben said. "One you've never seen before."

WE DROVE AROUND TOWN LOOKING FOR A GROCERY STORE so we could replace some essentials. We stopped at an A&P that had a big sign saying WE'RE OPEN 24 HRS A DAY, 365 DAYS A YEAR. Now, that's spunk. I grabbed two cans of tuna on the way out because I couldn't believe the price. Back in the truck I noticed that they were cans of cat food.

Out on the highway again, Mark got a charley horse (a Johnny Donkey he calls it), so I switched with him and took the wheel.

After we heard a soaring Allman Brothers instrumental ("Jessica"), Mark was kind enough to not remind me how I had passed up a chance to see them in concert. But I remembered anyway. The real Allman Brothers that is, with Dickie Betts and Duane and Greg Allman. That was in '71 when we were both still at home. Mark got two tickets for the concert and was going to take me. It was even in a small concert hall with great acoustics. Maybe it was because of my claustrophobia, but I didn't go, and I regret it to this day.

I was still awake when Mark got back from the concert. I remember asking him how it was and already thinking I might have made a bad mistake but secretly hoping it had been a letdown.

"Because I don't want you to feel bad," Mark said,

"let me put it this way. They stank. They were lousy. You didn't miss a thing."

"Holy balls!" I said. "Were they that good?"

"Unbelievable. The sound system was perfect. They were up. The crowd was up."

"How many encores?" I asked slowly, getting ready to flinch.

"Five."

"Five!" I said and couldn't believe it.

"I shit you not," Mark said. Then he must have seen my wounded posture. "Hey! We'll catch them next year. I'll get tickets again."

But he didn't. He couldn't have if he tried. Duane Allman was killed in a motorcycle accident six months later. I heard it on the radio. All that day the disc jockeys played Allman Brothers' tunes as a kind of rock 'n' roll memorial. And I remember wondering how close the two Allman Brothers were to each other.

WE JUST COULDN'T SEEM TO GET OUR OLD RHYTHM BACK. We exited for a Dairy Queen and chose a delight from their litany of treats. Then we stopped at a drive-in liquor store for a bottle of lemon sour. (I still don't really understand just what the hell a drive-in liquor store is.)

In a shopping mall parking lot, a live trout fishing pond was set up in a big rubber pool. Mark paid for a chance for Ben to hold a rod over the tank, but he didn't even get a nibble. Mark said you could do better by just throwing rocks at the fish.

LATE THAT AFTERNOON WE PASSED THROUGH A PARTLY built highway overpass. There was nothing to go under yet. Just a long double row of columns that in the lovely orange light of dusk gave it a ruined Greek temple look. I was driving. Mark didn't say a thing; he just turned full around in the passenger seat to keep his eye on the scene. I knew enough to stop on the shoulder and then back up to the site. Ben and I got out and stretched while Mark set up his tripod and did his photographer things. Even I could see that this was *National Geographic* material. *National Geographic*, and *Look*, and *Life* magazine, and *Arizona Highways*.

CHAPTER
23

FIFTY MILES DOWN THE INTERSTATE, WE HIT A BIG TRUCK-
station in Fargo. We had a pit-stop routine perfected
for those pre-self-serve days. Mark hopped out and gassed
us up. "Fossil fuels going down," he called out. "We're
dinosaur powered." I washed the insect-plastered windows and checked the oil. Ben got out and stretched. We
made like he was our ace, our Parnelli Jones. Meanwhile,
gas-station attendants got antsy.

The three of us walked into the cashier's area to look
at belt buckles and trucking magazines and electric cattle
prods. We could still hear the hypnotic drone of parked
semis and we were getting high on diesel fumes. A collie
sitting behind one of the counters yawned so wide that it
looked like it could have swallowed the cash register.
Mark and I caught it and yawned and then Ben heard us.
He fought a quivering lower jaw and lost. Medical science
has yet to develop an effective vaccine to prevent the
spread of a yawn.

Mark went back out and parked the Bronco next to a

row of idling semis. It looked like a rowboat among a fleet of huge ocean freighters.

Ben and I got a table in the attached restaurant. The place also had overnight rooms and showers and a TV lounge. This was no truck stop. It was a truck plaza.

Mark entered the eating area shortly after we sat down. "I'm going to bleed the lizard," he said as he walked by our table.

"Don't forget to wash your phalanges," I said.

One thing you get good at on the road is judging restrooms. Nothing compares to the great outdoors, of course, but we hit the whole spectrum of cans from the unfit to one that was actually labeled as a Certified Public Restroom. There was even piped-in music. I remember humming along to "Bridge Over Troubled Water." And you better believe that place was clean. I thought it was a health spa. It had a little dispenser of disposable toilet-seat covers ("Provided by the management for your protection") and it smelled like a florist's shop. There was also nothing written on the walls or if there was, it was taken off mighty fast. I hate the 180-degree version of that where you can't lock the door in a one-stool place with a springy toilet seat and high, greasy, yellow walls. And all the while you have to sit anxiously in the fetal position with one hand on the doorknob.

Actually, if you're coming off the road shaky and burned out, any lavatory with cold running water and a toilet that flushes will do. You rally. You get revived. You beat on your chest. They don't call them restrooms for nothing.

MARK CAME BACK TO OUR TABLE A SECOND TIME AND asked Ben to order for him. Then he headed for the pay phones to give Leslie a call. I read matchbook covers to Ben while we waited for some service. I told him how he could find success without college, or pick another career.

"Got any that are selling bust enhancers or X-ray vision glasses?" Ben asked.

"Afraid not," I said. "But here's a little bit of wisdom for you: 'Life is hard. Not only are we sometimes forced to eat shit, we can then be made to watch a videotape of it.'"

"Come on. It doesn't say that."

"Nah. I made it up," I said. "But somebody should put that on match covers or spray paint it on the walls of highway underpasses, don't you think?"

"It's a little bleak, you know. A bit gloomy."

"You're right," I said and leaned back in my chair. "I'd just like to see myself quoted someday."

WHEN MARK RETURNED, WE STILL DIDN'T HAVE ANY food. He looked radiant nevertheless. It was a case of phone magic. His loved-one's voice had just snuck along a wire right into his ear. He and Leslie had held hands from two hundred miles away. He was buoyed up. I feel like that sometimes after Mark calls me long distance.

That's one of the great things about travel in the great U.S. of A. Telephones. The telephone lines of our country are soul strings. Connections that keep us hooked up to the home front. It was very reassuring to me that no matter how far out on the American highways I was, I could call Mom or Dad or Mark if I was in a little emotional panic. Lewis and Clark couldn't do that. That's why I respected them so much. Forget pissed-off natives and blizzards and empty stomachs. They didn't hear voices that mattered for three years!

FUN FACT: Mr. Telephone, Alexander Graham Bell, was president of the National Geographic Society during its early years.

FINALLY, OUR FOOD CAME. I HAD ORDERED A MALTED milk and a cheese omelet.

"Who had the hard-boiled eggs?" the waiter asked.

"The young man over there trying to raise his sperm count," I said nodding toward Mark.

As high as he was after the call to Leslie, Mark can get pretty down about the state of the nation and the globe. And in that 1975 summer of our big trip, there was plenty for anyone to get down about. Even though Nixon had resigned the previous summer, Watergate was still daily news. Middle eastern terrorists were killing busloads of women and children. Patty Hearst was still on the run. India got nuclear arms. And talk of another Arab oil embargo would probably bring an end to the golden age of the American highway.

"Is there any hope for the old U.S. of America?" Mark asked Ben as he reached for one of Ben's french fries.

"There's no doubt about it," Ben said immediately. "We're just going through a little spasticity at the moment."

I guess I was expecting at least some minor contemplation from Ben. But it's so reassuring to hear someone give such a definitive answer.

Mark even looked a little better after that.

"Ben, what d'you say you and I get a couple of dog nuts for dessert?" Mark said meaning doughnuts and trying to puff up the cheeks of our Sherlock Holmes.

I WAS THE LAST TO FINISH EATING. I DRAINED EVERY BIT of my chocolate malt, the final pulls on the straw sounding like a toilet flushing.

"Well, I suppose," said Mark scraping back his chair.

I stood up and stretched. "Well, I suppose," I said.

"Don't we pay now?" asked Ben.

"No," said Mark. "We just thank them on the way out."

IT WAS DARK WHEN WE HIT THE ROAD AGAIN. 10:00 P.M. We had a good five hours of classic night driving ahead and it was about time we recovered our soaring form.

The big things seem to happen late at night. That's both on the road or otherwise. The exuberant thoughts, the dreams, the mind vistas. Things that during broad daylight you'd be afraid to talk about out loud.

But long-haul night driving has to be done cold, especially if you're on a solo. The windows should be down, the heater off. Loud radio can help, but if you're all alone and fighting the shakes and nods, I would also recommend driving with a full bladder. That will help keep your eyes on the road. It'll keep you sharp.

"Pull over, pull over," Mark said to me after we had just heard the 1:00 A.M. news. "I've got to do a Dr. Leaky real bad." Mark was not a believer in the full-bladder driving school nor was he driving. He started bouncing up and down in the passenger seat.

"No need to throw a shit fit," I said. I pulled onto the shoulder and parked with the engine running and lights on.

I got out and stretched. An inhalation of cool country air felt so good that I closed my eyes and did it again. There was no other traffic on the road and it was locked-in-a-closet dark.

I walked around the Bronco checking the tires, and stopped in front where I tried to warm my hands over the right headlight.

Ben had joined Mark and they were both standing in a little gully just off the shoulder. They were voiding, as the nursing-home lingo goes. Going tinkle.

"I won't look if you don't," I heard Mark say to Ben.

The radio was still on and I could just barely hear an early sixties instrumental, "Swingin' Safari." It's all horns and clarinets with kind of a bouncy beat. Suddenly, the radio was full blast. Mark must have turned it up. I happened to look out on the highway and there were Mark and Ben jitterbugging and jumping around. Right on the center line.

"Get the hell in here," I said. Then I hopped back into the driver's seat.

"Why?" Mark yelled. He and Ben were holding hands and bee-bopping on the loneliest highway in America.

"Because somebody might see you."

THE SONG AND DANCE EVEN GOT MY HIGHWAY JUICES temporarily going again. Mark and Ben napped. But I wasn't in a radio mood so I turned it off. The quiet and dark brought on a touch of the melancholy. I was lost in thought (or as Mark more appropriately says, found in thought). I was missing people back home and feeling like

I had my whole life to rearrange. There was graduate school to think about and getting a job. The Bronco needed a tune-up. If only I could have made a list right then and there, I would have felt a lot better.

I saw a lit-up, all-night drive-in theater screen from the highway and caught a subliminal glimpse of a hot, sweaty love scene. I laughed out loud thinking that if Mark was up, he would have made me stop right there in the middle of I-94 as he rummaged around for the binoculars and then fixed them on the screen.

I also got to thinking that Leslie was right about what she had said about me and Mark. I do overpower him. I don't give him enough rope. I don't give him a chance to return any favors. Then I thought that sometime after he moved to Chicago maybe I would ship my bicycle to O'Hare and then ask him to pick it up for me.

MARK TOOK THE WHEEL AFTER AN HOUR OR SO AND I napped in the front seat. I dreamed that my organic chemistry teacher, the beautiful and bumpy Miss Huxley, was helping me write up a lab report.

I think we were in the library. What was important was that she was sitting on my lap. I remember I had to reach around her to write anything down. I did a lot of writing. She was whispering answers in my ear. I don't know if the library was deserted or what, but we were having a great old time. I started to bounce her a little on my knee and we both started giggling. I felt the chair tipping over backward and we grabbed on to each other....

"Jesus H. Christ!" Mark yelled.

I snapped awake and hit my head on the dash. It took me a moment to realize I was in the Bronco. I wondered if I had been caressing Mark or something.

"Shit!" Mark said and pounded a fist against the steering wheel.

"What's up?" I asked. I was sitting kind of close to him.

"Dammit to hell."

"Come on," I said, "what's up?"

"You don't want to hear," Mark said.

"Hey, this is me. Your brother." Actually I thought for sure I had just violated our brotherhood.

"Remember when we left the truck stop at Fargo?" Mark said. "Well, we got on the freeway the wrong way. We've been heading back west for the last two and a half hours."

Jesus H. Christ! I said to myself. "Hey, that's okay," I said to Mark. "No sweat, we can handle it." Shit! Two and a half hours the wrong way.

We turned around at the next overpass. Ben was still out cold in back.

CHAPTER
24

ALL THE NōDōZ MUST HAVE BEEN IN THE BRONCO because it was running fine. But I wasn't. And Mark wasn't any better. We both had the shakes so bad we had to switch driving every fifteen minutes. Nothing worked to keep us sharp. Yelling and whistling. Full-blast radio. Putting our heads out the window. Somehow Ben slept through all the ruckus.

I eased off a little bad air during one of my stints at the wheel. Just a little poof. A bird fart. I glanced over at Mark. His eyes were closed but his nose twitched. Then he got a pained look on his face, like he had just heard a fingernail scrape across a blackboard. "Splatt," he said in a gravelly nap voice. Maybe by the twenty-first century the problem of offensive intestinal gas will have been worked out.

We crossed into Minnesota listening to an interview with Spiro T. Agnew.

I was on automatic pilot after a fitful doze in a wayside rest near Melrose. We were an hour away from the Twin Cities, so I just kept pointing the Bronco the right way.

Then I saw the gas gauge. It was on the wrong side of the big E.

I stopped at a Texaco station.

I knew Mark was out of money and I didn't want to wake Ben, so I reached into my pocket and found a buck twenty-five and three fossil hackberry seeds. I got a pop-machine Coke and one dollar's worth of gas, and then drove away with my comatose crew.

ON THE FREEWAY JUST OUTSIDE OF MINNEAPOLIS, I CAME over a hill and had to abruptly slow down for a several-hundred-car traffic jam. It was a daily rush-hour occurrence, but we hadn't seen this many vehicles in one place for three months. The skyline of Minneapolis popped up like a mountain range.

The slowing down woke up Mark. He didn't move from his modified fetal position, and his head remained propped against the window. His only movement was the blinking of his eyes in the new daylight.

"Looks like we went a little too far east," he said in a crackly, early morning voice as he looked out over the clogged highway. "Where are we? New York?"

"Minneapolis-St. Paul," I said. "Home of Twin City Triceratops."

Ben was unfolding in back and sat up stretching and yawning. The thirty-mile-an-hour pace was something else we hadn't experienced in a few months. It seemed like we weren't even moving.

Then I thought of a little slogan for Twin City Triceratops. I even imagined it on a sign that I would pound to the wall of some great big old warehouse in downtown St. Paul with bay windows and a skylight.

"TCT needs a motto," I said to Ben and Mark as if they knew what I was cooking up. "How's this sound? 'No one lies down on the job alone.'"

Maybe Ben and Mark were asleep with their eyes open, because they didn't say a thing. They didn't even nod or sniffle or shrug a shoulder. Or maybe it was just too early in the morning for company philosophy.

WE EVENTUALLY EXITED TO OUR NEIGHBORHOOD. WE looked around at the houses and lawns and parked cars in a bug-eyed daze. No one said a thing. I think I was even looking for fossil sign.

I went right through a stoplight and slammed to a halt, nose to nose with a vehicle that was where it should have been. You should have seen the stare I got from inside the other car. There is nothing quite like the cold, cruel look of a teed-off driver.

"Think he's pissed?" Mark said to me.

"Nah," I said backing up and letting him pass. "Probably just grossly disappointed."

ALL THREE OF US WERE RUMPLY AND STUBBLE-FACED. Petered out. The just-off-the-road look that wavers between looking like you've just gotten up, or like you've been up for a long, long time.

The Bronco itself didn't look much better. A partly eaten apple was rusting on the dash. An empty Mountain Dew can rolled around on the floor of the passenger side. And the back looked like a vacant lot. Crumpled candy wrappers, an empty box of graham crackers, loose gear trickling out of backpacks. All that was missing were some rodents running in and out among the garbage.

I STOPPED IN FRONT OF BEN'S HOUSE AND WE ALL JUST sat in the truck without saying a word. Early morning bird notes and children's playing voices wafted our way.

"Okey-doke," Mark said, suddenly opening up the passenger door. I got out too and met him at the back of the Bronco. He pulled down the tailgate to let Ben out. We all must have been car stiff because knees were popping and elbows cracking with every move.

Ben jumped from the truck onto the street. Then he started picking feathers off his tongue and spitting them out of his mouth. I looked in the back of the Bronco and saw that one of the goose-down sleeping bags had exploded.

"What happened to you, boy?" Mark asked as he

brushed some more feathers off Ben's back. "Look's like you just got laid in a chicken coop."

"I did," Ben said. Then he turned red-cheeked like the earlier, untainted Ben. "But I got found out by an old guy with a shotgun."

AS SOON AS WE DROVE AWAY FROM BEN'S, THE DEPRES-
sion set in. What the hell were we doing back in this beautiful, ordered city? What was Clarence up to just then? Were the Bakers back at the Bone Cabin? How were things in Ed, Wyoming? Where was Leslie? The trip really was over.

I still remember exactly how I felt at that time. Exactly. And it was totally different from how I thought you were supposed to feel and what you were supposed to do at the end of a long, character-building trip to the wilderness. I felt like shit. Grimy and grungy with a crink in my neck. I felt like pure, unadulterated shit.

What should have happened was for me to spring out of the Bronco when we stopped at Ben's and run over to Mark and clap him on both shoulders as I looked him square in the eyes. Then maybe Ben and I and Mark would all hug each other and bask in the glowing camaraderie like you see at the end of a great war movie as the credits roll over the closing scenes and the theme music builds and builds and the audience is collectively goose-fleshed and full of sniffles. That's what I expected our finish to be like. But except for the chicken coop bit, it was flat and burned out and had about as much zip as a stale, wet potato chip.

Actually, it's not until a few days after you're back that you can begin to savor a long trip like that. And then you realize that such a conglomeration of events will be hard to recapture. The moments of the dinosaur trip had had their own time. And that special aura of Mark and me and Ben and Leslie would be just as slippery. You can't do high school or college or the war over and have it be the same.

But the brain chemicals will always be there. The vision and smells and songs and feelings. Each and every one of them refrigerated in the head and heart forever, ready to bust out whenever they get warmed up by re-membering.

We don't have a slide of the end of the trip. The touching of home soil. The unpacking. Letting Ben out at his place. All of it went unrecorded. That wasn't like Mark; maybe he was out of film or just too beat to get it.

OUR HOUSE WAS LOCKED AND NO ONE WAS HOME. LUCK-ily, I still had a key. Dad was at work, and Mom and Pioneer Grandma were out. I suppose Anne was at school. We left the unpacked Bronco in the driveway. Mark stopped in the kitchen and opened the refrigerator. He took a long pull off the orange juice bottle and put it back without the cap on. I used the bathroom after catching myself from seeking relief in the backyard.

Mark called Leslie at her folks' several times but the line was busy.

Neither of us said anything. We looked at appliances and ran our fingers over furniture like we'd never seen the inside of a house before. The morning paper was laid out on the kitchen table and all I could think about was how it would look wrapped around a big fossil leg bone that was about to be plastered up.

"Let's hit the *NG* reading room," Mark said to me, meaning our old bedroom. In grade school, we'd stay up all night paging through *National Geographics*. In the morning there'd be magazines and maps lying all over the place. It gave the bedroom a ransacked travel agency look.

"I hope the folks didn't rent our beds out during our absence," I said as we climbed the stairs. I noticed Mark had grabbed a stack of old *National Geos* from the den.

MARK WAS SNORING BY THE TIME I HAD FINISHED MY second magazine. He was facedown on an opened 1956 *NG* that featured Nepal. I knew that because the last thing he said to me was something about us having to hit the Himalayas someday. Then he had held up the issue.

Mark sniffled and rubbed his face in his sleep. The little jerk-water was also probably drooling over a snow-covered Tibetan peak.

Sleep is such a vulnerable time. There you are out of control. You might pass gas or roll over or have something hanging from your nose and not be able to do anything about it. But it has its own beauty too. As I watched Mark rest, I felt like a dad who had just snuck into the nursery to watch his baby sleep.

I was grateful that however it worked out, Mark and I had been able to put a shoulder to life. Take a run at it full throttle. Together. Then Mark groaned in his sleep. A comfortable groan. There was a sunburned angel's smile on his face.

Sometimes I wonder if we would have been friends if we weren't brothers.

I KNEW MARK WOULD BE MOVING TO CHICAGO A WEEK or so after the big trip. He'd probably forget something important. Then I'd get a call. "Say, buddy, could you ship my thingamajig to Chicago for me?"

Of course, I would do it. Jump at the chance really. And then he might apologize and I will remind him that such things are a given within the laws of brothers in love, and that it is all something that was laid down a few billion years ago and is even more powerful and unexplainable than where the dinosaurs went.

CHAPTER
25

MARK DID MOVE TO CHICAGO. BEN DID GO TO WORK for the state. And I did nothing. Actually, I lived at home for the rest of that fall and winter and meditated about my future.

My room on the third floor became kind of an apartment. I got a hot plate and a little refrigerator and my own phone. The own phone is important, since Mark and I had twice-a-week long-distance talks, mostly at unholy hours.

Occasionally Ben got a call from Mark, but at human times like two in the afternoon. Mark usually called him at work. I'm sure that was so he could ask Ben outrageous questions like was he putting it to anybody in the office, or mainlining d-amphetamine to make it through the day. Ben told me all this, so I know he was glad the Chicago pervert was thinking of him from time to time.

I don't remember exactly what it was, but for sometime that year I was really teed-off at Mark. I mean like I never wanted to speak to the little beat-off again. So, for about two weeks I wouldn't answer my phone if it rang after midnight.

He owed me seventy-five dollars from the big trip and it seemed like every other day I was air freighting things that he had forgotten. But those were no big deals. It might have been something he said about Leslie. Ever since the trip, their romance was going belly up. I don't know. But I was burned up.

One night my phone rang every hour from ten o'clock on. Just four or five rings, but I knew it was Mark so I didn't pick it up. Eleven, twelve, one, the same thing. At 3:00 A.M. I answered it, since he probably would've kept calling for several days straight.

"Yah," I said. "What do you want?" I sounded a little harsh even to myself.

"I got a beauty for you, boy," he said. "It's the Kolbs." He was talking like there was nothing wrong. Like we had just talked that morning and didn't get to finish some important conversation.

"Hit me," I said. I was still wavering between apologizing and hanging up.

"Ellsworth Kolb got wind of some expedition to the Grand Canyon that the American Museum of Natural History was planning. Something to do with an isolated area by the North Rim called Shiva Temple. It was an unexplored forest-topped butte surrounded by desert. Scientists figured that there was a possibility that the Shiva Temple was a little island of ancient life. That living things unknown to man ran around up there. There was even talk about the last dinosaurs on earth being back in those woods."

Well of course I was into that story in about one sixtieth of a second. I didn't say anything, but Mark just churned away.

This was in the late 1930's. The Kolbs were probably the world's experts at Grand Canyon boating and hiking, not to mention that they were professional photographers. So, they offered their expertise at no charge. They'd lead the group to Shiva Temple and make a documentary film of the whole deal. But the museum not only turned them down, they said that only trained scientists would be members of the exploration team.

"They got dicked," I said.

"When I first read that," Mark said, "I wondered why they just didn't go ahead on their own. But listen to this. ... After eighteen months of planning, the official expedition began in September 1937. Without the Kolbs. The whole country was tuned in to the project by then. The papers called it the 'Journey to a Lost World.' A special telephone hookup was set up at the museum's base camp on the North Rim where over three hundred reporters and photographers had been hanging out for two weeks.

"Well, there weren't any dinosaurs in the Shiva Temple forest. Just a lot of squirrels and a few deer. The artifacts were the most interesting finds, but not the Anasazi pottery. The expedition leader found a large, framed black-and-white photo propped up on an easel. It was a self-portrait of the smiling and waving Kolb brothers with a little note that said, 'Welcome to the Lost World.'"

"That is a beauty, sweet," I said to Mark when he finished.

"I thought you'd appreciate it, sweet."

Then Mark caught me up on his own world and I told him that the walls of my room were still the same color. Mark told me a round-trip airplane ticket to Chicago was on the way up to me.

We talked for a good hour and a half until I said I had to salvage some kind of nap before daylight.

"Goodnight Moon," was all Mark said. Then he hung up and I held on to the receiver for a few seconds and even looked right at it wondering if he had really called but he must have because my ear was warm.

CHAPTER
26

THERE ARE SEVERAL PHOTOGRAPHS THAT I CONSIDER favorites, and whenever I think of them, they materialize in front of me like holograms. One I first saw on the wall of an old Czech dance hall. I assumed it was of a family gathering, a turn-of-the-century picnic perhaps. Twenty people are bunched together for the photo, but one fellow can be seen twice, on either end. With the seven- or eight-second shutter speeds of panning cameras, he must have changed spots in the middle of the exposure, shifting behind the group to the opposite side. His image is blurred in both places.

Another is Mark's and my Little League team shot. Three quarters of the ballplayers are not so subtly extending their middle fingers. (The swear word that you can make with your hands, as we used to call it.) Smiles are a little bigger than they should be and several lads are looking directly at the offending digits. This picture stood framed on my parents' mantel long after Mark and I had gotten our own private kicks out of it.

But my favorite of favorites is not really a photograph

at all. It's a more personal and private vision, unrecordable by any medium other than the chemicals of memory. It can be viewed with or without light, eyes open or closed. It is 3-D and five sensory and something I can step into and walk around in at any time. It's the mind film I have of Mark and me out in the field on the big trip with Ben.

I am not part of the scene right off. I see Mark cutting a tanned and strapping figure against the South Dakota Badlands. From outside the frame, I shake my head and smile. He is pacing back and forth, talking wildly to Ben about a find they are excavating. It looks like Mark is wearing a pair of tattered white gloves. But it's plaster on his hands. Fossil-hunter's blood Mark called it.

I usually enter at this point, about two ridges over from where Mark is. Stay right there, don't move, Mark hollers, running toward me. He tells me to keep my eyes closed and then he leads me by the hand to the site. I feel the hardened plaster on his palm. Then he lets me look. Ben is standing over the visible portion of a huge dinosaur femur. Fossil fragments are scattered over the surface. I yell and jump about in a manner appropriate for the occasion and grab Mark.

Then, in the picture we have a picture taken. It was dusk by that time. Mark's favorite lighting was that of near dusk. It supposedly brings out the exquisiteness of the red end of the spectrum and adds richness and depth to a photo. (The perfect light for a Pepsi commercial he always said.) First, the three of us together: two manic brothers arm in arm and Ben off to one side. This shot was time released, so there we all are smiling like everything for no one. Then just Mark and me, taken by Ben. Mark set Ben up behind the tripod and told him how to activate the cable release. Mark himself advanced the film and refocused between shots.

It turned out that there was a picture (35mm slide, really) of Mark and me in the Badlands. It is a fossil-hunting scene and probably time released.

I had found it taped to the west-facing window next to Mark's desk at his office in Chicago. It made me feel good to know that he kept an image of the two of us near him. And I noticed that from its mooring it could be seen best in the five-thirtyish light of the downtown Chicago afternoon.

On gray days or late at night when I can't sleep, I beam the slide up on the ceiling by propping the projector on a *Webster's New Collegiate Dictionary* and a paperback of Michener's *Centennial*. The images become a bit skewed, but they still take on life-size proportions. I can easily take it for a vision and reach out to touch my Kodachrome partner.

CHAPTER
27

CHICAGO IS NOT THE BADLANDS.

My last Chicago trip to see Mark was made under what you would call stressful circumstances. I got a phone call at work from him one day. At the time I had a part-time job in the admissions office of a community college. This was maybe nine months after the big trip. I could tell right away he wasn't doing well.

"How you been?" he asked. He sounded like he hoped I was better than he was.

"Fine. Fine. But you don't sound good."

"No, I'm all right." Then he asked me how I was again.

"Come on," I said, "what's up?"

"I don't know. It's Leslie. No, nothing really." He was speaking in a monotone. His voice petered out at the end of each sentence. I could hear the squeak of an inhaled cigarette. He was on the weed again.

"Hey," I said thinking of something that might get him fired up, "let's get to the Badlands next month. Fall might be a good time to bag a dinosaur."

He didn't bite.

"Can you come down?" Mark said. "To Chicago?"

Something real uncomfortable must have been going on.

"I guess so," I said. "When?"

"Now," Mark said and then I think he started crying.

"Well, sure. Let me check something out. Hell with it. I can skip a few days of work."

"Hurry up if you can."

Then I really got worried.

"What the hell's up?" I asked. My palms were sweaty. "Are you okay?"

"No," Mark said, "no, I'm not. Just get down here, will you?"

I tried to talk him down a little bit over the phone. Then I guaranteed I'd be there that night. When I hung up, I was ready to bolt out of the office and run my ass off all the way to Chicago. I got some leave time cleared, made a flight reservation, and called Mark again.

"I'm coming, buddy," I told him. "Sit tight. No, take a walk around the block. I'm on my way. See you tonight."

I didn't even go to my apartment first. Just cabbed it right out to the airport. I called Mark again before my plane left to make sure he was okay. No answer. I hoped he was just out on that walk.

I HATE PLANE RIDES. I'M NOT AFRAID OF THE PLANE crashing and me dying. Hell, that's nothing. It's just the thought of sitting in a claustrophobic little ball in that stuffy, packed fuselage for a couple of hours and not being able to open a window or step outside for some fresh air that does me in. So I usually get an aisle seat and then dive right into some reading. Any reading. Airline magazines, somebody's old newspaper, the disaster instruction cards. Something to let the words crowd out those nasty little claustrophobic panics that keep blistering up in my brain.

There's an okay part to flying once I settle down. It's really something to see mountain ranges and river valleys from the air. And it's rather twentieth century to take in a whole state in one look. But it's not like driving. You don't meet the people or get to sample regional radio or gas-station soda pop. Anxiety attacks aside, I'd rather drive than fly anytime.

Of course, on that particular trip I was worried about Mark, so the claustrophobia got left behind in the taxicab. I had never heard Mark so close to panic. I couldn't imagine what the hell was going on. He and Leslie were fizzling out again, but I had been down to Chicago three months before and he was fine. And all the other times too. I suppose I'd been down to see him two or three times since the trip. It's funny. I laugh even now. We hardly ever saw the big city during any of those visits. We stayed in his little, rat-piss apartment and talked and talked. All-nighter talks about American filmmaking and paleontology. Sometimes the subjects even merged. Mark wanted to do a big-time movie about Cope and Marsh and the nineteenth-century dinosaur bonanza. It was spring, and I was staying the weekend with him. (I had hitchhiked down!)

"It's all there," he told me as he jumped up from a couch and started dancing around the apartment. "Excitement, intrigue, the Great West. Indians. Conflict."

"What about the love interest, as they say?"

"Hell, yes. Got it. This brilliant, beautiful woman signs with a Cope field party as its illustrator. Only she cuts her hair an binds her chest and dresses as a man."

"I'm with you," I said.

"And she's not found out until months into the expedition, when a few of the boys catch her bathing and notice those wonderful and obvious reasons why their artist is not one of them."

"Eiyee, Gunga!" I said.

"So then, three men fall in love on the spot, one of them a Marsh infiltrator. You figure out the rest."

"Hey, that's all right!"

"Why don't you write the screenplay?" asked Mark.

"Sounds like it's already done," I said. "Why don't I just interview women for the bathing illustrator part."

And then on we'd go, both fired up and filling the room with great plans for more films and trips until our voices trailed off at about 4:00 A.M., just before the birds start up and the whole world is silent for one minute, as it takes its own deep, quiet breath.

GETTING TO CHICAGO FROM ST. PAUL SEEMED AMAZingly simple that day. With the cab ride and flight and express bus into Chicago from O'Hare, I was standing in Mark's apartment two and a half hours after his phone call. And I barely set a foot outside the whole time.

Just looking around Mark's place, I could see things must have been getting pretty bad. Mark was never Mr. Clean, but his apartment was always presentable. Dirty clothes sat in rumpled piles on the couch. Newspapers draped off two end tables and all the plants looked dead.

I touched a potted Norfolk pine, the only healthy-looking thing present. Every single needle fell off in one flick.

Mark picked up his guitar and started messing with it. He couldn't even play his one and only song.

We small-talked for a while and Mark started looking better. I would be staying two nights and a day. I was even going to follow him to work. He could tell me what he had to when he was ready.

"Looks like you're living in harmony with nature here," I said watching a cockroach crawl under a rug.

"You haven't seen the mice yet. I set out breakfast cereal bowls for them in the morning."

"How lovely," I said.

Mark told me what was going on at work. The legendary documentaries and Academy Award-winning feature films were in cold storage for a while, since things like food, clothing, and shelter were looming as nasty little realities. But sales-promotion films for liquor companies were softening those realities. So were food commercials. Mark was becoming expert at doctoring up food for the camera. Shaving cream didn't melt under hot lights and looked much better than the real stuff anyway. A little salt and liquid Ivory soap gave beer a nice frothy head. And it was standard to lacquer fresh fruit and vegetables. One of Mark's own innovations was to baste turkeys with several shades of brown paint and have burning incense hidden in the surrounding garnish.

"Those sons-a-b's looked so good," Mark said, "that people in the studio who didn't know picked at those turkeys between takes."

All of a sudden Mark jumped up and went into his bedroom. He came back with an old, beat-out 16mm projector that had a reel of film loaded and ready to go.

"You've got to see this," he said. He set up the machine fight in front of me. "This is some stuff I'm really proud of."

Then he turned out the lights.

"Flick the on switch," Mark said to me. He was standing two feet in front of the projector. I heard him unbuttoning his shirt. "Turn it on, brother," he said again.

I found the switch and the light shot out into the room but only as far as Mark's undershirt. Then I watched a little silent movie the size of an index card on my brother's chest. It was kind of his film portfolio. Snatches of black-and-white student films. Unused stuff from commercials. Some Chicago street scenes. It was all very nice, but I had to look around once or twice to see just where the hell I was. I mean here was this movie playing on the front of my brother's body.

"You've got a hell of an idea for a T-shirt there," I said to Mark when it was all done.

IT WAS OBVIOUS THAT WORK WASN'T CAUSE FOR MARK'S anxiety. Maybe it was all Leslie.

That particular week, Mark was working on a baked bean commercial.

"Anything special to hype up beans?" I asked.

"Nope," said Mark. "You just have to put the right light on a nice glazed pot of steaming Boston baked beans and they hold their own."

Baked beans hold their own, all right. Just ask Mel Brooks, who broke the passing-gas-on-film barrier with *Blazing Saddles*. Or ask the ghosts of thousands of real cowboys who lived on nothing but the famous prairie strawberries.

WE STAYED UP UNTIL 2:00 A.M. TALKING AND WATCHING *The Wizard of Oz* on late-night TV. My favorite part of *The Wizard of Oz* is when Dorothy and Toto hit Munchkinland and the film goes from black and white to color. Only we didn't get to see the switch that night. Mark's TV is a black and white.

In our prepuber years, it was a special deal to stay up late to watch something like *The Untouchables* on TV. That was the golden age of television. How little we appreciated the classics like *Omnibus* or *Howdy Doody* or *Rin Tin Tin*. I think I appreciated *The Mickey Mouse Club* show though. I was deeply in love with Annette Funicello.

After the national anthem, the TV went to static and Mark started talking about work again. But I wanted to get down to what was really going on.

"Cut the crap, babe," I said. "Tell me about you and Leslie."

He didn't answer me right off. His eyes misted up and he leaned back in his chair and looked at the ceiling. Then he got cranking. He went back to their high school and college days. All the little stuff about dances and parties and a couple of weekend trips I never knew about. Then he told me how they couldn't keep things together when he went to Toronto, but whenever he came home and they saw each other the old pilot light was lit again.

"So is that what's happening now?" I asked. "You're apart and the flame is low again?"

Mark took a full breath. He was rubbing his forehead with both hands. He said something I couldn't make out.

"What?" I asked.

Then Mark snapped forward in his chair and almost yelled. "The flame is out! O-U-T, out!"

Neither of us said anything for a good five minutes. Then Mark talked a little about the world and how it was all going to hell. He asked what Ben was up to and said we could sure use his mind in the White House of the United Nations.

"Or right here, right now," I said and laughed.

Well, that got us going on Ben for a while. Mark was looking better.

"You think Ben and Leslie are shacking up?" Mark asked. He was grinning like a maniac.

The phone rang and I picked it up. It was Ben. I held the receiver out to Mark. "Why don't you ask him," I said. "It's Ben."

Mark backed away from the phone like it was dangerous or evil, but then he took it in a daze. Pretty soon he was talking full bore.

Ben's call couldn't have been scripted it was so perfect. I had talked to him when I was waiting at the airport in Minneapolis and told him about Mark. I said a phone call would be nice, but to make it late. I forgot about it after that. I bet Ben set his alarm for 3:00 A.M. and then gave us the buzz.

Mark handed me the phone and went to take a shower. The earpiece was sweaty. Ben asked me if Mark was out of the room and could we really talk about him. I got kind of scared. Did I miss something? Mark was finally looking pretty good. Great even.

"It's not Leslie," Ben told me. "It's Mark. There in Chicago. I'm worried."

"So am I," I said. "I mean I was, then I wasn't, but now I am again. What the hell are you talking about?"

"What's happening now is just a little separation anxiety," Ben said. "An important relationship ends and the whole world goes bad. But he'll weather that."

"So what's the problem?"

"It's..." Ben said and then he sputtered and cleared his throat. I have never in my life heard Ben's voice waver until then. "I don't think we're going to have him much longer."

Ben's answer was so quick and clipped I thought I missed it.

"What, what?" I asked. "Who are you talking about?" But that was all Ben said and then he switched gears immediately to the Minnesota Twins or something. (Ben likes baseball less than dinosaurs.) So I shot the crap with him until Mark came back into the room and took the phone again for another ten minutes. While they finished their talk, I kept closing my eyes thinking that would make what Ben had said go away. I went into Mark's bedroom and rolled out a sleeping bag on the floor.

I heard Mark finish up with Ben. Then he came into the bedroom and stepped over me.

"Keep it down, girls," Mark said as he climbed into his squeaky bed. "My brother's staying over tonight."

I asked for a Kleenex and Mark tore a twelve-inch piece of toilet paper off an almost-expired roll sitting on his night table. It was the coarse, abrasive kind common to public restrooms. But it was functional.

"Didn't I tell you that boy was extrasensory?" Mark said about Ben.

"Goodnight Moon," was all I said. I might have smiled to myself for a second, but I couldn't get rid of what Ben had said.

"Goodnight cow jumping over the moon," said Mark.

SOMEHOW WE GOT UP AND MADE IT TO THE STUDIO AT more or less starting time. Mark didn't have an alarm clock. Hell, he didn't even have a watch anymore. He was on Indian time again, I suppose. If he ever did need the exact time, he looked out the window at a digital bank sign across the street. But you usually had to wait for a message and the temperature first.

Mark lived deep in the big city, close enough to walk to work. I was getting a bit claustrophobic on the way to the studio. I blew into town so quickly the night before, I forgot about the creeps I get in a big place like Chicago. You can't see the horizon or the sun. And those huge, hulking buildings press in on you like a humid day. I loosened my collar.

Mark must have seen my panic because he grabbed my arm. "Let's walk it off," he said and then quickened his pace. Hell, here I was supposed to be helping him out! We were two neurotic brothers whose fragile souls were leaning against each other like lightning-struck trees.

At the office, Mark introduced me to his main friend Tom as a screenwriter just in from the West Coast. I would have liked to play the role out, but my first question botched that. I had to ask what an editing table was.

I tried to keep out of everyone else's way and still stick pretty close to Mark. He looked all right. Preoccupied, but all right.

At lunch, Mark wanted to go for a walk. As soon as we got outside he started in.

"Watergate, terrorism, recession. Shit," Mark said running in front of me and walking backward so he could look my way. "I don't ever want to see a newspaper again or watch another TV news show. I don't want to hear about all that negative crap."

"You brought it up," I said. "It's just the American Dream turning into fecal matter."

Mark was walking by my side again.

"Let's just take a walk and not say anything," Mark said.

"Okay. No sweat. Whatever you want."

But we said a lot. I let Mark take the lead. He talked a little bit about Leslie again. But mostly, he got into what one's direction in life is all about.

"The tools are important," Mark said, "and the plan. You've got to have the tools and the plan."

It sounded for a moment like he was talking about equipping a dinosaur-hunting expedition.

"But you've got to have the fire first," he said shaking both fists. "Writing, making movies, raising kids. I don't care what it is, you've got to know what you're doing, and goddamit, you've got to believe in yourself. Believe in what you're doing. The fire is the name of the game!"

Mark was so loud and visible with his gesturing and all that people on the sidewalk stopped to look at us. Some cars even slowed down and rolled their windows open to hear what was going on.

I don't know what expression I gave to the lookers, but I do know that in my mind I was nodding my head and saying, "Folks, that's my brother."

We finally stopped at a Vienna Sausage Shop and ordered a couple of hot dogs to go. H. dogs Mark calls them. In the middle of a big crowd at the Sausage Shop I felt this horrendous sneeze coming on. I reached into my pocket for a Kleenex and kept pulling out a long, continuous piece of tissue. It must have been an easy four feet long. I did catch the sneeze with one end of it. People backed off from me like I had the Black Death or something, but more worried, I'm sure, about the toilet-paper streamer draped across my body and onto the floor than the sneeze.

THAT NIGHT MARK SUGGESTED WE GO TO A MOVIE. *Midnight Cowboy* was making a Chicago rerun.

Now *Midnight Cowboy* wasn't exactly what you would call escapist material. It's a nice film, but a little on the dark side. By the time only a third of the movie was over, Mark was a case and a half. At first he was just shifting around in his seat. Then he was hyperventilating. Halfway through the film, Mark was standing in the back of the theater. I got up and went to check on him.

"You all right?" I said putting a hand on his shoulder.

He didn't say a thing. He just stared straight ahead, breathing hard and fast.

"Let's get out of here," he said. Then he turned around and headed out into the lobby.

"Hey, wait for me," I said. "I've got to get my jacket." Then I did my best to relocate my seat, get the jacket, and run out again.

When I got to the lobby, I couldn't see Mark. I panicked. I was looking frantically for him in the lobby and the men's room and smoking lounge. No Mark. I felt like a parent who had just lost his baby in a state fair crowd.

I pushed a glass door open and started to go outside.

"You can't get back in once you leave," an usher told me.

Jesus! Where was Mark? I stood in the entryway holding the door open, looking over the lobby again and then back outside. There he was. Sitting on the curb. I ran over to him. His head was in his hands. He was one big muscle spasm.

"Motherfucker!" I said. "Don't run away like that. It's going to be all right."

"I can't breathe," Mark said.

"Slow down. Slow down," I said. "You're going to be

okay." I was sitting on the curb next to him with my arm
around his shoulders.

I stopped a cab and almost had to push him into it.

"Where to?" the driver asked as he drove off.

Mark didn't answer and I didn't know where he lived.

"Where's your place?" I asked Mark.

"Twenty-fifteen North Wells," he said.

"Twenty-fifteen North Wells," I told the driver. I was
holding Mark's hand now. I suppose the driver had his
own interpretation of the scene.

BACK IN THE APARTMENT, I OPENED THE WINDOWS AND
turned on the lights and the radio, which didn't work, so
I flicked on the TV just for some background noise. I was
going to get some life back into the dump.

Mark sat stiffly on the couch and I went over and sat
next to him.

"Count with me," I said thinking it would get his mind
off of whatever was paralyzing him. "One, two, three,
four, five . . ." He only breathed more quickly.

"My chest is so heavy," he was barely able to say.

I was sweating. My heart was doing double time. I was
scared too. How could I get him to an emergency room
I wondered. And if I did and if they locked him in a psych
ward, I'd stay right with him.

Mark's face was turning gray. He looked like he was
about to go under. I think about then I said some kind of
prayer. Yes, I'm sure I did, but I don't have the slightest
idea what form it took. And then it came to me. A bag.
A goddamned paper bag!

I jumped up and ran to the kitchen and started flinging
open drawers and cupboards. Thankfully, I found a brown
bag right away and returned to the living room.

"Breathe into this," I told Mark as I put the bag to his
face like a gas mask. Then I rubbed his back. "Slow down,
buddy, slow down."

His breathing and mine synchronized. "Nice," I said,
"and easy. That's it. Relax."

He began to loosen up and ease back onto the sofa.
Then he lay down. Thank God, it was over. I wiped my

forehead and stretched my neck and shoulders. Wow! We were both sweaty.

"God bless this home, sweet," I said.

"Amen, sweet."

I suddenly got very hungry and thirsty. A quick, standing-in-the-kitchen-doorway survey revealed your basic empty cupboard. I noticed Mark had been using a letter opener for a butter knife. When I was sure Mark was settled, I left the apartment to find an all-night grocery. Twenty minutes later I had a frozen pizza in the oven and Mark and I were sipping prune juice.

"Prune juice?" Mark said after a long pull from his glass.

"That's all they had left in the beverage department," I said. "Unless you're into baby formula."

"I guess not. But you better get back there and get some diapers for the both of us."

It wasn't just Leslie that Mark was all topsy-turvy about. It was also the state of the world. The universe. Humanity in general. It was some of the things he told me about on the walk at lunch. He had been having these crippling anxiety attacks for about two weeks. A great song or a moving story would set it off. Mark always did like to tie into the global picture.

"I have so little faith in the human race," Mark was saying. "I'm not talking about terrorists and wacko sociopaths, I'm talking about our everyday you and me. We pollute. We lie. All we want to do is make a fucking buck."

I really didn't know what to say but something that sounded reasonable came out.

"You've got to take the human race on a one to one," I said. "There are good people left. Look at Clarence. Look at Pioneer Grandma and our own folks. Good solid human beings who care about each other."

Mark went over to a window that was held open with a twelve-inch ruler.

"There's a lot of assholes out there," Mark said looking outside. "All I see here are these beat-off account people in Mercedeses who think the world hinges on buying TV time."

"We need to hit the road again," I said. "You've got to clean out your system."

"The product hype you get just turning on the radio or TV or looking at *People* magazine is so bullshitty," Mark said. "So small. All this go-for-the-gusto and life-in-the-fast-lane crap. As if life gets its meaning from beer and mouthwash and tight jeans. And I make some of that crap."

"The world's always been screwed up," I said. "There's just more of us doing it now and we find out about it sooner."

"It's a chickenshit world," Mark said. "And not just in the ad world."

"You got it," I said. "Nobody wants to take a stand. The country can't pass an equal rights amendment. Domed football stadiums get more backing than schools. Millionaire jocks hold out for more money. Shit. Now I'm getting depressed."

"And they're all just nice people doing their jobs," Mark said.

"The world is full of nice people doing their jobs," I said.

"Think of the greed, the ungratefulness. People don't know how good they've got it. They should be glad just to be alive or to see a sunset or to take a whiff of a country breeze. Does it matter that they have friends or brothers and sisters or parents? Is there anybody left who gives a shit?"

"There's you and me," I said. Then I tried to lighten things up. "We've got out priorities straight. Fame, money, and power are the big three. Then somewhere down the line is family, church, and state."

"From top to bottom," Mark said. But he was just humoring me. "Hey, who the hell are we, anyway? Just because we're lucky enough to dig dinosaur and drive all night and visit sick grandmas, what makes us so righteous?"

"Somebody's got to have the right answers," I said. "And it might as well be us."

Mark stood up and started pacing back and forth.

"I've been going to church again," he said as if apologizing. "Do you believe it?"

"Do what you've got to do, man."

"Not on Sundays though. In fact, not even for Mass. I'll just go there and sit. After work. It's quiet and it smells just barely of incense and nice old furniture. Sometimes I think I hear beautiful voices warming up with a little Gregorian chant. I get goose bumps."

"Sounds like the Badlands," I said.

"It's not the genuflections and every Sunday Masses and holy water fonts. It's the feeling. The feeling that somebody, something bigger than all of us put together, has been here before, has laid down the path, and is taking care of us."

"That is mighty fine," I said.

"I don't know what it is," said Mark. "But as much as we human animals need each other, we need something else too."

"The Badlands?" I said. "Dinosaurs? The solar system?"

"The feeling that they all give is what I'm getting at. That to know how minuscule we feel by looking at the moon or trying to imagine the millions of years back to dinosaur time is really just to know how great it is that we are all part of one mad, grand plan."

"What about," I said and stopped, carefully measuring what I wanted to say, "you and me? As brothers? Do we fit into that plan?"

"We are the other end of the scale," he said hitting fist to palm. "That's what life is all about. On the one hand is the astounding wonder of earth and nature, and on the other hand is you and me. People who matter. Friends, family. The real reasons we get out of our sleeping bags every morning."

Mark was walking around the room again. Then he turned to me.

"Hey!" he said kicking a footstool so hard that a poof of dust rose off it. "And you and me, we are as tight as they make them."

I think I just sat there biting a quivering lower lip. Then

I said something crazy, although it was true. As if it followed from what Mark had just said.

"The Russians are trying to implant frozen woolly mammoth sperm into modern-day elephants."

Mark sat down on the footstool and looked at me. He ddn't say anything, but I could see that he was misty-eyed and that he understood.

I WAS LEAVING THE NEXT DAY BUT I WALKED MARK TO the studio first. He told me he was going to give Leslie a call when he got up to the office, but that it really was over between them and they would both be okay. Then he asked me to knee Ben in the nads for him.

From a bus stop across the street, I watched Mark climb the steps to the main entrance. I'll never forget how he looked. An occasional car or truck passed between us, but I could see that he had regained some of the old vigor, even though he still looked a little tentative. My heart crossed the street to him. Before entering the building, Mark turned my way and let out an ungodly whoop. Then he signaled the thumbs-up, it's okay, high sign. I bused it out to O'Hare. That was the last time I ever saw Mark.

CHAPTER
28

THERE WERE TIMES WHEN I WONDERED IF MARK WAS as committed to our brotherhood as I was. I'd get to thinking that maybe I cooked it all up. That Mark merely tolerated my weekly long-distance phone calls. That he really could give two shits about dinosaurs and the Badlands and us someday being film-crew partners. That's about when he called me late at night or I'd get a book from him in the mail (wrapped in newspaper and plaster, like some fragile fossil).

We actually did kind of start the film-crew bit when Mark first moved to Chicago. He was in Texas for six days to shoot the International Chili Festival for an Alka-II commercial. He got the job on last-minute notice, so he was down there by himself. He hired a lighting and sound man in Dallas and they headed two hundred miles through the desert to Dust Bowl, Texas. The actors and actresses were coming for the final three days. I got a call after the first day of background shooting.

"Sweet, get your ass down to the Dallas Airport."

"What'd you do, forget something there?"

"I need you down here for a big commercial shot," he said. "Alka-II. We're doing it in 35. It's the big time for a change."

Hell yes I'd be down there. I wasn't working at the time, but I had enough cash for the round trip, which Mark said to put on the IOU sheet.

THE NEXT DAY I WAS STANDING AT THE LUGGAGE CLAIM of Dallas Airport. It was early evening. My major concern at that moment was if my underwear would come streaming out of the baggage chute one by one. Then I got a little tap on the shoulder.

"Emery Kolb, I believe?" said Mark. "The great Grand Canyon cinematographer?"

"Yes," I said in fake disgust, "and who, may I ask, the good Christ are you?"

MARK AND I LOVE TO STAND AROUND IN AIRPORT LOBBIES and make spot assessments of people. We were sure we could pick out the rock stars and athletes and writers and people sneaking out of town for affairs in warmer climates. All that was easy. We'd get into the finer points too. Like how many kids some businessman had at home or where a lonely-looking, skin-headed marine was off to and what was on his mind. And Mark swore he could tell a divorced woman at a glance. We just kind of did on-the-spot vignettes from the conveyor belt of people moving by.

We had a quick orange juice and roll in the Dallas Airport coffee shop. Mark was eyeballing this beautiful middle-aged woman with a little poodle on a leash who had sat down at a table across the room. Mark said he wanted me to go over and introduce myself and start talking to her. "She's lonely," he said. "Newly divorced. And rich. But she no longer has the attention and affection she's been accustomed to."

I don't know if Mark had me under hypnosis or what, but I stood right up and walked over to her table. I started blabbing about Russian literature and Impressionist painting and the ecology movement. The woman didn't say a thing, but she was smiling and nodding her head so I just kept on talking. Then I got into how Mark and I both worked in the movies and what big plans we had for our cinematographic futures. Mark came over about then and sat right next to her. When I stopped talking for a moment to take a drink of ice water, she asked us just what it was we did with film. Then Mark tells her straight out that we were ushers. I kind of looked around like I didn't know where that answer came from, but she didn't ask anything further and then Mark said it was nice visiting but we had to get going.

Actually, we had to be back in Dust Bowl by the next morning, so it really was time to vamoose, as they say.

We whipped out of the airport in a new white Ford station wagon that was buffed with red Texas dust. All the film gear was in back and there was a half-eaten pizza in a box on the front seat that I didn't want to see go to waste. The pizza, that is.

It was dark on the road and Mark was going an easy eighty-five or ninety. It was Halloween night.

"Say, where'd you get this car?" I asked. "Is it hot?"

"The big Number Two," Mark said. "They try harder."

The tires whined like I've never heard tires whine before. Like they were about to disintegrate. I suppose Mark had laid an airstream to the airport in the first place, and there we were winging back through the desert without the tires or the car having cooled off.

"Maybe you better slow down a bit," I said. The red temperature light had come on.

"If we aren't in that little shit-kicking town by morning," Mark said, "I'll lose the job." Then he actually sped up.

I think it was about 9:30 P.M. when the left rear tire tread separated from the main body of the wheel. We wumped to a stop on the side of the highway. We were lucky the car didn't flip or spin out of control. Mark jumped out to change the tire. Steam slipped from between the hood and fenders. Mark was swearing in back. I got out to help.

We had to handle the destroyed tire with a towel it was so hot. After the spare was put on, the car wouldn't start.

"Jesus H.!" Mark said. He got out and paced back and forth alongside the wounded vehicle. "We've got too much gear to hitchhike."

Somebody stopped and then went on ahead to call a tow truck that pulled us to a gas station in the next town. The station was closed and the car still wouldn't start. Mark called Avis back in Dallas and they said they'd send a car along in two hours.

We couldn't leave the vehicle with the camera gear and it being Halloween and all, so Mark and I tried to get some sleep hunched up against our respective doors. Usually I can sleep anywhere. On my feet even. But not that night. The car was pelted with eggs at least three times, and every fifteen minutes, the hollering face of a costumed kid would look in one of the windows.

About midnight the reinforcements arrived. Ours. An Avis mechanic with a new vehicle. We got the better end of that deal, although I suppose he could fix the dead car.

We transferred the equipment and away we went. Originally, I was hoping to do some fossiling on the way to Dust Bowl, but not after that. I was just hoping that Mark wouldn't burn out this car and blow the commercial.

Mark does not learn well from experience. Speedometers in 1976 cars still went up to 120 mph. Mark used it to the fullest.

There was a little radio and a little talk, and then I conked out.

WE WERE STOPPED ON THE ROAD WHEN MARK SHOOK ME up. I thought I had dreamed about getting the replacement car. Then I saw that this one was blue.

"Hey, look at the sunrise!" Mark was saying. 'We've got to get this."

The mountains were purple and copper. Outstretched saguaro arms were silhouetted against red beams of light. It was the holy sunrise scene known so well to the Indians of the southwest. The ones that were supposed to be drug freaks. Hell, I bet peyote is a placebo. You can hallucinate just looking at the wonder of the earth down there.

We climbed a foothill for a better angle. I carried a big tripod and equipment bag. Mark was telling me to watch out for rattlesnakes and scorpions and poison cactus. I was looking for dinosaur bones but only saw a couple of rusty beer cans.

The tripod wouldn't hold on the side of the hill, so I had to brace the thing up while Mark shot the panorama. (It turned out to be a beautiful opening for an entirely different commercial.)

We made it to the festival in time to meet the talent and the client's agents. I was a hotshot film gofer for the next three days. Clapping the slate, holding reflectors, changing film magazines, and eating lots of chili. The worst thing was trying to ease off voluminous amounts of bad air while standing next to these incredibly beautiful actresses. You smile and clear your throat a lot.

CHAPTER
29

I SUPPOSE IT WAS FITTING THAT I FOUND OUT OVER the phone. Mark's and my brotherhood was a long-distance affair that was nurtured along by AT&T. Mark told me that sometimes when he called from Chicago and I wasn't home, he let the phone ring and ring. Maybe fifteen or twenty times. Just enough, he said, to stir up the air in the room and let me know that he had been there.

I have such a naïve wonder about something like a long-distance phone call. To me, Mark's area code and phone number were a magic set of Arabic numerals that in the right combination materialized my brother's voice.

Pioneer Grandma told me that Mark used to call the telephone a "hello." In grade school, I strung up one of those homemade phones between our rooms that they tell you how to make in Cub Scout manuals. The orange juice cans with wire between them. I guess they worked, but Mark did have a loud voice.

* * *

THE BAD NEWS CALL WAS NOT FROM CHICAGO AND NOT from Mark. It was from my father, five miles away on the other side of St. Paul. I had just come into my apartment from an afternoon bike ride and was eating a whole-wheat bagel with Swiss cheese when the phone rang. I recognized my father's voice. It was shaky. I knew something wasn't right.

"What's wrong?" I said. "It's Grandma. Grandma's gone, isn't she?"

"Come to the house right now," was all my dad said. He said it in a tone that I'd never heard before.

"Tell me!" I said and then I swore, which I usually don't do in front of my parents. "Tell me right now, goddamit!"

"It's not Grandma," he said. "It's Mark."

"What?"

"Mark. He was in an accident in Utah. He was killed in a car wreck."

"Oh no!" I said. I sat back in a chair and felt like I'd just been kicked in the gut. "No, no."

"Come over right now," my dad said. Then I think he started to cry.

I hung up the phone in a daze. It was a Saturday. Four P.M. An otherwise beautiful June weekend afternoon. Outside, people were bike riding and washing windows. Lawns were being sprinkled. Insects buzzed around on new wings. The streets and houses were all ordered and unchanged. And my brother was gone.

I called my dad back and told him I'd be there in an hour. Then I went outside and ran. I'm not a jogger. I just ran because I didn't know what else to do. I ran and ran. My windpipe burned. My sides ached. My nonrunner's clothes were all sweated up. But I ran harder. I wanted to make it hurt. By the time I got back to my apartment, I suppose I had run seven or eight miles. Then I drove to my parents'.

Anne was there. Pioneer Grandma was up in her room and my mother said she didn't know yet and that maybe we'd better leave it that way for a while. Other than that we didn't say much. We just kind of leaned together and let the tears go.

I don't remember exactly what happened after that. I know the phone started going and didn't stop. I became the family telephone dispatcher. It seemed like I spent the next two days on the phone. I put off calling Ben and Leslie.

MARK'S CHICAGO PEOPLE WERE AT THE STUDIO WHEN I called. I talked to his friend Tom first. When he heard my voice he sounded happy. I remember thinking that maybe there was some horrendous mistake and maybe Mark was in Chicago working at that very moment.

"Is Mark there?" I asked Tom. I don't know if I was sounding Tom out to see if he knew or if I wasn't sure about the news myself.

Tom told me I'd be lucky to catch Mark at work during the week let alone on a weekend. Mark was doing some filming in Utah. Then he was going to start BS'ing in general (I would have too if I didn't know what was up), so in a panic I just blared out that Mark was gone, killed in a car accident the night before.

"No way!" Tom said. "I just talked to him yesterday. Don't mess with me on this."

I told him three or four times and he still wouldn't believe it. It was a mistake he said. Some bad joke. Then he told me he was going to hang up and call the Utah highway patrol himself.

BEN ALREADY KNEW AND HAD BEEN TRYING TO CALL our house for over an hour. He said he heard it on the radio—Chicago filmmaker drowns after driving off mountain road. That was too much and not enough for me to hear, so I didn't really process what Ben said. Ben was coming to the house when he could get a ride.

I think I could feel Leslie's heart stop when I told her. She was crying so hard she had to hang up and I figured she'd be right over too.

Sometime in there, I went for a ride in the Bronco. I really didn't go anywhere, I just drove around town. I was feeling kind of other-worldly. Like I was floating along.

I drove through stoplights and didn't look at intersections. I turned the radio on but snapped it off before I heard anything. Then I stopped at a little overlook above St. Paul.

Mark had been dead about fourteen hours before we knew about it. I think I was at a party when it happened. Goddamn, he drove off a cliff! I was thinking that I should have been there to fend it off. I should have talked to him that day and told him to be careful. At least I should have felt a stab to the heart the moment he was killed.

Back at the house there was a new set of relatives and friends. I saw my mom and Leslie sitting on the couch with their arms around each other. I hadn't seen Leslie in months. I know that she and Mark talked only occasionally but had still been on good terms for former sweethearts. Leslie had a new boyfriend I heard.

Ben had gotten a ride over and he was, well, he was Ben. The stalwart. Composed but grieving in tone and posture.

"I lost a good friend," I heard him say to Anne. "I can't believe I'll never see him again."

I squeezed Ben's elbow and steered him out of the crowd into the TV room. I had to ask him about that late-night phone call back in Chicago. He sat down on the couch and I stood in front of him.

"You knew all the time, didn't you?" I said.

"About what?" said Ben.

"About Mark," I said. "About Mark going to die."

"I have no idea what you're talking about," Ben said. He looked mad. Then he stood up and walked right past me. Brushed me aside almost. I watched him find his way back into the living room and sit down by Leslie and my mother.

We soon dropped into the ritual of the leftover of the loved one who has died far away. It's not something you read about or rehearse. You just dive into it and are glad you have something, anything, to do. Anne and Leslie were looking through old pictures of Mark trying to find one for the undertaker. They were laughing and crying and holding up photos for us to see. Growing-up pictures. Baby pictures. Some of Mark's own first dreadful artsy-craftsy pictures. Anne put a nice shot of him sitting in the backyard on the mantel. People who came over gathered around it like it was a little shrine.

There was a lot of talk about the young dying so unnecessarily. What the hell, I don't know if there's any good time for the lights to go out. But maybe the mid-twenties is the worst. A baby dies and a cuddly bundle of love is missed. At fifteen or sixteen we say he or she was a good kid, but what we don't say is that actually it was a life without meat. At eighty, it was a full life. But Mark at twenty-three? We're talking about a finalized human being who was just taking the first full strides forward.

Tom called me back and sounded pretty bad so I knew that he knew for sure. He got all the specifics from a highway patrolman in Salt Lake. Mark had been in Utah making a short documentary film about ski areas in summer. (We knew that.) The patrolman figured Mark was coming home from a party at Alta in a borrowed car and missed a turn. He estimated the time of death as 4:00 A.M. Instant death he had told Tom, with no pain. (I don't know how the patrolman knew that, but I wasn't going to question it. I didn't care if he made it up.) The body was discovered almost right away when a bread delivery driver noticed the wreck in a ravine below the road.

Tom must have felt just like me because I wanted to know everything about what happened, and he had it all. Mark was found faceup in a shallow stream twenty yards from the car. He probably wasn't wearing a seat belt, because he went through the windshield. And so on and so on. At the time, I needed to know as much as there was to know.

I GUESS ALL OF THIS TOOK CARE OF SATURDAY AND SUNday. Monday, Mark's body was going to be flown in. The wake would be Tuesday, the funeral Wednesday. Somewhere in there the Chicago people would be coming in.

Pioneer Grandma stayed in her room upstairs the whole time. We hadn't told her yet. Mark was always right up there on her list. She thought he would be President.

That's President of the United States of A. Mark thought that would be like being sent to the penal colonies, but for Grandma it was about the best thing she could say.

I was camping out at my parents'. I think it was late Sunday night that I heard Grandma moving around. Everyone else was asleep. I got to thinking that maybe she did know what happened. She must have heard some of the coming and going downstairs. I got up and went into her room. She was in bed but still awake.

I was going to be the strong, silent comforter. I would be there if she wanted to ask me anything or maybe cry a little. I lay down next to her on the bed, outside the covers. When I put my arm around her, she squirmed a little bit.

"Is my arm too heavy?" I asked.

"No. It's not heavy," she said. "But are you staying all night?"

MONDAY MORNING LESLIE AND I WENT TO THE AIRPORT in the Bronco to pick up Mark's gear. She had asked to go with and I was glad to have her along. She knew Mark and I had had quite a talk on that last Chicago visit. Leslie and I had quite a talk of our own on the ride out.

"How did he look when you left him?" she asked. "Was he okay?"

"He was great," I said. "He was fired up. Ready to go at it."

"I thought so," said Leslie. "I hoped so."

Then Leslie told me Mark had called her right after that visit and told her how glad he was I had come down. "Goddamn fucking glad" were the exact words, she said.

"I am so grateful for that visit," I said. "It scares the shit right out of me to think how I'd be now if I hadn't gone."

We were pulling off the highway onto the airport exit ramp. Leslie reached over and grabbed my wrist and looked right at me.

"I hope you don't think this is cold," Leslie said to me. "I'd gotten over Mark and me as sweethearts. Not that it was easy. If he was sitting here right now I'd probably be in love all over again." Then she started shaking and sobbing and I do believe I was in a similar state.

By the time we parked the Bronco and walked to the baggage claim office, we were both a little steadier.

Mark didn't have much with him. Just a suitcase and a couple of backpacks. The camera equipment had been rented and that was sent from Utah straight back to the Chicago supply house where he got it.

We started looking through his stuff right there in the baggage claim area. His wallet didn't have any money in it, but that wasn't any different from when he had it on him. Leslie buried her face in an armful of sweaters and shirts. "You little bastard," she said when she came up for air. "You dear, wonderful, little bastard."

I pulled a book out of a pack. *The Moviegoer* by Walker Percy. It was my copy. I had sent it to him before the Utah trip. There was a Raleigh coupon sticking out of it marking pages 136 and 137.

We had thought about meeting Mark's body too, but figured that would be best left up to the undertaker.

It's funny, but Mark's and my best talks were either on our trips or coming and going to airports. As far as the airports go, there were plenty of those times. Mark was always zipping in and out of town, so in those fifteen, twenty or thirty minutes we usually got right down to the bone.

I couldn't get hold of Mark the day before he left for Utah. I called four times without connecting. But really there was nothing left to take care of. Things were as cleaned up between us as they ever would be.

I drove Leslie back to her parents' house. She asked if she could have *The Moviegoer* and I was glad to hand it over.

BACK AT THE HOUSE, MORE PHONE CALLS, MORE PEOPLE, more sorrow. But our sorrow as a family was being numbed and diluted. We were starting to console others who were hearing for the first time that we had lost a son and brother and fellow dinosaur digger. Your own soul is still weighted down, but you're actually feeling sorry for the people you have to tell.

MONDAY AFTERNOON I WENT BACK OUT TO THE AIRPORT to pick up the Chicago people. Tom and I kind of stuck close for the next couple of hours. We never really knew each other but in a way we kind of did because we knew Mark. We had this silent rapport that sometimes takes over in times like that. He called me a little whorelet after I mentioned something about matey to him. But I think we both knew that neither of us could replace Mark for the other. Besides, Tom hated dinosaurs and I couldn't operate an Instamatic camera if you paid me.

THE WAKE WENT BY LIKE A LONG MOVIE THAT I WAS sometimes in and sometimes just watching. Aunts, uncles, cousins, work people, school people, friends, neighbors. I can't tell you how many people I saw actually double over when they were hit with the sight of Mark lying there in the open coffin. Ben stayed with Leslie for most of the service.

I never understood the need to see the laid-out loved one until that night. The grief is not whole without that sight. You need it for your sorrow to peak. Then it can turn to the long, gradual down slope.

I touched Mark on the hand when no one was looking. He was mighty hard. I thought I saw plaster under his fingernails. Maybe he'd been doing a little fossiling out there in Utah.

At a wake, everyone feels bad, but you can pick out the ones who've been down that road before. I felt the worst for the people who hadn't talked to Mark in maybe two or three years.

AFTER THE WAKE, I SHOWED AN HOUR AND A HALF'S worth of trip slides back at the house. Five full trays. Mostly from the big trip with Ben.

A lot of people got turned on to the Badlands that night.

There was a time when Mark and I could barely talk about where we were going because of the crap we got. There were enough people asking to go to the Badlands that night so that I could have formed a major expedition right then and there.

Looking around in the slide-show light, I saw quite a few beaming, misty-eyed faces. I think Mark's soul had slipped into the room and put its arm around all of us.

ANNE AND MY MOTHER HAD MADE ALL THE FUNERAL arrangements. Casket, grave site, pallbearers, church. Leslie did two readings and Ben took care of the music. "Day by Day" from Godspell, an instrumental that he composed, and a booming, soaring version of Seals and Croft's "We May Never Pass This Way Again" that left the packed church short of breath. "Johnny B. Goode" and Handel's Hallelujah Chorus would have been perfect finales, but maybe a little too schitzy.

Mark was buried in a Catholic cemetery just outside of St. Paul. Farmland lapped up against the edge of the grounds. Prairie land. And just a little farther west was dinosaur country. While I didn't actually see any digging or shoveling or even the casket being lowered into the grave, I thought that Mark's return to the earth was kind of a reverse fossil-hunting procedure.

I had put a few things in Mark's casket to be buried with him. The old picture of the two of us on a teeter-totter when with and so did a film can with four little fossil hackberry seeds inside. But I'm sure what Mark appreciated most was the extra set of Bronco keys I slipped into his coat pocket.

THERE WAS A FINAL GATHERING AFTER THE FUNERAL AT my parent's with about fifty or sixty people. So many people brought food and silverware and extra plates and were helping in the kitchen that my mom couldn't find some utensils for months afterward. I myself found a dried-up piece of ham in the fork drawer a week later.

It was a glorious gathering on a glorious day. Mark

stories and anecdotes flew about the backyard like sparrows. In fact, I was pointing out from which upstairs window Mark had shot a sparrow with his new BB gun. That was in the eighth grade, when the hormonal explosion of puberty often clouds the sense of reason.

And photographers. Other than at a celebrity's funeral, I couldn't imagine more cameras at a burial party. Shots were being fired almost matter-of-factly, but there would be later tears in the darkroom.

One wonderful group shot of all our family with the Chicago crew and Ben and Leslie is so happy that it looked like a reunion of the long lost.

Tom took the shot and sent me a negative, which I had blown up to 11 X 14. In the photo store, I pulled the print out of the envelope before I paid the bill. The attendant peeked at it with me.

"Happy crowd," she said. "Fourth of July picnic?"

"Nope," I said. "My brother's funeral." And then I started laughing because it sounded like the punch line to a joke. She laughed too. Hell, I would have if I were her. How can you explain seventeen beaming faces at someone's funeral?

MY MOM AND I TOLD GRANDMA THE DAY AFTER THE funeral. She sat up straight in her bed and her gaze took on a faraway look. I was actually shook up by her lack of what I thought should be the appropriate emotion for such news. She cried more when her Yorkshire terrier died. I had to ask her about that.

"The little dog I will never see again," she told me. "I will be seeing Mark in heaven." But then she said something else. Something that made me start bawling. She said that the biggest griefs are deeper than tears.

So. Mark's upstairs, the little beat-off. He knows all. Sees all. Wish he could beam me the directions to the whereabouts of a perfect *T. rex* head. The little whorelet also actually knows what made the dinosaurs extinct.

*   *   *

SOMEWHERE IN THAT ONSLAUGHT OF WAKE, FUNERAL, and burial, an old boyfriend of Anne's told me that he had lost a brother several years ago, but since they weren't as close as Mark and me, it wasn't as bad. This was news to me, because I always thought that would be a lot worse.

People told me I was strong through those days. But what is strong? Even now, I could cry every day. At first, I tried to find some consolation in reading, but I couldn't take more than three paragraphs of anything at a time. What would you read anyway? The Bible? Kübler-Ross? Wayne Dyer? About the only thing I even remotely felt like looking was at the *Rand McNally Road Atlas*.

Three days after Mark's death, Anne gave me two photocopied pages of an Anne Morrow Lindbergh book. Anne Morrow Lindbergh, whose writing Mark and I both used to laugh off as being too artificially sweetened and sentimental. The thoughts of a rich lady who had nothing to do all day. But, my God, this was it! My exact feelings. After the death of a loved older sister, she wrote that the worst and most powerful thing in her life had just happened. The rest of her life would be easy. Nothing else in her remaining days could be so terrible. And nothing else would give her as much strength.

If I knew where Anne Morrow Lindbergh lived, I would have sent her an apology.

Strength. Power. The fire! Yes, that was it. That's what Mark's passing did to me. We had such a passionate brotherhood that played itself out right to the end. It was a clean finish. No old sores, no apologies. No business to finish up. His death would fuel me onward. Mark had handed me the lit torch, flame first.

Depression continued to interrupt that little bit of euphoria, but always it was the fire that pulled me up and out. There was no time to waste anymore. No time for negative bull shit or Ultra Brite commercials. Something was blowing up inside me like a tire about to bust. I felt like I had so much to say and do, but I didn't have the slightest idea what it was other than some vague directive Mark had passed on to me. I had the Fire, but I had no idea what the Tools or Plan should be.

ON THE DAY OF MARK'S FUNERAL I GOT A LETTER FROM him that somehow got hung up in the mail. That was frightening. A message from a dead loved one. It was like a séance. Or something extrasensory. I carried it around in my back pocket for two days afraid to open it. Afraid that it might be dated after he died or something. Afraid that it contained some beautiful testimony to our brotherhood that would reduce me to a state of terminal emotional instability. When I felt up to it and I thought the time and place were right, I opened the letter late one evening in my bedroom. All it said in big printed letters covering the whole page was *S P L A T T* !

CHAPTER
30

M Y BROTHER IS NOT A SAINT NOW JUST BECAUSE OF an untimely death in the prime. As a matter of fact, he's a little asshole to go and check out on us the way he did. He was probably partying and got lit up and then was driving too fast. Well, so what. He's gone, that's the main thing.

Two days after the funeral, I drove down to Chicago in the Bronco to pick up Mark's stuff.

I went alone. At night. On the way there, I was thinking that maybe I should stay in Chicago for good. Just take over where Mark left off. Follow his paths. Make movies. Carry on.

It was a pretty sad ride actually. The protective glaze of the wake and funeral was wearing off and I was beginning to realize that my most important person had slipped away on me. I think I even considered putting the Bronco in a ditch and calling it quits myself.

I looked at the faces of the road people that I saw in a truck-stop restaurant and wondered if they knew what it was like to have your life picked up by the collar and then flung into a corner.

Back on the highway I started thinking that maybe all the vehicles on the road to Chicago that night were there for the same reason as me. To pick up after a dead loved one. It was kind of a strange thought, and I laughed a sick laugh thinking that I was part of a long, strung-out funeral procession.

I was too tired to drive straight through, so I napped for a few hours at a wayside rest in southern Wisconsin. When I did hit the big city, I went straight to the studio.

I guess my voice bouncing off the walls and hallways startled a few of the Chicago people. Tom said I sounded exactly like Mark. I know my taped voice does.

Tom helped me evacuate Mark's corner. We pulled memos off the wall and took down pictures and threw away a pile of papers. I boxed up some books and film magazines that I was going to bring back to St. Paul and read myself. In a desk drawer there were letters and a few agates and a pile of old long-distance phone bills that looked like travel schedules. Chicago to St. Paul; St. Paul to Chicago; Chicago to Aspen; Beauty, South Dakota, to Chicago; Glendive, Montana, to Chicago....

There was some talk of a funeral reunion trip out to the Badlands. I think the studio folks were really wondering what the hell Mark and I did out there.

I went to the bank alone to pay a thirty-dollar overdraft. (I was surprised that was all there was.) I imagined Mark standing at one of the same marble counters for some little transaction. And if I know him right, probably every so often while he stood there he wondered how easy it would be to knock over a bank. He would just wonder is all. He wouldn't ever have done it.

I don't know if I was trying to put off going to the apartment or what, but I went to lunch after the bank.

I knew the apartment would be the soul wringer.

The caretaker let me in and told me how sorry he was. He meant it too. You can tell when someone is really sorry. It's in the eyes and the tilt of the head. A pained posture that says they've been there too.

Mark's place was in much better shape than when I

was down to help him over the blues. It was straightened up anyway. The dead plants were gone and it seemed brighter.

I spent the rest of the day looking at Mark's things. Photos. Rocks. Camping gear. Just kind of passing a hand over his goods. It was a little bit like an archaeologic dig. I felt like I should have been tagging and photographing specimens.

For all practical purposes, the refrigerator was empty. Unless you like to eat mustard or lemon juice or 35mm slide film. I pulled out the vegetable drawer and found a package wrapped in a brown paper bag. An unopened present I supposed. It had my name and address written on it so I opened it up. It was a beautiful, old leather-bound copy of *Experiences in the Grand Canyon* by Emery and Ellsworth Kolb. The book version of their 1914 *NG* article. What a find! What a present! Standing in the refrigerator doorway, I opened the book and put my nose to the cold pages. It smelled like a great old book with just a trace of aluminum ice-cube tray thrown in.

Mark told me once that the safest place to put something valuable was in the refrigerator. It was obviously fireproof he said. You'd never forget where it was and a thief wouldn't think of looking there. I suppose if Mark had had any extra cash he would have stashed it in Tupperware and put it in the freezer.

After a quick going-over, I settled in to really biopsy all the stuff before I packed it up. The clothes were scary. I tried not to smell Mark on them.

Mark had a shitload of books and I read the inscriptions. Some were from Leslie. Some of them from me. ("Let's go for it, sweet. Your Bro, 8/73.") Mark wrote in a lot of them himself. Like they were autographed copies of the classics or something. In a paperback of Mark Twain's *Roughing It*, he had written "To another great traveler. All the best, S. L. Clemens." A few of the books had crushed black flies on the pages. Little Alaska mementos. Back home I had some personal salutations from authors in books that Mark had given me. I can remember Count Leo Tolstoi, Flannery O'Connor, and Homer for sure.

I read some letters and looked at bills and boxes of old checks. You can get someone's routine down pretty good by looking at their canceled checks. I found one made out to the Chicago Transit Authority for seventy-five cents. Mark probably landed on the el once without any money. (Once! Maybe once a week.)

Around suppertime, I left the apartment for a little walk. I was wearing a nice rust-colored corduroy sport jacket of Mark's. In one of the pockets I found a piece of fossil turtle shell about the size of a torn ticket stub.

Mark lived in Old Town. Kind of the shabby side of Old Town. I felt rather artsy just being there. After checking out a few of the joints, I walked the alleys. Alleys are good places to nurse along a little melancholy. The garbage cans and old junk. The netless basketball hoops. The dirty backyards. There's a lot of the past in alleys.

I had to hurry back to the apartment because I had to go number one and number two real bad and out there in the alleys and streets of Chicago I wasn't about to do a wilderness-type disposal.

Mark had a stack of *National Geos* and *American Cinematographers* next to the toilet. That boy loved to read on the can.

Tom came over about ten o'clock and we had a last visit. I gave him a load of things to give to people back at the studio. A cap, a backpack, some books, two or three fossils. Power objects for friends to hold on to for a little while. I wanted Tom to have Mark's ten-speed and his copy of Romer's *Vertebrate Paleontology*.

The caretaker looked in after Tom left and I gave what measly furniture there was to him. I helped carry the stuff down to the basement.

By midnight there was just a four-foot pile of boxes in the middle of the living room. I spread Mark's sleeping bag on the floor and stretched out to recuperate for the St. Paul return. I closed my eyes and thought I was laid out on good old South Dakota prairie.

The next day I drove straight back to St. Paul with only two quick gas stops.

THREE WEEKS AFTER THE FUNERAL, I INTERCEPTED THE autopsy report from my parents' mailbox. I read it alone. My God, I didn't realize he was so crumpled! Broken neck, fractured ribs, severed thoracic aorta, depressed skull fracture. That was Mark, my sweet. I was not that intimate with what a hurtling automobile could do to the human frame. You skin your knee or sprain an ankle or maybe even break a wrist. But this?

My mother told me that for months she couldn't stand the thought of Mark's injured body lying in that ravine all alone. She wanted to have been there. To have held him and smoothed his hair.

I remember explaining how Mark died to a little cousin who had asked. I thought I'd make it quick and just say he hit his head. But that wasn't enough so I said he hit his head and his heart stopped and he died. Then she wanted to know how come his heart stopped if he hit his head.

EVERY TIME I'D SEE SOMEONE IN THE MONTHS AFTER the funeral who knew Mark or me I'd face the same minor dilemma. Did they or didn't they know about Mark? If their conversation was too nonchalant, I'd know that they didn't. Then it started. Should I tell them before they ask how Mark is? Should I hold my breath and hope that they don't, or should I just get out with it? Now, I take a respectfully aggressive tack. Did you hear about my brother I might say right off to someone I hadn't seen in a while. Then I let it out, trying not to make them uncomfortable.

Anne had the first bad taste Mark joke. It was a beauty. The day before what would have been his twenty-fourth birthday, she told me that this year we wouldn't have to get the little jerk a present. I loved it. Then it hit me that Mark would be a young man forever. We would all get older, but Mark would be an everlasting twenty-three.

THE FOLLOWING FALL I PLANNED A SOLO TRIP TO THE Badlands. I left all cocky and hippity-hop. I was going to shoot straight through to Wall and then Beauty, but I petered out near Mitchell and moteled it there for the rest of the night.

When I did get to the Badlands, there was a different show playing. Clarence and Goldie were visiting in Rapid City. The Longhorn was boarded up and Mr. Jordan had had a stroke and died. I hiked out to our old campsite and found some peanut shells on the desert pavement. Little remnants of Mark and me. One anxious night was all I could handle. I legged it to the truck the next day and slung back to St. Paul.

I'm sure that I'll go to the Badlands again. I just wasn't ready for that first trip alone. Maybe it'll be better if the Chicago people ever go out. Or if Ben and Leslie want to get going again.

THE BRONCO CALLED IT QUITS THE FOLLOWING SUMMER. In one week I had a fender-bender, the floor boards rusted through, and the transmission dropped out. It was the end of the road for the old Bronchitis. It had made it to the respectable age of a hundred fifty thousand miles. I sold it to an auto salvager for two hundred bucks. Lots of good parts on her yet the guy told me.

The Bronco would never run again on its own power, but pieces of it would be recycled into injured but more youthful models. A fender here, a radiator there, a steering wheel somewhere else. I laugh whenever I think that Mark now knows that the Bronchitis is still on the road, going eight or nine different directions at once.

Parts of Mark were recycled too, before his funeral had even begun. His driver's license had the donor box checked, and being a healthy product of millions of years of evolution, why should his heart or kidneys or corneas go to waste? I don't know the details of this at all, but I found out that his heart went to the University of Utah and was transplanted into a forty-five-year-old man the next day. An undamaged kidney was flown to the University of Minnesota for a young diabetic girl.

For a while, I actually wanted to track down those folks—maybe see them for a few minutes or talk by phone.

After all, since they now had parts of my brother in them, they were my relatives too. But I never did. I guess I don't need to pay my respects to any of his former organs or even his body for that matter.

I don't visit his grave. That's not my boy there. It's only the husk, the shell. His spirit is what I'm after and that's elsewhere—sitting at an editing table in Chicago, roaming around the Badlands, or listening to a busy signal in a phone booth along the AlCan Highway.

I can sense his presence anywhere now. Not a ghostly or lurking window-peeper presence. More like an early evening breeze or a before-the-rain smell. The little whorelet is still with us.

I suppose that the rest of Mark's body is also being recycled. Into the earth and its minerals and waters. A process no doubt delayed by twentieth-century funeral practices. But one day, he will come down again as part of some cloudburst. Not knowing that exact moment, I will have to collapse my umbrella in the middle of absolute downpours or go running out of the house into the rain and assume I am being drenched by him.

CHAPTER
31

WELL, THAT'S IT. WHAT ELSE CAN I SAY? THE SHOW is over, the lights come on, you blink your eyes, and the slide projector fan hums through the silence. If this had been a slide show with a gathering of friends, somebody would get up and stretch and say that it was pretty good. "Yah," three others would say, "that was good. Real good. What kind of camera did you use?"

It's been three years now since Mark died. The first Christmas without him, Pioneer Grandma couldn't figure out why one stocking was missing from the mantel. "Weren't there three of you?" she said and nobody felt like explaining it again, but then she had her own answer. "That one is always away on a trip, isn't he?"

Leslie has since moved out to Seattle and is doing some community theater there. We write a little bit. She keeps suggesting a reunion trip out to Beauty and Clarence country. By the way, old Clarence, the last time I heard from him, says he's turning into rock from the inside out. He claims he's got gallstones and hardening of the arteries and a touch of the gout crystals. He's proud of it. He says that's the way an old rock hound should go.

Ben still works for the state's department of education. He's in the planning section. You should see that guy whip out on a braille typewriter. Dear, wonderful Ben. He can still remember exactly what Mark or I said on what day of the big trip. He'll hear a song like "My Baby Does the Hanky Panky" and he tells me we heard it in Glendive, Montana, on August 27 and that Mark made us turn the radio off. Ben's got his big piece of petrified wood in his office and a dinosaur vertebra that Mark gave him.

Me? I'm a raving photo waver. I carry several pictures of Mark, including his license, which has a pretty good likeness of him on it for those penitentiary-type shots. Somebody says the least little thing about Mark, and I whip one of my pictures out like the proudest and most puffed up grandparent.

I started getting into a little photography myself. I have Mark's light meter and I bought a cheap 35mm. Two weeks ago I did a sunrise over the Mississippi. Got there about 4:00 A.M. It was still cold and dark out but I got all set up and it turned out kind of nice.

Actually, my main mission in life these days is getting through medical school. I know that if Mark were around now, he'd be calling me Zhivago or Dr. Sax. I'm a sophomore. Me, who can't stand the sight of blood. Me, the claustrophobe. Me, the shy one who now has to ask women when their last periods were and men what color their bowel movements are. Maybe I'll be a dermatologist.

I get a lot of compliments on Mark's clothes. The hand-me-ups I got after Mark's exit. I've been wearing this very natty camel hair overcoat of his that gives me a banker look. He had a couple of nice corduroy sport jackets that fit me just right and five Pierre Cardin shirts. The taped-up boots don't quite make it in my wardrobe anymore.

The trip slides Mark took never made it into *National Geographic*. Of course, we never sent them in. I don't know if we thought they should call us first or what. But Clarence will be in *National Geo* someday. So will the

Bone Cabin and Ed, Wyoming. It's just a matter of time before a real *NG* photographer spots them.

I've been thinking about a memorial for Mark after seeing a couple of beauties. On a black highway in southern Minnesota I came across the Billy T. Snyder Bow and Arrow Target Range, and in a library in Rapid City I found the Helen Cliborne Memorial Agate Display. Remembrances of loved ones in their element. Maybe for Mark I could dedicate a men's room stall in some South Dakota truck stop.

MY BROTHER REALLY IS GONE. FOR GOOD. MY LITTLE sweet. My love boy. I still can't quite believe it. I keep thinking of him as just being on a trip. He was always somewhere else. Toronto, Chicago, hitchhiking to Alaska. So to me, right now, Mark is simply away. On the road. Doing a job somewhere on the other side of the globe. I'm waiting for the late night when I get a call. I'll pick up the phone and hear the long-distance hum. It will be a collect call from Mark. He will speak first.

"Hello, sweet. I love you."

And I will answer, "The charge is reversible."

—Goodnight Moon—

ABOUT THE AUTHOR

TIM RUMSEY was born in St. Paul, Minnesota. Formerly a rock musician, he is now a family doctor and amateur paleontologist. He lives with his wife and two young children in St. Paul.

The sights, sounds and feel
of AMERICA

from FAWCETT BOOKS